THE GIRL WITH THE FIERCE EYES

SOPHIA VAHDATI

One More Chapter
a division of HarperCollins*Publishers* Ltd
1 London Bridge Street
London SE1 9GF
www.harpercollins.co.uk
HarperCollins*Publishers*
Macken House, 39/40 Mayor Street Upper,
Dublin 1, D01 C9W8
This paperback edition 2025

1

First published in Great Britain in ebook format
by HarperCollins*Publishers* 2025

Copyright © Sophia Vahdati 2025
Sophia Vahdati asserts the moral right to be identified
as the author of this work

A catalogue record of this book is available from the British Library
ISBN: 978-0-00-873216-5

This novel is entirely a work of fiction. The names, characters and incidents portrayed in it are the work of the author's imagination. Any resemblance to actual persons, living or dead, events or localities is entirely coincidental.

Printed and bound in the UK using 100% Renewable Electricity
by CPI Group (UK) Ltd

All rights reserved. No part of this publication may be reproduced, stored in a retrieval system, or transmitted, in any form or by any means, electronic, mechanical, photocopying, recording or otherwise, without the prior permission of the publishers.

Without limiting the exclusive rights of any author, contributor or the publisher of this publication, any unauthorised use of this publication to train generative artificial intelligence (AI) technologies is expressly prohibited. HarperCollins also exercise their rights under Article 4(3) of the Digital Single Market Directive 2019/790 and expressly reserve this publication from the text and data mining exception.

For Lulu, who has always been my shining star, and because we made a promise.

CHAPTER 1
HOVER

JANTSIA

Mrs Naz's Teahouse was one of the only places in Densolid where Jantsia didn't stick out like a sore eye. As a gathering place for immigrants and outcasts, it was a space where her olive skin and dark, frizzy hair didn't mark her out as different. As foreign.

The air hummed with foreign accents, and an icy breeze carried the rich smell of Parsian herbs downwind. Behind the steamed-up windows of the restaurant, customers lounged on satin cushions and intricate Parsian carpets, sheltered from the glacial weather. Annoyingly, Jantsia had arrived too late in the day to snag a table inside.

Jantsia took a large sip of hot, jammy zhoozh as she scrolled through learning materials on her Tile. The cold of the metal chair pierced her facsfur-lined tracksuit, entering her bones.

Where on Shariza was Kain? He should've been here by now.

The revision texts on her Tile blurred as her eyes lost focus. Fladden forsake her, studying for hours in the biting cold had left her completely exhausted; she wasn't concentrating at all. Better to take a break than scroll mindlessly.

Swiping left on her Tile, she opened up the *Densolid City Times* news site and glanced at the headlines.

A local outbreak of shadowbird flu, the annual Imperial Inspectors' Gala scheduled for the end of the lunar cycle, and a speculative report into the whereabouts of Topper Luxo, the most-wanted mercenary in the whole of Albin. Aside from that, there was little else going on, at least not in this backwater city.

A 'breaking news' notification popped up.

One she couldn't ignore.

LOVE THAT KILLS: A TALE OF FRATERNISATION AND CROSS-PROCREATION
An exclusive scoop from *The Albin Independent*

Her gorge rose, stomach writhing in knots. And her hands shook so violently she almost let go of her Tile. As she manoeuvred her arm to stop it slipping from her grip, her elbow knocked into the mug of zhoozh, tipping half of it onto the floor. Steam rose from the dark blue paving stones where the drink had spilt.

'Fladden be merciful,' she whispered, unable to look away from the purple liquid and the web of ice growing around its edges.

The ice cracked away as the spilt zhoozh rose back into the air, forming a bubble that hovered over her mug. The eponymous Mrs Naz appeared in front of her, deep-set eyes glowing bright turquoise. In a flash, the zhoozh poured back into the cup and a handful of grit dropped onto the table.

'You still cannot manage a simple oculary kinesis and filtration?' Mrs Naz said, her accented voice rich with elongated vowels and soft consonants.

Jantsia grimaced. 'Not yet, Nazanin *khunam*.' She hoped the Parsian term of respect would soften Mrs Naz's reaction. 'Although, I hope to have my awakening soon.'

The creases around Mrs Naz's eyes deepened. Jantsia's basic use of her language hadn't softened a thing.

'It is pronounced *khanoom*, take better care with our language. And with your future. You must awaken, Jantsia *jaan*,' Mrs Naz said. 'Otherwise, you will not pass your oculary practice exam. You should study more, final exams must be soon.'

As if Jantsia needed reminding, the threat of exams remained ever present in her thoughts, and these days she studied almost as much as she breathed.

Biting back a retort, she smiled sweetly. 'Good advice. I'll do my best.'

With a final stern look, Mrs Naz rushed off to seat more customers.

As she returned her attention to the article, Jantsia's heart started to thump loudly in her chest, obscuring the bustle around her. The home screen featured a lengthy exposé denouncing a couple who'd broken the segregation law: the rule that mandated against romantic relations between oculary orders.

Her head jerked up, mouth dry.

Was she safe?

Was this a sign?

She scanned her surroundings. Mrs Naz darted between bustling tables, carrying steaming mugs of zhoozh, plates of sweet shirini, and heaped bowls of safra rice. Heavily clothed migrant families argued over the last slices of juicy kookoo.

She let out a breath. No shadowbirds. No Inspectors. She was safe ... for now.

'Have you ever been on a hoverbike, boss?'

'Oh, my eyes,' Jantsia exclaimed, searching for the source of the cheeky voice that could only belong to her best friend, Kain Trovit.

Floating above her table, Kain sat proudly astride a monstrous white hoverbike plastered with graffiti of scantily clad women. Warmth spread up Jantsia's neck to tickle her cheeks. Everything would be fine now Kain was here.

She was about to grin and tell him how great it was to see him, when she caught herself. Better to play it cool...

She pouted. 'What are you playing at? Sneaking up on me like that after leaving me high and dry for hours?'

'All right, all right. No need to get snarky.' The hoverbike roared as he reengaged the engine and lowered it to the ground. He turned to face her, a coy half-smile playing across his lips. 'I wouldn't exactly call this an inconspicuous mode of transport. Didn't you hear me coming?'

Jantsia's eyes darted between her Tile and Kain's expectant expression. She didn't know what to say. She hadn't heard a thing.

'I... I...' she stuttered.

Kain frowned, hopping off the bike and taking a seat. Messy locks of ice-white hair flopped over his snow-pale face, falling across electric blue eyes in a way that always seemed to make her smile.

'What are you reading about, anyway?' He leaned towards her, squinting at her Tile.

The last thing she needed was to rouse his suspicions. She had to pull herself together – and fast.

Kain snatched the device from her shaking hands, face screwing up in distaste as he scrolled. 'The Sepia and Veridian couple that gave birth to a dual-oc baby... This is what's got you so worked up?'

'What do you think happened?' Jantsia asked, so quietly the words were almost lost to the wind.

'To the parents? Executed, I guess.' He paused and scrolled some more. 'Yeah, that's what it says here.'

'And the child?'

'Poor kid didn't stand a chance.' Kain handed her back the Tile. 'Dual-ocs are born sick, aren't they? Never make it past two or three years old. Can you imagine what the parents must've been smoking to think cross-procreation was a good idea? It's pretty selfish, if you ask me. I don't think I'd even be attracted to anyone who wasn't Azure.'

His words hit her like a shot of Fireglug to the eye.

Masking the hurt, she scrolled to the end of the article. It wouldn't be fair to blame Kain for his harsh words. He wasn't to know, and if she had her way he never would.

Grief clenched her heart as she finished reading. The Inspectors had killed the child. Well, that wasn't exactly the wording the journalists had chosen. They'd *terminated the aberration*. A maelstrom of emotions whirled in her gut, and she struggled not to let them reach her face.

'Stop reading that calabash and take a look over here at Densolid's new illegal couple,' Kain announced, leaning back to stroke the bike suggestively.

Jantsia folded the Tile and placed it inside her fluffy facsfur jacket. Pushing against the silent scream rattling inside her, she flattened the emotion into a sarcastic smile. 'Exactly what I need, a saviour to fly me away on ten-thousand tokens' worth of shiny, sexist, *stolen* machinery.'

Kain grinned, running a hand through his silky white hair. Dressed in dark, close-fitting thermal pants, a navy waistcoat and matching jacket, his unique style and impish smile made him stand out from the other boys her age.

Tiny snowflakes danced through the air, settling on his long white eyelashes. He was so out of her league that sometimes it hurt to look at him. To be so close and know they could never be more than friends...

'Well, have you or not?' he asked, flicking a stray lock of hair from his eyes.

Shariza wept, she'd completely zoned out. What had they been talking about again? She racked her brain and came up short. 'Have I what?'

Kain raised a silver-blond eyebrow. 'Been on a hoverbike, stupid.'

She clicked her tongue in annoyance, she might have lost focus, but she was far from stupid. 'It's obviously stolen.'

'Borrowed!'

'Your brother has a hoverbike. If you were going to borrow one, it'd be his.'

'So?'

'So, this one is obviously stolen.'

'It's not,' Kain groaned. 'If you must know, Daezen took his bike to The Pipes to pick up some stuff for Ma, else I would've borrowed his.'

'Who does the bike belong to, then?' Jantsia demanded.

'Unseeing eyes, unhurt heart,' Kain replied with a shrug.

She shuddered. A phrase she repeated to herself far too often.

He stood up and patted the bike.

'This ... is a bad idea,' she said, already imagining the warmth of Kain's body as she snuggled up behind him and flew around the city.

'Oh, come on, Jantsy. Live a little.' He extended a hand.

Her mouth was already forming a resounding no when she found herself taking his hand.

Her parents' voices echoed through her mind.

Reckless.

Dangerous.

Stay invisible. Stay alive.

Her grip loosened. Still time to retreat. To head back home like a good little Azure servant...

Kain's fingers tightened around hers and he forced her arm up, punching the air. 'Yes! Us against the world.'

She smiled involuntarily. As she caught his eye, he winked, sending gooey light bubbling through her stomach. Doing her best not to blush, she threw a few tokens on the table, more than enough to pay for the zhoozh, and let Kain help her onto the bike. With a nimble hop and a skip, he jumped in front of her and pressed an array of strange buttons. The engine buzzed beneath them.

While riding a stolen hoverbike wasn't exactly the best way to avoid being noticed by the Inspectors, she needed a distraction. After all, it could be her name in the headlines tomorrow. And what was the point in staying alive if she wasn't allowed to live?

A slight dropping sensation tickled her stomach as they took off.

'Hold on properly, boss,' Kain instructed, adjusting her hands so they clamped firmly around his waist.

Sparks tingled at her fingertips as she pressed up against him, breathing in his scent of elderflower and sage.

Then they zoomed into the sky.

CHAPTER 2
FLY

JANTSIA

Rising high above the streets, the bike broke through a cloud of twisting fumes. Factories and production centres surrounded the city, exuding rainbow-coloured smoke that curled upwards, clouding the horizon.

For a brief second of stillness, life seemed to pause.

Wings beat behind them as a flock of black-feathered birds flew past in perfect formation, eyes marbled dark, like the eyes of an Obsidian.

Shadowbirds were eerie creatures, almost exactly like the wild birds they'd learnt about at the academy, but with fundamental differences. Their movements were smooth, feathers uniform, and instead of fleeing from humans – they monitored them.

The stillness drew longer, and a set of little black eyes locked on to Jantsia. A shadowbird separated momentarily from the flock, swooping over to perch on her shoulder. Talons gripped her coat. Feathers tickled her cheek.

They'd found her.

Don't scream.

They were watching.

Don't react.

They were *always* watching.

Stay invisible. Stay alive.

The bird returned to the flock, but a sense of sickly unease remained in her stomach.

What had she been thinking when she'd agreed to ride the bike with Kain? She wasn't like other people. She couldn't take risks.

'Kain, we need to land. The shadowbirds are—'

And they were off.

Leaving the still moment behind, they rocketed back into the turning world. Kain pushed the hoverbike onwards, executing several nauseating loops with reckless abandon. Jantsia squeezed his waist, burying her face in his coat. It smelt like him. Like safety.

Just as she started to enjoy their closeness, they turned upside down again and her stomach flipped. Rushing air deafened her ears and the pulsing knots in her gut made her worry the zhoozh might make another appearance.

Shariza wept, if she vomited on Kain she'd die from embarrassment.

After having a stiff word with herself, the bile in her throat retreated, and she attempted to appreciate the panorama as if she were a distant observer, not a teenage girl a slip away from death.

The shadowbirds hadn't seen anything that would

incriminate her. They were just two seventeen-year-old Azures having fun. She concentrated on this thought, slowing her breaths, holding on to Kain's slim frame with all her strength.

At a distance, the segregation of the city was visibly pronounced. A mess of metal-roofed huts and gloomy, terraced housing sat at the centre of Densolid Minor, a slum-like maze with two clearly marked areas: the Azure section and the Veridian section. Water-wielders and root-renders.

They dropped lower, flying over a relatively well-to-do Azure zone. Neat, navy bricks caught the fading sunlight, reflecting into Jantsia's eyes. As they crossed into the slums, carefully coloured tiles became tarmac and mud, sloppily splashed with thick luminescent green paint.

'Keep in Azure airspace, son,' an emerald-eyed, uniformed soldier shouted, gesturing menacingly with a buzz-baton. It wasn't like he could actually hurt them, Ver-sec and Az-sec didn't have real weapons. Still, the short, sharp electric shock of a buzz-baton wouldn't be pleasant.

'Let's get back to Azure streets,' she said, pulse racing. She couldn't afford to get into trouble. She had to cut this ride short.

Kain didn't respond, so she pinched his right side and leaned forward until her lips almost touched his ear.

'Let's get back to Azure streets,' she repeated, trying not to let her voice shake. Though she knew there was nothing romantic between them, it didn't stop moments like this sending electricity through her bones.

He scowled, not seeming to notice she'd almost kissed his ear. 'Fladden forbid we forget to stay on our own ocking side. Screw that mud-munching Ver-sec soldier. We're getting out of Veridian Minor anyway.'

Jantsia understood why the rules bothered Kain, she just

wished he'd think through the consequences of his actions. The danger of his words. Surviving had to be the priority, and the way to do that was by staying below the radar. Besides, Azures had a key part to play in Sharizan society, even if they were at the bottom of the oculary pile. There was a place carved out for everyone in the Empire.

Well, for almost everyone.

Speeding forward, they left Densolid Minor and skirted the edge of Densolid Major. Freshly cleaned tiles of onyx sparkled on the ground, and skyrises wreathed with twisting black metal edges shot into the air. From this distance, Jantsia could hardly see the demarcation of the streets. It was all Obsidian. But she didn't have to see the markings to know they were there, everyone knew they were there. The thin paths drawn out in shining turquoise, emerald-green, and dark amber, spread across the streets like a network of barely visible veins.

Jantsia's fear faded away as she sat up tall, relishing the rush of the breeze on her face and the snowflakes melting on her nose. She tracked the trajectory of several egg-shaped mahogany pods as they transported citizens to the factories at the city's edge. The Sepia district was just about visible from this height, a functional grid of utilitarian terracotta houses.

They rose higher.

A sudden jolt dragged her back to her body, and she made the near-fatal mistake of looking down. A new, dizzying perspective assailed her with vertigo. They were so high she could barely make out the tops of the skyrises. The city beneath them transformed into a shimmering blob of darkness surrounded by endless arctic tundra.

'Oh, my ocking eyes! CALABASH!' she shouted.

Kain slowed the descent so they could hear one another.

'I was trying out different flight modes. We're fine, no worries, boss. Did you look down?'

'Yup.'

'Gonna vom?' he taunted.

'Mmm,' she squeaked.

Gradually, they descended further and looped the main city, turning back before reaching Densolid Meridian. A shining forcefield protected the southern Obsidian neighbourhood, giving it the feel of a mirage. Only select vehicles were capable of breaching the bubble, and a stolen Azure hoverbike wasn't one of them.

'I still can't believe you live there,' Kain shouted over the wind, directing them back to Densolid Minor.

Jantsia couldn't believe it, either. Nothing in her life made sense, let alone her living situation – and Kain didn't know the half of it.

They whizzed over ramshackle streets and half-finished buildings, back in the slums of Azure Minor. Crowded around a dank-smelling heated fountain, a bunch of Azure kids sprayed one another with water. A young girl's eyes flashed bright blue, sending tiny droplets of water towards what looked to be her younger brother. The boy squealed and jumped into the fountain, creating a splashback that sprayed Jantsia's hair.

'Watery little brat,' she exclaimed.

Kain beamed. 'I think I've heard you curse more times in the past half hour than I have in the whole time I've known you.'

'I blame the hoverbike.' She pressed closer to Kain, letting the warmth of his body soothe her irritation. The light snow had dissipated, leaving behind clear crisp air.

'As long as you don't blame the driver, that's fine with me.'

She'd never blame him. Never. He was a ray of truth in her life of lies.

They picked up speed, zipping down alleyways and over carts, crossing back into Veridian Minor. The smell of freshly laid manure rose from a small allotment where locals tended to their crops. Even though Kain made fun of Veridians, Jantsia found their oculary abilities mesmerising. An old Veridian man, knees covered in dirt, smiled broadly at her. With a rhythmic tap of his fist on his chest, the earth spat out a large root vegetable. His eyes shone emerald.

They rocketed upwards, and this time Kain seemed determined to see how high they could go. The initial thrill of the ride hardened into an ice-cold marble of fear. They were too high. Far too high.

'Kain, what the ock are you doing?' Jantsia cried.

'Hold tight, nearly there, just want to get the perfect view. Think of it as a belated birthday present. You'll see.'

The air bit down with frozen teeth. The higher they went, the harder it was to breathe. Glacial wind tickled the back of Jantsia's throat and the hoverbike shook, emitting a warning chirrup.

'I can't breathe. This can't be safe. Let's go back down. Now!'

Her teeth chattered. Panic flared in her chest. The bike jolted violently to the left, knocking her off balance. She tried to grab hold of Kain, but he was leaning forward, frantically pressing buttons.

'Do something! I'm slipping!' Jantsia yelled, hands flailing for purchase on the edge of the seat. There was nowhere to hold, the stupid thing was all gloss and spurs. They continued rotating sideways.

Jantsia screamed as she fell from the side of the hoverbike, managing to grab the footrest at the last moment. After all the worrying, all the carefully constructed lies, she was going to die because of an ocking stolen hoverbike?

Fingers slick with sweat, and upper-body strength nigh on non-existent, she wouldn't last another jolt. The engine whirred. Nausea spiked through her limbs. She closed her eyes and waited for the bike to buck one last time.

It didn't.

'Phew.' Kain exhaled. 'You know, I really thought I'd lost control then. You all right back there?' Peering over his shoulder, his already pale face whitened, draining of all colour.

Jantsia Brittle was about to fall to her death.

'Just hold on. It's going to be okay,' Kain shouted.

He sounded so sure of himself she almost believed him.

A terrifying thought flashed to the front of her mind. If she died now her mother would deem Kain responsible. And he wouldn't stand a chance against her mother.

Jantsia's chest heaved. She wanted to live. To be part of something. She couldn't die now, she just couldn't.

'I've got a plan; you hanging in there?' Kain yelled.

'Just about,' she panted. Her arms screamed in agony, fingers turning white from the effort of maintaining the grip. 'Kain?'

'Yes, boss.'

'I don't want us both to die,' she sobbed.

Pain flickered across his delicate features. 'Us?'

She couldn't do it. Even now, moments from death, she couldn't reveal her secret. At least this way, she would die with their friendship intact. Kain would be none the wiser.

Unseeing eyes, unhurt heart.

The bike lowered and she risked a glance downwards. They were only a few hundred feet above the roof of the Red Ruins; a patchwork building of clay bricks, corrugated iron, and ancient minarets. If she held on for another few minutes, they'd be close enough to the roof that the fall wouldn't kill her. She'd make it.

Jantsia's undeveloped muscles tore.

Her heart hammered a mantra against her chest.

Stay invisible. Stay alive.
Stay invisible. Stay alive.
Stay invisible. Stay alive.

Her fingers slipped.

She lost her grip.

A final howl tore through her throat.

Closing her eyes and hoping the end would be quick, she let her body go limp and plummeted towards the hard, icy ground.

CHAPTER 3
FALL

DAEZEN

As Daezen Trovit mounted his hoverbike, he was surprised to see a girl falling from the sky. But that didn't mean he wasn't ready.

Pushing the bike to top speed, he zoomed through the air so fast his eyes stung. A warm body smacked against him, sending a spider web of pain through his legs. Without faltering, he scooped the limp form into one arm while lowering the bike to minimise the force of impact.

The girl's chest rose and fell.

She was breathing.

She was alive.

A brutal gust of exhaust fumes burnt his lips and shook his bike off course as someone on a large white hoverbike nearly crashed into them. Daezen scowled. Thank Fladden the idiot had pulled up at the last minute. He couldn't make out the face of the rider in all the smoke, but he saw the bike veer off to the roof of the Red Ruins.

'Watch where you're flying, twack-face,' Daezen called, tightening his grip on the girl. That was when he realised his packsack had been knocked loose. The bag had fallen from the bike and landed in a dirty, stinking puddle next to a market stall, where an eagle-eyed vendor picked it up and pocketed it.

Daezen bared his teeth at the silver-haired Veridian merchant, ready to turn the bike around and crash straight into his stall of faulty, brass contraptions and bogus potions. His finger hovered over the accelerator, the girl coughed and wheezed. Ocking avalanches, he didn't know how badly injured she was, what if charging down the merchant did her more harm?

The thief doffed his cap then disappeared into the dark maze of The Pipes, where it'd be impossible to track him down.

Daezen winced, his hesitation had cost him exactly 340 tokens. His mind whirred through calculations, assessing the sorry state of the family's finances. That packsack contained expensive herbal meds and his latest withdrawal of Duty credits. Without it, he couldn't afford to buy more food for the quart-cycle, let alone pay off the latest installment of the family debt. Ma would have to go without. They all would.

'Daeze, is that you?' Kain shouted, his impish face appearing between two minarets on the top of the Red Ruins. His face was whiter than the tips of the Ice Cap mountains. 'Did you get her? Is she all right?'

Of course, his reckless little brother knew the girl who'd fallen from the sky. Most likely he had something to do with her failed skydive.

'Oh, my eyes,' the girl wheezed.

As she tried to sit up, a mess of wild dark curls brushed against Daezen's face along with the soft aroma of spiced chai. She wasn't an Albiner, that was for sure. Maybe an immigrant from Laminos, or Parsia.

'Stay down,' he said. 'You took a pretty bad fall.'

'Jantsia,' Kain called. 'Are you okay?'

'Kain,' she croaked, ignoring Daezen's advice. She spun to look him in the eye, her deep olive complexion reddening.

'Daezen?' she exclaimed. 'What are you doing here? I—' She choked on a cloud of acrid opine smoke that floated up from The Pipes.

The familiar taste of chemical regret stung Daezen's mouth as he manoeuvred the bike up and over the Red Ruins, docking at the side farthest from Kain. Then he turned his attention back to Jantsia Brittle, his younger brother's best friend.

Bright eyes, expensive facsfur coat, silver-tipped snowboots, and curls sticking out at all angles with a force and vigour that smacked of excellent health and nutrition. Great, so he'd sacrificed his packsack to save a pampered little princess. He fixed his jaw, dark rage threatening to crack his mask of indifference.

He wouldn't let his emotions reach his face. The one thing that kept him and his family alive was his ruthless discipline. One moment of weakness, and the shadowbirds would swarm to pick the flesh from his bones before he'd taken his last breath. This girl might be Kain's friend, but she had powerful people on her side. People who could take away everything he'd worked for on a whim.

Daezen dismounted, and Jantsia's hands trembled as he took hold of them to help her down, too. He treated her to a half-smile. 'Don't worry, princess. I didn't save you just to mug you.'

She chewed on her lip, still avoiding his gaze, then pulled her hands from his and tried to scramble off the bike. One of her legs caught on the seat and she fell headfirst towards the floor. He lunged, catching her and placed her down gently. She flinched at his touch.

'Oh, thank Fladden, you're okay,' Kain gushed, hurrying over to embrace Jantsia. Her whole demeanour changed as he wrapped his arms around her; her face softened and her shoulders relaxed.

Daezen moved closer to the crumbling edge of the roof. From here, he had a shadowbirds'-eye view of The Pipes, the black market he'd scoured all day in search of expensive herbal meds.

The streets below were the market's arteries, haphazardly crossing one another and illuminated by flickering neon signs. Large, navy-and-camouflage-coloured canopies sheltered the market stalls where nomadic merchants sold their wares. From psychoactives, like flash and opine, to necklaces adorned with weld-wolf fangs – anything and everything could be found in The Pipes. For a price, that is. A price that he couldn't pay.

Daezen spun on his feet, ready to demand answers from the troublesome duo, when the glint of shiny metal spurs caught his eye. At the sight of the white hoverbike painted in colourful graffiti, a sickening certainty settled in his gut. Well, ock him sideways, Kain had officially surpassed Daezen's expectations of his stupidity. Without a doubt, this was the most idiotic decision his little brother had ever made – and that was saying something.

Daezen paced, cold white anger shooting through his veins. He'd been too preoccupied with the lost tokens to rationalise anything. Kain didn't own a hoverbike, so it made absolutely no sense that he'd be riding one. Unless he'd stolen it.

And who in their right mind would steal the hoverbike of a wanted assassin? Kain must have pinched his key to the shared neighbourhood lockup where Topper occasionally stashed his bike. His little twack of a brother had risked his life to impress a girl – and almost ended up killing her.

Daezen's breaths came hot, fast, and laced with venom. He wanted to kick the icy gravel beneath his feet. To pick up a stray tile and hurl it into the air. But the way he felt didn't matter. He had to stay firmly in control. That was how he helped his family.

That was how he stayed alive.

Daezen was the only one around capable of looking out for Ma and Kain. So he didn't have the luxury of making sticky, teenage mistakes like these two.

He let out a deep breath, focusing on the situation at hand. Evaluating the players on the board. He toyed with the idea of heading back to The Pipes to pickpocket a few shoppers, but a handful of tokens here and there would hardly touch the edges of his family's need, let alone pay off the debt they owed to the Health Centre. Besides, he wouldn't steal from his own. That was a line he'd never cross.

Kain's voice pulled him back to the present. He was apologising to Jantsia with all the elegance of a mudmole. 'I'm so sorry, boss. I just wanted to show you the tops of the Ice Cap mountains. I don't know why the bike did that, I'd already done a test run and it was fine. I never would've done it if I'd thought something might happen to you. I ... I... I don't know what to say.'

Tired of listening to Kain ramble on, Daezen cut in, 'How about "Thanks, brother" – that sounds about right to me.'

He felt in his pockets. No tokens there, either. May Fladden strike them down, these kids were going to be the death of him. No meds for Ma. No tokens for food. No credits to pay off this cycle's instalment of their debt.

The wind picked up, howling and shaking mosaic tiles loose from the dilapidated rooftop.

'I'm okay, really,' Jantsia said, extricating herself from Kain's grip. She took a few steps, then addressed Daezen without looking him in the eye, 'Thank you for saving me.'

Kain's eyes grew round, bottom lip quivering. Seeing him like this made it hard to believe he was seventeen years old. Only a year and a bit younger than Daezen. What he'd give to be Kain's age again. The age where his biggest worries were exams and which girl to ask to the Savin family's end-of-year party.

Daezen winked at Jantsia. 'I would say anytime, but I hope my brother doesn't make a habit of risking your life,'

'Look,' Kain said, 'Jantsia has nothing to do with this, I didn't tell her that it was Topper's bike or—'

'I can't imagine you did,' Daezen interrupted. 'I doubt Jantsia would be stupid enough to take Topper Luxo's newest toy for a ride. After all, he's the most-wanted mercenary in the whole country.'

Jantsia gasped.

'Oh, come on,' Kain groaned, 'I know Topper's big time now, but he's still your mut, your friend. It's not like he'd've cared.'

Once upon time, Topper Luxo had been one of Daezen's best friends. They'd gone to the same academy and gotten into all sorts of trouble together. But when Daezen was forced to leave before graduation, they'd grown apart. At some point along the road, Topper had decided violence was the best way to gain status as an Azure, and the chasm between them became an abyss.

A shadowbird flew over their heads, diving down to perch on a lamppost illuminating the glazed eyes of the opine addicts sprawled on the dirty floor. Daezen's jaw ticked. They shouldn't spend too much time out here in the open. Any clear association between them and Topper could peak the Inspectors' interests.

'I'm flattered you think I can control what Topper Luxo does. But the next time you get the bright idea to steal from someone like him, why don't you try using your brain?'

'Borrow...' Kain mumbled.

Daezen kept his voice low, allowing a slither of anger to wind through his words. 'What the ock did you just say to me? Do you understand what we've lost because of your recklessness? Did it even cross your mind that there might be more important things going on than your stupid teenage crush?'

'I said I ... I'm sorry, Daeze. You're right, I'll try to do better next time. I promise.' Kain puffed up his chest. Earnest to a fault, his brother. The world needed people like Kain. Young men who dared to dream. He didn't want the spark of mischief to leave his eyes, but would it kill the kid to think before acting, once in a while?

Daezen needed to make him understand the consequences of his actions. He couldn't bear this weight alone. 'That packsack contained Ma's meds and our allowance of tokens for the rest of the quart-cycle. Give me one good reason why I shouldn't make you leave the academy so you can start earning your way for a change.'

'That's not fair,' Jantsia murmured, her head in her hands.

Daezen's rage coiled like a serpent. 'What was that, princess? Not fair? What would you know about fair, huh? Kain isn't like you. And if he has to miss a few quart-cycles of academy to get that straight in his thick skull, then that's what's going to happen.'

Jantsia's fingers shook and her legs trembled. Was she hurt? Cold? Or simply afraid of what he might do?

'Leave him alone,' she growled. Her eyes shot up, piercing straight through him with a defiance he hadn't thought her capable of. 'And listen to what I'm saying. It's not fair because it wasn't Kain's fault. I accept full responsibility for what happened. I'll do whatever I can to make it up to you.'

His anger ebbed away, replaced by pleasant surprise. Daezen laughed, a genuine, full belly laugh. Jantsia hadn't been shaking from cold or from fear, it had been anger. This was the first time he'd seen her like this – and he liked it.

In his mind, he'd filed her away as Kain's strange, quiet friend who'd attached herself to their family during their grieving period. A sort of morbid little mountmouse.

He beamed. It was rare for people to surprise him. 'And how exactly are you going to make it up to me, princess?'

Jantsia narrowed her eyes. She looked like a different person with her chin pointed upwards and feet planted firmly on the ground. 'I'm open to suggestions. Reasonable ones. Just leave Kain out of this.'

By the ice, he hadn't expected this. She must have picked up a thing or two from her patron. Very few Azures emanated as much status and power as Jantsia in this moment. He took in her easy, powerful stance. As if she thought the world and everyone in it owed her something.

An idea sparked in his mind. There was something she could help him with. Something that had the potential to solve all their problems.

Kain scrunched his nose, eyes darting between him and Jantsia as if he had no idea what was going on. His little brother had a lot to learn.

'Kain,' Daezen called. 'Did you turn off the engine on Topper's bike and slam the safety on? We don't want anyone sneaking it from under our noses, do we?'

Kain's eyes widened before he dashed to the other side of the roof towards Topper's bike.

Daezen sauntered closer to Jantsia, imitating her posture. 'I need you to get me into Meridian. There's something I want to discuss with your father, and I've been having trouble getting hold of him. It has nothing to do with today, I promise.'

'They won't let you in,' she said, 'why don't I give you Baba's shortcode and you can arrange to meet somewhere else?'

He took a single step closer, dropping his voice to a whisper. 'This is how you help us, Jantsia. If you care about Kain at all, you'll do it.'

Jantsia faltered, dropping her gaze and tugging at her coat. 'Okay.'

He had to admit, it was a little disappointing to watch the fiery young woman morph back into an unassuming little mountmouse.

Never mind, he'd get what he wanted and that was all that mattered.

'What was that?' Kain stormed between them. 'What did you just say to her?'

'It's fine,' Jantsia smiled sweetly. 'He's got some business with Baba, that's all. Guess you'll finally see it for yourself, now.'

'See what?' Kain asked, still frowning.

'What it's like inside Meridian, of course.'

'You're going to sneak us in?' Kain asked, rocking on the balls of his feet. 'No way. You're actually going to sneak us in?'

She shook her head, curls flying loose in the wind. 'Nothing as exciting as that. It sounds like there's been a bit of miscommunication about Daezen's application to join the waitlist for the Ice Warriors. I can get us past the guard and then Baba can smooth things over from there.'

Wow. This girl had the unassuming act down to a T. Daezen couldn't believe he'd never seen through it before. As impressed as he was, it was unnerving to watch his brother's closest friend spin silver lies out of thin air. He made a mental note to warn Kain to be careful around her later.

'Right,' Daezen said, 'Let's go, then.'

'What about Topper's bike? We can't just leave it here,' Kain said.

'Nobody in The Pipes is stupid enough to touch Topper's bike, except my own brother, apparently,' Daezen shot back, mounting his hoverbike.

Kain and Jantsia followed his lead, squishing onto the bike in awkward silence. He handled the machine steadily in spite of the extra weight, pushing it up into the air and towards Meridian.

At the edge of his vision, he thought he spied the black raven-feathered wing of a shadowbird, but when he turned to get a better look, there was nothing there.

CHAPTER 4
MERIDIAN

DAEZEN

With steady hands, Daezen steered the bike towards Meridian, approaching at ground level and landing near the entrance checkpoint. His bottom lip curled down in disdain at the shimmering force-field encasing the decadent neighbourhood.

So perfect.

So sheltered.

The wealthiest Obsidians lived in this bubble of safety and opulence, while Azures like him licked the dirt off their shoes and were expected to be thankful for it.

A hulking Sepia security guard decked out in a brass-buttoned brown uniform walked out of the checkpoint hut, mouth tightening as he appraised them. 'Permission ID?'

Jantsia wriggled, unsuccessfully trying to get off the bike.

Kain hopped off to help her to the ground. Ever the gentleman, his brother.

Daezen kept his face neutral, eyes firmly on the Sepia. Sepsec were infamous for their love of violence and destruction, making them excellent security guards. Most lighter colours wouldn't dare approach this man. His dark brown eyes could open a sinkhole beneath them in a flash of amber.

Daezen rolled his neck. Well, he wasn't *most people.*

The guard scanned the code on Jantsia's Tile and ran a retina scan on her eyes. The positive beep set Daezen's pulse racing. So far, so good. The engine of the hoverbike hummed beneath him. This was going to work. He'd get inside Meridian and finally have a chance to confront Benyamin Brittle face-to-face.

His finger hovered above the accelerator switch.

'Not so fast, Azure.' The Sepia placed his bulk between them and the entrance gate, a large archway of black metal that glowed eerily in the fading light. 'Permission is for this Azure girl only. No vehicle and no guests.'

Daezen's hands itched to press down on the switch, ram the Sepia aside, and speed through the gate. He was so close. So close to getting answers. He couldn't let this hulk of a man get in his way.

The Sepia guard's eyes flashed amber in warning. 'I don't want any funny business, Azure.' The ground trembled.

Kain grabbed Daezen's jacket, pulling him off the bike.

He struggled, shoving his brother away. 'Get your hands off me.'

Kain murmured, 'Leave it to Jantsia, mut. She knows how things work around here.'

Daezen shook his head, temper cooling rapidly. He'd lost

focus. It was rare for Kain to be the voice of reason in any situation. He had to put a lid on his emotions and *calm the ock down.*

As if to prove Kain's point, Jantsia crept closer to the guard, hands raised and head bowed. 'No funny business whatsoever, Mister Sepia. My patron has requested that I be accompanied by an escort during the night. However, if it is of great bother to you, I can make the journey alone. Just promise that if something happens to me, walking alone at night through Obsidian streets, you will tell her that I tried to bring an escort.'

The Sepia's small mahogany eyes flicked back and forth. 'And your patron is?'

Daezen grinned. She'd surprised him, again. Who would've thought the little Azure princess would come up with such a good idea?

'My patron is ... the Musika, Zuleikha Riviera Rostamani.' Jantsia bowed her head even lower in respect.

The guard's reaction was priceless. His narrow, beady eyes opened as wide as they could, and his mouth sucked in like a butthole.

Yeah, that was more or less the reaction Daezen had expected. Not many people would risk the wrath of Zuleikha Riviera Rostamani. As the offspring of an alliance between two of the Great Elite houses of Parsia and Laminos, she was only several degrees removed from the Empire's rulers. To top things off, she was a Musika, the title given to world-famous oculary musicians – it didn't get fancier than that. She even had the Brittle family indentured as her live-in servants, a privilege afforded only to the Great Elites.

'Leave the bike here. You'll both be back in an hour, or I'll set the Inspectors on you,' the guard mumbled.

Jantsia's trick had worked. The guard was letting them in.

And for the first time since Pa died, hope flickered in the shadows of Daezen's mind. He ran through the odds, the potential outcomes, the pinch points. It was still a long shot, but it was something. A chance to change his family's situation. A chance to sleep through the night without waking up drenched in sweat.

He submitted to the mandatory, thorough ID check, intimate body search, and retina scan. As invasive as the process was, he was used to it. Security guards regularly searched young Azure men for no other reason than the colour of their eyes.

The air shifted as they walked through the forcefield barrier, setting foot on an immaculately clean and symmetrical street. The wind stopped, replaced by a warm stillness. Daezen licked his finger and placed it high in the air. Not even the ghost of a breeze.

From the outside, Meridian seemed perfect, beautiful even. But on the inside, the bright colours glared artificially, the air tasted sickly sweet, and danger pervaded the atmosphere. One step wrong and the Inspectors would come down on them hard. Not to mention that if they so much as looked at an Obsidian the wrong way their ears could be bleeding for weeks. Soundbenders could cripple a member of any other oculary order with a well-aimed screech-note – and they regularly did.

He frowned, unease prickling through him as Jantsia led them around circular neighbourhoods until they reached the innermost streets. This place was strange. He felt small. Unsafe. Glass houses became never-ending cubic mansions, and white float-lights hovered in the air, grotesquely elongating their shadows.

A rush of blood pounded at his temples as he slowly followed the trail of blue bricks, even though his feet barely fit inside the lines. Next to it, was an equally narrow line of green, then a healthy few feet of mahogany paving that blended into a sea of smooth black stone. He couldn't shake the feeling he was trespassing. This place wasn't meant for Azures like them.

Passing Obsidians shot them scathing stares, making no effort to hide their disapproval. Some whispered insults, others didn't bother whispering.

'Drowned little rat.'

'Watery scum.'

'Tasteless servant girl.'

'Sewer children.'

Kain scowled at the Obsidians once their backs were turned, but all Daezen felt was a growing wave of guilt at how he'd manipulated Jantsia. How he'd been so quick to judge. He'd always thought her privileged, but she wasn't an honorary Obsidian at all. She was a prisoner, trapped in an artificial bubble and surrounded by apex predators. Weren't they all prisoners in the end? All Azures were trapped in this system one way or another.

'This is it,' Jantsia said, indicating a mind-bending construction of white and glass cubes, just about visible from behind the marble gate.

He couldn't help comparing the monster of a house in front of him with the tiny, damp apartment he shared with Kain and Ma. He gritted his teeth, his resolve strengthening.

The doors slid open and a domineering Azure man walked out to meet them. Daezen rolled back his shoulders, standing straight.

The elusive Benyamin Brittle.

The leader of the Azure performance troupe known as the Ice Warriors, a personal slave to Zuleikha – and Jantsia's father.

'What happened? The guard sent a message to say that you were coming back with two Azure men in tow.' Benyamin eyed Kain and Daezen. 'I was ... worried.'

Once upon a time, Daezen had believed this man worried about his and Kain's welfare, too. Pa had sworn to him that Benyamin would support them in the event of his death.

That'd been a short-lived hope.

Benyamin hadn't even bothered attending Pa's funeral, let alone checking in to see how they were doing. Whatever promises Benyamin had made to Flint Trovit, they'd died along with his father.

Daezen took a step forward, bowing respectfully then raising a hand. The overpowering scent of roses invaded his nostrils. 'I am Daezen Trovit, sir. The head of the Trovit family. It's a pleasure to finally meet you. Pa spoke highly of the great Benyamin Brittle.'

'It is good to meet you, young Trovit,' Benyamin said, raising a hand in reply. 'Condolences for the loss of your father. He was a good man.'

His bright blue eyes glistened with sympathy. Was it genuine or was he as good at acting as his daughter? Unlike Jantsia, Benyamin was tall and lithe, his light skin tone and strawberry-blond hair clearly marking him as an Albiner. Her foreign heritage must come from her mother's side. Daezen didn't know anything about Jantsia's mother. Kain had never spoken of her. He guessed that the woman had abandoned her family long ago.

'May I speak with you privately, sir?' Daezen asked, straightening his posture. He didn't miss Jantsia's barely perceptible nod towards her pa.

'Yes, please come in. Jantsia, why don't you show Kain

where Luz likes to play? I think I saw him stalking a flutterby in the rose bushes.'

Benyamin led Daezen through a pair of large glass doors, leaving Jantsia and Kain in the rose-infested garden.

Trying not to gawk, Daezen followed Benyamin through a never-ending open-plan space of granite worktops, spotless cream sofas, and ambient light. They reached the kitchen. Sweat beaded on Daezen's forehead. The high-end furnishings and spotless marble floor made him feel insignificant, *dirty*.

Benyamin clicked his tongue. 'Go on, then, tell me. What did those two get up to now? Are they in trouble?' He shook his head. 'Honestly, Jantsia is old enough to know better than this. We have Zuleikha's reputation to uphold, after all.'

'No, they're fine. No trouble at all, if anything they spend too much time studying for their own good.' He hoped Benyamin's searching gaze wouldn't see through the lie.

'So, what did you want to speak to me about? I'm afraid I won't be able to give you much information about Flint. We played water darts together every half-cycle, but we weren't close,' Benyamin said, establishing eye contact.

'He spoke about you a lot. Said you had places reserved for me and Kain in your performance troupe.'

Benyamin raised his eyebrows. 'Really? There must have been crossed wires. I'm not currently recruiting and it's not easy to get new members past the security check...'

Daezen wasn't under any illusions about getting into the Ice Warriors. He hadn't graduated from the academy, let alone gone to performer's school. Even if Benyamin put his name on a waiting list, he'd be right at the bottom.

He closed his eyes. Benyamin hadn't displayed the slightest of emotions. He needed to dig deeper. 'Why weren't you there?

At the funeral. Pa insisted you'd look out for us when he passed. He said I could trust you.' Daezen's voice faltered as painful memories knocked on the closed door in his mind.

'Trust me? Trust me with what?' Benyamin's cool stare gave nothing away.

Daezen fixed his gaze on the shine of a glorious chatrang set, made entirely of silver, half the squares on the board purposely oxidised to give them a darker, rustier colour. Displayed on a shelf next to heavy leath-bounded blocks of ... were those books? Bound books of parchment? He'd only seen a few books before in the restricted areas of The Pipes.

After the roll-out of Tile-tech, the Empire had decreed printing a waste of resources, choosing to upload everything online. Daezen had his suspicions that the real reason they wanted knowledge behind a digital gate, was to limit access to knowledge among lighter colours.

Benyamin caught him staring. 'Do you play?' he asked, picking up a silver King piece and rolling it in his hands. 'I used to, but I must admit, I'm a bit out of practice.'

'Yeah, I do,' Daezen replied, 'Pa made me a set out of wood, nothing fancy like that, but it does the job. I play *every* night.'

Daezen didn't trust this man one bit. In spite of everything Pa had told him, Benyamin hadn't lifted a finger to help his family and now he was almost definitely holding out on him. Daezen was many things, but he was not a fool. The great Benyamin Brittle was a good liar, just like his daughter.

Clenching his fists, he forced himself to speak softly, 'You promised him you'd look out for us. And don't lie. Pa would never have said it otherwise. What made you break your word, Benyamin?'

Benyamin faltered, seeming to really see Daezen for the first time. Then he turned away, reaching for a tall crystal glass and filling it with water from a spotless chrome-steel tap. 'I apologise, Daezen. I know nothing about this.'

Calabull. The man was good at playing it cool, but Daezen hadn't missed the tremor in his hands.

Benyamin took a sip of water. 'And please, call me Beny, no need for formality among friends.'

Daezen's hands were shaking now, teeth clenched to hold back the insults gathering in his throat.

Liar.

Blood traitor.

Gilded slave.

'Beny,' he said, sounding out the traitor's name. What kind of man turned away their friend's family in need? A man with no idea of the true plight of Azures. 'Things are bad. We need help. I'm struggling to keep up the payments to the—'

'Let me stop you there, son. I'm afraid there's nothing I can do for you.'

Nothing he can do, huh?

Pressure built in the front of Daezen's head, blood rushing to his temples as he grinded his teeth together. 'May I use your bathroom, sir?'

'Of course, down the hall on the left.'

Benyamin's gaze weighed on his back as he walked down the hall. Daezen's clenched fists shook, rage boiling his blood as he entered the bathroom. It was an enormous room full of large grey tiles and hanging plants that trailed diamond-shaped leaves down the walls. Bigger than Daezen and Kain's bedrooms combined.

Even as he opened the tap to splash water on his face, he feared he might sully the chrome-steel finishings with his grubby hands. He stared hard at his reflection, willing his rage to cool and his burning shame to fizzle out.

What had he been thinking? He was an idiot. He should never have degraded himself by asking for help. By being so vulnerable in front of Benyamin Brittle, of all people.

This was a stupid idea.

In Densolid, nobody kept their word. Nobody gave out charity.

It was time to get out. He didn't want to spend another second in this Obsidian mansion.

A flash of silver drew his eye to the other side of the corridor. A room with a door slightly ajar, through which he could see a dressing table covered in shiny items.

This household has riches pouring out of its windows and gold puffing from its chimney.

With a quick glance back to check Benyamin wasn't observing, he ducked into the room and was greeted by a strong smell of burnt hair. His nose crinkled. A large bed with purple-silk finishings and decorative pillows took up most of the room, the stark colour complementing the lush cream carpet.

At the far end of the room was a large marble dressing table with a fluid design of gold flakes swirling on the surface. Words were painted on the mirror in beautiful calligraphy.

Stay invisible. Stay alive.

Whose room was this? It looked too personal to be a guest room but far too luxurious to belong to Benyamin or Jantsia.

A silver box engraved with shooting stars and intricate, geometric patterns drew his eye. The box opened with a soft click that had Daezen's heart thumping. On a black-velvet bed, two diamond earrings sparkled, accompanied by a matching diamond necklace with offshoots in gold that looked like they could be letters.

This couldn't be Jantsia's room. No Obsidian master would give their Azure servant valuable jewels. His fingers shook. Benyamin had refused to help. He'd gone back on his word.

Daezen was alone and his family were counting on him.

He had to do whatever it took to keep them going – even if that meant stealing from the most dangerous Obsidian in the city. Tension pricked up his neck, the tendrils of headache at his crown.

He chose to leave the necklace be and pocketed a single earring. A diamond would go for at least five-thousand tokens down in The Pipes. This little jewel would settle their debt and keep them fed for several cycles.

A wave of nausea had him swaying on his feet. He wasn't stealing from Benyamin or Jantsia. He was taking from Zuleikha, a wealthy Obsidian Elite. No Azures would be harmed. So why did it feel like the walls were closing in on him?

Footsteps echoed down the hallway and Daezen rushed out of the room, barging straight into Benyamin Brittle.

'What are you doing in here?'

Tension knotted in Daezen's chest as his headache intensified. 'Er, Beny, sir. Forgive me, I got lost. I've never been to a house this big before.'

He pushed past Daezen and made a beeline straight for the dresser.

Ocking avalanches. He knew. Somehow, he knew. Were there cameras in this room or was Daezen's crime written on his face for all to see?

Beny's lips tightened as he popped the silver box open.

'I can explain,' Daezen said. He definitely could not explain and he wasn't sure how he was going to try, but it seemed like the right thing to say.

Beny marched back towards him, eyes glistening. It took all his willpower not to fall to the floor and beg for forgiveness. Daezen retreated, raising his arms as Beny's closed fist rushed towards him. Waiting for the blow, he tensed his core and closed his eyes.

It didn't come.

Instead of a painful right hook knocking him from his feet, he felt the cool edges of the second diamond earring against his palm.

'Take it,' Beny said, 'Zuleikha has no need for it.'

Daezen narrowed his eyes, searching Beny's face for a trace of trickery. For his angle. Because there was no way anyone in their right mind would catch a thief then give him more stuff to steal.

'What do I owe you?' Daezen asked.

The corners of Beny's mouth turned down, eyes red and weary. 'I'd like your forgiveness, though I don't expect it. You're right. I promised Flint I'd keep an eye on you. There were complications. I didn't realise you were struggling this much. I thought you were exaggerating – looking for quick wins, like all kids do. Jantsia only ever talks of Kain's jokes and good humour. It never crossed my mind that...' He trailed off, as if he remembered where he was and who he was talking to. 'You shouldn't be here.'

Daezen's mind spun. He didn't know how to respond, let alone how to feel. Beny was gifting him financial freedom for many, many cycles. That was no small boon. His headache flared, burning up his forehead. It was too good to be true. What game was Beny playing?

'Why did you lie? What's going on with you?'

Beny scowled. 'You need to leave. People like you do not belong in Meridian. You draw unwanted attention. Take the jewellery and go. I'll do my best to help in the future, but you have to understand: mine and Jantsia's situation is far from secure. I cannot do anything to put her safety at risk. If you need me, don't come here. Get a message to the old barman at Tavern Blue. His name's Glent.'

A cryptic response. One that didn't answer Daezen's questions at all. But it would have to do for now. 'Thank you,' he said before rushing to exit the house. The anxious look in Beny's eyes hadn't comforted him one bit. If he didn't get out of here fast, the man might come to his senses and call the Inspectors.

The glass doors slid apart. Jantsia and Kain sat cross-legged on the heated tarmac at the edge of the garden, taking turns to throw flower heads for the small feline creature rolling on its back between them. Was that a firecat? Daezen would've sworn they were extinct.

He rolled out his neck. Benyamin and Jantsia may be Azure, but they didn't know a thing about the hardship their people faced every day. Extinct animals frolicking around warm, blooming gardens were nothing but synthetic dreams for those who lived in Azure Minor. Still, Beny had done them a favour, at least he hoped he had. There was still a chance this whole thing could be an elaborate trap.

'Well,' Daezen said, 'Kain and I should get going. Dinner won't cook itself.'

Beny stood at the open door. 'I'm sorry I couldn't be of more help. If you think of anything else, you know where to find me.'

Daezen put a hand across his chest and bowed. 'Thank you, sir.' Then he spun on his heel and made for the exit.

Kain scrambled to his feet, face scrunched up in confusion, and followed Daezen to the slowly opening gate. Jantsia followed suit.

'Watch your step, little Brittle,' Daezen said.

'See you later, boss,' Kain added, with a big toothy grin.

Jantsia waved them off, her face burning with an endearing pink tinge that highlighted the freckles on her nose.

'What was that all about?' Kain asked, peering over his shoulder as a group of Obsidians stared them down.

'My application for the Ice Warriors was rejected,' Daezen responded without pause.

'That sucks, mut. Was it about your graduation certificate?'

'Yep.' Daezen increased their pace, feeling as if the weather-controlled bubble was contracting. Closing in on him. Ahead he saw the glow of the metal archway and forced his breaths to even out. 'He said you still have a chance, though. I'm sure Jantsia could put in a good word for you.'

Kain puffed out his chest, doubling his pace to keep up with Daezen. 'He really said that?'

'Yep.' Daezen repeated, and forced his legs to go even faster. He needed to be out of here now. Out of here before someone stopped him.

He was trapped.

He couldn't breathe.

Almost at a sprint, Daezen burst through the gate and looked up at the open, starry sky. The bitter cold slammed into him, and it was glorious.

He didn't know how he'd managed it, but he was leaving here with freedom glowing in his pocket. He raised his hands to the sky and started to laugh. He hadn't felt this free since Pa got sick.

Kain came up behind him, eyebrows arched as Daezen continued to laugh.

They got onto the hoverbike.

'What's got into you, mut?' Kain said as they rose into the sky.

'Just happy to be alive, brother. Happy to be alive.'

Stars glinted in the blackness of the night. The markets and skyrises of the city glowed with neon lights. Rising higher and higher, Daezen increased the bike's speed, relishing the cold rush of icy air.

CHAPTER 5
INSPECTOR

SOBA

The stories of the city played out on the shadowstream.

The gruesome gut of Densolid Minor lay far beneath Inspector Soba Nite as she scaled buildings and stalked the shadows. Navigating the entrails of the city's slums, she leapt onto the crumbling roof of the Red Ruins. Moonlight glinted off the polished surface of a clunky hoverbike.

Topper Luxo's bike.

A perfect fifth.

Soba had spent the day watching the shadowstream, a live video stream recorded through the shadowbirds' eyes. The Inspectors of the Sharizan Empire had invested centuries in genetic and ocular engineering to make the shadowbirds a perfect tool for surveillance. Unlike a creature of pure tech, they had instincts, self-awareness, even a degree of autonomy.

Useful they may be, but their beady black eyes sent chills down Soba's spine.

In Densolid, the birds served to monitor the activities of the lower oculary orders. The rollout of the video capture upgrade had provided hours and hours of often tedious footage for the Inspectors to peruse. And today, Soba had drawn the short sword.

After hours of watching Azures and Veridians stumble around, off their heads from street psychs, the thankless job had finally paid off. She'd caught sight of a hoverbike covered in obscene drawings flying above the Red Ruins. The hoverbike of a wanted Azure assassin.

Topper Luxo was a man with ideas far above his station, and terrible taste in transport. Over-glossed and overdone, the vehicle boasted an array of superficial upgrades and crass customisations.

Here's the bike, but where's the rider?

Soba hadn't gleaned any idea of Topper Luxo's whereabouts from the shadowstream. He hadn't even been driving the bike. Two young Azures were shadowsnapped riding it, little more than teenagers taking a joyride.

Scanning the citizen database, Soba had matched their faces against identity files. Kain Trovit and Jantsia Brittle, Azure finalists registered at the Azca 9 Academy. They seemed harmless enough, but she would still add them to the report. Her mentor would welcome any information that led to the capture of the notorious Topper Luxo.

Continuing her journey, Soba skipped unseen between tin roofs and canopies. Never once touching the earth, high above the filthy streets; her domain was the sky. One floor high, then two. Five floors up. Ten. She prowled the urbanscape as easily as she breathed. For this was breathing ... at least it was for her.

A sharp intake of vertigo as she peered off the edge of a fifty-metre drop. The subtle flow of sliding down a copper-coated drainpipe, one hand extended to catch the icy breeze. Holding her breath, she hopped along a broken window ledge. Then came the rhythmic beat of her feet on the vertical wall, propelling her upwards to roll, roll, roll across the roof's surface.

Exhale.

Between breaths, she surveyed the upper network of dilapidated, steaming rooftops. Yellow smoke oozed from the chimney pipes, clouding her vision and clogging her throat. No sign of Topper or the young Azures. The cycle began again.

Inhale.

Exhale.

Inhale.

Exhale.

Once every quart-cycle, Soba's mentor set her a new physical challenge to complement her investigative work. The tasks ranged from scaling buildings and sparring to trekking through the tundra in the dead of night. Her mentor had believed in her from the very beginning, pushing her to hone her agility and strength since the day she'd turned fifteen.

Now, at the age of nineteen, the parameters of the challenge had elevated, conditions becoming infinitely tougher and targets ever harder to locate. Soba savoured the thrill of it, the chance to prove herself.

Jumping from rooftop to rooftop, landing silently, rolling between the shadows; only at times like this did the city feel like home. In the dark of the night, her dark brown skin, jet-black braids, and white-ringed Obsidian eyes were tools in her armoury, rather than markers of difference. Unlike her pale-faced colleagues, Soba could leap the gaps between buildings without worrying that a stray lock of flaxen hair or glassy skin would catch the light. She worked best at night, that's what her mentor had always told her.

Soft footsteps came to a halt. She paused before a looming skyrise. The final part of the test.

Crossing the boundary line between Densolid Minor and Major, she vaulted off a rooftop, landing silently on the jet-washed onyx stones of the city proper. A flash sparked from a high window in the Inspectors' skyrise.

The signal.

Frost bit at her exposed neck as she craned her head. Her gaze fell inwards. The sounds in her vicinity tickled her awareness. More than ordinary noises, they were vibrations. Oscillations that moved through the frigid air carrying silent songs on the wind.

Breathing in the soundwaves nearest her, she forced her heart to change its beat in time with their universal hum. They answered her call, ready and willing. Zoning in on the pattern of acoustic particles, Soba twisted them together, forming a sonar call-out and sending it up the skyrise. In half a blink, the waves returned.

Thirtieth floor.

Soba bit the inside of her cheek, hard enough to draw a single drop of salty blood. A mountain of a climb lay before her.

Several hours later, she reached the twenty-ninth floor. She held her core tight, gripping all four points of the skyrise's slightly indented side panel. Bracing herself, she heaved her body to the ledge, biceps burning as her chalked hands fumbled for purchase. The grip was lazy, but she felt impatient, so she pushed off her feet with the remaining strength in her thighs.

At first, she thought she'd gotten lucky. Her right hand darted out, catching the final ledge. But as she swung to place her grip, something tore in her left upper arm.

Soba howled in agony, right arm straining under the added weight. Slowing the swing, she used breathing exercises to distract from the roaring pain of her injury and the rising panic in her chest.

If she fell now, she would die.

A dark, mellifluous voice whispered inside her head. *Would it be so bad?*

'No,' Soba breathed, silencing the voice. She would find a way. She would never give up. Tightening her abdominals, she curled her legs upward so the soles of her malleable shoes rested against the panel. Filling her lungs with air, she let her gaze slip into second sight. The unseeing.

The air around her burst to life with bustling black, acoustic waves. Like a broken harp, strings of particles wrapped around the wind, pouring from open windows above and below her.

Another set of vibrations, smaller and stronger, lay dormant in her chest. With a reverent bow of the head, she made her request in the way she'd been taught long before taking the name of Soba Nite.

Long before arriving in this cold and bitter land.

Soba may have left her home country behind, but her connection with sound originated from that fateful day in the Desert of Eyes. The day of her awakening.

Loyal acoustic energy lit up her chest, trailing forward in a line of white noise. The particles flew through her vocal cords and out of her mouth. What came back was their echo. A sonar map imprinted in her mind. Soba knew of no one else in the whole of Albin with this ability. Her unique skill had earned her the moniker, *Bloodbat,* in the Inspectors training academy.

The echolocation map showed a second, broader ledge above the one where she hung. Flames of pain burnt up her bicep. Sweat dripped into her eyes. No matter how much her muscles screamed for her to let go, she couldn't quit now. Resigning herself to her fate, she widened her stance and pushed off tired legs. In spite of the crippling pain, she forced her arms to grab at the second ledge and swing her up. By some miracle, it worked.

She crashed through the window, screaming with equal parts relief and agony.

'Hello, Soba.'

A honeyed voice met her ears, sweetening the aches and silencing the small part of her that whispered unsayable things. The part of her that wished she'd fallen.

'Chief Inspector Vox,' Soba said between heavy breaths, unable to get to her feet and salute. She would recover, she just needed a few seconds.

'I told you not to call me that. Not when we're alone,' he replied.

A strong pale hand, adorned with golden rings, stretched out in front of her.

'Elias,' she said, ignoring the hand and placing aching elbows against the floor, ready to push up. Her injured bicep burned. If she didn't get it healed soon, she'd be unable to carry a weapon for at least a half-cycle.

'An impressive performance,' Elias said.

She didn't deserve the praise. She'd been reckless. Worse, she'd been weak. Shakily, she manoeuvred her way to her feet.

The mirrored walls of the small office reflected her dishevelled appearance back at her.

She grimaced. 'I apologise for my weakness.'

'There's no need to be so formal when we're alone, Little Night-Eyes,' Elias said. 'And you were hardly weak. I expected to see you at least ten floors below in one of the usual rooms. In fact, I'd even had them prepared. This was supposed to be an impossible task.'

A flash of admiration in his dark-treacle eyes.

She cocked her head. 'Why would you set me an impossible task?'

'So you would learn your limits.' A wide grin spread across his full, parted lips. Starlight caught the waves of his shoulder-length golden hair. The sight of him almost made her fall back to her knees.

'I thought you knew me well, Elias. My only limits are my orders.'

'I'm starting to see that.' Elias took a step forward, reaching out to twist a dark braid that had fallen from her ponytail during the climb. Being near him was like scaling a building without a harness. Constantly aware of how far she could fall if she placed her weight in the wrong place, but unable or unwilling to return to the ground.

Trying not to let his musky scent distract her, she began the debrief. 'Topper Luxo's bike is on the Red Ruins. It's definitely his. No sign of him, though.'

'If he rode the bike there, it should be on the shadowstream.'

'He didn't,' Soba replied, relaxing into the familiar routine. 'Two children drove the bike there. Azures finalists by the names of Jantsia Brittle and Kain Trovit. They were later collected by Daezen Trovit, Kain's older brother and San-centre worker.'

'Hmm. The Brittle girl is Zuleikha's servant. And the Trovit boys ... Flint's sons. Well, that is very interesting.'

Soba trembled at the glint of hunger in his eyes. At the way he could so easily transform from a kind mentor, a gentle lover, into someone who bent the world to his will.

Burying the errant thoughts in the sand dunes of her mind, she continued, 'I'll keep monitoring them, then pass the mission to you if we make headway tracking Topper.'

'No, no. I'll be far too busy organising the Gala. Aunt Greta has agreed to hold it in Densolid this year, something which is nigh on unheard of. This is my chance to finally prove myself in front of the entire preening Empire. They think themselves better than us, you know. Well, we'll show them why Albin was once the heart of oculary science. We'll show them what the Empire could've been.' Elias was behind her now, tracing her shoulder blades with his fingertips. 'I plan to show Greta what I could do if I were granted more responsibility among the Vox Elites. And I think you can help me do so. Take the lead on this mission. Watch the children. The older Trovit boy, too. Watch the bike. Give me a win to talk about at the Gala, and I'll make it worth your while.'

'I will try my best,' Soba whispered. Her heart ached to make Elias proud, but she also feared what would happen if she failed him.

'I thought your only limits were your orders?' Elias whispered in her ear. 'The Albin City Inspectorate has been lauded to no end for the capture of the illegal couple and their dual-oc offspring. Just think of it. This time, I could be the one to claim the accolade, with you at my side, of course.'

She didn't need reminding of Albin City's discovery; she'd followed the case closely. Dead memories long buried, began to stir. No. She wouldn't look at them. She must never look back.

Elias's teeth grazed her bare throat, and a twinge of lust melted away her misgivings. She reached up a hand to tangle in his silky hair. What an honour it was to be desired by such a man. He may be ruthless, but he only did what was necessary to protect the Empire. To protect her.

From humble beginnings, Soba had broken records by becoming the youngest qualified Inspector in Albin's history. She was also the only Inspector of Octengion origin to gain a golden pass from the Densolid training academy. All thanks to Elias.

He spun her around, lightly kissing her on the lips. Warmth spread across her lower stomach as she pulled him closer, desperate for release. He returned the passionate embrace with a heated kiss of his own. His reciprocated love would never cease to amaze her. She didn't deserve it.

But one day, she would.

Every mission, every torturous training session, took her one step closer to being worthy of his charity. Of his love.

She owed him everything.

CHAPTER 6
MEDICINE

JANTSIA

The morning after the hoverbike fiasco, Jantsia awoke from feverish dreams to a firecat purring on her chest. A rough tongue grazed her cheek as she blinked open her eyes. The strange dreams left a tightness in her chest.

'Good morning, Luz.' She yawned, finding comfort in the softness of the cat's scruffy fur.

In spite of a full night's sleep, exhaustion weighed her down. She snuggled back under the duvet. Another ten minutes of snoozing couldn't hurt. After all, she nearly died yesterday.

Soft rays of the morning sun reflected in Luz's golden eyes as he issued a stern meow. For a small furry creature with a tiny brain, he sure knew exactly how to manipulate her. In theory, almost all animals in the Sharizan Empire had been bred and engineered to serve humans, but every time she'd tried a command on Luz, he'd shaken it off as if it were a light dusting of snow rather than a binding order.

Luz wailed, patting Jantsia on the head with velvet paws as if to say, *I'm not going anywhere, stupid human. It's time to wake up.*

She placed her hands together in a prayer position. 'Luz, stay still.'

Ignoring the command, he dashed around the bed and pounced on her foot, claws outstretched.

'Oh, my eyes,' she screamed as little hot needles lanced through her foot.

Fladden forsake him, this creature didn't understand a thing about authority and status. It wasn't appropriate to rebel against orders issued from above, and it definitely wasn't smart to bite the hand (or foot) of one's guardian. She'd have to teach him a lesson.

She grabbed hold of Luz, bracing a single finger to deliver justice with a well-timed flick. His button nose twitched, shifting from black to orange as he squirmed to free himself. His fur warmed several degrees, heating her hands. With a final chirrup, he broke free.

Shariza wept, she couldn't shout at this little fluffball, let alone flick him. The little tyke was far too adorable to ever be disciplined. She stared into his eyes and blinked slowly. A golden glow spread up her arms and nestled in her chest as he returned the gesture.

Once she'd dragged herself out of bed, the mischievous firecat twisted and rubbed himself against her legs, ensuring she walked straight to his food bowl with a well-timed nip of her foot.

'Bred to obey humans,' she muttered. 'Guess nobody told you that.' She skipped backwards to avoid another foot bite, then bent down to scratch him under his chin. 'Well, I'm not supposed to exist, so we make a good pair.'

Scruffs of white and black fur protruded from his ears and slitted pupils drifted together in his golden eyes. Perhaps she'd named him incorrectly. Luz was the Laminosian word for light, but the more she got to know him the more the name 'Loco' suited him better.

She filled his bowl with fresh food before shuffling to the shower in her en suite and beginning the torturous process of getting ready for the academy. No teenager enjoyed waking up at the crack of dawn to prepare for a day of lessons and classroom politics, but the process was especially excruciating for Jantsia.

Every morning in the shower, she'd repeat the lies she had to tell the world. The lies that shaped and enveloped her in a protective blanket, smothering her so tightly she could hardly breathe. But she was still breathing, and that was the whole point.

Thanks to her blue eyes, she looked like an ordinary Azure; the lowest caste of the four oculary orders. But beneath the surface, she was anything but ordinary. Deep inside her, a war was raging.

A war for her life.

Jantsia Brittle was a dual-oc. The illegal offspring of her Azure father and Obsidian mother. And by all rights, she shouldn't be alive...

According to the Empire, all dual-oculary children were born with a sickness in their blood that resulted in their death. Despite all this, Jantsia was still here, having made it to the age of seventeen. Every breath she took was a threat to the Empire. And if anyone found out the truth and reported her, she'd be 'terminated', just like the child the Inspectors had discovered in Albin City.

She was lucky to be alive.

Or at least, that was what her parents had always told her.

Jantsia scowled at her reflection, aggressively pulling at clumps of uneven curls with her heat brush. 'Nothing about this feels lucky,' she mumbled.

Out of nowhere, Luz launched at her hand, claws on fire, knocking the heat brush to the floor where it sizzled against the carpet. Jantsia screamed, dropping to the floor and deactivating the heat brush while Luz clung to her hand.

'Hurry up, Jantsy *jaan*. What's going on in there?' her father called.

'Nothing. I'm coming, Baba,' she called back.

Luz's rough tongue licked at her hand, instantly cooling the burn and healing the surface scratches.

She tried to force authority into her voice. 'Don't think you're forgiven just like that.'

Checking herself in the mirror, she grimaced at the fuzzy wisps surrounding her hairline. The spirit of her hair writhed in its final death throes, desperate to spring out and take up space. Tugging her burnt locks into a plait, she gelled down as many of the wisps as possible. A far cry from the poker-straight, pale-blonde hair of her peers, but it would have to do.

As soon as she opened her bedroom door, Luz dashed toward his favourite scratch-post: a cream velvet chair. She sighed, equal parts exasperated and jealous. He held more defiance in the tip of his tail than she had in her whole body. Most of the time, she tiptoed through life, watching the world pass her by as if she were an observer.

But not always.

The memory of the wind rushing through her hair as she flew across the city with Kain flashed to the front of her mind. The blood-shaking feeling of surrender. Of daring.

Now *that* was living.

In the open-plan living space, Zuleikha stood at the floor-to-ceiling windows while Baba prepared breakfast. Zuleikha wasn't looking at the pristine garden of pink and black roses, nor at the black-marble sculptures in the middle of their patio. She was looking up.

Hundreds of metres above them, thousands of ant-like pods buzzed out to factories and in between skyrises, jammed full of citizens travelling to perform their Duties for the Empire. The people in those pods would think Jantsia lucky. She may be an indentured servant, but she lived in luxury, nonetheless. Unfortunately, and unbeknownst to anyone outside Jantsia's family circle, her Obsidian patron wasn't just her master – *she was her mother*.

A curse almost as bad as her illegal genetics.

Lengths of purple satin swished as Zuleikha spun around, glancing disdainfully at Luz before surveying Jantsia. Displeasure creased her perfectly contoured face. What Jantsia wouldn't give to look like her.

Zuleikha was about the same height as her, but with her wide-set hips and powerful shoulders, she had the air of tallness. Smouldering eyes of pure Obsidian flecked with embers, skin the colour of burnt umber, and long dark waves of hair that twisted down to her waist. She embodied everything Jantsia lacked: beauty, power and talent.

'Get your pet under control, please,' Zuleikha said. 'And what have you done to your lovely hair?'

Here we go again.

Jantsia tugged at her hoodie and hunched her shoulders, folding in on herself.

Zuleikha smiled thinly. 'Your natural hair is beautiful. If only you stopped trying to deny your heritage. Why don't you try to line your eyes and highlight your eyebrows the way I showed you? You are a descendent of the Riviera and Rostamani Great Elites. Be proud, *miha*.'

If she'd inherited her mother's beauty and Obsidian oculary, then maybe she would be proud. Instead, she was an awkward mix of both her mother and father. Not pale enough but not tanned enough, either. Too broad, but not curvy. Azure eyes, but no power. It was like the universe had mixed two beautifully coloured paints and ended up with an ugly grey.

Jantsia grimaced. 'Whatever you say.'

'Anyway,' Zuleikha continued, 'Baba told me you pulled some kind of trick on the guard to get two Azure boys into Meridian. Care to explain what you were thinking?'

Beny's eyes widened as he flipped a pansweet in the frying pan. 'Hmm.' His eyes darted between them. 'Those weren't my exact words.' He stirred the saucepan, avoiding Zuleikha's glare.

Irritation prickled down Jantsia's spine, flaring up like an itch that couldn't be scratched. 'Now I need to explain to you why I have friends?' If Zuleikha had her way, she wouldn't even leave the house, let alone have friends.

Zuleikha paced back and forth. 'Friends are the weakest link when it comes to keeping secrets, especially at your age. There's no loyalty among teenagers. Besides, the Trovit boys would receive a large reward for informing on us. Artium knows, the Inspectors would pay them handsomely if they handed you over. Remember to keep a distance, Jantsia. Don't let kind words and actions fool you into trusting them.'

Rules, lies, fake smiles. Every part of her life was a scripted performance to keep her and her parents safe from the Inspectors. Her friendship with Kain gifted her brief moments in which she didn't have to pretend. Where she relinquished control, even for a few seconds. Without those moments, life wouldn't be worth living.

Jantsia narrowed her eyes. 'You always say things like this. But you don't know anything about Kain or his family. Just because your Obsidian friends are all snakes, doesn't mean Azures are the same. I'm going to be eighteen soon, you know. Would it kill you to treat me like an adult and not an ocking servant child!' Luz's claws dug into her skin as he leapt on to her shoulder and hissed.

Zuleikha's neutral expression cracked, her mouth twitching. 'I know pretending is hard on you. Like you say, you're nearly an adult, and there are things you must accept. Life is nothing but one big show, the ultimate pretence. We wear many masks and hide the truth so we can keep on living, but don't forget that it's a façade. I am not your patron. I am your mother. Your maman. And I would do anything to keep you safe.'

Hot tears rolled down Jantsia's cheeks. 'You're not a mother. You're a jailer.'

Zuleikha's eyes widened revealing inflamed red veins, a sign of sleep deprivation. 'Jailer? Me? You think I want to live in this cursed backwater city? Everything I do is for you, you ungrateful little—'

'Zuli, that's enough,' Beny interjected in a low voice. The fine lines around his eyes were more pronounced than usual.

Jantsia wiped her tears on the back of her sleeve, guilt seeping into her bones. It hadn't escaped her notice that her parents had been sleeping in separate rooms for the past few lunar cycles. Whenever they argued it was always about her. Why did everything she touched have to fall apart?

'Now, who's hungry?' Beny asked in a weirdly upbeat tone.

He always did this; try to make light of their ocked-up family situation. She sniffed. As fractured as her relationship was with her mother, she didn't want Baba to pay the price. 'What's cooking?'

'Pansweets and Parsian nectar spread,' he replied, leaning over two large pans on the stove.

'Thank the Empire, finally! A breakfast fit for a descendant of the Great Elites.' Jantsia kissed him on the cheek, then inhaled the scent of sweet, cinnamon mixture.

Zuleikha swished back around to look out of the window, ignoring Jantsia's sarcastic remark.

Beny slapped two fluffy pansweets on a plate. 'I guess it's too much to ask that the women of this house make an effort to coexist?' He doused the pansweets in thick, gooey nectar. 'Or is this the fate that awaits all fathers of fiery teenagers and dragon mothers?'

Jantsia scoffed, grabbing the plate from her father's hands and devouring the food. Her plate was empty before he'd finished plating up the other two dishes.

'See you later, Luz.' Jantsia tickled the cat under his chin then started for the door.

'Wait,' Zuleikha's musical tone urged her to slow. Her mother wasn't an expert in persuasive harmonics, a strand of Obsidian oculary power that manipulated a person's vocal tones to make others follow orders, but she was proficient in charging her voice with power. Not enough to make you believe everything she said for too long, but enough to make you consider it for several minutes.

Zuleikha drew closer, exchanging a look with Beny. 'I'm sorry for being so strict with you. I'm ... under a lot of pressure at the moment.'

'Forget it,' Jantsia replied. Empty words for an empty apology.

Zuleikha forced her face into a smile and raised her eyebrows as if she were waiting for Jantsia to say more. The silence grew long and heavy. 'Is there something you'd like to say to me?'

Jantsia shrugged. 'Not particularly.'

'How about an apology?' Zuleikha placed her hands on her hips, a fake smile straining. 'Apologise, now.' Another dark look from Benyamin. 'Please.'

Jantsia could almost see the acoustic particles gathering around her mother's vocal cords, imbuing her words with power. Well, if her mother wanted to use words as weapons, then so would she.

'I apologise for disrespecting you, patron,' Jantsia said curtly, bending at the waist in an awkward bow and crossing a hand over her chest. If Zuleikha wanted respect, she'd give it to her. The respect that a servant owed their master.

Zuleikha scoffed. 'Jantsia, you are a miracle. You're our miracle. One day, you'll understand what Baba and I have sacrificed to keep you safe.'

'You mean what I've sacrificed so you and Baba get to play cross-eyed lovers with a mutant kid. It's not like anything would even happen to you if we were caught. They'd kill me and Baba, and your oh-so-powerful Rostamani and Riviera Great Elites would get *you* off the hook!' she shouted. 'Did you even bother to read *The Albin Independent* yesterday?'

She hadn't meant to be so blunt, but it was as if all her

anxiety from reading about the dual-oc child, her fear of failing exams, and her lifelong struggle to fit in had erupted inside her.

Zuleikha's black-marble eyes glowed with rage. 'You're going to be late, *so leave*.'

Jantsia stared back defiantly, unmoving.

She was not a docile animal bred to follow orders. She was her own person, and it was time to stop being a meek little mountmouse and be more like Luz. It wasn't like she'd chosen to be born into a secretive half-life, fleeing from shadows and jumping at the sound of flapping wings. She'd been raised alongside secrets so poisonous that they devoured her from the inside, corroding any sense of self she might once have had.

She didn't choose any of this. Her parents had been the ones making the decisions, as they continued to today. Well, she'd be an adult soon, so it was time they started treating her like one. Fladden be damned, she wouldn't apologise for her words. Today, she wasn't going to back down.

'Leave!' Zuleikha's voice boomed.

Trails of vibrating waves shot towards Jantsia, clapping with a force that pushed her towards the door. Unable to combat the sonar attack but unwilling to let her body move with it, she tripped and landed hard on the floor. Her head knocked against the marble and sharp pain melted through her crown.

A low, feral growl sounded as she pushed herself to her knees. It felt like a flock of shadowbirds were pecking at her head. What had just happened?

Zuleikha rushed to her side, checking her eyes and stroking her hair. 'Jantsia ... daughter ... please, give me a chance... I didn't mean to hurt you. I... I...'

Luz arched his back and hissed.

Her father stormed between them, helping Jantsia up and pulling her away from Zuleikha. 'You knocked her down. Our own ocking daughter. Do you have no control over yourself?'

Jantsia pulled away from her father, unsteady on her feet as her memories reordered themselves. She'd been knocked to the ground by a sonar wave. Exactly what an Obsidian master might do to their servant, and not at all what a mother should do to their daughter. The sharpness of the pain in her head gave her clarity. This woman was her mother in biological terms only. Nothing more.

Zuleikha would never understand what it was to be Azure in an Obsidian world, let alone a pale imitation of Azure, a ticking timebomb inside the chests of everyone she loved.

Her father's hand gripped her shoulder. 'Jantsia, you look pale. Shall I get you some analgesics? Have you already taken your pills?'

'No, I forgot,' Jantsia murmured. Those Fladden-forsaken pills.

Zuleikha swished away, and if she didn't know better, Jantsia would've said there were tears in her eyes. 'You see, I didn't push her that hard, it was the withdrawal. We should control her doses, Beny. I've said this before I—'

'She's nearly an adult, remember. I for one don't advocate treating her like a prisoner!'

Her parents continued to argue as if she weren't there, so Jantsia dusted herself off and went to her room to retrieve her packsack and take her stupid medicine.

Another wonderful benefit of being an illegal dual-oc freak was that she had to take special pills her mother had sourced from Fladden-knew-where. She popped a pill from the pack, eyeing it warily. These tiny things were the only reason she hadn't perished from the blood sickness. The only reason she was still alive.

She swallowed, ignoring the lump in her throat, and rushed out of the house. Though she tried to ignore the shouts and insults her parents dealt one another, every word crept under her skin, constricting her veins.

It hadn't always been like this. At least, she didn't think it had. Her memories from before they'd arrived in Densolid were foggy, tinged with a metallic colour that didn't seem real. Staying in small fishing villages on the southern coast of Albin. Sleeping in makeshift cabins to the roaring sound of the sea. Foraging for food. Splashing in the waves. Even though they'd had nothing, not even a home, they'd been happy. They'd been a team.

Time to pull herself together and prepare for the day ahead. Cold, icy air constricted her airways as she exited Meridian through the glowing metal gate. The sudden change in temperature had her unsteady on her feet, and her temples began to throb. She hadn't hit her head that hard, had she?

A green-and-blue striped multipod clanked and rattled to a stop in front of her. She eyed the egg-shaped vehicle; metallic tiles flapped on its sides and the cage protecting the power core looked awfully rusty. The doors slid open revealing at least fifty Veridians and Azures, stood together so tightly they were practically a wall of flesh. She screwed up her nose and pushed her way through, grabbing a stray cable that hung from the ceiling to secure her balance.

The vehicle shook, gaining height. The transport jerked in

one direction, then another, slamming Jantsia against the tinted window. She held tightly to the loose cable, trying to ignore the fact that her face was practically in a man's armpit.

This was going to be a long ride.

CHAPTER 7
OCULARY

JANTSIA

The multipod slowed, dropping to ground level as it reached the Azure 9 stop. By some miracle, she'd lasted the entire journey without having a panic attack. Every time she fought with Zuleikha, her hands trembled for hours. With the added bonus of the blow she'd taken to the head, it'd been a struggle to stay upright during the bumpy multipod ride.

The smell of sweat and rusted metal had her gorge rising as she squeezed her body through a wall of Veridians and Azures, hopping out before the automatic doors closed behind her. The shaking blue-and-green striped transport took off to resume its route.

She scrunched her nose. Of course, the only place where Azures and Veridians were permitted to mingle was a sweaty, overcrowded multipod. Unlike personal pods, there was no seating inside the communal vehicles, just rows of sticky handles and straps. If only the Great Elites would—

Jantsia caught herself mid-thought. She shouldn't think like this. She had to stay unnoticed, unemotional, *undetectable*. Whatever she felt, whatever she believed, it didn't matter. As much as she resented the leash her parents kept her on, it had kept her alive, hadn't it?

Stay invisible. Stay alive.

The phrase beat in time with her heart. She was no longer an innocent child frolicking in the waves on the shores of Sumavig. She knew what awaited her if she dared to challenge the system. A small disagreement with Zuleikha, and she'd almost cracked her head in two. What would happen if she roused the anger of the Inspectors?

Well, she was alive, and that was enough. There was no dream worth dying for.

'A Brown got you down, mut?' Kain appeared at her side.

'Same old cack, ice-eyed twack,' she replied, as was their custom.

Jantsia had never learnt Azure patterns of speech, instead absorbing an eclectic mixture of her mother's high register and her father's neutral tone. She and Kain often greeted each other in a lowborn, Azure manner. It was their in-joke. A gentle poke at the difference in their upbringings. A way to prove it didn't matter to their friendship.

'Jantsy, your eyes are all red. Is this about the hoverbike thing?' Kain took a step forward, placing a hand firmly on her shoulder.

Jantsia cast her gaze to the ground, her traitorous eyes still bore signs of the argument with her parents. Kain wouldn't understand. And she couldn't tell him that all the lies she had to remember hung over her like a dirty shadow. Nor that if she didn't take those stupid pills, she'd be dead within a few days.

Unseeing eyes, unhurt heart.

Grappling with her emotions, she forced them down, locking them away in a secret space in her chest.

Kain's electric-blue eyes glistened with worry.

Jantsia pursed her lips. 'I had to stand downwind of some of the worst body odour I've ever had the misfortune of inhaling in the multipod. It could have been the end of me.'

Kain's face relaxed. 'That'll explain the tears. Who was it this time? I bet it was a Greener. All dirt, no soap for those unlucky plodders.'

'Kain,' she giggled, 'you shouldn't say stuff like that.'

'I'm right, though, aren't I? It was a stinkin' root-render!'

'It might've been,' she said, muffling her laughter with her sleeve.

'Knew it.' Kain grabbed her arm. 'Come along, my intoxicated friend, we're running late.'

As they ran toward the dark, metallic fence marking the perimeter of the academy, Jantsia relaxed her face muscles into a neutral half-smile. Time to forget her cursed genetics and her ocked-up family. She had to focus on something more tangible: exams. At that thought, her heart raced with a different type of stress. Exam day would be here in no time at all. And no matter how much she lied to herself, she wasn't ready.

That day would decide her future.

Students lined the courtyard, standing in formation for the morning hymn. Jantsia and Kain rushed to take their places at the end of the line. Girls and boys alike ogled Kain, passing over Jantsia as if she weren't even there. She didn't mind. Better to be invisible than plastered over the home screen of *The Albin Independent*.

Mere seconds after they'd stepped in line, the digital gong sounded. The metal gates drew closed, and the familiar synthetic notes of the Empire anthem started up. Without exception, every single student opened their mouth to sing.

> *One Shariza united*
> *We thank the Great Elites*
> *For fighting to create*
> *Peace and prosperity*
>
> *All colours invited*
> *To make the Empire great*
> *Separately we strive*
> *To maintain our peaceful states*
> *Obsidians you lead us*
> *Sound-benders speak the truth*
> *Sepias give us strength in strife*
> *Earth-breakers fight on through*
> *Veridians placate us*
> *Root-renders heal and feed*
> *Azures, they support the rest*
> *Water-wielding as we need*
>
> *Oh, glorious Shariza!*
> *Victorious Great Elites!*
> *In Fladden's steps we follow*
> *By Artium's grace we reap*
> *The wonders of the oculary*
> *Long live the Empire's creed!*

As the song came to an end, a holo-Tile depicting an animated flag rose above them, extending in all directions, so that everyone could see the flag of the Sharizan Empire. An all-seeing Obsidian eye ringed with Sepia, Veridian, and Azure. It blinked and scanned the students, watching over them, surveilling them.

Nobody moved a muscle until the screen was at full mast. The synthetic gong sounded once more.

By the time the gong rang out again, she and Kain were seated in the Oculary Practice classroom along with the rest of the finalists. Each desk held two ceramic bowls; one filled with purified water, the other with dirtied liquid.

'Right, Level Tens, you know what to do.' Educator Leanne entered the room. 'Final examinations are just around the corner, so prove to me that you've learnt something other than how to send each other messages when I'm not looking.'

The students laughed. Although Educator Leanne had always been strict, when they'd entered final year, she'd started to treat them more like equals than children.

As usual, Flossie Savin was the first to complete the task, separating the grime from the clean particles of water in her bowl in no time at all. Her long, silvery-blonde hair sparkled in the light, complementing her perfect porcelain skin. A paragon of Azure perfection and oculary control.

Oculary power required the user to adopt the special state of unseeing, a shift in perspective that revealed the particles of one's particular oculary affinity. Once a student grasped the unseeing, they were said to have had their awakening. By Level Ten, all the students had awoken. All bar one.

Because when Jantsia looked at water, she simply saw ...

water. No particles. No lights. Just plain, transparent water. Thanks to her parents, she'd been born broken.

Broken, but not beaten.

Jantsia had intensively studied oculary theory, mastering the multitude of mental exercises necessary to send commands towards the particles in the water. However, without knowing where to direct the calls, the effects were weak. Very weak.

Today was no different. Jantsia was unable to see or unsee anything. Her stomach riled with anxiety as the students around her finished purifying water with varying degrees of finesse. She hung her head. How on Shariza would she pass these exams if she couldn't see anything? An image of her and Kain exploring the world as travelling performers flickered and disappeared completely from her mind. It was impossible.

The dull throb in her temples returned.

'Jantsia, is something wrong?'

Educator Leanne appeared in front of her, bright blue eyes full of kindness. The stark sapphire colour contrasted with her creamy-white skin.

'Just the usual,' she mumbled, hunching her shoulders and trying not to wince at the web of pain in her crown. Leanne couldn't help her, no matter how hard she tried. Nature beat nurture – and her nature was rotten to the very core.

'Still can't see a thing?'

'Not a dot.'

Leanne was young for an Educator, barely in her thirties. She kept her hair closely cropped and dyed bright pink. Wearing the dowdy, navy jumpsuit as she did, rolled up sleeves and trousers legs, with a fuchsia sash at her waist, it looked more like a fashion statement than a mandated uniform. Jantsia adored her, which was why the idea of disappointing her yet again was so repugnant. In an alternate world somewhere, a world where she had normal parents, she'd want to be like Leanne when she grew up.

Ordinary but cool.

Ordinary and kind.

Educator Leanne unfolded her Tile, spreading it on the desk in front of them where it melded with the desk's internal screen system. She called up a diagram Jantsia knew by heart and loathed with every fibre of her being.

An image of a bowl filled with moving blue dots materialised on the screen. Leanne zoomed in on the dots, bringing up annotations that detailed the names of each group of particles.

Periphery Particles
Connector Particles
Central Particles

Leanne tapped on the 'Central Particles' label, highlighting the thickest group of blue dots, the group right at the bottom of the bowl. They vibrated slightly, but apart from that they barely moved. With another tap, she conjured up a paragraph of text.

The central-particle group is the foundation of the body of
water. These particles glow brighter than surrounding water
droplets, indicating their pivotal role in holding the water
grouping together. By focusing on asserting one's will over
this group, the Azure ensures a steady and full control over
the water, as long as it is small enough in volume. Large
volumes of water have several central groups, with naturally
occurring rivers and streams nigh on impossible to

manipulate due to the presence of hundreds, if not thousands, of central groupings.

Jantsia nodded, she knew all this. In fact, she'd read that particular explanation over a hundred times. It never made a difference.

'Now, locate the central group in your bowl,' Leanne said. 'Let your gaze slip, change the perspective,'

Jantsia focused on the water, her face flooding with heat. Blinking slowly, she willed her vision to switch, imagining the joy of finally seeing the dancing particles she'd read so much about. She wasn't going to give up. Her eyes were blue after all, that in itself should be impossible for someone like her. Why not aim for one more impossibility? Whatever tomorrow might bring, she was alive today. Time to make it count. Her bottom lip quivered, and she stared so hard she went cross-eyed.

Her eyeballs twitched, unsteady in their sockets.

Nothing happened.

Raising her hands, she pushed her will at the water, imploring the liquid to reveal its secrets. Imploring the water to recognise her as Azure. As a valued member of the Empire.

A single drop of water rose from the bowl then fell back down with an anti-climactic plop.

'Okay,' Leanne said, 'you've established a minor kinetic connection, that means...'

She wanted to scream that it meant nothing. That it wasn't good enough. That she had to do better.

But she didn't.

Taking a deep breath to steady herself, she responded, 'A group of peripherals felt the oculary-pull and reacted in kind.'

'Yes, that's good.'

No, it wasn't. It had been good last year, when she'd finally managed to make the water move, but now, with final examinations looming, she couldn't bring herself to enjoy the small victory.

Leanne smiled, seemingly oblivious to Jantsia's inner turmoil. 'Why don't we try something different?'

Something different? Relief washed through her. Yes, something different was all she needed. A new approach to which she could apply herself.

Swiping the Tile, Leanne brought up an altered version of the diagram and Jantsia's mood darkened. The same sketch of a bowl, but this time the blue dots were accompanied by brown dots, representing impurities.

Leanne cleared her throat. 'You seem to have had more luck with the cleansing task. Why don't you show me how you did it?' She indicated the small vial of clean water on her desk.

Jantsia hadn't had any luck at all, unless by 'luck' the Educator meant Kain Trovit. When Jantsia couldn't handle any more failure, Kain would step in to complete her oculary tasks, not minding that Flossie finished first instead of him.

Educator Leanne tipped the clean water into a white ceramic bowl encrusted with dirt. Then she raised her hand, eyes flashing sapphire as a tiny vortex appeared, mixing the clean water with the dirty residue. Jantsia stifled the urge to groan.

'Let's have a go, shall we?'

She tried her best to follow the steps. Focusing her gaze on the water, willing the particles into existence. But no matter how much she strained her eyes, she couldn't see a single dot, let alone the different groupings or the empty spaces where the contaminants were. All she saw was a bowl of dirty stinking water.

Fladden be merciful, why couldn't she see anything?

In a last-ditch attempt, she shouted the key message in her mind.

Push up. Push up. PUSH UP.

A single drop of dirty water flew out of the bowl and landed squarely between Jantsia's eyes.

The sound of snorting reached her ears. Kain covered his mouth, trying not to laugh out loud. The little twack. The least he could do was feel a bit sorry for her. Her vision darkened; he didn't know how lucky he was.

He tapped the middle of his forehead and mimed wiping something off it. Taking the cue, she used the sleeve of her hoodie to wipe her brow clean.

'Good try.' Educator Leanne's voice lacked conviction. 'You'll get there in the end.'

In the end? When on Shariza was the end? She needed progress and she needed it now.

'But Educator, we've got finals in a few lunar cycles. I have to pass the oculary practice test or I'll never get a permit for international travel.'

'I know, Jantsia. A pass in oculary practice is required for all Duties, apart from...'

'Apart from Jan-Duty,' Jantsia finished, hanging her head.

Jan-Duty, or Janitorial Duty, ranged from sweeping the streets to collecting waste and cleaning public bathrooms. While it wasn't as disgusting as the entry-level water-purification jobs, it was the lowest paid of all Duties, barely providing enough tokens for a child's rations.

'You'll be fine, Jantsia. I'm sure your patron will ensure that you're assigned to her household if necessary. Which it won't be. And, anyway,' she said, seeing Jantsia grimace, 'you're going to pass the exam, you just need to awaken. It'll come. I see it in you.'

Jantsia wished she could see what Educator Leanne saw. Spending her life as a maid in her parents' house wasn't exactly something to look forward to. Perhaps an early death from the blood sickness would be a blessing in disguise.

'It does work with your name,' Kain shrugged, appearing behind her.

'What are you talking about?' Jantsia snapped.

'Jan-Duty, like Jantsi-Duty.' He flashed her his best impish smile and stepped out of arm's reach.

Jantsia's hand itched to slap him, then she had a better idea. Narrowing her eyes, the command echoed in her mind.

PUSH UP.

A bead of dirty water flew up and out of her bowl and splashed into Kain's eye.

'What the ock!' he yelled, rubbing his eye vigorously as his face turned bright red.

Educator Leanne laughed. 'Now, now, children. Don't make me give you Level One treatment again.' She walked back to the centre of the room, glancing over her shoulder to mouth, 'Good shot'.

It was a shame Jantsia had been aiming for his forehead, not his eye.

'Right, that's enough for today. Make sure to read up on past exams this evening. Tomorrow, I want to see you all make a start on your routines,' Educator Leanne said to the class who were already packing up their things and making for the door.

'Flossie, Kain, stay behind for a minute, please.'

Jantsia stormed into the courtyard, rushing past the heated metal fountain that funnelled water from a spout at its centre. Coloured lights illuminated the trickling water, filling her with embarrassment from head to toe. Even the rusty old fountain had more power than her.

In a while, Kain caught up with her and nudged her playfully.

'You still here, boss?'

'I'm here.' She turned to him. The confusion in his bright eyes was enough to make her smile. 'Anyway, weren't you supposed to stay behind with Flossie?'

'No,' Kain said. 'I'm supposed to be here with you.'

Warmth rippled through her.

What did he mean by that?

'Educator Leanne's right,' he said. 'You'll get there. I was just joking with that thing about Jantsi-Duty. Even if the worst does happen, Daeze started out on Jan-Duty and he got promoted in the first few lunar cycles. There's no shame.'

She hadn't thought about Daezen. It was hard to believe that someone like him had started out in Jan-Duty. He and Kain were so different. They shared the same high cheekbones and electric blue eyes but that was where the similarities ended. Kain was a beam of golden light, an explosion of joy and silliness, while Daezen was all shadow. His wiry body was laced with muscle, his naturally pale-blond hair trimmed short and dyed reddish brown. It gave him the air of an Az-sec soldier or a mercenary. Someone to fear, like Topper Luxo.

If she were honest, he scared her. His calculating eyes saw

far too much of her. Not the pretend-her. The real her. As grateful as she was to not be splattered across the dirty floor of The Pipes, the idea of being in debt to someone like him was terrifying. Well, she'd done what he'd asked, so maybe now he'd leave her alone.

CHAPTER 8
MIRRORS

JANTSIA

Jantsia's heart skipped several beats as Kain took her arm and they joined the queue for the cafi van. In moments like this, she'd wonder if he felt the same way about her. If his skin warmed whenever their hands brushed together. If her smile made his chest lighten the way his did for her.

But even if he did feel the same, what would she do? It wasn't like she could act on her feelings when so much of what she'd told him was a lie...

They reached the front of the queue, and a wave of nausea had Jantsia doubling over. What was wrong with her? She muffled her groan in her sleeve, not wanting to attract any attention.

'Two cafis for us, boss.'

'Ya want stardust up top?' asked the barista.

Pain sparked from her head to her neck, swirling in her chest.

'No, ta. Just straight cafi,' Kain replied.

Dark stars expanded and inverted before her eyes.

'And ya?' the barista asked the person behind them, eyes flashing turquoise as he prepared multiple orders at the same time. His face distorted, the glow of his eyes trailing in Jantsia's vision.

Flossie Savin's floral voice drifted through the air. 'Nothing for me, thank you. I'm just here to have a word with Kain.'

Pressure built inside Jantsia's chest. From the space where she cried silently at night, the pressure took root. Tendrils expanded to the self-critical part of her mind, to the voice that called her horrible names. Deep inside the secret space where she once wished she'd never been born, a darkness arose.

She trembled.

Kain was saying something to Flossie.

Blinking rapidly, Jantsia tried to focus on her surroundings. Her vision wobbled, morphing the room into a sinister shape. Faces around her sharpened and shifted.

They looked ... *unfamiliar*.

An overwhelming certainty descended on her psyche, tearing her stomach to pieces. She was surrounded by strangers, by alien faces with horrible gaping mouths, opening and closing.

Opening and closing.

Holding her hands in front of her, she saw they were shaking. But instead of fear or panic, she felt ... nothing. She felt ... *empty*. Her arms vibrated faster, then her head followed suit, blurring her vision until the world around her morphed into strings of colour and light etched in the air. Until suddenly, she couldn't see at all, nor could she feel the solidity of the floor beneath her. Trapped in continuous movement, rotating round and round and—

'Jantsy? Are you all right? What's happening?' Kain's worried voice reached her ears, battling through a haze of darkness to prick at her awareness.

A sharp, stabbing sensation cut through her temples like dark light.

Her throat tightened.

Was she dying?

Was the blood sickness finally taking hold?

Ice burned through the pain, dispelling her blurred vision and throwing everything around her into frightening clarity. Except, when she opened her eyes, she wasn't in the academy courtyard anymore. She was…

She didn't know where she was.

Enormous mirrors lined the seemingly never-ending hallway that lay before her. But wherever she was, this wasn't an ordinary hallway. She lifted a foot and the grey viscous substance beneath her boots wrapped around the edges of her shoe, pulling it firmly back to the ground. Instead of open sky, vast emptiness blanketed the ceiling, like the depths of a cavernous cave or the inside of a mine.

The mirrors flickered, shuffling until a single, reflective surface stood before her, displaying her own fearful expression. Her reflection reached out, touching the surface of the mirror. Her stomach heaved. She hadn't felt her arm move.

Oh, my eyes, have I completely lost my mind?

Looking down at herself, she saw her hands clasped together. She hadn't moved her arm at all. Strangely, the thought that her limbs might be moving without her knowledge had scared her more than suddenly appearing in the bizarre place. If this really was a symptom of the blood sickness, it was far weirder than she'd ever expected.

Her reflection rippled until it hardly resembled her at all. The woman before her stood up straight. Eyes of swirling oceans. And instead of hair, a mane of sea foam. Dark blue lips creased into an unnerving smile.

'Let me out,' her reflection said, in a voice that sounded like a stream trickling over pebbles.

'Who are you?' Jantsia stuttered.

Her reflection took a step forward, leaving puddles of water in her wake. Her strange smile widened. 'I am you. Or at least, I could be. I heard you call for me, so here I am.'

Jantsia tried to step back. To flee. But the thick grey substance on the floor kept her trapped in place. Her breath caught in her throat. 'I think there's been some kind of mistake, Miss. I don't know where we are or who you are. And I definitely didn't call for you.'

The water woman bit her dark bottom lip, looking more like Jantsia than she cared to admit. 'I am you.'

Jantsia glanced around at the empty space. The infinite line of mirrors extended as far as the eye could see. 'Where is this place?'

'It's not important,' her reflection replied. 'Now, don't you want to be Azure?'

Jantsia clenched her fists, breathing heavily. 'I am Azure, sort of.'

'Don't you want to be a real Azure? To feel the thrill of oculary control?'

She wasn't under any illusion. This whole thing was most

likely an hallucination brought about by the blood sickness. 'Yes,' she replied.

The woman's seafoam hair expanded, her skin rippling and roaring like white water waves. 'Take my hand.'

Jantsia bit her lip. Heart rate rocketing. 'Is this the start of the blood sickness? Am I going to die?'

Her reflection's eyes glowed like two gems of turquoise; her arm swished and extended towards the glass. 'Everyone dies. Now, take my hand.'

'If I do this, I can go back to the courtyard?'

The water woman's voice roared like waves crashing down on rocks. 'You never left.'

Hand trembling, Jantsia reached out to touch the surface of the mirror.

Ice burned through her fingertips, travelling up her arm and threatening to encompass her entire body. Her mind. At the last moment, she snatched her hand away.

The world of mirrors faded as she slammed back into her body in the freezing courtyard. Blinking through bleary eyes, she saw Kain's face split into an enormous grin. At least the pain in her head had vanished. And the people around her ... they looked normal. Although, it was a bit strange that they were all moving their hands back and forth like that.

Her eyes grew wide as she took in the scene before her.

Everyone in the courtyard was clapping, even the barista. Jantsia searched Kain's face for an explanation, but he just clapped harder and gave an almighty whoop.

A soft, lily-white hand reached out to take hers, accompanied by an overpowering scent of jasmine and a swish of silver hair.

'Congratulations, Jantsia. You've finally awoken!' Flossie

Savin announced, flamboyantly squeezing Jantsia's hand and raising it high into the air, as if she'd had something to do with all this clapping business. Jantsia smiled warily at Flossie, bemused by this strange behaviour. Then her words sunk in.

You've finally awoken.

Jantsia scanned the courtyard, expecting everyone to start laughing. This was obviously a joke. Some cruel prank masterminded by Flossie to humiliate her. But as her eyes reached the fountain in the centre of the courtyard, her mouth dropped open. It was completely empty. The water that had been inside it just moments ago floated in a large mass above their heads.

It was beautiful to behold. An uneven spherical globe, light shimmering strangely inside it. An entire rainbow of colours in flux.

Had she done that?

But where were the particles? The peripherals? The central groups?

Jantsia moaned, feeling a small spherical light inside her pop and whoosh out of existence. The water mass hovered for a second, then crashed down, soaking everyone in the vicinity.

She turned to Kain, not caring that her hair dripped with icy water, that her clothes were sodden through. A fire crackled in her belly. 'I did it,' she said. 'I had my awakening.'

It didn't take too long for the Educators to pull the water from the students and pass around facsfur blankets for those still shivering. Then they were all ushered into the canteen and provided with food and hot drinks.

While causing a scene was pretty high up on Jantsia's 'don't even think about it' list, she couldn't find it in herself to care. No matter how impossible it was meant to be, all signs pointed to one thing.

She'd *awoken*.

Her chest brimmed with pride. Now she could graduate, move out of her parents' home into more traditional Azure accommodation and live out her own life. For Fladden's sake, she might even get the hang of things quickly enough to graduate top of the class. Flutterbies danced in her stomach, what a life lay ahead of her. The life of a normal Azure – not an aberration that needed to be terminated.

But how?

Everything her parents had ever told her about her condition pointed towards her either remaining powerless or imploding from the unstable mix of oculary energy that thrummed in her blood. A dark, velvety cloud of fear began to encroach on her joyous mood. Had she really managed to banish the Obsidian part of her for good, or was this some unexpected reaction to her medicine?

Was this the onset of the blood sickness?

Her breaths quickened as the dark cloud disturbed the positive flow of her thoughts.

Kain sat at her side while she played with her food, yapping about her *awakening* and what it meant for her career. It seemed that he'd decided she was going to become a performer like him. Without needing to consult her, he'd taken it upon himself to invent an entirely new path for her future, for *their* future. Whatever was happening to her, she could count on Kain's support. He'd always be there, right up until the end.

Jantsia reached out, taking Kain's hand and squeezing it hard.

He stopped talking, opening his mouth to say something, but before the words were fully formed someone called Jantsia's name. She turned around to see that it was none other than Flossie Savin, Ice Queen Supreme.

Flossie was talking to *her*.

'Hey Jantsia, I'm pronouncing your name right, aren't I? Jant-si-ah. It's so exotic, just like you!'

A wave of flowery perfume filled Jantsia's nostrils as Flossie drew closer. 'Anyway, Pixa and I are going out tonight for a ... cafi. You want to tag along?' Flossie raised a perfectly plucked blonde eyebrow, flicking her gaze between Jantsia and Kain. 'You can bring your boyfriend if you like.'

Boyfriend?

Jantsia's heart slammed against her chest, beating so hard she feared the others might hear it. She let go of Kain's hand. She must have gone as red as a Veridian's prize-winning tomato crop. And she didn't dare look at Kain for his reaction. He was either going to make a stupid joke or say something that would crush her heart. She had to get in first before he got the wrong idea.

'He's my friend,' she stuttered. 'Not boyfriend ... just friend.'

Flossie batted her long white lashes in Kain's direction. 'Well, *friend*. You're more than welcome to join us. We can get a head start on the project Educator Leanne was telling me about. I bet Jantsia will have great ideas for our special performance, now that she's finally awoken.' She swished her hair, turning back to Jantsia. 'After all, your father is Benyamin Brittle, is he not?'

Unease mixed with warmth inside Jantsia's stomach. Hope fluttered in her chest. As much as she envied the girls, she'd always wondered what it would be like to be accepted by Flossie's group. To be popular.

And now that she'd awoken, nothing would stop her from finding out.

Kain frowned, glancing at Jantsia. 'I don't think that—'

Channelling the confidence of a descendant of the Great Elites, Jantsia interjected, 'Sounds navy, Flossie. You've got my shortcode, right? Send me the details and we'll see you this evening.'

'Wonderful,' Flossie announced. With a final swish of her silky locks, she wandered off to join her friends.

Jantsia turned to Kain. 'You don't mind, do you? I just ... I'm so fed up with being the useless, quiet girl all the time.'

A series of emotions flickered across his face before they were eclipsed by a giant grin. 'Not at all, boss. I'm looking forward to sharing a few bevvies. We've got to do something to celebrate your awakening, right?'

Her cheeks ached from smiling so much. She'd awoken, and later she'd be celebrating with Kain and the two of the most popular girls in the academy.

For the first time in many, many years, a frisson of hope ignited inside her. Maybe, one day, she'd be able to forget her secret altogether. Though the threat of the blood sickness hovered in her mind like a dreaded spectre, she had to believe there was hope. After all, wasn't her existence supposed to be impossible? Maybe her awakening was just another in a long chain of impossibilities.

Maybe one day, she'd be just like everyone else.

CHAPTER 9
ENCOUNTER

DAEZEN

As Daezen went about his Duty, sifting excrement from water, he couldn't stop thinking about the diamonds he'd left at home. He could be at The Pipes right now, selling the jewels for more tokens than he'd ever seen in his life.

And yet, he was here.

A fresh batch of sewage ran down a large funnel, stopping in a deeper pool where it was held by a lock system. From the reservoir, the waste made its way through a maze of pipes into the upturned basins in front of each worker.

Daezen's basin filled with foetid liquid. He coughed, swallowing acidic bile. After time, he'd expected to get used to the smell, filtered as it was through the san-suit's breathing tube. But after many lunar cycles of this Duty, it still made him sick to the stomach.

The thrill of taking the diamonds had calmed rapidly overnight. When Daezen had woken up that morning there'd been two things clear in his mind. One, things were too good to be true. Two, Benyamin's strange behaviour did not warrant immediate trust.

And where did that leave him? At his stinking, ocking Duty, that's where.

Sanitary Duties took place underground at a facility on the outskirts of Densolid, near the wasteland of the arctic tundra. The San-Duty workers stood on small platforms either side of the metal tunnel that linked the sewage pipes with the water filtration works and composting centre.

Daezen took in the blank, pale faces of his colleagues. Green-tinged skin, faint lines around their mouths from choking back vomit all day, and a sheet of dusk in front of their eyes. If he didn't find a way out of this Duty soon, he'd end up just like his colleagues. That's why it was good to come here. To keep doing this Duty. It reminded him of where he'd be trapped forever if he didn't find a way out. A permanent way out.

Even if he got a favourable price for the jewels, the money wouldn't last forever. Ma's meds were expensive, and he'd have to pay a penalty to settle his entire debt with the Health Centre early.

Pushing his will on the particles of water, he grasped hold of the central grouping, guiding it out of the mess. A flick of his wrist, and a command sent to the peripherals, had the pure liquid flying down the water tube that led to the filtration works. His Tile, melded to the wrist of the san-suit, indicated that seven points had been added to his total. He glanced at the scoreboard. He had the highest score, again.

Azure San-Duty workers were ranked by the quantity of pure water they amassed in a day. And Daezen consistently led the scoreboard. For all his faults, his oculary control was second to none. If he kept it up, he'd be transferred to the water-testing facility in less than a full solar loop. He should feel proud, excited. But when he thought of another twelve lunar cycles of San-Duty, something twisted inside his gut. A sickness that had nothing to do with the stench.

As soon as the shift ended, he went to the lab to take off the san-suit and wash himself down in the sterilisation showers. While putting his clothes back on, he caught sight of his reflection in a foggy mirror. Body pink and pinched, ribs jutting out, blue veins visible through translucent skin. When did he get so thin?

Wrapping himself in thermals and a facsfur fleece, he headed to the bike shed and mounted his hoverbike, relishing the momentary rush of freedom that came with flight. Cold air pounded his ears as he directed the vehicle toward Azure Minor.

The cold rose with the setting of the sun. Autumnal weather marked the season of smoky street-side firepits surrounded by crowds of chatty merchants. As winter approached, the merchants travelled up to Densolid from the Parsian straits, keen to flog the next generation of double-lined facsfur clothing and Sepia-made thermal underclothes.

After stowing his bike in the shared lockup, Daezen walked through the maze of market stalls, subconsciously taking the long way home. At every turn, a shadow caught his eye. An awareness at the corner of his vision. But he looked to find nothing there but empty space.

Shadowbirds flocked overhead, dropping down and scanning individuals at random with implanted reti-scan Tiles – a recent upgrade. As if the video-capture feature wasn't enough to keep them in line. Daezen didn't know who they were searching for, but he bet that they hadn't done anything that bad.

In Azure Minor, it was commonplace to see shadowbirds stalking innocent citizens while they went about their day, bioengineered eyes streaming everything they saw to the cyber unit of the local Inspectorate.

Azures were the lowest caste in the eyes of the Sharizan Empire, and as the human spirit is wont to rebel against injustice, they were the class with the highest volume of rebels, thieves, and gangs. After Pa's death, he'd sworn to himself that he'd stay on the right side of the law. That he'd do everything in his power to be a role model for Kain. But when hunger came knocking, it'd gotten harder and harder to stick to his morals. Azures had been held down for so long that crime was one of the only ways they could make a stand.

Sometimes he wished he could go back and accept the job that Topper Luxo had offered him. But he had to remember why he hadn't. Ma was a lost cause, Pa was dead. Kain needed some semblance of order, just until graduation. Then Daezen could do what he liked. Follow whatever twisted path that called him.

Against the darkening sky, he spied the silhouette of a shadowbird perched atop a minaret of the Red Ruins. Squinting up, he could've sworn there was a figure standing next to it. A figure in a black, armoured suit. An Inspector.

A rush of nausea overwhelmed him, and his heart began to thud. Forgetting his exhaustion, he tailed back, heading for the most direct route home. As he neared his apartment, a strong hand clasped around his wrist, dragging him out of the crowds and into a dark and narrow alleyway. The dank walls drew inwards forcing him closer to his aggressor.

He blinked rapidly, eyes adjusting to the darkness as he

readied himself to fight. As soon as he focused on the woman before him, he relaxed his stance, letting a slight smile curve his lips. She was small in stature, tawny skin and large angular eyes indicating Taoan heritage. Unusual. There weren't many Taoans left in Albin. Since the country had rolled out the Empire's shadowbird programme, many of them had fled back to Arq-Tao, the only country in the Empire where shadowbirds didn't thrive.

Daezen appraised her, observing the details. She wore a full snowsuit and a utility belt. Inner-city dwellers never kitted themselves out so completely unless they planned to travel imminently. The white material stuck close to her slight frame, accentuating light curves. Her silky black hair was pulled back in a severe ponytail, which hung long and iron-straight. She looked familiar.

He breathed in her scent: sandalwood and smoke. By the ice, she smelled good. He considered overpowering her and demanding to know who she was, but part of him delighted in the thrill of all this. If he spoke, he'd break the spell. Loosening his muscles, he let her drag him further down the dark passageway until they reached a dead end.

She turned to face him. 'I'm bringing a message from a friend.' Her lips thinned and the angles of her face caught the shadows, becoming more prominent. 'He needs your help and wants to meet.'

The woman stank of danger. He considered his options. On one hand, he really should head home, he was bone-tired and he'd told Kain he'd make dinner tonight. On the other hand, there was something about this woman, something familiar, something ... intriguing. She made him feel like he still had a chance. Like it wasn't too late.

He'd asked the universe for a way out. Was this some kind of sign? Fladden save him, he didn't believe in stuff like that. Much more likely was that this woman was trying to trick him into buying her services. She wasn't dressed like a woman of the night, but what in the ock did he know about how ladies of the night dressed. He wasn't Topper Luxo. He had neither the inclination nor the tokens to pay for sex. Maybe full snow gear was a new kink for the Azures that hung around here.

'Look, love,' he said, easing his hand out of her grip. 'Although I'm flattered, I'm not buying what you're selling. You're gorgeous, but even if that was my style, I doubt I have enough tokens for what you'd charge.'

Her opal eyes narrowed with barely suppressed rage, then her face abruptly softened.

'My name,' she said, extending a hand towards him, 'is Tala. And I promise that if you follow me, you won't regret it. Don't give up on life just yet, Daezen Trovit.' She brushed the tip of her tongue over her bottom lip.

Lust clouded his mind. Didn't he deserve a moment of surrender? A drop of pleasure in his ocean of discipline and sacrifice? Before his tired mind came to its senses, he took her hand and followed her into the dark.

CHAPTER 10
REUNION

DAEZEN

Tala led Daezen to the back of Prenderghasts – a debaucherous late-night hangout in the heart of Azure Minor. Letting go of his hand, she walked to the back entrance and knocked four times in quick succession. Each knock was a beat on Daezen's heart. Was he really doing this? He'd told her he couldn't pay for it. Had she just liked the look of him and wanted some practice?

The door opened and an Azure security guard beckoned them in, his grave expression pulling tight on Daezen's nerves. The guard didn't speak as he ushered them into a dim office, the walls lined with dark-red velvet and faux-flame wall lights.

His hairs set on end at the sight of the man sitting behind the swanky white desk.

'Long time no see, you icy little bastard,' Blink said, grinning from ear to ear.

'Blink? Is that really you?'

He hadn't seen Blink in years, not since his friend had disappeared from the academy without a trace, a few cycles before Pa had got sick. And now, without any warning, he was back?

'As I shit and breathe, my old friend.' Blink beamed, walking towards him with open arms.

Daezen hesitated. He'd tried to get hold of Blink when Pa got sick, but he'd seemingly disappeared from the face of Shariza. Blink hadn't been there when he'd needed him, in spite of their promise to one another. But pushing down feelings of rejection and abandonment, he rushed forward and locked Blink in a tight embrace. Whatever happened before didn't matter. Blink was back.

'Where on Shariza have you been?' Daezen asked, pulling back to look at Blink properly.

Since they'd last seen each other, his friend's boyish features had sharpened into manhood. There was something different about the young man before him, and it wasn't just the light stubble, long hair, and broad shoulders. He had the same irritating smile, but there was a hardness to his face that Daezen didn't recognise.

'Here and there,' Blink said with a wink. 'I hope you don't mind that I sent my sister to fetch you. I've got to be careful where I step these days.'

Daezen raised his eyebrows. So, that woman wasn't a sex worker. She was Blink's sister. It made sense, the familiarity, the half-recognition. Tala bore a striking resemblance to her brother.

Tala cleared her throat. 'I know I'm the better-looking sibling, but the fact you didn't guess the connection doesn't reflect well on your mental aptitude. And I'm not a whore, thank you very much. Just because I'm a Taoan woman in Albin, it doesn't mean I'm a sex worker. You'd do well to check your prejudice.' She came closer, close enough that he could smell the delicious scent of her hair wash. 'And you...' she placed a finger on his chest, 'couldn't be further from my type, so don't get any ideas.'

Daezen bit back a nervous laugh. 'Message received, loud and clear.' He turned to Blink. 'So, why're you back? When, where and how?'

'It's temporary.' Blink's smile broadened. 'But I've got a job. A mission, as it were, and I want you by my side.' He slapped Daezen on the back, surprising him with his strength. He must have been doing some serious working out. Strange, because the Blink he'd known had avoided exercise at all costs.

A wave of nostalgia crept up on Daezen, joyous memories tinged with sorrow. The dim lights flickered, throwing shadows across the velvet-lined walls.

This didn't feel real and Daezen' forced a laugh. 'Not a chance. I haven't forgotten what a failure all your previous schemes were, mut. I'm not signing up for any plan that comes from your empty head.'

Blink's smile turned cold and he glanced at his sister. 'Was he like this when you tracked him down, or has my friend been replaced with a body double?'

'I tire of these games.' Tala rolled her eyes. 'You asked me to fetch him, and I did.'

'Fetch?' That harmless word didn't exactly match the aggression with which she'd dragged him down an alleyway and pretended to lead him to a whorehouse. 'I came, didn't I?'

'Thanks to me,' Tala said.

'You did,' Blink agreed.

'So, what's all this about, then?' Daezen asked, a creeping sense of unease spreading through him.

Blink moved back to his previous position, lounging in a kitsch, red armchair with his feet on the desk. He nodded to the chair opposite him. 'Take a seat, Daeze.'

Tala scrunched up her face. 'I'll stand guard.' She left the room without so much as a backward glance.

Daezen took a seat on a rickety wooden chair, grimacing as the door slammed shut. 'I'm sorry for thinking your sister was a whore, mut,' he said, caught between anger and amusement.

'Nah, no worries. I told her to do whatever it took to get you here. But hands off, right? She's off limits. Anyway, to more important matters. The job.' Blink took his feet off the table and sat up straight, his gaze boring into Daezen's.

Daezen stared back at him. He wasn't going to be the first to show his hand. He tapped his foot, anxiety reaching a crescendo. The room grew smaller. There were no windows. He couldn't breathe.

'Okay. You're right,' Blink said, breaking the tension. 'I used to be a fool, only interested in the quickest way to scrape together a scrap of wealth. I need you to understand that I've changed.'

Daezen believed him. The man opposite him had the old Blink's erratic energy, but he also had a new edge. Something had happened to Blink to change him. Just like his pa's death had changed Daezen.

'I left because those *schemes* ended up getting me in more than a bit of trouble. But also, because I was suffocating, mut.' Blink pursed his lips at the faux-flame light on the office wall. 'Look around you, this tasteless, fake display of power is the best we can hope for. We have no prospects, no rights, and no chance to prove ourselves. Look at you! You're intelligent, strong, brave. You have a blinding, insane control over your oculary. And where has it got you, eh?'

While Daezen mulled over his response, Blink continued, 'Mut, you don't need to say it. I know...'

'Know what?'

The ghost of their friendship danced between them. They were no longer children playing games of rebellion, they were young men. Their wills pushing against one another, vying for dominance.

'I checked you out,' Blink said. 'You're on Sanitary Duty.'

So, he was here to insult Daezen's life choices. How wonderful.

Daezen stopped tapping his foot, shoulders stiffening. 'It's an all right Duty. I get by.'

'Do *not* be ashamed. And do *not* lie to me. And most of all – don't ever tell me it's okay!' Blink slammed his fist on the desk. 'They are using you, my beautiful, powerful friend, as if you're no better than a piece of tubing, a machine, a genetically engineered sewer rat! You deserve more!' He leapt to his feet. Beads of sweat dripped from his brow.

Daezen choked out a laugh. Blink sounded like a rebel. 'Who would've thought that out of all of us, you'd be the one still holding on to the dream?' he said. 'I seem to remember you saying something like – better to be enslaved and warm than free-zing to death.'

Like a flower wilting in the frost, Blink slumped back in his seat. He had no idea what Daezen had been through these past years. *No idea.* It boiled Daezen's blood to see him here, acting like they were still in the academy playground.

Blink smiled wanly. 'Yes, I did say that. Things are different now. I was wrong. When I left, I went back to live with some of my family in Arq-Tao. Life is different there. No shadowbirds, more freedom. Many still believe in the old ways.'

A Tao acolyte as well as a rebel. Of all the theories Daezen had run through after Blink's disappearance, the image of his friend dressed in robes and offering prayers to an imaginary god had never crossed his mind.

'I reconnected with my sister. It was wonderful. She's so similar to me in many ways. Similar but better. One day, she invited me to go to the temple with her. Obviously, like the cynic I am, I said no. You know me, can't hack collective praise, to the fire with collectivism – that's what I say.'

'Get on with the story!'

'All right, yeah.' Blink's pupils dilated in the low light. 'You see, it wasn't exactly what it said in the shortcode. The temple wasn't just some whack religious meeting. The Azure Angels were there. The resistance is real and alive.'

Blink's words punched Daezen in the gut. After all these years, he'd assumed the resistance to be a myth. An urban legend whispered by Azures to create the illusion of hope.

'Are you ocking with me, Blink?'

Blink shook his head several times, and for a second, he looked like the boy Daezen remembered. Then the light shifted, the hardness returned.

'I asked to join them, and they accepted. Now I've got a chance to really prove myself. To be someone important in the organisation. And I need your help to seal the deal.'

The weight of expectation pressed down on Daezen's shoulders. Why in the ock weren't there any windows in this ocking office? He'd give anything to feel a fresh gust of icy wind on his face, to see the stars. He and Blink were entering dangerous territory. Resistance was futile, the Obsidians were simply too powerful. Surely Blink could see that.

Blink continued, 'To earn my place among the leaders, I have to pull off a solo mission. And to do that, I need people I can count on. People I trust with my life.' He rushed on, tripping over his words as he grew more and more animated. 'I've got a plan. The annual Inspectors' Gala is in Densolid this year, and I want to make it a night the Empire never forgets. I managed to get a copy of the guest list and there are some real important people going. We're going to break in, cause a scene, and escape with some VIP hostages.'

Daezen laughed, a hollow and bitter sound. 'You've lost it, mut. Can you hear yourself? The security is going to be insane at the Gala, how on Shariza are you going to break in and break out with a little stop in the middle to kidnap Obsidians? The Empire Hall's surrounded by a forcefield, only one way in and out, had you thought of that?' A niggle of disappointment ran up his neck. Part of him had really hoped Blink was here to pull him out of this grey and stale life. But no, he was still the same idealistic fool. Daezen wasn't going to get involved in a suicide mission just to feel alive. He wasn't that guy.

'*Kumalma ka*, brother. That's why I need you. I need your brains on this. Anyway, it's not as crazy as it sounds. I've got a lead on some experienced rebels in the area who might be able to help. Besides, the Inspectors here are too comfortable – they won't see it coming, trust me. There hasn't been a true militant resistance in Albin for decades. But if my contacts fail me, I'm going to need you to step up.'

'Step up?' Daezen said, unsure if he'd understood Blink correctly. 'Mut, I'm not getting involved in this. And it's not like I have anything special to offer.'

Blink smiled sadly. 'Do you really think that?'

Did he? He wasn't sure. Since Pa's death, everything had centred on moving forward and keeping his family afloat. He'd hardly given himself a second thought. 'I don't know, mut. I have my family to think of. You know I'm the only person Kain has. He could really make something of his life. You should see him now. You probably only remember him as a snotty little rune-pup.'

'I know about Kain. I know about Cathy ... and Flint... It must've been tough.'

In spite of Blink's soft tone, the words froze Daezen to the core. He'd known about Pa's death?

No word from Blink for two solar loops, not even a message on the day of Pa's funeral. At the time, Daezen had assumed Blink was too far away, unaware of the tragedy that had befallen his family. But he'd been wrong. Blink had known, and he hadn't even bothered to reach out.

The stale smell of chemically cleaned carpet curdled Daezen's stomach.

'So, that's why you lost sight of the dream?' Blink asked.

The nerve of the man. 'We were kids. I wouldn't say I lost sight of a dream, I'd say I grew up. I have responsibilities.' Daezen fixed his jaw. 'So, you know that I can't be involved in whatever you're doing.'

'Daeze, you still don't get it. This is for your brother. For Cathy. For Flint.'

He dared to speak his parents' names?

'My father is dead,' Daezen replied through gritted teeth.

'But Cathy isn't. Nor is Kain.' Blink's eyes glittered.

Daezen ran a hand through his hair. 'And they rely on me to stay that way, for blinding sake.'

Blink raised his hands. '*Kumalma ka*, brother. *Kumalma ka.*'

Daezen took a deep breath. 'I'm okay, Blink. I just... You know more than ever that I'd love to do something with my life. I'm happy that you went home and found your sister. Ock, I think it's crazy and mad exciting that you found the Azure Angels.' Biting down on the treacherous sparks of hope, he continued, 'My beliefs haven't changed. I still dream of an uprising. Of freedom. But that's all it is... A dream.' He stared Blink straight in the eye. 'I wish it was more than that.'

'So, believe in it, mut. Be part of the wave of justice. Fight with me. Fight with me and Tala. You're the smartest guy I know, D, but you're too cautious. You think about things too much. I'm offering you the opportunity, and the means, to be the Azure that masterminded a break-in at the Inspectors' ocking Gala. Don't tell me that doesn't tempt you.'

His voice rang true, conjuring up traitorous sparks of excitement in Daezen's chest. But how did getting involved with a rebel mission fit with his responsibilities? Blink was asking him to risk everything, and the odds were definitely not in their favour. If they were caught acting against the Empire, they'd be executed. Then what would happen to his family? What would happen to Kain?

Daezen stood up quickly, hope and fear singing in his veins in equal measure. How could Blink do this to him? Arrive like a demon in disguise to disrupt his life and tempt him to throw everything away?

His indecision thickened the air as his mind whirred through possibilities. He still had the diamonds he'd taken from the Rostamani Riviera household. He didn't need to take a risk this big. Things were good. Things were fine. There was no need to rock the boat.

The phantom stench of the San-centre sewage curled up his nose.

The tokens from the diamonds won't last forever. What will you do when they run out? Are you really so set on a life spent in the sewers? Don't you want to be someone?

'What's in it for me?' he said. He wouldn't agree to anything without factoring in Blink's history of broken promises. Rebellion be damned. He wouldn't risk his life for an ocking idea. For a dream.

'For you, mut? Isn't it enough to fight for a better world for Azure-kind?'

Daezen set his jaw. 'No, *mut*. It's not.'

The sound of Blink's laughter echoed around the room. There wasn't anything funny about this.

'All right, all right... Sit down, mut. I'm sure I can sort something. What do you want? You want in with the rebels? Easy, if we pull this thing off, you'll have rebel leaders all over the Empire fighting to have you on their team.'

'Tokens,' Daezen said. 'Enough to never have to spend my day wading in shit ever again.'

Blink looked him up and down, smile fading. 'I promise you, mut. If you get us into the Gala, you'll never have to worry about tokens ever again.'

Join the rebels? Endless tokens? Wasn't that what he'd always dreamed of?

'What about Kain and Ma?'

'They could come with. If you impress Command, the sky's the ocking limit.'

Sweat coated Daezen's neck as he spoke through clenched teeth. 'Do you mean it? If I do this, if I take this risk, do I have your word that the rebels will look after me and my family?'

The door crashed open.

'Temples burn, how long does it take to outline a simple plan?' Tala said, breathing heavily.

'What's going on?' Daezen demanded, his heart racing.

'There were too many birds, I had to cause a diversion then double back. We shouldn't stay much longer.'

Blink pulled on his snow kit, retrieving a utility belt with an assortment of contraband weapons.

Not only was Blink a rebel – he was packing gear. That belt alone was enough to get him locked up for a long, long time. Daezen stared at the belt, packed with a short sword, a curved knife and a spiked hammer, unsure whether to be impressed or terrified.

'Ah, you'd better come with us, we can keep talking on the way,' Blink said.

Daezen assembled the chatrang board in his mind, imagining Blink's offer as a pawn. A soldier piece. Usually cannon fodder, expendable. But if, against all odds, this unassuming piece reached the other side of the board, it would transform into the most powerful piece of the game: a Queen.

But was he capable of such a thing?

In theory, an in with the rebels and access to tokens was just what his family needed, but could Blink be trusted? The opponent's knight shot across the board, knocking Blink's pretty words and silver promises out of play.

Blink tapped his foot impatiently. 'Come on, mut. Tala doesn't like people who delay our emergency exits.'

Tala's cheeks still burned red from her recent exertion, but her back was straight, eyes alight with exhilaration. Daezen stopped his thoughts in their tracks. She was Blink's sister, and she was strictly off limits. Besides, she hadn't exactly seemed into him.

Tala shot out her hand, gripping his forearm with violent force, then dragged him out of the door.

Trusting the wrong people could be his downfall. He, Blink and Topper had been close friends once upon a time, but Blink had never been known for his honesty. What if this was simply another one of his self-interested schemes and after Daezen had sacrificed everything, Blink disappeared again?

An idea sparked in Daezen's mind. A glowing, chatrang piece. A Rook to defend the pawn-turned-Queen.

As much as he hated to admit it, their old friend Topper Luxo would be a valuable addition to this tentative alliance. The elusive assassin could teach them a lot about evading the law and using the shadows of the city to their advantage. Besides, with Topper on board, Blink wouldn't dare to double-cross them, not if he valued his head.

'I'll agree to help if we bring Topper in on it,' Daezen said breathlessly, struggling to keep up with the pair as they whizzed down the damp alleyway. Though the idea tasted bitter on his tongue.

'Topper?' Blink said, increasing his pace. 'That mad dog won't work with us for free. As much as I'd love to have him on the team, I've heard the stories, I know who he is now.'

They turned abruptly, heading down a dingy alleyway that stank of piss.

Tala's eyes were on the sky. 'I think we're losing them.'

They paused. It was true that Topper wouldn't help them for free. He wouldn't even help them for the promise of tokens. To get the rook in play, he'd need cold, hard cash.

Two diamond earrings glowed in Daezen's mind. Without a

doubt, one would be enough to settle his debt with the Health Centre. He could front Topper the second diamond as a down payment for joining Blink's mission. Sweat gathered on his forehead.

It'd be a gamble. Giving up cycles of financial freedom for the hope of a bigger jackpot.

Was it worth the risk?

'Look, Blink, I want to help. But if the rebels haven't seen fit to arm you with more manpower, we need to find our own. Like it or not, Topper is the most competent mercenary in the city. I'll sort it with him, make sure he behaves. But without him, there's no deal.'

Blink's eyes widened. 'You got some secret stash of stolen goods you haven't told me about?'

Tala smirked. 'As if.'

'I don't know, Daeze. I don't know if I can trust Topper with something this important.'

Daezen didn't trust Topper. He needed him. If he was going to put his neck on the line and try to achieve the impossible, he needed some assurances. First, he needed to know the Inspectors wouldn't crash the game before they'd cashed out, and second, that Blink wouldn't double-cross him and flee without fulfilling his promise of tokens and safety. Bringing in Topper solved both those issues.

'Topper's in, or I'm out,' he said.

With their friendly neighbourhood assassin on the team, he could be sure that Blink would keep his word. Besides, they needed someone like Topper if they wanted a chance at infiltrating the Inspector's Gala without getting caught. While it made Daezen sick to the stomach to think they had to rely on him, he'd evaded the Inspectors' grasp for so long, his skill couldn't be denied.

Tala ducked behind a bin. 'I saw another bird. We can't hang around any longer. Make this quick.'

'Fine. Fine! Me and the sis have to split,' Blink said. 'Find Topper, get him on side. We'll work out the rest later.'

In spite of his misgivings, hope blazed in Daezen's chest. Of course it was dangerous to trust Blink. Dangerous to be involved with anyone who plotted against the Empire. But nothing worth having in this life came without risk.

Without embracing danger.

A cool, hard voice in his head told him that this was his last chance. His last chance to stave off the shackles of a common, sewer rat and do something worthwhile with his life.

The Azure mastermind behind a break-in at the Inspectors' Gala.

He liked the sound of that...

The siblings broke into a run, heading towards another alleyway, even narrower and dingier than the previous one.

'How will I contact you?' Daezen shouted.

'Topper will find a way,' Blink shouted back, before Tala grabbed him by the shoulders and dragged him down the alleyway, leaving Daezen alone in the cold of the night.

A light spattering of hail fell from the sky, hammering home the truth of what he'd done. He'd agreed to commit treason against the Empire.

A cool sensation spread through his temples.

He'd never felt more alive.

CHAPTER 11
OPPORTUNITY

SOBA

Black rose petals stuck to Soba's skin as she rolled off the silk sheets of the Empire-sized bed. Elias stood by the door, already dressed and making to leave. He and Soba were off-duty, so they'd planned to spend the whole evening together, exploring each other's bodies in the black-velvet luxury rent-room.

Her heart sank. 'You're leaving?' she asked quietly, covering her naked body with a satin throw. Her injured bicep twanged as she adjusted the material.

Elias avoided her gaze. 'I want to stay, but Aunt Greta asked for a last-minute call. She booked a table at the Albinesque, she'll videocast me from there.'

Soba's body tensed. Last year, Elias had become the youngest Chief Inspector on record, rising to the top of Densolid Inspectorate's ranks before he'd even turned twenty-five. Though he was only six years older than Soba, he had more power and responsibility than she could ever wish for. Power that he'd earned through his actions, not some stupid birthright.

Though he was part of the Vox family, one of the Great Elites of Albin, he'd been all but disowned after disobeying his father's wishes. Elias' father had planned for him to become a diplomat, but Elias had known he was destined for more. He'd enrolled at the Inspectors Academy, working his way up from the very bottom, until his aunt, Greta Vox, the Director of all the Inspectors of Albin, had no choice but to take notice of him. It was one of the reasons Soba admired him so.

His drive was second to none.

Elias walked around the bed and brushed a rose petal from her collarbone. Her skin tingled where he touched her. 'You know I don't want to leave, don't you? I'd much rather be here with you.' Her knees trembled at the soft tingle of his touch.

'I know, Elias. I know.'

And she did. He couldn't be seen with her in public. Not yet. In the eyes of Densolid society, she was far beneath his station. It would cause him embarrassment, shame even. She didn't want that for him. When she finally proved herself worthy to be at his side, they'd go public with their relationship.

'I would invite you to come, you know?' His breath tickled her neck. 'I *want* you to come along. But Greta told me that the leaders of both Albin Elite families have been in touch. You don't have the security clearance to be there.'

She pulled back. What could the leaders of the Albin Elites want from the Densolid Inspectorate? Had they discovered her true identity?

Elias gripped her waist and pulled her back towards him, his hold on her unbreakable. 'It's not about you, Little

Night-Eyes. Those stuck up Parsians have unreasonable demands, yet again. And of course, they expect us to roll over like faint-eyed fools.' A muscle twitched in his jaw. 'Anyway, you can relax. I'll keep you safe. You keep your end of the bargain and I'll keep mine.'

She breathed in his musky scent, letting it overpower her doubts. The lilting cadence of his words calmed her. But somewhere deep inside her mind, she knew them to be a lie. Elias couldn't protect her from everything. He couldn't protect her from *them*.

A council of ten Great Elites governed the Empire. Each country housed two of the Great Elite families, and each family elected a head of house. While the Council leader always came from Parsia, all the houses held a level of power and influence over the Empire. Over the Inspectors. Over Elias.

Over her.

'Of course,' she said. 'I'll see you later, though?' She hated the flimsy sound of her voice. Too vulnerable, too weak.

'No,' Elias said firmly, 'I have other things to do.'

Crawling insects teamed through Soba's veins and rushed towards her rotten heart. At some point she'd let the satin blanket slip to the ground. Glimpsing the scars on her belly and thighs, she grabbed her clothes and quickly covered up.

Elias left the room without giving her a goodbye kiss, leaving her with an emptiness in her chest that grew cold and heavy. In times like this, to keep herself from giving into the off-key suspicions singing in her head, she'd cast her mind back to the day she first met him. The day she'd shed the name Adelola Sàlàkọ́ and became Soba Nite.

Nine years ago, Elias had found her half-starved, sheltering under a wooden boat in a small coastal village east of Densolid.

She'd just turned ten years old, and her life revolved around stealing rotten fish and staying hidden.

On being discovered, her first instinct was to fight. She'd bared her teeth and let her oculary sight take over, giving herself to the will of the air. But as she'd started to whip up a sonic storm, Elias had spoken with a voice that tasted of honey. Soft vowels and serene sibilance had calmed her childlike fear. Dark treacle irises had met her eyes of onyx, ringed with a thin web of white. He'd instantly seen her potential.

Elias had taken her to a shelter in Densolid city proper, where he'd cared for her as if she were a wayward younger sister. His boundless kindness had dulled the sharp edge of her self-preservation. Enraptured, she'd acquiesced to his every whim.

He'd offered her a deal. A way out of the nightmarish world of a life on the run. He would take her in and be her sponsor, enabling her to start a new life in Densolid. But first, she had to swear her loyalty, and choose a new name.

That was when she'd seen it. A glimpse of the path to who she could be. To who she was *meant* to be.

Upon shedding the weight of her old name, her corrupted past, she made herself a promise. From that moment onwards, she would only ever look forward, never back.

And yet here she was, nearly a decade later, looking back.

By the time Soba reached her capsule flat, her breaths flowed evenly, blood running clean. Her apartment was little more than an ode to matte grey-and-chrome steel finishings. Not a single personal object or unique feature on show.

On her desk, she spied a note sitting atop a small black box.

I'm sorry for leaving, little Night-Eyes.

Elias must have known his early departure would upset her

and sent a gift to her apartment this afternoon after she'd left to meet him. A smile tugged at her lips.

She opened the box. It contained a bouquet of black roses and a sonic meal. Retrieving the food, she followed the instructions to reheat the vacuum-packed tray. It wasn't dinner at the Albinesque, but it would do.

Soba sank into second sight, relaying the frequencies and timings to the corresponding acoustic particles around her. They responded without emotion, without heart.

It never felt the same when she used her power like this.

It felt flat and sterile, like a song without rhythm. A tune with no heart.

In less than a minute, she had a hot, creamy, high-protein meal of dumplings and beef right in front of her. She didn't have grounds to complain. Elias looked out for her. He always would.

As she finished the food, her Inspector-issue Tile vibrated with a new message.

> **Inspector Rutkitz**
> Spotted some odd activity while tracking the elder Trovit boy.

Soba tightened her grip on the Tile, then typed back a response with one hand. By Artium's grace, she'd need to see someone about her blinding arm. If it wasn't healed soon, it could seriously impact her ability to perform her Duty.

> **Inspector Nite**
> Send me the file.

> **Inspector Rutkitz**
> No please or thank you?

Soba scowled, irritation prickling up her arms. Inspector

Rutkitz had made her life almost unbearable back in the training academy. She had tried to tell herself that these taunts came from a place of jealousy, but in her heart, she knew it had as much to do with the colour of her skin as it did towards the way Elias favoured her. Soba had been the only Octengion student at the Inspectors' training academy, and in the Empire of Shariza, it was always dangerous to be different. During every group session, her dark brown skin had felt like a beacon, separating her from the sea of white faces. Singling her out. Though the War of the Splicing had occurred centuries ago, the Albiners still resented foreigners, blaming them for their own failed imperial ambitions.

> **Inspector Nite**
> Just send me the file, Ratkiss.

> **Inspector Rutkitz**
> Whatever, Bloodbat. Sending it through now.

Soba's breath quickened as she clicked on the footage. Daezen Trovit stumbled out of an alleyway, squinting his eyes and rubbing his head. Rewinding the shadowsnap, she saw him on the other side of Azure Minor standing in a crowd of people, before ducking and disappearing down another street.

Soba squinted. Was that someone's hand around his wrist? She slowed down the footage. It was hard to tell. One thing was clear, between disappearing down a street in Azure 9 to reappearing near Azure 12, the Trovit boy was unaccounted for.

Her heart skipped a beat.

There was hardly any evidence to go on. He could easily have been scoring street psychs or loitering, but her instincts wrapped around the doubts like a constrictor snake, squeezing them to death with certainty.

This was a lead. A chance to prove her worth. To demonstrate her investigative skill to Elias and all the other Inspectors in Densolid. Anticipation rushed through Soba's fingertips as she typed another message to Rutkitz.

> **Inspector Nite**
> Did you run an infrared scan on the area where he disappeared?

> **Inspector Rutkitz**
> No, assumed he was engaging in typical, debauched Azure behaviour. When I saw him reappear in Azure 12, sober as song, I realised something was off.

Soba cursed aloud. Didn't her colleagues understand that it was exactly this type of incompetence that made Elias favour her? All that training, and they couldn't even get a simple thing like this right. No wonder Albin was the least-respected country in the Empire. They blamed others for their own inadequacies, rather than learning from their mistakes.

> **Inspector Nite**
> So, there's no way of telling where he was or who he was with?

> **Inspector Rutkitz**
> We can't all be the chief's golden girl like you, Bloodbat. Now, shall I bring him in for questioning? Chief says you're leading this opp.

Soba bristled. Arresting the Trovit boy would kill the mission. Sure, he had tenuous links to Topper Luxo and a tainted family history, but there was no guarantee he'd be able to help them find Topper Luxo. Not yet. Brute-force wouldn't win this mission. It needed tact. Intelligence. If only there was a way she could get closer to him without having to rely on those blinding shadowbirds...

A chorus of song erupted in her chest. Now, this was an idea that would make her career.

> **Inspector Nite**
> Don't make a move and don't lose sight of him.
> I want updates on his movements every hour.

Inspector Rutkitz
You really need to get a life, Bloodbat.

> **Inspector Nite**
> That's an order, Ratkiss.

Inspector Rutkitz
Heard, loud and clear.

Chewing her lip, Soba scrolled down her contact list until she found the name she was looking for – Dr Alhaadi Popoola. An old friend and elite scientist from the Salog Inspectorate in Octengion. She tapped on his shortcode.

He picked up after less than two rings.

'Alhaadi?'

'*Ọmọ-binrin ọba*, what a pleasure to hear from you.' Dr Popoola's rich voice echoed through Soba's Tile, the soft sound completely at odds with how it felt to hear him use her former title.

'Don't call me that,' she snapped.

Dr Popoola had been friends with Soba's mother. When everyone turned against her, he'd remained silently supportive. Aside from Elias, Dr Popoola was one of the few people in Shariza who knew the truth of her background.

Dr Popoola smacked his lips. 'Business rather than pleasure,

I see. Well then, Inspector Nite, what can I do for you? I am your humble servant.'

Soba smiled, the song of victory already resounding in her mind. Where all other Inspectors had failed, she would triumph.

'I want to try the...' Soba paused, she'd have to word this carefully. All calls were recorded and she didn't want to get him in trouble. '*New product*,' she said.

A pause. Her heartbeat drummed in her ears.

'You're not supposed to know about that,'

'And you're not supposed to use my old title, *òrẹ́ mi*.' Soba hadn't spoken Yoru in many a solar loop, but she knew that by referring to Dr Popoola as her friend she'd have a better chance at getting what she wanted. The words felt clumsy on her tongue.

'All right, all right, *òrẹ́ mi*. I could do with more trial subjects. I'll drop by your apartment tomorrow morning, I have business tonight.'

'Thank you, thank you so much. I owe you one.' Soba cut off the call, pride swelling her chest.

To catch Topper Luxo, she would have to think like him. She would have to act like him. And that meant infiltrating his world.

The excitement of the challenge roared inside her, she didn't want to wait till tomorrow.

Her Tile buzzed again.

She read the message and smiled, glimpsing her reflection in the window.

Perhaps she didn't have to wait.

CHAPTER 12
UNHEARD

JANTSIA

Luz was the first to greet her when she arrived home. He scampered down the corridor, claws clicking against the grey tiles, then jumped into her arms.

'I thought firecats were meant to be independent and aloof,' she said as he nuzzled her chin.

She pressed her face into his fur, inhaling the cosy scent of bonfires and cloves. 'I've awoken, Luz. I'm a real Azure now.' Saying the words didn't make them true, but it lifted her spirits.

It strengthened her resolve.

If she believed hard enough, it would be true. Because she couldn't for a second entertain the other explanation for what had happened today. For the way she'd moved the water. For the strange hallucination of the water woman. The hall of mirrors.

'Jantsia? Is that you?'

At the sound of Zuleikha's voice, she let go of Luz,

automatically tensing up. Part of her couldn't wait to tell her parents about her day. To let them know they no longer needed to fear the Inspectors because she'd awoken. That she was just an ordinary Azure now. But another part of her feared their reactions. If she told them about the hall of mirrors, they probably wouldn't believe her.

Not probably. They definitely wouldn't believe her.

Thinking her mad, they'd disregard everything she said.

Her hands were clammy, heartbeat erratic. What would she do if they told her this was the beginning of the end? Hallucinations and power surges sure sounded like signs of the blood sickness.

No.

She wasn't ready to die. She was ready to prove the impossible possible. And as a real Azure, she would be free to live a full life like an ordinary person. And that was all she wanted: to be ordinary.

Footsteps echoed down the corridor and her father appeared in front of her, a strained smile on his face. 'Hi Jantsy, how was your day?'

She stood up straight, pouring confidence into her posture. 'Amazing. I've got something pretty incredible to tell you.'

'Good, good. You can tell me all about it over dinner.' He raised his eyebrows. 'Your mother cooked.'

She screwed up her face. 'Really?'

Zuleikha had barely cooked three meals since they'd settled in Densolid, often claiming she was too busy to manage her workload and engage in menial, domestic tasks. Never mind the fact her father worked a full-time Duty as the leader of a performance troupe and was still expected to act like Zuleikha's servant both in and outside of the house. What was the woman up to? In spite of her determination to stay positive, Jantsia's stomach filled with lead.

The dining hall smelt of fried cheese and corn, with a rich hint of safra. Atop the golden-edged tablecloth lining the long, glass dining table, was a dish of white and yellow safra rice, a pile of fried maize pancakes, and a cast-iron pot filled to the brim with bubbling tomato and aubergine stew. Despite her misgivings, Jantsia's stomach rumbled, her mouth watering at the delicious smells.

At the head of the table, Zuleikha sat upright, a black facsleath apron tied over her purple satin gown. Elegant and graceful, even after cooking.

'Take a seat, Jantsia. I've cooked cachapas, your abuela's secret recipe, of course. And that is polo safra,' she said, indicating the mountain of rice, 'and the stew is khoresh bademjoon. I watched Maman Bozorg cook them all from scratch in Shizar City.'

Tentatively, Jantsia took a seat and let her mother serve her a portion of each dish. After thanking Zuleikha for cooking, all three of them began to eat in uneasy silence. The flavours tantalised her tongue and warmed her belly. Even though Zuleikha was a lousy mother, she cooked like a professional.

'How's the food?' Zuleikha asked.

'Yeah, it's good,' Jantsia said through a mouthful of buttery rice.

'Now, there's something we need to talk to you about. Your father and I have been making plans for the future.'

Her father snorted. 'You mean you've been making plans for the future. It seems my opinion is worth very little in this household.'

Jantsia fidgeted in her seat. Couldn't her parents make it through a single meal without fighting?

Zuleikha whirled fizzwine around her golden goblet. 'I'm not making plans, Beny. I'm offering suggestions. If you have worthwhile alternatives, you're welcome to voice them.'

Her father's expression darkened. 'You know very well what I think. What I would have us do.'

'I said *worthwhile* alternatives. Not naïve and reckless ideas that'll get us all locked up or executed. Say what you want about my family, but they helped us set up here. Thanks to them we have some semblance of an ordinary life, just like you wanted.'

Ordinary? Nothing about any of this was ordinary. Hearing them talk like this made the food become tasteless and dry in her mouth. They needed to work together, not against one another. Jantsia took a deep breath. 'I actually have something to tell you both, too. Something good.'

Zuleikha dismissed her with a wave of her hand. 'In a minute, Jantsia. If your father would just let me present my plan first.'

Benyamin took a large gulp from his goblet and banged it down on the table. 'I for one would like to hear Jantsy's news. I actually care about what she has to say.'

'And what is that supposed to mean?'

'You know *exactly* what it means.'

Tension curled up Jantsia's shoulders. She balled up her fists. 'I've awoken.' Raising her head, she forced strength into her voice. 'We don't need to worry anymore about the Inspectors discovering I'm a dual-oc. I've become a real Azure. Today, after OP class, I had my awakening. Educator Leanne said she'd never seen an awakening like it. I emptied the entire fountain. I think I managed to completely banish the Obsidian part of me.'

Her father's goblet clattered to the ground.

'Impossible,' Zuleikha whispered to herself.

'Are ... are you sure of this, Jantsia?' her father said; his face had turned as white as snow.

The silence thickened.

'Yes, I'm sure,' Jantsia snapped, red heat infusing her cheeks, her forehead. 'I think the right response is "congratulations".' She looked between her parents. Sweat trickled down her back. 'I've solved all our problems, haven't I? Is nothing I do ever good enough for you?'

Her baba's face fell. 'Of course we're happy for you. We're both happy for you, it's just... This isn't supposed to happen.'

'I'm meeting my contact tonight,' Zuleikha said to Beny. 'I'm sure there's something he can do about it. There has to be. If the blood sickness is overpowering the medicine, she'll need something better.'

'What if it's too late?' Beny responded. 'What if—'

A silent scream tore through her chest, forcing her to her feet. 'I'm right here. You can't keep talking about me as if I'm a little girl. I'm standing right here.'

Zuleikha glanced at her, then carried on talking to her father as if she hadn't said a thing. 'Don't say that. It'll be fine. He's the best in his field, he'll have an explanation.'

Jantsia banged her fists on the table then stormed out of the dining hall to her bedroom. As she slammed the door behind her, her father called her name.

See if he likes being completely ignored, she thought, pulse racing as frustration and anger sparked in her limbs.

This was exactly what she'd feared. Her parents had immediately jumped to the worst possible conclusion.

The blood sickness was taking hold.

Why couldn't they just be happy for her? Why couldn't they believe in her? Was it really so impossible that she'd accessed her oculary through sheer willpower? There was no point telling them about the hall of mirrors and the water woman now. All they'd do was twist and turn her words until she felt powerless to resist their point of view.

She scooped Luz into her arms. 'I'm not dying, Luz. I'm not. I would know if I were. I'm Azure. I have to be.' The sleepy feline croaked a feeble protest. Jantsia ignored him, needing the comfort of his warm furry body more than his approval. Tears gathered in the corner of her eyes. And even the feel of Luz's satin-soft fur couldn't crush the niggling feeling that something was wrong.

She wiped the tears from her eyes. She needed to get a grip on her emotions and get ready. Flossie, Pixa and Kain would be waiting for her at Tavern Blue in a few hours. Just because her parents were determined to ruin her awakening, she wasn't going to let them stop her from celebrating. Even if her worst fears were true. Even if the blood sickness was taking hold, she deserved to live. To experience at least one evening of being an ordinary Azure teenager before everything fell apart.

As she gazed at the heaps of clothes spread out on her bed, a different kind of fear rose in her gut – what on Shariza was she going to wear?

Luckily, Luz was good for more than just moral support. Once Jantsia had placed all her outfit options on her bed, Luz made her decision easy by kneading his paws on top of his favourite ensemble before curling up into a ball of purring fluff.

Jantsia turned to the mirror to begin the next challenge: eyebrow plucking.

Flossie and her friends all had fine, blonde hair that hardly showed on their faces. She didn't want to look like a dark, hairy monster hanging out with a group of slender princesses. This thought distracted her from the task at hand and she accidentally caught a fold of skin in the tweezers.

'Oh, my eyes!' she exclaimed.

Luz chirruped in agreement.

Worried her frustration would lead to more unnecessary pain, she paused the eyebrow torture and moved on to her complexion. Freckles, blemishes, and moles everywhere. They would have to go. Jantsia liberally applied petal cream to her visage.

After an hour or so, the transformation was complete. For once, her reflection made her smile.

Thin, lightened eyebrows arched neatly around her eyes. Snow-white lashes extended from her eyelids, making the usually dull blue of her irises shine like cobalt. Her hair hung straight and loose in a low ponytail after ages spent straightening and greasing her curls into submission. Blue leath wrapped around her legs, covered with a long turquoise gauze that masked her powerful thighs. A flexi-vest squeezed her chest and abdomen. Not exactly comfortable, but when combined with the loose tunic, she almost appeared slim and slight of chest.

A loud knock tore her attention from the mirror, and her bedroom door swung open.

Luz hissed.

'Jantsia, we have a visitor.'

Her renewed good mood faded at Baba's stony expression.

'It's okay, Luz,' Jantsia soothed. 'Everything's fine. Stay here, I'll be back in a sec.'

Shutting Luz inside her room, she hoped with all her heart that she'd spoken truly.

Jantsia followed Benyamin into the open-plan living area. Someone decked out in a suit of black armour was sitting opposite Zuleikha.

Her heart slammed against her chest.

An Inspector was inside the house.

CHAPTER 13
TROUBLE

JANTSIA

Nausea writhed in her stomach.

Sweat dripped down the back of her neck, leaving a trail of sticky warmth atop her clammy skin. The muscles in her legs twitched. Every instinct, every inch of her body, screamed at her to run. To flee.

She'd been discovered.

They would kill her.

They would execute her entire family.

Zuleikha didn't even glance up as Jantsia entered, her focus fixed on the Inspector.

Jantsia clenched her fists, tucking her thumbs inside and squeezing them hard.

The Inspector glanced over his shoulder, revealing a chiselled, handsome face and cruelly arched nose. 'This is she?'

Catastrophe had knocked on their door. Catastrophe was sitting at their ocking dinner table. Jantsia squeezed her fists tighter. She wouldn't panic. She had to hold herself together – even if her life was falling apart in front of her eyes.

Stay invisible. Stay invisible. Stay invisible.

'Yes,' Zuleikha answered. 'Servant girl, come here.'

Zuleikha's stern tone triggered a flare of resentment. How was she supposed to stay invisible if her mother was presenting her to this man on a silver platter?

'Go on, Jantsia. Everything's going to be okay,' her baba whispered in her ear, gently pressing a hand against the small of her back.

Her heart pounded against her ribcage as she walked toward the Obsidians.

This was it.

The moment she'd been waiting for.

The end of everything.

With that thought, a morbid sense of calm took root. Her worst nightmare had become real. There was nothing left to fear.

'Master Musika,' Jantsia said, bowing and crossing an arm over her chest. Just this morning she'd performed the very same gesture to irritate her mother. Fate had a sick sense of humour. Then she saluted the man that could rip away everything that meant anything to her. 'Mister Inspector.'

'Take a seat, servant girl,' the man said, a soft smile playing on his full lips.

His smile made Jantsia feel uneasy. The man was beautiful, no doubt about that, but something sinister shadowed his features.

'Now, Azure. Do you know why I'm here?'

Jantsia gaped. What was she supposed to say to that? *Yes,*

Mister Inspector. I'm a dual-oc and you're here to kill me and arrest my family.

Zuleikha's eyes widened. 'Get to the point, Elias. The girl has chores to do, and I'd rather not have her working through the night.' She held her ribcage high with her shoulders relaxed, her chin raised; a countenance that smacked of power and wealth. Of dominance. This wasn't Jantsia's maman, it was her patron.

The Inspector smirked. 'Of course, she looks ... ready for maid duties.'

Jantsia remembered her dressed-up appearance and shot her mother a pleading look.

Zuleikha turned away, resting an elbow on the table and placing her chin in her hand. 'I prefer my servants to be easy on the eye. You must know that about me. I appreciate beauty, in all of its forms.'

Greasy sickness flipped Jantsia's stomach as she watched her mother rake her gaze up and down the Inspector's body.

The Inspector responded with a lascivious smile. 'I bet you do.' His voice was low and rough. 'Now, servant girl. Let me refresh your memory. Yesterday, you were shadowsnapped on the back of a wanted criminal's hoverbike.'

He unfolded a golden Tile, bringing up an image of Jantsia and Kain on the back of Topper's bike.

Fladden be merciful.

'Well,' Zuleikha demanded. 'What do you have to say for yourself, servant?'

Her stomach writhed and she feared that if she spoke, she'd bring her entire dinner back up again. 'I ... I ... I didn't know whose bike it was. Not until we landed and Kain's brother—'

'So, you've never met Topper Luxo?' The Inspector didn't even look at her as he spoke, too busy consuming Zuleikha's curves with his dark eyes. 'And you have no idea of his whereabouts?'

'No, Mister Inspector. I don't even know what he looks like,' she said, her voice small.

'That's a pity,' he drawled, still staring at her mother. 'Musika, I'm willing to let this ... *indiscretion* go unpunished. In exchange for a favour. You know, a boon from one Great Elite to another.'

What did he think he was doing, leering at her mother like that? Her insides churned and it took all her strength to stop herself from calling him out. From revealing her truth.

Then she remembered her mask and let her expression go neutral. She wasn't Zuleikha's daughter, she was her servant, nothing more.

Zuleikha cocked her head. 'What kind of favour? And I didn't know that you had been officially welcomed back into the family. Congratulations.'

Why was her mother acting like some kind of courtesan right in front of Baba? Heat and sweat crept up Jantsia's neck. Embarrassment entwined with anger.

The Inspector flinched. 'You're one to talk, Zuleikha. You know it's always struck me as odd that you would establish yourself here, so far from your family. Some people might say you have something to hide. In my experience, most immigrants arrive here with secrets. Why else would they come to this frozen and forgotten land?'

Jantsia bit down hard on her bottom lip, relishing the clarity that came with pain.

Zuleikha shot him an enchanting smile. It didn't reach her eyes. Jantsia's breaths evened out. Of course. She was just pretending. They were all pretending. Whatever ill will there was between them, no matter the arguments and the rage, they would do whatever they had to do to keep each other safe.

Reality twisted in front of her, and a pressure began to build in her chest.

'There's no need to indulge in gossip, Elias. I'll be happy to help you out however I can. I could never resist your charms.'

The Inspector puffed out his chest. Pathetic. He was a fool if he thought he had a chance with her mother. Her vision darkened at the edges.

'I'm organising the Inspector's Gala this year. We'd be honoured if you'd grace us with a performance of your latest work.' He abruptly turned his head, acknowledging Benyamin. 'And we want your man-servant's performance outfit, too. Something banal, inoffensive. You know, light entertainment for the troops. Something to laugh at.'

Benyamin's voice rang out, devoid of emotion. 'As always, Mister Inspector, my Master Musika commands and I obey.'

Needles prickled up Jantsia's spine. These people weren't her parents. They were strangers. Dark stars danced in her eyes, and for a second, she thought she could see mirrors all around her. She bit down harder on her lip.

No, she couldn't lose control. Not now.

The Inspector stood, then walked around the table and offered his hand to Zuleikha. The moment she took it, the loathsome man bent down and kissed her mother's hand. Jantsia wanted to shout. To fight. To do anything other than keep silent and still.

Frozen in the centre of a nightmare.

'We have a deal, then?'

Zuleikha gently led him towards the corridor. 'As you said, it would be my pleasure.'

The water woman's face appeared at the fore of Jantsia's mind. Dark blue lips whispering into her ear. Eyes like stormy oceans. *'Use me. Free me.'*

At those words, particles burst to life in the air, shifting her perspective. And all of a sudden, the jug of water on the table upended, soaking the golden tablecloth. The glass jug rolled off the table and shattered against the floor.

The Inspector looked back, curiosity sparking in his dark eyes.

Benyamin dashed to the table, faking a stumble. 'My apologies, Master, Inspector. In my haste, I knocked into the table. I will do better.'

The Inspector continued down the corridor. 'I don't want any of that clumsiness in my performance, Azure. Zuleikha, I'll be holding you responsible for his troupe, you know. We can't afford any breaches of security.'

The glass doors slid open.

Jantsia held her breath.

Please leave.

Please leave.

Please leave.

Before crossing the threshold, the Inspector spun back.

'I'll be in touch. I'll want to attend your rehearsals. A few private performances wouldn't go amiss.' He clicked his jaw, eyeing Zuleikha hungrily.

She raised a perfectly arched eyebrow. 'Don't push your luck, Chief Inspector.'

He chuckled, sending another wave of shivers down Jantsia's spine. He looked back at Zuleikha one last time before leaving the property. Jantsia didn't even dare to breathe as the Inspector entered his golden pod. The vehicle hovered above the ground, then rose, disappearing into the sky.

Jantsia unclenched her fists. Her hands trembled. It felt like her stomach and heart had swapped places, pounding, writhing, nauseating. Her tongue felt too big for her mouth.

Zuleikha remained still for several minutes, the tension in the atmosphere so sharp it could cut flesh. Jantsia didn't dare speak. Then her mother slumped in a cream-velvet armchair, clutching her head in her hands.

Jantsia braved a word. 'Maman?'

Her mother's head shot up, Obsidian eyes ringed with red. 'Jantsia, you moved the water. You ... you...'

Benyamin rushed to her side, helping her to her feet. Jantsia remembered the way the Inspector had gripped her mother's hand, like she belonged to him. She tasted bile.

Zuleikha shook her head. 'I must go. My contact is waiting for me. The medicine. We need it urgently. Beny, what if she...' Tears streamed down her face, smearing lines of kohl down her cheeks.

Jantsia had never seen her mother like this before, it filled her with dread from head to toe. The world around her drained of colour.

'I'll come with you. You can't go out like this by yourself,' Benyamin soothed.

Zuleikha's face softened, folding into Benyamin's embrace. 'I shouldn't let someone like him get to me so. He wanted to humiliate me, but only because he knows he'll never get what he wants. I'm sorry for arguing with you, Beny. We must be united in this. Let's go.'

Jantsia's breathing quickened. 'You're leaving? Now? What if the Inspector comes back? You can't leave me here you—'

'Enough,' Benyamin boomed, his face a steely mask. 'You've done enough, Jantsia. We're going to meet the man who makes your medicine. That's the most important thing right now. Keeping you alive. Now make sure you take your evening dose, double it if you have enough spare. We'll talk later.'

A scratching noise came from Jantsia's bedroom, Luz protesting his confinement. Jantsia went to let him free, hoping he would provide what her parents hadn't: comfort.

Luz yowled and jumped into Jantsia's arms.

'It's okay, Luz. I told you I'd come back, didn't I?' Luz licked her face eagerly.

Holding him tight to her chest, she turned to address her parents. To apologise. To beg for forgiveness.

But they weren't there.

In the fading glow of the garden's float-lights, she glimpsed them walking through the gate, leaving her behind. The marble-gated doors closed with a clank. Jantsia squeezed Luz so hard that he issued a small, irritated squeak. She let go and he sprang free, dashed to the armchair and extended his claws.

For a single moment, an awful moment of surrender, Jantsia had dared to act like a normal Azure teenager. She'd dared to live. And look what happened.

Look what she'd done.

Something as banal as a hoverbike ride had nearly unravelled her world and placed her family in jeopardy. The family that, in spite of her mistakes, had ventured out in the cold to procure more medicine.

And now she was alone.

Unable to live, but not ready to die.

A bird-shaped shadow, wings extended, swooped across the garden. Sweat slicked her temples and her fingers trembled.

Rage and guilt and anxiety swirled together like a tornado inside her skull, rattling her brain until she couldn't think straight.

'What am I supposed to do?' she shouted.

Luz took little notice of her raised voice, he simply zoomed around in circles and chirruped enthusiastically. Her parents would be home soon. Things only got worse from here. A cowardly solution slithered through her thoughts.

She could leave. Head to Tavern Blue as planned and delay the inevitable punishment her parents would impart upon her. Delay the shame. Spend one last evening living a fanciful lie. One last evening before it all came crashing down.

Ock it. What was the worst that could happen? Catastrophe had already knocked on her door and she was still here to tell the tale.

She was still alive.

Bursting to her feet, Jantsia checked her make-up in the mirror, the pull of the idea too strong to resist. Locating her pills, she swallowed two of the capsules dry, leaving a lump in her throat. After feeding Luz a few treats, she rushed out of the house to the pod-stop.

It was time to live. Really live.

Because for Jantsia, tomorrow was never guaranteed.

CHAPTER 14
TOPPER

DAEZEN

The stench of sweat and vomit brought bile to Daezen's throat. He needed a drink, and he needed one fast. This locale was not a place to frequent sober.

'Blink is back?' Topper exclaimed.

Having second thoughts about his decision, Daezen appraised his friend's screwed-up face, blood-red hair and tattooed arms.

They weren't boys anymore. This was serious business. And he'd promised Blink that Topper could be trusted.

'Daeze, buddy. You can trust me,' Topper added, almost as if he could hear Daezen's thoughts.

Daezen flinched. 'My face that easy to read?'

'Nah, boy. Only for me. I know you, see. I *really* know you.'

In scarcely three years, Topper had made enough of a name for himself to strike fear into the heart of any Azure, Veridian or

Sepia. Az-sec and Ver-sec turned a blind eye to trouble if Topper Luxo was involved. Several cycles ago, the Inspectors had issued a fifty-million token bounty for any person able to deliver him to the doors of their HQ in Densolid Major, and they were still no closer to apprehending him. Topper had all the locals in the palm of his hand. Nobody would rat on him, especially not here.

Topper stretched out a hand, fingers capped with sharpened iron nails. The edges glinted in the low, artificial light of the drinking den. He caught Daezen staring.

'They're called body-mods not brain-mods, I'm still the same person, mut.' Topper smiled wide, showcasing his lethally modified canines.

Daezen shook his head with a wry smile. 'You're not the same person, Tops.'

Topper leant forward, slamming his mug of Fireglug on the table. The wood was so old and worn it would probably leave a permanent mark. Two intense cat-eyes bore into Daezen, alight with curiosity rather than anger.

Daezen's jaw twitched. As if things were that simple. As if he could just turn to a life of criminality without it sending ripples through the rest of his life, affecting his family, and most importantly, corrupting his mind. 'Mut, don't tell me that killing doesn't change you. I've been open about how I feel about your ... *job*. I don't like it.'

The assassin ran his split tongue across pointed teeth, clearly trying to unsettle him.

Well, he'd have to try harder than that. Daezen leant forward, lowering his voice. 'Don't forget that I know you too. *Really* know you.'

Topper laughed. Slapping a hand on Daezen's shoulder, he

whispered against his cheek, 'Of course killing has changed me. But you haven't changed one bit. And I still love you, you wet little sewer rat.'

Then he did something Daezen hadn't expected – he kissed him.

'Get off!' Daezen shouted, pushing his cackling friend away. 'What's wrong with you?'

Topper continued to laugh, taking a large sip of Fireglug and gesturing to Daezen's cup. 'Drink up, boy.'

Daezen grimaced. Sometimes the kill and the cure were one and the same. He gulped down the bubbling fizz, wincing as the bitterness hit the back of his throat. Topper looked at him expectantly.

'What?' Daezen demanded.

'Just waiting,' Topper chuckled.

'For?'

'For the Fireglug to do its magic and pull that navy stick out of your tight little ass.'

Daezen shook his head at his friend's vulgarity. The embers of the liquor ran down his throat, sparking up a steady flame in his twisting stomach.

'Okay. Yes, Blink's back. And he brought his sister along for the ride,' Daezen announced, throwing caution to the icy wind.

Topper raised his multicoloured eyebrows. 'She hot?'

Daezen was about to roll his eyes but took another sip of Fireglug instead.

If you can't beat them...

'She's steaming, mut. Absolutely steaming.' The words were out of his mouth before the fire in his belly had cooled. Despite his promise to stay away, Daezen had thought about Tala a fair few times since they'd met. Of course, he'd never betray a friend like that. And it'd been clear that Tala hadn't thought much of him.

You can't touch, but that doesn't mean you can't look.

Topper grinned. 'So, what's he doing back here? Last I heard he was nestled up near Iambe, going to temple and being a good little Tao acolyte.'

'How did you know that?' Daezen asked, unnerved at how Topper kept so well-informed when he spent most of his time stealing and maiming.

'I've got my ways, mut. I've got my ways.'

Daezen cocked his head. 'You'll have to tell me about these ways, one day.' He glanced around them, ensuring that no one was close enough to hear what came next.

'Ooh, let me guess. This is the part we don't want anyone to hear,' Topper teased.

'They're involved in the ... *fight*,' Daezen said in a low voice.

Topper's eyes widened, modified cat-pupils bleeding into bright blue irises. 'Daezen, are you telling me that Blink and his sister are here on a mission for the Azure Angels?' he spoke in a velvety tone, the words blending into background noise.

Daezen tensed, fearful someone may have heard them. The uninterrupted melody of rowdy shouts and heavy bass indicated otherwise.

'I know how to play these things, brother. Subterfuge is my vocation. What was that thing Blink used to say to us? Oh yeah. *Kumalma ka.*'

The Tavern was filling up now, the line at the bar heaving with young Azures who glanced surreptitiously at their table. Daezen wasn't arrogant enough to think they were looking at him. The old man was working tonight, cheeks red from a life of selling and consuming psychs. Benyamin had told him that this was the man who could get in contact with him, should Daezen ask Benyamin to meet? Force him to take back the diamonds in exchange for tokens?

He wouldn't do that. Token transfership always leaves a trace. That's why the merchants in The Pipes prefer to barter over goods.

'Mut, what dirty things are you thinking about?' Topper's voice interrupted the flashbacks.

'Huh?'

'You're as red as a dead man.'

'Why are dead men red?'

'They are when I'm done with them,' cracked Topper.

Taking another large gulp of Fireglug, Daezen recounted his meeting with Blink. By Topper's silence, he could tell the assassin understood the gravity of the situation.

'I'm not gonna lie, mut. It sounds interesting. But if I'm going to help you boys with this suicide mission then I need something upfront. I'll have to cancel my next few jobs and I'm running low on capital.'

'How can you be low on tokens? You're rolling in it.'

Topper ran his hands through his spiked red hair, artificial talons glinting. 'Spend it faster than I can make it, brother. Mods and sex don't come cheap.'

Daezen grimaced. 'You're not telling me you still have to pay for sex.'

'I don't have to do anything, my man. I just prefer the best of the best. With my line of work, I ain't got time for amateur fumbling in the dark. I go straight for the goods.'

He ordered another round of Fireglug. The psychs sang in Daezen's blood, loosening his mind – and his tongue.

A fiery smile curved his lips. 'Did I tell you that when I first met Blink's sister, I thought she was selling herself.'

Topper splurted Fireglug from his nostrils. 'No mut, and what ... you told her thanks for the offer but you're dirt poor?'

'Something like that.' Daezen emptied his muglet. He'd been too quick to judge Tala. Too quick to assume. Perhaps she'd been right to tell him to examine his own prejudices. 'You want another?'

Topper frowned in amusement. 'You trying to get me drunk? I'm telling you, mut. I love the idea of us three working together. But I don't work a job without taking a deposit. A hefty deposit.' He kicked back in his seat, showing off his ruby-lined boots.

With a lopsided smile, Daezen withdrew the diamonds from his pocket. 'How about this?'

Topper's mouth dropped open. 'What's a sewer rat like you doing with those bad boys?' He took them from Daezen's palm, rolling them over his fingers.

'Stole them, didn't I?' Daezen said, pride swelling in his chest. 'Kain's friends with the Brittle girl. I got her to let me into the Meridian. Swiped them from Zuleikha Rostamani Riviera's house.'

Topper erupted in maniacal laughter. 'Who the ock are you and what have you done with my wet blanket of a friend? Getting in the Angels and stealing from Great Elites... Wow.'

Daezen raised his glass. 'Needs must. No Azures were harmed.'

Topper's gaze softened as he stared off into the distance. 'I remember when I first broke into Meridian, a rite of passage my mut.'

'Go on, then,' Daezen groaned. 'You know I want to know how you did it.'

Topper's feline eyes sparkled in the low light. 'It's the force-field, you see. There's always a point of confluence in the energy. A point of weakness. They set them up to stop vehicles coming in, but no one ever expected an Azure to drop in from the sky. That's where you got to enter. Right at the top, bodies pass through, vehicles don't.'

Daezen narrowed his eyes. It was an interesting idea. For the mission to go ahead, they'd have work out how to get into the Empire Hall in the first place and there was no way they could go through the front door. But if Topper spoke truly, and there really was a way to get through the forcefield by skydiving in ... well, it meant there was hope. 'You did not work that out yourself, no way.'

'Didn't anyone tell you that imitation is the highest form of flattery?' Topper's expression turned grave. 'Seriously, though, you promised you'd tell me if things got that bad. I've got loads of jobs you could help with. You didn't have to risk the wrath of an ocking Great Elite.'

Ice crept into his veins. 'Things aren't bad. It's all under control.'

Topper burst into laughter again. 'Control? Mut, nothing's under control and the sooner you realise that, the better.'

Daezen fixed his jaw. 'So, do we have a deal? You can take those diamonds, all I need is three-thousand tokens of it.'

Topper sipped his drink. 'One thousand.'

'Two.'

Topper extended a hand, metallic nails sharpened and shining. 'You've got a deal, Daezey-boy.'

With a firm grip, Daezen shook his hand, but inside his mind a cacophony of thoughts spun together like a vortex. A thousand tokens was enough to settle his debt and the rest would tide his family through the next few cycles. What happened after would depend on the mission.

He and Topper were an odd pairing.

The assassin and the sewer rat.

'Glent, my man,' Topper called over to the old barman, 'another round, please.'

The red-faced old man brought over a tray of Fireglug.

'How do you know him?' Daezen asked, thinking of Beny's cryptic words. 'Who is he?'

'Who, Glent?' Topper asked, taking another gulp of Fireglug. 'He's actually the man who told me about the weakness in the forcefields. He used to pilot an old Azure pod and moonlight for robberies. There's a lot of shiny things in Obsidian households, mut. Though, you already know that...'

Daezen screwed up his face, a plan to infiltrate the Gala starting to take shape. The opening move was clear in his mind. To break into the hall, they'd need to parachute in. He took another drink of Fireglug, he could worry about the rest of the suicide mission later. 'So,' he said, slurring his words, 'Blink said you'd know how to contact him.'

'Oh, that's easy. If he needs manpower, he'll be headed to the Asabreks to try and make contact with the Dissidens. I know someone there, I can get a message to him. Though I could've saved him the trouble. Those lazy dipshits are the worst kind of rebel there is.'

He shifted on his seat, head spinning after that last drink. Through a haze of drunkenness, he tried to form words. Tried to insist on more details.

Then a tall, beautiful Octengion woman sauntered towards them. Her features were striking, long black braids, strong muscular thighs and tight abs all on show thanks to that flimsy piece of blue fabric he supposed was a dress.

'Hello, my name is Millie.' The words left her full dark lips like whispers of song. She was slim but muscular with legs for days.

What was a vision like this doing in Tavern Blue? And why had he never seen this woman before?

Topper's fangs glinted. 'Why, hello, my dear. Can I interest you in joining me and my ratty friend?'

CHAPTER 15
FIREGLUG

JANTSIA

The smell was the first thing she noticed. A pungent cocktail of sweat, saliva, and citrussy chemicals. The second assault on her senses was the noise. Digital guitar, synth and percussion set the backdrop for raucous laughter, shouting, and off-key singing.

In one corner, a group of middle-aged Azures sipped at golden liquid in tall glass muglets, playing water darts and mumbling to one another. On the other side of the long oak bar lay a makeshift dance floor equipped with legacy Tile-tech. Rows of stained wooden benches separated the two areas, every inch of the tavern occupied by rowdy groups of Azures.

Jantsia had never felt such a loose and wild energy before, her heart matched the beat of the tinny music.

When she'd stepped out of the doors of the multipod in front of the tavern, she'd wondered if she was at the right place. It was a dive. A glorified wooden shed, with a wonky half-lit sign hanging off a rusty half-open door. Smoke and steam filtered out of cracked windows. The place exuded the smell of grease and poor life-choices. Not in a million years had she imagined Flossie and Pixa would frequent somewhere like this.

Now she was inside, it was obvious that the place *was* a dive. But the people inside it gave it life. Flossie and Pixa stared at her, identical smug grins on their porcelain faces, draped in floaty tulle and full-length, hooded facsfur coats.

Nerves jittered inside her belly. What was she supposed to say to them? How was she supposed to act?

'Erm?' she said, simply to say something, cheeks heating.

'Oh, Jantsia, your face! It really is a picture,' Flossie said, the corners of her eyes sparkling with silver-shine.

'Come on, Floss. Our table's free,' murmured Pixa, tugging on Flossie's floaty sleeve.

They sat at the only free table, right next to the dancefloor and the booming bass.

Flossie turned to Jantsia. 'So, Little J – does it bother you if I call you that?'

'Erm?' Jantsia repeated. *Super smooth.* It appeared she'd lost the capacity for speech. She pressed her lips tightly together. It was better to be a mute than show herself up like this.

'You know, it's just you're so...' Flossie sat up tall, stretching out her long legs and kicking Jantsia playfully under the table. 'Little.'

It wasn't the worst nickname in the world. As someone who constantly worried about the roundness of her hips and the density of her thighs, the word 'little' was a blessing, even if it was just another signifier of difference.

'Nope, I don't mind.' Jantsia smiled earnestly. At least she hoped she appeared earnest.

'You're probably wondering why we come here, right?' Flossie said in a sing-song voice.

Pixa cackled, bringing to mind Kain's collective nickname for the girls: *the Harpies*. A small smile crept onto her lips. Hopefully, he'd be here soon to break the ice. With all the drama of the past twelve hours, she hadn't even considered what it'd be like to be alone with them.

'Something funny, Little J?'

'No, I just, erm...'

'Do you like Peri-water or are you more a Fireglug girl?' Flossie asked.

Jantsia's eyebrows lifted, realisation dawning. They weren't here for cafi or chai. They were here to drink something stronger. They were here because it was the only place where no one would bother to question their age.

It was illegal for Azures and Veridians to consume psychoactive substances under the age of eighteen, and that was the lowest entry-age among all oculary orders. Sepias were forbidden to experiment with mind-altering substances until the age of nineteen and Obsidians were expected to keep their minds clear until they were twenty-one, at the very least. It had something to do with oculary development and the effect of intoxication on one's power.

Flossie stared at her expectantly, the weight of her gaze sending shivers down Jantsia's spine.

Jantsia didn't know what the drugs would do to her *unique genetic composition*. Besides, whenever she'd watched her parents consume psychoactive liquids, they'd always embarrassed her, acting strange and awkward, loud and cringey. She didn't want to act like that. But she did want to fit in. To stop thinking about what awaited her at home.

The decision was made.

'Peri-water,' she said.

'Nice choice,' replied Flossie, her smile broadening as if she knew that Jantsia had never drunk a drop of anything psychoactive in her life. 'You heard the girl, Pixa.'

Pixa pouted but didn't protest. She headed to the bar and returned with three large glasses of sparkling pink Peri-water. Flossie handed the first one to Jantsia, then took one for herself.

Flossie took a large sip. 'So, Little J. Where's your *friend*?'

'Erm.' She clenched her teeth. Why was she being so weird? After a lifetime of trying to stay invisible, it was hard to switch back and be herself – whoever that was. It had been a bad idea to come. Kain had ditched her and now she was stranded with Flossie and Pixa in this drunken cesspit. She should've stayed home, faced her parents. She should've—

'Jantsia, you haven't touched your drink,' Pixa cooed. 'Go on, it'll loosen your tongue. Among ... other things.' Her eyes glinted with mischief.

'Pixa, don't be such a whore,' Flossie admonished. 'Drink up, Little J. Pixa's an irredeemable flirt, but she's got the right idea.'

After the slightest hesitation, Jantsia took the glass and brought it to her lips. It tasted like rose syrup and bitter grapefruit.

By the time they'd finished the first round, Jantsia's face was flushed. Warmth trickled through her stomach. Anxious thoughts became silent. Bright words tumbled from her lips with ease. These girls were amazing. Trustworthy. Fun. All three of them had a special connection.

This was it. She was finally making friends.

Before her eyes, the sticky table and cramped space

morphed into a banquet hall with music swirling around her ears, cushioning her frantic heart.

'Now, take a look at that walking, talking piece of candy.' Pixa pointed a dainty finger toward the entrance, her silver-lined eyes slightly glazed.

Flutterbies danced in her stomach as Kain sauntered into the tavern. He'd come. He hadn't abandoned her. He was here.

Spotting Jantsia, Kain's face broke out in a giant grin.

'Hey ladies.' Kain scooted in next to Jantsia. 'What's the craic?'

'Well, Jantsia was about to explain why you and her are "just friends" when you're practically connected at the hip,' Pixa said, slurring slightly.

Kain grimaced, glancing at Jantsia questioningly. 'What's she on about?'

'It's nothing.' Jantsia's blush deepened. The pink haze clouded her mind. She had to think of something better than that to say. She had to—

Flossie swished her hair and leaned in closer. 'What Pixa was trying to ask in her roundabout way was ... are you two shagging?'

'No!' Jantsia blurted out.

Pixa burst into giggles.

'Well,' Flossie said, waving her manicured hands in the air. 'Why the ock not?'

Kain shrugged, fiddling with the lapels of his leath jacket. 'I mean, that'd be weird. She's like a sister to me, aren't you?' He put his arm around Jantsia's shoulders and squeezed.

Her back stiffened.

His words were a poison pervading her body, slowly killing every inch of the excitement she'd felt at seeing him.

Like a sister?

So, when he'd been planning their lives together as performers touring the country he'd been imagining her there as ... a sister? She'd tried to prepare for this. Tried to tell herself again and again that he didn't like her that way. That he was out of her league. But, oh Fladden be merciful, it wasn't easy to hear.

A heavy emptiness grew in her chest.

She shouldn't be so disappointed. It was always going to be impossible for them to be together. Even if he did see her that way, what would she do? Risk telling him the truth of her heritage, or do what she did best and lie through her teeth?

Flossie looked Kain up and down, lips parted. 'So that means you're fair game, then?'

A writhing serpent of jealousy ripped through Jantsia's guts. It didn't matter that they couldn't be together. She didn't care if it was impossible. She wanted him and didn't want anyone else to have him.

Kain laughed awkwardly. 'I guess it does. Listen, I think I need to catch up with you girls. You're way more buzzed than I am. I can't keep up.' He slid off the bench and made his way to the bar.

'Kain,' Jantsia shouted, her voice wavering.

He turned around, raising his eyebrows.

'Get me another drink.'

He saluted. 'Yes, boss.'

'Little J,' Flossie whispered theatrically. 'I don't want to break girl code, but I have my eyes on Kain. Is it definitely okay with you?'

An image of Kain embracing Flossie flashed in front of her mind, and her stomach cramped further. What was she supposed to say? She knew what she *wanted* to say, but the difference between what she thought and what she *should* say was becoming less and less clear, her sense of reason lost to the fusty, tavern air.

She bit her lip. Desperately grasping at her train of thought. She was sinking. Sinking into a pit of drunkenness and resentment. This wasn't how she wanted the night to go. This wasn't how she wanted to feel.

A dark voice whispered inside her head, *'He's made it brutally clear that he's not interested in you. Don't waste any more time on him. Don't alienate your new friends.'*

She fumbled over her words. If she wasn't careful now, she'd reveal more than she should. Better to keep her answers short. 'It's fine.'

Flossie's ice blue eyes bore into her, sparkling at the edges. She was so beautiful. So perfect. So sure of herself.

Kain returned, slamming two glasses of bubbling red liquid on the sticky table. His pupils vibrated. He couldn't be drunk already, could he?

'Saw Daeze at the bar. He's here with Topper. They're heading off to Prenderghasts in a bit. You girls want to join?'

His words vibrated through the air, spinning and dancing before they made sense to Jantsia. Daezen was here? An unexpected flutter of wings took root in her stomach. She remembered how he'd stared her straight in the eyes, really seeing her.

She couldn't see Daezen now, not like this. He'd see through her smile to the violent turmoil beneath. The memory of the Inspector leering at her mother sliced through her mind. Her parents would be getting home now to find no one in the house apart from Luz. What would they say? Would they come to find her? And what if her mother's contact had told her that Jantsia's awakening was a clear sign of the blood sickness? A sign that she wasn't long for this world.

Her heart raced, beating violently against her ribcage.

Kain nudged her, tearing her away from spiralling thoughts. 'What's up with you?'

Before Jantsia could reply, Pixa started to squeal.

'The Topper Luxo? How navy. He'll get us into Prenderghasts, right? We don't have ID.'

'Yeah, he's got flash on him, too.' Kain indicated his pupils. 'Might've popped one myself back at the bar.'

Flash was a low-grade psych, mainly used for partying by Azures and Veridians. Jantsia knew they'd be bad news for her. Unlike drinks, they distorted oculary vision, turning particles into dancing lights and colours.

Jantsia opened her mouth to say that she should go home, but the words stuck to her tongue. It was dangerous to stay out later, especially with someone like Topper Luxo who casually gave out flash. She should go home.

She had to stay invisible.

Stay alive.

Flossie licked her lips. 'I'll go if you dance with me, Kain?'

'Aha, Flossie, you should be so lucky,' Kain said with a wink.

Desperate to be free of her mind's incessant chatter, Jantsia grabbed the drink and gulped it down in one. The liquid burned and fizzed as it travelled down her throat, sparking a fire in her belly. Her internal flames mixed with the sweaty atmosphere. Shapes blurred at the edges.

Pixa whooped and followed Jantsia's example.

They went through several more rounds of Fireglug as the bass boomed louder and the background noise became rowdier. With the thrum of her head and the beat of the music, Jantsia could barely hear anything anyone was saying. But it didn't matter, she could see their smiles. Feel the connection. Taste the burning liquid lighting her up from within.

'Steady,' Kain shouted, a hand on Jantsia's shoulder. 'Fireglug is strong, boss.' He moved his lips closer to her ear. 'Are you okay?'

Okay? An Inspector had invaded their home. Jantsia had almost been exposed. And now? Kain and Flossie were flirting like there was no tomorrow. All of this proved once and for all that Jantsia was nothing. Worse than nothing. An abomination. An aberration.

She tried to focus on Kain, but her eyes were buzzing. They couldn't stay still. Kain was only being nice to her because they were friends. If she left now, he'd probably just join his brother with the Harpies. He'd be happier with them. He deserved their beauty. Their status.

She gulped down another shot.

Fladden be damned, she wasn't going to let Kain and the Harpies have all the fun.

The elusive Topper Luxo didn't make an appearance in the end, but Daezen managed to get them all into Prenderghasts just by mentioning his name. When he'd joined their group, Daezen hadn't even acknowledged Jantsia, he was too busy talking to Kain in hushed tones.

As the bouncer let them pass, though, Daezen held the door open for them, finally looking at her.

'Didn't think I'd see you somewhere like this, princess,' he said. 'Keep an eye on Kain, eh? He shouldn't be taking flash on a weekday.'

'I think he's got eyes for someone else,' she said.

Daezen smirked. 'My brother doesn't see further than the

end of his nose. Don't be too hard on him. And don't be surprised when he finally sees you, all right?'

She wanted to ask him what he meant, but a waitress wearing a bright pink wig and white leath dress was approaching them and ushering them to the dancefloor. Bass drummed in Jantsia's chest and the strobe light sparked a numbness within her.

There were bodies everywhere. Gyrating, sweating, dancing bodies. She quickly lost sight of the Harpies as the crowd swallowed her up. By the time she pushed free of the rush, she found herself trapped in a circle with two handsome young men with golden skin and dark hair. From the way they danced, easy and sensual, she bet they were Laminosian. The beat embedded itself in her bloodstream, rolling through her hips and her shoulders. Her body moved almost as if of its own accord. The music danced around her, telling a story without words or images. Leading her down a path of pure feeling without judgement.

The men cheered as she danced.

'*Epa, mami, ¡Qué show! Bailas como una angelita.*' The boy whose bright eyes were lined with kohl spoke Lamino, confirming her suspicion.

A rush of confidence and pure bliss whirled in her mind as they passed her a drink. It tasted strange. Peri-water with a side of something chemical.

'*¿Qué tiene?*' she said, asking them what was in the drink.

'Ahh, I told you,' said the taller one, raven-coloured hair gelled into spikes. 'She's Lamina, one of us.'

Warmth spread all through her limbs as she continued to swing her hips from side to side. One of us, he'd said.

Right here and right now, she belonged.

'I sprinkled a bit of flash in the drink, *nada más*. I'm Ramón, nice to meet you, *señorita*,' said the Laminosian with cold sapphires for eyes.

They continued to shout over the music, every now and then dissolving into a dance-off when the beat dropped.

A hand gripped her shoulder, spinning her around to face Kain.

He was bouncing up and down and chewing his cheek, eyes as wide as saucers. 'Hey, we lost you back there. We're over by the bar, follow me, I'll show you.'

'*Putas, tiene que ser el novio*,' shouted Ramón, lamenting that her *boyfriend* had arrived.

'No, he's not my boyfriend. Not my *novio*,' she shouted back. 'We're just *amigos*, right Kain?'

Kain gave the men a dark look then grabbed her hand and pulled her away.

The music wasn't as loud near the bar, and Jantsia found herself missing the free and easy energy of the Laminosians.

'I didn't know you spoke Lamino,' Kain said.

Jantsia looked back at the dancefloor, swaying on her feet. 'Well, Kain. Maybe there are a lot of things you don't know or notice about me.'

Hurt crumpled his face. 'What?'

'Kaiiiin, over here!' Flossie called, indicating a line of shots waiting for them on the bar.

The way she looked at him sparked anger in Jantsia's core. She tore away from Kain's grip. 'Stay here with Flossie or come with me, I don't care. You can do whatever you want.'

Lights trailed the air, drawn in rainbow colours, as if by an invisible artist. They wanted her to go back to the dancefloor. They wanted her to belong.

Her head spun.

Kain grabbed her arm again. 'Don't go. What are you doing?'

She slapped his hand away. 'Stop being an overprotective *brother*. I can handle myself.'

He retreated. 'What's going on with you?'

'I want to have some fun for once. And those guys over there, they don't see me as a sister. They see me as a woman,' she spat.

His face scrunched up. 'I don't understand what you're saying. You're not making any sense.'

The music tingled and vibrated, caressing every part of her.

Whispering dark thoughts inside her head.

He doesn't deserve you. You could be so much more than him. You're the descendent of a Great Elite. He shouldn't speak to you in this way.

Defiant rage soared within her, a shadowbird in flight. The voice was right. Kain had disrespected her. By refusing to recognise what she was. By not seeing the real her.

'Well, I'll make things clear as water for you, shall I?' She raised her chin and sneered. 'You only wanted me around because I was powerless. Thought of me as a useless little sister that needed your help, I bet. Someone to keep around to make you feel good about yourself. Well, let me tell you. I am so much more than that.'

Kain's bottom lip trembled.

The haze of strobe lights and deep bass faded into the background. The mirror world came partially into view, overlaying on the scene around her. A single mirror stood before her, reflecting back an imperious black-marble statue of a woman. A woman who looked eerily like her and whose eyes glowed like burning coals as she stretched an arm towards Jantsia. The arm passed through the surface of the mirror and clasped hold of Jantsia's mind. She snapped back to her body, limbs coursing with power.

Kain's wide eyes met her gaze.

'*Leave me alone, watery scum.*' Power imbued her voice. A voice that was undeniably hers, and yet somehow not.

Kain's eyes went blank. Like a zombie, he turned on his feet and walked back to the bar.

A sharp headache sliced through Jantsia's mind as she danced deeper into the centre of the crowd.

What had just happened?

Had she somehow forced Kain to walk away?

All of a sudden, Jantsia's legs were made of lead, strength draining from her body. Her stomach heaved and pulsed. She was going to be sick. The high roof of the warehouse seemed to be caving in on her.

She had to get out.

She had to get out, right now.

Jantsia rushed toward the neon exit sign, throwing herself out of the door and into the cutting cold of the night.

Blood thumped in her temples. Voices shouted in her mind. A dark, marble presence was crushing her, absorbing all the light.

'You doing okay, princess?'

She looked up. Daezen was leaning against the brick wall, puffing on a smokestick a few metres from the exit.

'Daezen, what are you doing here?' She breathed in the fresh night air, filling her lungs. The voices quietened. Her vision stilled.

'I needed some air,' he said, walking closer. Shadows accentuated his sharp cheekbones in the glow of blue light.

'Yeah, me too.'

From around the corner, a buzz of intoxicated conversation floated through the air along with a low sound of beating drums and electronic steps.

He cocked his head, gaze raking over her, stirring a strange heat in her lower stomach. She trembled.

He took a drag of the smokestick, vapour curling from his full lips. 'Want some?'

Tendrils of smoke danced and twisted between them.

'No, thanks,' she said with a grimace. Stars popped into her vision then disappeared again. 'I don't think psychs really agree with me.'

The side of his mouth curled upwards, the ghost of laughter in his eyes. 'They don't agree with anyone, princess. I shouldn't offer it to you, really. I shouldn't even let you and Kain be here. With exams coming up, you shouldn't be drinking.' He examined her face, piercing eyes seeing to her very core. 'Or taking flash.'

Her breath caught in her throat, her clothes suddenly feeling incredibly restrictive, squeezing her centre. She shouldn't be out here with Daezen. He was too dangerous. He saw too much. She should leave.

'So, why did you let us come here?' she said, not breaking eye contact. Though she knew what she should do, she didn't want to. She didn't want to be safe. She wanted to be here. With him.

His jaw ticked, sharp edges softening. 'Because I can't hold it together all the time.' He took another long drag on the smokestick, staring at his boots.

The tension in her chest eased into a cold trickle of sympathy and understanding. She'd never considered how it must be for him. Never thought that his glacial manner might just be his own form of protection against this world. His own mask.

It wasn't easy to live a life of pretence.

To sleep inside a paper house of lies.

She steadied her breaths. 'I'm not a princess, you know. I get that I don't have the same challenges as you and Kain. But that doesn't mean my life is easy.'

He licked his lips, chucking the smokestick on the ground where it fizzled in an icy puddle. 'I'm starting to see that. You should lean on Kain more. He wants to make it up to you, you know?'

Jantsia struggled to make out his words, he was speaking so quietly his voice was almost lost to the wind. She took a step closer. 'Make it up to me?'

He raised his chin. 'For all the ways you've helped him. You were the only one there when he needed someone. Emotionally, I mean. You know, when Pa died.'

The strong chemical smell of smokestick mixed with leath reached her nostrils. Daezen's smell. Even with the stony mask of indifference he wore firmly in place, his fingers shook slightly. His breaths quickened.

Jantsia took another step closer, until she could hear his breaths. See them dancing in the air like dragonbees. 'And who was there for you?'

His brow creased, ruining the smooth marble surface of his skin, folding like paper. He looked so alone. So lost. She wanted to comfort him somehow. To let him know that she knew how he felt.

She knew what it was to carry a burden that no one else could know.

Her heart pounded in her ears as he turned to her, fingers grazing her cheek. He tucked a strand of her hair behind her ear. 'Interesting look you went for tonight.' His lips parted. 'I prefer the curls.'

She shivered, not understanding the tension that held them in place. Confused by the lights that popped in the air.

The smile fell from Daezen's lips. He stepped back, arms at his side. Eyes gazing off into the distance. 'It's cold, we should get back in. Feeling a bit more sober?'

The space between them pulsed. Nausea spiked at her temples. 'A bit. I think I'd like to go home, actually. Could you help me hail a pod?'

Daezen nodded, not a trace of feeling in his expression. 'Sure. Didn't you bring your Tile out?'

'No, I didn't want my par— I mean my Pa, to track it.'

'Makes sense.'

He walked around the corner to the main road, raising his hand and whistling, looking so much older than nineteen years old. A pod lowered from the hover rank and came down at his gesture.

'Thanks,' she said, heading towards the spot the pod landed.

'Don't mention it.'

The pod door slid open and she was about to get in, when she turned, inhibitions relinquishing the question on her tongue. 'Earlier, when you said Kain would see me eventually. What do you think he'll see?'

Daezen's expression didn't shift. A mask of stone and porcelain. 'If I knew how to explain what I see in you, then I'd probably be after you myself.'

The pod door slid shut, shooting off into the night sky.

CHAPTER 16
INTEL

SOBA

On the approach to the sleek metallic entrance of the Inspectors' skyrise, Soba removed the blue-coloured contact lenses from her eyes. They dissolved in her hands, stinging her palms. Just as she'd thought, her oculary was far too powerful for coloured lenses to last more than an hour in her eyes. She'd made the right call to leave when she had.

After discovering that Daezen was headed to Tavern Blue, a down-and-out nighttime venue with the reputation for the sordid and the illegal, Soba had thrown caution to the icy wind. While any long-term investigation would have to wait for Dr Popoola and his invention, without waiting for Elias's approval nor for Dr Popoola's visit, she'd gone undercover.

And thank the sands she'd taken that risk. Not only had she passed as Azure and failed to rouse Daezen's suspicion, but he'd led her right to the one and only Topper Luxo. The universe must have been singing her song tonight.

Cold wind blistered her skin through the low-quality fabric that passed as a coat among those Azure animals. The Tile at the entrance emitted a laser blue light that scanned her eyes. The door slid open. Warm air from the heated hallway enveloped her, lessening the bite of the cold. She almost groaned in pleasure.

Upon seeing her tottering blue heels and floaty tulle coat, Inspector Babitut cast her a bemused look from behind the security desk.

'Been on a hot date, Bloodbat?'

She ignored the jibe. Inspector Babitut was fresh out of the academy, keen to grasp at superiority whenever he could. She wouldn't dignify him with a response. Besides, the information she had couldn't wait. No matter how much she ached for a shower and a change of clothing, there was no time. The grease and sweat of that disgusting Azure hovel curdled on her skin.

Reaching the door of the cyber control room, she knocked three times, heart thrumming in her chest. It had been risky to approach Daezen Trovit and Topper Luxo the way she had. Even riskier to plant a tracker on Topper's clothes. Nonetheless, the reward had been second to none.

The door opened, revealing Inspector Jenna Rutkitz, her flowing red hair falling all the way down to the waist of her black leath jumpsuit.

Jenna gave Soba a once over. 'You look like an Azure whore.'

'That's kind of the point, Ratkiss.' Soba pushed past her, making a beeline for her desk.

At the far end of the room, a large screen encompassed the

entire wall, cycling through the live streams from the shadow-birds' eyes all around the city. The eerie blue light of the night-vision videos illuminated rows of black-marble desks, each one equipped with holo-Tile functionality.

Soba's fingers skipped across the display, bringing up a large holographic map of the city. In Azure Minor, a bright red dot flickered, moving towards the upper ranking Azure neighbourhoods. She closed her eyes and exhaled, relief relaxing her tensed muscles.

The tracker had worked.

Jenna peered over Soba's shoulder. 'Who're you tracking?'

Pride glowed in Soba's chest as she spun on her chair to look the Inspector in the eye. Her smile grew wide. 'Topper Luxo.'

Jenna's eyebrows shot up, crumpling her alabaster skin into deep lines. 'You got close enough to Luxo to plant a tracker on him? Why didn't you bring him in?'

It was a good question. Uncertainty over the decision to let Topper go weighed heavy on Soba's mind. It hadn't been difficult to lure him out of the tavern and down a dark alleyway with a flutter of her eyelashes and a few sycophantic comments. However, it wasn't the assassin's horrific attempt at charm that had stopped her from arresting him. It was what she'd heard before approaching his table.

'There's a bigger plot at hand,' Soba said, irritation bleeding into her voice. She didn't have to justify herself to Jenna Rutkitz. Soba was the superior here. Elias had trusted her to take the lead on this mission. 'I have a lead on the location of two suspected Azure Angels. Topper's small fry in comparison.'

When she'd entered the tavern and immediately spotted Daezen, it was by some stroke of luck that he was talking to

Luxo. But unlike the rest of the Azure drunks, they'd kept their voices low, movements measured. So, she'd twisted on the acoustic particles in the sweating dive of an establishment and heard every single word of their conversation. The essential information being that Daezen had met with a member of the Azure Angels and they were working on some kind of secret terrorist plot. Now, that was the kind of intel that transformed an Inspector's career.

'Did you check that with the chief? Seems a bit risky to me. What if he discovers the tracker?'

Maybe Elias would've wanted her to bring in Topper. Without a doubt, he would've been pleased. But catching an Azure mercenary that stole and killed from other faint-eyes wasn't going to move the needle for her. No. There was a bigger prize on this horizon. If she could uncover a terrorist plot and get the inside scoop on the Azure Angels' next moves, it would be a far greater achievement than capturing a wayward assassin.

She wanted to earn greatness.

Soba gritted her teeth. 'He won't. And the chief has given me authority in all matters pertaining to this case.'

Withdrawing her Tile, she started to write a message to Elias.

Jenna drew closer, invading her personal space. 'Ooh, inviting the chief to your apartment are you? Does someone have to make up for their little boo-boo?'

Soba folded up her Tile. Her skin crawled from Jenna's insinuation, and a night spent cavorting with Azure scum. 'Watch what you say, Jenna. Before long, you're going to be reporting to *someone like me.*'

'Oh, come on, I'm just playing. But tell me, how does the chief like it? Does he ask you to get on your knees and—'

Soba slid into the unseeing, capturing the words as they exited Jenna's gossiping mouth. She twisted the particles together, swirling them around until they dissipated in the air, silencing whatever filth the woman had been about to say.

Jenna tightened her fists, mouth opening and closing before she was finally able to form words again. 'How dare you use your Bloodbat nonsense on me.'

Soba stood. 'I don't have time for your games, Jenna. Enjoy the night shift.' Turning on her heels, she made her way to the door with as much grace as her scanty outfit allowed.

She recalled the heat of Topper Luxo's breath, the feel of his dirty hands on her waist. Getting close to him may have enabled her to place the tracker, but it made her stomach churn. Of course, she'd pushed him away and left before anything had happened, but still... She needed a shower as soon as possible.

Tomorrow was going to be an important day. The day she finally took hold of her destiny and engaged in her first ever solo mission.

The day she earned her place in this world, all of her own accord.

Nausea overtook Soba as white light erupted behind her eyes. Her body convulsed. This was nothing, she reminded herself through gritted teeth. She could cope with pain. Physical discomfort was little more than a sensory message. Messages could be ignored. But it wasn't the pain that caused a fist to tighten in her chest. It was the *silence*.

'You will be fine, Ọmọ-binrin ọba. This is the latest in Octengion science. A true oculary miracle.'

She winced at the sound of her old title.

Propping herself up on her elbows, she hissed at the sting in her left arm. She was lying on her grey cotton sofa in the living room of her apartment. The man next to her wore a white coat and a matching pair of white-framed spectacles that contrasted with his rich brown skin. Warm eyes of liquid coal and a friendly larger-than-life smile filled her vision.

The memories returned.

Early in the morning, Dr Alhaadi Popoola had knocked at her door, ready to administer a new experimental drug at her request. Dr Popoola may be the star scientist of the Salog Octengion Inspectorate and a leader in oculary research, but whatever he'd stuck her with burned like the desert at high noon.

'I don't feel fine.' Soba's voice sounded alien to her ears. As she looked around, it took all of her strength to keep her heartbeat steady, her breaths even. She'd known the serum would disable her oculary abilities, but she hadn't been prepared for how different everything looked. For the empty silence weighing on her chest.

Where was Elias? He was supposed to be here.

Not wanting to get Dr Popoola in trouble she hadn't been able to communicate the full details of her plan in her message. Despite the way she'd shaken off Jenna's questioning, she wanted Elias's approval before she started her mission. She wanted to see the look in his eyes when she told him what she planned to achieve.

Soba's forehead was damp with perspiration. A vacuum encompassed the place in her chest where acoustic particles usually lay dormant. Without her oculary, without Elias, she was utterly alone in this frozen land.

Dr Popoola reached a hand to her forehead to check her temperature. 'The fever is leaving you. I predict that you'll be back on your feet in half an hour or so, maybe less. You are strong. Perhaps, after this mission, you will consider the offer I brought to you last time we met. The people of Octengion are ready for a change.'

Soba pushed herself to a sitting position, doing her best to mask the pain from her arm. 'This is my home. You know what Elias did for me. When I arrived here, I was nothing. He treated me like family. I have no interest in leaving.'

'Hmm,' Dr Popoola said, checking her pupillary responses. 'Whatever you say, Lola.'

'My name is Soba.' She winced as he shone a light stick in her eyes. 'And I still don't understand why you couldn't simply have made a sturdier pair of coloured lenses.'

'Òrẹ́ mi.' Dr Popoola smiled widely, revealing a set of bright-white teeth. 'You know the lenses don't work for long. Obsidian oculary power dissolves them far too fast for infiltration missions, especially yours. But you know this. You know why. That's why you asked for my help.'

He placed a small packsack in her hand.

'What's this?' she asked.

'Oral doses, you'll need to take them throughout your mission.' Dr Popoola's large forehead creased. 'Is there something wrong with your arm?'

She avoided his gaze. 'I injured it while training.'

Dr Popoola's smile disappeared. 'And Ọgá didn't send a healer?'

'It's not his fault,' she replied. 'Elias is very busy.'

Dr Popoola sucked on his teeth, then reached into his briefcase and withdrew another needle. Gently, he injected the swirling liquid into her torn bicep. 'That should speed the healing. Now, how are you feeling? Will you be able to stand?'

Soba nodded. She was starting to feel better, physically, at least. She got up from the sofa, legs trembling. 'So, it worked?'

'Take a look for yourself,' Dr Popoola said, holding up a hand mirror.

Soba's legs gave way, and she fell back on the sofa.

In place of the dark onyx eyes she'd grown used to seeing in the mirror, her eyes were dull and blue.

'Take that away.' She batted the mirror out of his hand. 'Have you tried it?'

Dr Popoola seemed taken aback. 'Of course not. It would not be very scientific to try the inventions out on oneself. I can assure you that the serum has been adequately tested on a range of randomly chosen participants, the trials controlled and peer reviewed.' He continued prodding and poking her, taking more readings and noting them down.

Elias still hadn't arrived. Would she dare to start the mission without his approval? No, she couldn't. There'd be no point in the endeavour if Elias wasn't by her side, ready to recognise her greatness and publicly announce their relationship.

'There was a full moon last night, did you see it?' Dr Popoola asked as he noted down the readings on his Tile.

She remembered the white light of the moon illuminating her scanty Azure outfit as she'd walked the streets of Densolid Minor. 'I did.'

He adjusted his glasses. 'What did you see on the moon's face?'

She bristled, then thought through the question. 'I saw a face howling in silence. Their pain unable to reach us across the vast emptiness of space. The sound of their suffering reduced to a mere snapshot, an image frozen in time.'

'Very poetic. You remind me of your mother you know, she would always—'

Pain cracked the wall of ice separating Soba from frozen memories. 'Get to your point.'

His smile strained. 'One of the Aunties used to say the moon was warning us. That they'd seen our cursed fate from the moment we began to reach for the stars.'

Soba raised an eyebrow. Was he judging her ambition? 'Well, that's a bit rich coming from you. Or am I to believe the serum hasn't been tested on others? Wouldn't you say your actions count as reaching for the stars?'

'I have made peace with my actions. However, I wish I had thought through them more before embarking on my experiments. You have yet to act, and all your choices float before you like fireflies. All of them, Ọmọ-binrin ọba Adelola. You would be welcomed back with open arms. There are enough of us to support you know. He will not win.'

She squirmed with discomfort. 'You speak out of turn.'

'I wonder ... if Tiwa had lived, would you be making the same decision, or would you choose to come home?'

Soba clenched her hands into fists.

The sound of someone clearing their throat brought Dr Popoola to a pause.

'Chief Inspector Vox. Ògá, I did not know you would be coming by. Accept my apologies for not officially announcing my presence in your—'

Elias cut him off. 'It's fine, Dr Popoola. You can go now. I'll take things from here.'

Dr Popoola frowned, pushing his spectacles up the bridge of his nose. 'If I may, Chief Vox. I should observe the lady a little longer, this is the first active use of the Azuserum in Albin and—'

'I said you can go,' Elias ordered.

'I'll see you at the Gala?' Soba asked. 'If your invention doesn't blind me, that is.'

'Of course.' Dr Popoola bowed his head, shooting Soba a worried glance before scurrying out of the apartment.

'I am grateful that the Salog Inspectorate is so generous with their scientist's time and ... inventions. But that man irritates me to no end.' Elias approached her, hands casually tucked into the large pockets of his cream-fur waistcoat. Then he stopped and stared fixedly at her eyes. 'Extraordinary. You look just like one of them. The files said you might even be able to mimic their oculary power to a degree. Have you tried?'

Soba's mouth dropped open. 'You know about the serum?'

Elias took a seat next to Soba, flashing a feline smile at her. 'Of course. Aunt Greta has been monitoring Octengion communications for the past solar loop. Once Inspector Rutkitz informed me of your ... activities last night, I looked through your call history and put two and two together.'

Her chest tightened. He'd looked through her history? While it was standard procedure in the Inspectorate, she couldn't help but feel disappointed. She wasn't just another Inspector to him, she was his lover. His shadow. And soon she'd be his equal.

He reached across to stroke her hair. 'Don't get upset, Little Night-Eyes. I just wanted to make sure you were safe. I don't want anything bad to happen to you.'

Soba shook her head, trying to ignore the gaping hole where her oculary sense should be and concentrate on the feel of Elias's hands on her hair. 'I ... I can't hear properly. My oculary ... will it return?' She hated the desperation that rang in her voice.

He smirked. 'You think I would've allowed that man into your home if I thought he'd leave you like this permanently? Frankly, Soba, you look disgusting. Of course, you'll return to normal. Aunt Greta assures me the Octengions have been experimenting with this stuff for years, in spite of what they say. As much as we have our disagreements, there's no questioning their scientific prowess.'

Soba flinched at the distaste on his face, but quickly masked her reaction. She would not appear weak in front of him. He deserved more than that. 'Of course. I didn't mean to question your judgment.'

'Quite right. So, run me through your plan. What are the objectives?' Elias asked, still staring at her eyes in disgust.

'From a conversation I overheard between Topper Luxo and Daezen Trovit, I discovered the presence of Azure Angels in the city – and I have a lead on their next destination. Evidence points to the fact they are planning something. I decided against arresting Topper, fearing it would put my infiltration plan at risk.'

Elias caressed her neck, tracing down her shoulders to her collarbone. Sparks lit up in her stomach, skin exploding with warmth at every place he touched.

'Shut your eyes,' he said, 'and continue.'

She scrunched her nose. 'My eyes?'

He pulled away, leaving a coldness where his fingers had been. She didn't want him to stop. She wanted to feel the comfort of his touch, the only thing that would help her forget the sharp emptiness carving through her chest where her power should be.

'By Artium's grace, Soba. I don't want to look at you, let alone touch you, with your eyes that watery colour. So, shut them.'

She acquiesced, pushing down the vertigo of being plunged into darkness. Usually, she could sense all her surroundings, even with her eyes shut. Dr Popoola's serum was stronger than she'd expected.

Elias grasped her shoulders and pulled her closer to him, resuming the light caress. Desire stirred in her lower stomach and she wriggled against him, desperate to be closer.

'Continue,' he whispered, breath heating her ear.

'I ... I...' She struggled to catch her breath. 'I got close to Topper and placed a tracker on him. That way, whatever happens we'll still be able to arrest him when the time comes. I plan to locate the Azure Angels, infiltrate their operation and report back with all information I obtain about the militant movement.'

His fingers danced lower, drawing broad strokes across her stomach that seemed to burn through the thin fabric of her shirt.

'Did Topper Luxo touch you?'

She tensed up, opening her eyes and arching her neck to look up at him. 'What?'

'Close your eyes.'

She followed the order.

'Good. Now, did he touch you?' He rubbed his thumbs in circles across her hips. 'I'm taking your silence as a yes.'

Her breaths quickened, a coil tightened in her lower stomach, pleasure entwined with fear.

'Where did he touch you?' He gripped her shoulders. 'Was it here?' His hands moved down to her waist. 'Or here?' Fingers grazed Soba's breasts. 'Or here?'

All of a sudden, he pushed her off him and stood, leaving her alone on the sofa, unease and rejection thrumming in her blood. She opened her eyes. Elias grasped his hands behind his back, peering out of the large windows that overlooked the city.

'It's a good plan.' He nodded. 'And the fact that they're headed to the Asabrek forest proves they're planning something and looking for support. The Dissidens are the closest known rebel outcrop.'

She tried to steady her breaths, still reeling from his touch. 'Do I have your approval?'

He spun around. 'Of course you do. Don't make any hasty moves, and report back on everything you hear at the Dissidens' encampment. The right kind of information will be more beneficial to us both than the capture of a few rebel youths. Now, on your feet, Inspector.'

She stood to attention, keeping her eyes down to avoid seeing disgust crumpling Elias's handsome face. She didn't want him to see her like this, not after his initial reaction.

'I've uploaded all the intel we have on the Azure Angels and the Dissidens to your Tile, along with a cover story. Make sure to read through it all before you head out. This is your first solo mission, Inspector, and a positive outcome will do wonders for both of our careers. Are you ready for this?'

'I'm ready,' Soba said. And she realised that she was. Ready to make history. Ready to protect the Empire. Ready to make Elias choose her.

'I need to go,' he said, checking the time on his Tile. 'And you need to get started. Crossing the tundra isn't for the faint-eyed.'

He approached the door, looking back at the last minute. 'And when this mission is done, I will imprison that Azure assassin and chop off every finger that dared to touch what is mine.'

CHAPTER 17
MILLIE

SOBA

Soba travelled to the outskirts of the city and took a cross-country pod to the sparse settlements on the edge of the icy desert. From there, she began the trek towards the Asabrek forest. The journey would've been quicker and smoother on a hoverbike, but the intel file had been clear – she must approach by foot.

The Ice Cap mountains towered above the dark green mass of trees, casting a monstrous shadow across the tundra. Sleet smacked into her face as she pushed through the snow. A day spent trekking across snow wasn't enough to tire her. She'd trained far harder than this before and could keep going for miles. Cold and pain were just sensations. Feelings could be ignored. Even the aching silence in her heart was just another feeling.

At least that's what she told herself.

She paused, double-checking her eyes in the reflective

surface of her heated water canteen. Two ocean-blue eyes stared back at her. In the Dissidens' encampment, citizens of all eye colours mingled and lived side by side, but Soba's mission was to ingratiate herself with the Azure Angels. To do that, she couldn't enter with any other oculary than Azure. The Azure Angels were known for their extremism, their blatant disregard for innocent life when it came to pursuing their goals. Until Soba had overheard that conversation between Topper and Daezen, there'd been no detection of Azure Angels in Albin for over thirty years.

It was disconcerting. Almost as disconcerting as the silence.

It wasn't like there was no noise. The arctic wind roared around her, and the snow crunched under her boots. But separated from her oculary ability, it sounded far away and hollow. Her brain filled the silence with unwanted thoughts and memories.

Dr Popoola had offered her a chance to go home. Should she have taken it? And why had he brought up her mother and Tiwa? He knew how she lived. How she made it through each day. Never look back, that was what she'd promised herself. And she'd never even entertained the possibility of *going back*.

As if nature had heard her thoughts, the wind picked up, and a spattering of snow rained down upon her. Her fingers and toes burned from the extended period of time spent trekking the tundra. This place couldn't be further away from the thick humidity of her home city. Settled deep in the lowland forests, Salog, the capital of Octengion, was known for its advanced integration of the city and the natural world; thick green leaves blended into large, rounded complexes and underground laboratories.

The oppressive white blankness of her current surroundings

encroached upon her will, making her doubt everything from the mission to Elias himself. The chemistry between them was undeniable, but out here, away from the city, a small niggling fear took root. Was her love for Elias trapping her in this place? Would it keep her from who she was meant to be?

By the time she reached the edge of the forest, the snow had thinned, revealing the barren earth beneath. Towering high above her, fir trees spiralled into the sky, trunks covered in criss-crossing rope-like vines that melded into thorny bushes. It was almost impossible to see inside, let alone traverse.

She pulled a blade from her belt and hacked through the brush, making her way through to the heart of the forest. Her limbs warmed from the exertion, and each satisfying thwack at the plants strengthened her resolve. Elias was helping her to become her own person, separate from the tragedy of her past. With him at her side, she'd rise all the way through the Inspectorate ranks all due to her own merit, nothing more. She didn't need to go home.

She had everything she needed right in front of her. It was up to her to reach out and take it.

After hours of searching the forest for the Dissidens' encampment, despair was setting in. Everywhere she looked were skeleton trees and empty forest, not a sign of life, human nor animal. Her head pounded from dehydration, having consumed the last of her water several hours previous. A darkness fell upon her, bringing negative voices to the fore of her mind. Falling at the first hurdle by failing to locate the Dissidens' secret camp didn't bode well for her mission.

And if she couldn't complete her first solo mission, what use was she to Elias? What use was she to anyone?

Her shoulders hunched as she tripped over a thin line of stones, landing hard on the frozen ground. She cursed and scrambled to her feet, teeth grinding together as she searched her mind for her next steps. Nobody who knew her would ever describe her as clumsy, but the inability to access her oculary had her unbalanced in body and mind. If only she could use her power to scan the area, then she'd find the Dissidens in no time at all.

The sound of footsteps crunched through the forest.

Her pulse raced.

From behind her, a voice boomed. 'Who goes there?'

Two tall men dressed in brown cloaks and furs came into view, each with a bronze mask covering their face and a sharp pointed staff in hand.

Her heart pounded as she schooled her features into a meek smile and cast her mind back to the intel file. She swallowed past the lump in her throat. The icy wind howled through the trees. Though she knew her cover story by heart, it felt different with these men looming over her. Lost in the forest, alone with armed, masked men, unable to access her oculary and with only a small knife for self-defence. She shivered.

You'd better be convincing.

'Ho,' Soba called, her index fingers and thumbs formed a triangle shape. According to the file, this was the Dissidens' established manner of greeting one another. By some miracle, her hand remained steady. Beneath her heavy tracksuit, her knees wobbled.

The taller man banged his staff against the ground and Soba didn't have to fake a flinch. 'Wherein lies the way of the truth?'

'The path of dissidence leads the way,' Soba responded, keeping a weak and docile smile on her lips. Tentatively, she brushed the snow from her hair, taking care to tremble overtly. The aroma of fresh pine pervaded the bitter air.

While reserves of strength still coursed through her body, her new persona, Millie Kuti, the Azure performer escaping from her troupe, would not be so hardy. The trek across the tundra would've taken her to her limit, and Soba had to act the part as well as look it.

'My name is Lazlo,' the man responded, removing his mask to reveal a thin, sallow face and shrewd brown eyes. He searched her face, eyes narrowing before flashing amber.

The ground beneath them trembled and Soba's shaking legs nearly buckled. Her breaths became shallow. Fear seeped into her blood like a toxin, contaminating her focus.

'Brenwyn,' Lazlo said under his breath, 'keep your weapon on her, if I give the signal do not hesitate. Run her through.'

The other man, Brenwyn, stepped forward, angling his staff towards her. Dark brown stains covered the sharpened point of the staff. Stains that looked like blood.

'Please,' she said, voice trembling in earnest, 'I come seeking shelter, I mean you no harm, I promise.'

The staff in Brenwyn's hands lowered slightly. He was listening to her, of course he was. He wasn't about to ram a pointed staff through a defenceless Azure woman found in the woods. Soba elongated her breaths. She could do this.

Lazlo banged his staff on the ground again; it felt like a blow directly to her ribcage. 'Don't lower your weapon. Protocol is protocol,' he sneered, circling Soba. 'The last time I found an Azure out here, they were Inspector scum with high-grade coloured contact lenses. I won't make that mistake again.'

She breathed in the scent of the forest, she decided to let herself feel the full weight of her fear for five seconds and five seconds only. She started to count.

One.

She dropped to her knees.

Two.

She would never see Elias again.

Three.

She wasn't good enough for this mission.

Four.

She was doomed to fail and she'd die a slow and torturous death.

Five.

She gritted her teeth as old demons raised their ugly heads.

Then she exhaled, banishing the emotions from her body. It was an Inspector-taught technique. The best way to vanquish an emotion was by feeling it to its full for a limited amount of time then letting it go. She widened her stance. Whatever these men threw at her, she would handle it. Everything was under control.

'State your name, that of your Dissidens contact and the purpose of your visit. Brenwyn, search her things.'

She passed her packsack to Brenwyn and reeled off the answers from her cover file while Lazlo verified her answers by searching for the details on his Tile.

'All checks out,' Lazlo said with a thin smile. 'Brenwyn?'

'What're these?' Brenwyn asked, producing the pack of pills Dr Popoola had given her.

'Analgesics,' Soba said without skipping a beat. Dr Popoola's notes had assured her the packaging was consistent with standard painkiller blister packs. 'I get terrible migraines.'

'We'll keep hold of them for now, if they pass our herbalist's tests then you can have them back, Millie Kuti,' Lazlo said, pronouncing her fake name with sharp vowels.

That wasn't ideal. She had to take the pills every day or risk reverting back to her natural state, but she'd worry about that later. 'That's fine,' she said, 'is the interrogation over? Did I pass your test?'

Lazlo nodded slowly. Brenwyn lowered the staff.

She didn't let herself relax. Lazlo may look weedy and appear friendly, but she saw past his amicable persona. She hoped he couldn't see past hers. The men began to lead her through the forest, before Lazlo turned around, raising a hand.

His mahogany eyes glinted and the trail of rocks she'd tripped on reassembled into a perfect line. 'I forgot something, silly me. The retina-scan check. Brenwyn, do you have the machine?'

'Oh, yeah, I've got it somewhere, let me just...'

While Brenwyn searched his bag for the retina-scan Tile, Soba tried to recall the way out of the forest. Nothing in the file had mentioned the Dissidens having access to advanced tech, there was no guarantee that Dr Popoola's drug could fool a scan. She needed an escape plan. She needed to be ready.

Artium be damned, she had no idea how she'd arrived at this part of the forest. In her despair at not finding the Dissidens earlier, she'd lost track of her paces. If she were discovered, fleeing would be too risky, it was just as likely she'd run into another group of Dissidens security or stumble across the camp rather than finding her way out. If things turned sour, she'd have to fight, and without her oculary ability, hand-to-hand combat was the only tool at her disposal.

Soba took a step back, reaching into her facsfleece bodywarmer. Her fingers rested on the hilt of a knife. She could do this. She was trained to do this. If these men were to be her first kill then so be it.

'Ah,' Brenwyn exclaimed. 'Here it is.'

Lazlo took the Inspector-issued golden Tile from Brenwyn's hand. Soba's palms grew clammy. How had these savages got hold of an Inspector-issued Tile?

The sounds of the forest faded. The corners of her vision blurred. Soba's entire being focused on Lazlo's neck as he approached her with the Tile.

'Open your eyes wide, please, *Millie*.'

Soba recalled her training, slowly reaching to the inner pocket of her coat. *Spin, duck, pull the head up with one hand, press deep, and slice across the neck.*

Thud, thud. Thud, thud.

Her heart beat a battle cry as she tightened her grip on her knife.

The Tile issued a beep as a thin ray of blue light extended into her eyes.

Thud, thud. Thud, thud.

'A bit wider please.'

Spin, duck, pull the head up with one hand, press deep and slice—

'Okay, the reading's registering...'

The cold metal handle of the knife's grip against her palm.

Spin, duck—

Soba's fingers twitched. Her eyes itched to blink. But she couldn't. She had to be ready.

'And it looks like...' Lazlo squinted down at the Tile.

Thud, thud.

Brenwyn banged his staff, raising it up high.

Her fingers closed around the knife. Her back muscles tensed, ready to throw.

The Tile issued another chirrup.

'Yes,' Lazlo said, his face relaxing. 'You are indeed, Azure. I can welcome you into the camp for now. But don't get comfortable. You'll have a half-cycle to prove yourself loyal to us and convince Gambit he should let you stay. Until then, I'll be watching.'

Soba's fingers trembled inside her pocket, her heart beating at a hundred miles per hour. It would take some time for her body to sync up with her head, that was fine. That was normal.

Excitement took the place of fear as she followed the men through the forest. She'd done it. She was through. She was infiltrating the rebel camp.

Sending a silent prayer of thanks to the moon for Dr Popoola and his genius, Soba entered the Dissidens encampment.

CHAPTER 18
TRUCE

JANTSIA

Mirrors. Everywhere she looked there were mirrors.

Fists of dark marble, translucent ice, tanned skin, golden rings, leath gloves; knocking. Long, painted nails scraped down glass.

A thousand versions of herself whispered, screamed, sang to be free.

Jantsia awoke drenched in sweat. Heartbeat messy and off-tempo. Fragmented memories cut through her mind like broken glass.

She coughed, her mouth tasted dry and bitter. Well, she'd managed to get home in one piece, at least, though how she'd got here eluded her.

What exactly had happened last night? She knew she'd argued with Kain about something, and consumed far more psychs than anyone in their right mind would on their first time, but apart from that, the entire evening had been reduced to flashes of emotion and movement. A pounding resounded in her head, and her stomach curdled with regret.

Luz snored lightly, curled up in the crook of her arm. She stroked him as she pieced together patchwork memories, realising several things with sickening certainty. Last night, Kain had made it painfully clear that he had no interest in her as anything more than friends, and with the way she'd acted, she wasn't sure he'd want to be friends anymore. She'd embarrassed herself by acting like a jealous little brat. Said things she couldn't take back.

Before they became friends, Kain had been one of the most popular guys in the class, the male equivalent of Flossie and Pixa. Although Jantsia had always admired him from afar, she'd never dared to talk to him. They'd only really had one, mortifying, encounter.

She still remembered the flames of embarrassment that had engulfed her when Kain had approached her singing a stupid song.

'She's the girl that never smiles, she's just a girl that never smiles.'

Not knowing what to say, she'd blushed and quickly rushed away while he continued to sing. From that day on, Jantsia resolved to practise her neutral, unthreatening smile.

Everything changed when his father died. Dark clouds and smoke replaced his golden moods and electric energy as he withdrew into himself. It wasn't long before he was as much of a pariah as Jantsia. Well, almost. Without knowing how to talk to him, his friends distanced themselves, turning their attention to other, more jovial members of the class.

He must have spent cycles without speaking to anyone at the academy, until one day, Jantsia gathered all her courage and approached him.

'Well, would you look at that,' she said.

He squinted at her from under messy strands of unwashed hair.

'He's the boy that never smiles,' she sang, ignoring the pounding of her heart and the reddening of her cheeks. 'He's just the boy that never smiles.'

And by some miracle, a smile had broken through the darkness of his expression and laughter had trilled from his lips. A real laugh, not the bitter shell of it he'd sometimes issued in classes. From then on, it had been the two of them against the world.

Until now.

Her heart fluttered, recalling her conversation with Daezen. It was clear he struggled to cope with the burden of his responsibilities. She didn't know how he did it, managing their mother's ill health, and keeping their family together through grief and financial insecurity. His determination and will of steel were admirable. She wished she could be more like him. Strong and relentless, rather than weak and pathetic.

Her mouth grew drier. Reaching for the glass of water at her bedside and glugging down half of it in one go, another thought sprung to mind.

Kain's blank expression as she'd told him to leave her alone. The mirror-woman of dark marble, grasping hold of her mind.

Had she somehow used Obsidian oculary power? But if she had, then what on Shariza did that mean? Fear filled the pit in her stomach.

Had her awakening been a fraud? And did this mean she really was succumbing to the blood sickness?

Steadying her focus on the glass of water, she tried to reach for the unseeing.

Nothing.

Her head throbbed, but she wasn't going to give up that easily. Yesterday in the academy courtyard, she'd moved the water. She had to be able to do it again. She had to prove that she was Azure, not some Obsidian chimera. Not a dual-oc dying from the blood sickness...

Jantsia narrowed her eyes and screwed up her face, begging the particles to reappear. Her stomach clenched and she let out a savage cry. Luz jumped several feet into the air and with a flash of claws and fluff, disappeared under the bed.

She tried several more times, but all she succeeded in conjuring up was a Fladden-awful headache. Mood sinking, she hid beneath the covers of her bed. Tears grew in the corner of her eyes and her chest heaved with sobs.

A clattering of pots and pans drew her attention, spiking fear through her heart. Someone was rustling around the kitchen and the moon hadn't even fully set. Someone could've seen her last night. An undercover Inspector might've seen her use of Obsidian power and now they'd come back.

Back to raid her home.

Wiping her eyes, and trying to be brave, trying to be like Daezen, she crept into the hall.

Facsleath apron resting over purple, velvet loungewear, Zuleikha pottered around the kitchen, talking to herself while sorting through ingredients. 'Varzesh this, Varzesh that. Well, it's not that simple, my dear. It is not that simple.'

Jantsia let out a deep breath. Relieved to discover her fears were unfounded. Then she cocked her head. What was Zuleikha on about? And what was Varzesh? The word sparked familiarity in her mind. Was it a Parsian word she'd learned as a child?

Jantsia blinked, bleary eyes adjusting to the bright lights of the spacious kitchen. 'Maman?'

Insecurity blazing through her heart, the word had slipped out. Even though Zuleikha hadn't acted like her maman for an age, that's who Jantsia needed right now. Not a patron, not a protector; her maman.

Zuleikha spun around, shoulders tensing. 'Oh, Jantsia *jaan*. Don't mind me. I couldn't sleep so I thought I'd get a head start on breakfast.'

Jantsia blinked several more times, unsure if she'd heard correctly. Surely Zuleikha should be berating her for going out last night, not making her breakfast. 'Where's Baba?'

The silver frying pan fell from Zuleikha's trembling hands, clanging against the marble floor. Jantsia swooped to pick it up and place it back on the counter.

'You don't remember?' her mother asked.

Jantsia's headache curled around the back of her ears and stiffened her neck. 'Remember what?'

Zuleikha rubbed her fingers on her temples, then started cracking eggs into a large ceramic bowl. After several minutes of breaking eggs and whisking the mixture, she looked up at Jantsia. 'Are you going to stand around like a gormless Sepia guard or are you going to help?'

At first, they worked in silence. Jantsia took care to chop the spinach and the rest of the greens as finely as she could while Zuleikha prepared the cornbread dough. Then, as Zuleikha began to form patties from the mixture, Jantsia chanced a question.

'Why aren't you angry with me?'

Zuleikha worked the dough between her hands, forming perfectly circular flat patties. 'Last night when you sauntered through the door, high as a hoverbike, I was angry with you.' She smiled. 'As I'm sure you can imagine, we exchanged several a stern word.'

'And now?'

Zuleikha sighed. 'Let's just say, my priorities have shifted. Your baba and I disagree on many things, but he was right in one regard.' She slapped the final patty onto the worktop. 'I've been too harsh on you. Artium knows, I had my fair share of wild nights out at your age. I think it's one of the reasons I act the way I act. I'm afraid you'll be like me.'

'Ouch.' Jantsia's finger slipped and she sliced the knife into the soft pad of her index finger. Blood dripped onto the steel. A warm sensation burned at her fingertip; not enough to really hurt. Her mother rushed to her side, eyes glowing as she reached for her hand and examined her finger. Jantsia let Zuleikha lead her to the sink and place her finger under cold running water.

Wisps of perfect fifths and melancholy harmonies echoed around the room, taking Jantsia's mind off the cool sting in her finger and transporting her to her childhood. Whenever she'd tripped or fallen, her mother would twist acoustic particles together to create this very same song, and envelop her in a tight embrace. That's all Jantsia had ever wanted from her mother. That feeling of love. Of comfort and recognition. She didn't need a patron watching out for her. She needed this.

'I'm sorry, *miha*,' her maman whispered, 'I'm so sorry.'

Pushing doubts and suspicion aside, Jantsia wrapped her arms around her maman's strong body, tears growing in the corner of her eyes. 'I'm sorry, too.' She thought back to Daezen's strained expression as he spoke of the burden that weighed on his shoulders. 'I never thought about how all of this must be affecting you. Having to pretend to be my patron and suck up to people like that horrible Inspector all the time.'

Her maman held her tightly. For once, the scent of her lavender perfume didn't make Jantsia tense up. It smelled like safety.

When her maman pulled back, she stared straight into her eyes. 'You have nothing to apologise for. Yes, the hoverbike ride was ill-advised, and you picked a terrible night to go off the rails, but you're seventeen years old. And you're strong and clever.' She wiped a tear from Jantsia's cheek with her thumb. 'Now, are you ready to eat?'

They'd prepared two dishes, a Parsian dish called kookoo, a thick, juicy omelette jammed full of greens, as well as fried arepas.

Jantsia's stomach rumbled. 'Shouldn't we wait for Baba to wake up?'

Zuleikha's face fell. 'We argued when you came back last night. He left the house, and I don't know when he'll be back.'

Jantsia stiffened. What could her mother possibly have said to make her baba leave in the middle of the night? The last thing she wanted to do was break the easy truce they'd established. Still, she couldn't help but feel that this was all Zuleikha's fault.

As they ate, Jantsia recounted the events of her night. Her maman laughed as she told her about the Laminosian guys, providing her own anecdotes of scandalous Laminosian beach parties where she'd danced until sunrise. However, just as Jantsia was about to share the argument she'd had with Kain, she paused. An hour of understanding didn't make up for almost a decade of being a patron first, mother second.

Whatever was happening between her and Kain. Whatever was happening inside her, in the hall of mirrors. She would work through it herself. Her parents didn't need to know. Not yet.

Unless...

'Am ... am I dying, Maman?'

Her mother's eyes hardened from swirling black marble to opaque jet. 'I won't let that happen.'

Zuleikha rushed out of the room, swiftly returning with a pack of what looked like standard analgesics. 'With all the drama, I forgot to give you these. They're next-generation pills from my contact. He assured me they'd calm whatever oculary instability you're experiencing.'

Jantsia's heart sank. 'So, I'll be powerless?'

'You'll be alive.' Her mother's eyes glistened, mouth turning down. 'There's a slight hiccup though... After this batch, he will no longer be our supplier.'

Her grip tightening on her cutlery, Jantsia stared down at the remaining food on her plate. Stomach churning. Fists trembling. 'So, I'm okay for now. But once this pack is done for ... I am, too.'

'No,' Zuleikha said through gritted teeth, 'I have a plan. I've been working on something for a while. At first, I was careful. Slowly reaching out to my brother, feeling out opportunities to reconnect with my family. Now that the Inspectors have turned their dirty eyes on us and our source of medicine has dried up, I've accelerated the process.' She sighed. 'The family is willing to overlook past grievances and shelter us at one of their villas in Laminos. We'll be safe there. Protected. And once we're settled in, I'll reach out to some old friends with exceptional knowledge of oculary science. They'll be able to reproduce the medicine, I'm sure of it.'

Jantsia's breaths quickened. 'Do we have enough to last until then? What if I run out?'

'My contact assured me that these new pills will tide you over to the end of this lunar cycle. He also recommended you avoid stressful situations, keep your emotions steady, they could well be a trigger. I've got a link for meditation exercises on my Tile, I'll send them over to you.'

Jantsia's mind whirred, struggling to process everything her mother had told her. Her shoulders tensed. 'Wait, we're leaving Densolid?'

'That's what I'd prefer, though your father seems to have other ideas... Why? Do you want to stay?'

Cold, dark sadness pooled in her chest as she thought back on her nightmarish exchange with Kain. If she didn't have him, what was the point in staying in this frozen hellhole? 'No,' she said, 'I don't want to stay.'

Was that true? Could she really just leave everything behind and start again?

'We'll leave straight after the Gala, that's a few days before your exams, isn't it? At least that'll be one less stress for you.'

She wasn't sure she was ready to trust her mother fully. Not after everything that had happened between them. And a part of her hated the idea of running away. Of losing the opportunity to excel at exams and prove herself. Of leaving Kain behind. But all of that paled into insignificance when she thought of what she had to gain. A fresh start could be just what she needed. Perhaps it was what her family needed, too. Besides, if all Laminosians were as friendly as the guys she'd met at Prenderghasts, she might finally find what she'd spent so long looking for.

A place where she belonged.

CHAPTER 19
ORIGIN

JANTSIA

Baba had yet to return home by the time she left. Though she was starting to seriously worry about him, she didn't want to risk ruining the newfound peace between her and her mother by questioning her further.

No one was waiting for her when she arrived at the Azure 9 pod-stop. Though she hadn't expected Kain to be there, his absence settled in her bones, alongside the bitter cold of the frozen air. She tried to tell herself that it didn't matter, not anymore. After all, before long she'd be in Laminos, dancing the night away at beach parties, far, far away from this cursed wasteland.

Kain stood next to Flossie, avoiding Jantsia's gaze throughout the morning hymn, acting as if she were invisible. Her chest tightened as she followed the Level Ten students to Educator Vortil's cabin. There were no Oculary Practice classes scheduled for today, instead the finalists would head to Oculary

History, Numeration, and end the day with Janitorial class. At least, she wouldn't have to reveal her loss of Azure power to anyone. She had another day before dealing with that unique experience of humiliation. Who'd ever heard of an Azure that had their awakening and then immediately lost their connection to water?

She shuffled into the classroom last, eyeing the empty seat next to Kain.

He looked up at her, electric-blue eyes ablaze. Tightness spread through her aching chest, filling the pit in her stomach. Fladden forsake her, if she was going to leave Densolid at the end of the lunar cycle, shouldn't she at least try to make things up with him? Shouldn't they be spending every last minute they had together?

Electricity shot between them. The spark of words unsaid. Jantsia blinked rapidly, squashing her vortex of feelings into a box. There was no going back from what she'd said. Even if she blamed it on the Fireglug and flash, it wouldn't be the same. Their easy friendship had evaporated in the sweaty air of Prenderghasts.

Vortil, a learned ancient man with scruffy grey hair, paced the classroom, barely noticing the students' arrival. Jantsia took a seat at the back of the class, trying not to stare at the back of Kain's head. His silky white hair was ruffled from the wind. What would it feel like to run her hands through it?

As if he'd heard her thoughts, Kain peered over his shoulder, jaw set and expression dark. 'Hey, aren't you going to—?

'ANCIENT HISTORY!' Educator Vortil boomed, making Jantsia jump out of her seat. Kain turned back to the front of the class and sat up straight. What had he been about to say? Was he going to ask her to sit next to him? Jantsia cursed the old

Educator, wishing he'd chosen a less opportune moment to start his lecture.

Vortil continued, lowering his voice to its usual monotone. 'A lesser-studied epoch that is absolutely key to understanding the formation of the Empire as we know it today. While rarely appearing in examinations – mindless, pointless exercises, if you ask me – the ancient past holds the key to our present, and indeed our possible futures.'

Jantsia gave a silent groan. She didn't want to listen to extended ramblings, she wanted to speak to Kain. To know what he was going to say to her.

Vortil continued in his usual monotone. 'The world before the Empire is shrouded in mysterious and contradictory tales. But only one is accepted as truth. The tale of a greedy, careless society that afforded utmost individual freedom to its citizens, to the detriment of the natural world order. As the planet changed position, the stars aligned to afford a great alteration in Shariza's atmospheric components. Yes, I am indeed talking about The Splice. The moment oculary powers came into existence.'

Jantsia frowned. Her mother had told her a different story. A story of how the Albin military had invaded Parsia and Octengion, aiming to set up their own empire. In Zuleikha's version of history, a Parsian warrior known as Shariza Farzhad had bravely fought against the Albiner invaders, using her newfound oculary power to overthrow their reign and establish the Empire they knew today. The Empire of *Shariza*.

'WE LEARN FROM OUR MISTAKES!' Torvil shouted. 'That is why the Empire established the four pillars of a peaceful and stable society. Segregation, Purity, Unity, and Status. Through ensuring that oculary lines are kept pure and separate, we ensure a healthy and ordered population. Segregation is the greatest gift the Empire could bestow upon us. We are united in our difference. The correct attribution of tasks according to one's oculary power encourages us to be a productive society, one in which everyone has a place no matter how small. Yes'—the old man blinked as Kain raised his hand—'you! Flint, no Dazin... No ... Dazoon! Daezen Trovit is it?'

'Kain Trovit, Educator. Daezen is my brother and Flint ... was my father,' Kain said, mouth tightening.

Oh, my eyes, Jantsia thought. Why on Shariza was Kain interrupting the Educator? He knew better than this.

'Ah yes ... Kantrov, what do you have to say about the great pillars of our Empire?' Vortil said.

Kantrov. Jantsia held back a smirk. If they ever spoke again, she'd tease Kain about this.

'Well, there's something I don't get,' Kain said.

The rebellious glint in his eye wiped the smirk from her lips. For all his admirable qualities, Kain didn't have an ounce of tact. There were so many things she didn't understand about his behaviour. Like why he chose to get in trouble by asking impertinent questions when he was so talented. If he actually applied himself, he could be a top student with a bright future.

'Ah, a philosophical doubt, is it? Come on, son. Share your confusion with the class.' Behind his oversized circular glasses, the Educator's pale blue eyes zoned in on Kain.

'I guess, I don't get how they decided which oculary group gets which status. Water is life, without it there wouldn't be the Empire. So why are we at the bottom of the pile? And who even has the right to decide something so ... so...'

A low murmur crept through the class.

'Arbitrary,' said Educator Torvil, peering over his spectacles.

'Yeah,' Kain said, 'And why do most of us live in slums like Azure Minor when they get to lounge around in places like Meridian? They can't know what it's like to be us, not really. So how's that fair? Why can't we be equals?' He cast a look back at Jantsia that made her stomach churn.

'We are equal, in a way.' Coldness laced the Educator's voice. 'We work in the most effective and natural—'

'But how do we know it's the best way if we haven't tried other things?' Kain continued, cutting off the Educator mid-sentence.

Jantsia shot up her hand. She'd have to head off the discussion before the Educator, old as he was, became suspicious. She doubted Vortil would report Kain, but it wasn't worth the risk.

Whispers surged through the room. Jantsia wasn't the only person who'd noticed the treasonous tinge to Kain's questions. Anyone in here could report him to Az-sec. The last thing his family needed was a raid. Especially if his mother was going through one of her bad patches. So, Jantsia would step in and help the only way she knew how.

'Yes, Brittle girl. Erm, Janet, yes, Janet Brittle. More philosophical doubts?' Educator Vortil snapped.

'No, Educator. I simply thought it might be good to explain Artium's Law and how it served to designate the ocularly order system. Perhaps that would clear things up for ... *Kantrov*.'

Kain's head turned a little so that she could see his profile, and scowled. Jantsia couldn't tell if it was his usual mock-scowl from when they teased one another or a genuine expression of displeasure at her comment.

Vortil continued to recount how Artium Jansen had been Fladden Scope's partner, both Albiner scientists who later became leaders. According to the Educator, Shariza Farzhad had established the Empire alongside the two scientists, including them in her inner cabal and taking their counsel regarding all things oculary. Artium had gone on to publish a seminal text dictating that the natural order of oculary powers followed a colour spectrum, from dark to light. Obsidian, Sepia, Veridian, Azure.

'Of course,' Vortil continued. 'Artium's Law was not adopted without extensive testing and failsafes, many of which academics are still unravelling. The founders of the Empire had an exceptional depth of understanding in the field of oculary science and arts. Rumour has it that before Shariza Farzhad's death, the three founders enshrined one of these failsafes in blood. A mechanism to challenge unfettered power and trigger change in the Imperial Order. By all accounts, it was an act of oculary science and art far beyond anything we are capable of today. However, the Varzesh Clause has not been activated for hundreds of years by my count.'

There was that word again. *Varzesh*. She'd known she'd heard it somewhere before. Before she could think through her actions, her hand shot up again.

'Yes, Janet? Would you like me to elaborate further on the minutiae of Artium's Law?'

Many of her classmates groaned and mumbled to one another. But Kain turned around, fully this time, his eyes alight with curiosity.

Her heart beat rapidly and she focused on the Educator, ignoring the weight of Kain's gaze. 'The Varzesh Clause, Educator. How exactly is it triggered?'

A bead of sweat formed on the Educator's large, lined forehead. He turned away from the class, mumbling something to himself.

'Educator?' Jantsia prompted, well aware of the hypocritical nature of her line of questioning. If Kain's words had been reckless, hers were downright treacherous. But if there really was a way to change the structure of power, all while following the Imperial Laws, then she had to know. Maybe, one day, she wouldn't have to hide what she was. Maybe, one day, someone would take control of the Empire and abolish the segregation law...

'No harm in saying... No harm in telling them,' Vortil muttered as he paced the length of the classroom. 'Miss Janet, the Varzesh Clause is only activated if a direct descendent of one of the Great Elite families issues a public call for—'

A tinny voice through the tannoy system interrupted Vortil's sentence. 'Students, please vacate the classroom. Students, please vacate the classroom.'

Vortil's eyes darted around the room as he fiddled with his specs. 'No, no ... I didn't say anything wrong. I didn't cause harm.'

Two burly Az-Sec soldiers burst through the door, pushing the desks aside to take hold of Vortil. In quick succession, they blindfolded him, removing his access to his oculary power, and clasped bright blue handcuffs around his wrists. Jantsia stared in horror as they marched Vortil out of the classroom.

'What are you looking at?' one of the soldiers snarled at her.

'Watch your words, kid,' said the other.

The students shuffled out of the classroom. Jantsia remembered her mother's words and tried to steady her breaths. To melt the ice in her veins. She had to keep her emotions under control. She had to slow the onset of the blood sickness until they got to Laminos.

'Hey.' Her heart rate rocketed as Kain approached her, hands in his pockets.

'Hi,' she squeaked.

'I want to talk,' he said. 'About what happened last night.'

Cheeks heating and blood thrumming in her temples, she broke eye contact to stare at the frosty ground. Dark stars danced across her vision. No matter how much she wanted to make things right with Kain. She couldn't. She couldn't talk about what happened. Not now.

That conversation was too dangerous.

That conversation could kill her.

Stay invisible. Stay alive.

Her breaths slowed. 'I don't think that's a good idea, Kain. Please leave me alone. I need space.' She didn't dare look at him. Didn't dare see the anger or hurt or whatever he was feeling in his eyes.

She remained shivering in the corner of the courtyard, gaze firmly fixed on the ground until she heard his footsteps. Until he walked away, leaving her completely and utterly alone.

CHAPTER 20
FOREST

SOBA

The Dissidens had prepared a small cabin for Soba to stay in, right at the centre of the camp, in full view of their treetop watchtowers.

They may have let her in, but they didn't trust her.

It had been impossible to sleep that first night. The bed was hard, mattress thin and lumpy, and as soon as the sun set, the forest came alive with noise. Howls, hoots, crunching twigs, rustling branches, the groans of the wind. All of it set her hairs on end, tightening the knot of fear in her chest.

She was alone. Trapped among enemies, lost in the depths of a frozen forest, with only a small knife to defend herself.

How would she make it out here without her oculary ability?

How would she make Elias proud?

How would she survive?

But morning had come, like it always did, and with it a

newfound determination to retrieve Dr Popoola's medicine and gather intel on the Dissidens. If she held her mettle, sooner or later she would find the Azure Angels. Sooner or later, the opportunity would arise to show Elias who she could be. Then she'd show the world what she could achieve all by herself.

After grabbing one of the large fur coats hanging in the small, creaky hut, Soba had set out to explore the encampment. But before she'd been able to make much headway, a plump Veridian woman named Linda approached her proffering warm bread and offered to give her a tour.

The small forest town consisted of treetop watchtowers, lodges, cabins, a makeshift barracks, a communal kitchen and small farm. The inhabitants came from a mixture of oculary orders but Artium's Law still rang true. From what Soba had observed so far, the most important duties were assigned to Sepias, including the role of camp leader. Veridians supported them by growing crops and cooking subpar dinners, while Azures took responsibility for menial tasks. What a bunch of tree-dwelling hypocrites.

Halfway through the tour, Soba's stomach growled with hunger and a migraine crept up the back of her neck.

Pain is only sensation.
Pain is only sensation.
Pain is only sensation.

'Are you all right there, petal?' Linda asked.

It took all of Soba's willpower to bury the instinctive snarl deep in her chest and force her features into something that resembled a smile. Without another dose of Dr Popoola's oculary imitation serum, her Obsidian power would resurface, and the mission would be over before it had even begun.

Linda's rosy cheeks and bright green eyes met her gaze. The

woman's frizzy ginger hair was plaited and styled with leaves and small white flowers, as if she were some sort of forest creature.

Another spasm of pain laced Soba's head, thorns piercing her skull. This time she wasn't able to control her flinch. 'Migraines,' she said through gritted teeth. 'Lazlo confiscated my pills. Said the herbalist needed to check them.'

Linda's eyes creased. 'Oh, petal, I suffered from those when I was pregnant with my first. An awful affliction.' She rummaged through the large pockets of her apron, miraculously retrieving Soba's packet of pills. 'I'm the herbalist,' she continued, 'and we can't have you feeling like this ahead of the party tonight.'

Careful not to move too fast, Soba slowly took the pills from Linda and placed them inside her heavy furs. 'Party? What party?'

'Well,' Linda said, 'you're not the only newcomer to have arrived here recently. And while the others aren't like you, we want to welcome you all to our camp anyhow.'

Soba could hear the bells of opportunity ringing in Linda's voice. 'What do you mean they're not like me? Not Azure?'

'No, they are Azure. I just mean, they're not here to stay. They're visiting from another settlement like ours.'

A perfect fifth.

She must be referring to the Azure Angels. And the party tonight would be the perfect place to locate them. Nervous excitement sang in Soba's veins.

It was hard to believe a woman like Linda could hold a position of authority in a rebel camp. From the way the others deferred to her, Linda was someone important to the Dissidens. But she was also a bleeding heart who had shared far more information than she should've with Soba.

And the Empire of Shariza wasn't a place for the kind-hearted.

～

Soba's nose crinkled at the plate of plain vegetables and nutloaf in front of her. Flaming torches flickered in the breeze, illuminating the crowd of rebels sitting at wooden tables in the clearing of the dark forest.

Set in a circular formation with a large bonfire at its centre, the impromptu dining arrangement had been hastily put together that afternoon. Soba supposed she should act grateful, so she reluctantly placed a forkful of vegetables in her mouth.

Insipid. Watery. Tasteless.

Nothing like the protein-rich, heavily seasoned food to which she'd become accustomed.

Instead of gagging, she grinned and nodded at the expectant faces of her hosts. 'Mmm, it's lovely,' she said, hoping her smile didn't look too much like a grimace.

Sepias, Veridians and Azures mixed as if the segregation law were nothing but a myth. She clenched her teeth; among a sea of pale faces, she was the only person not of Albin heritage. Nor was there a single Obsidian among them either.

These rebels may consider themselves diverse and liberal, but every community feared something. Every community created castes. At least the Empire was transparent about their model for society. The Dissidens weren't morally superior, they were a collection of eccentric lambs dumb enough to welcome a weld-wolf into their flock.

The tasteless vegetables turned bitter in Soba's mouth. Among the people gathered at the feast, it was impossible to tell which of them were the Azure Angels. She had to hope they would reveal themselves soon. That thought made her scowl. Hope. Luck. Only fools counted on such things.

At the far end of the table, a tall, wiry man got to his feet, tapping a wooden spoon against his goblet. 'Settle down, settle down.' His eyes were deep mahogany, hooded and creased with age, but from the gravity of his posture, it was clear he was someone important.

The buzz of voices hushed as people stopped their conversations to listen.

'My people, it is with great pleasure that I welcome several newcomers to our community. For those who I have yet to meet, I am Gambit, the camp leader of this small community. Every new member to arrive here gives me hope that we might one day shake off the shackles of this oppressive regime and be free to live together. Azures alongside Sepias, Veridians alongside Obsidians. For obvious reasons, we have yet to welcome an Obsidian into our camp, but I still dream of the day when our lost black-eyed brethren can join the flock. Our eyes may appear different, but our hearts are one and the same.' As he spoke, he placed his hand on his chest, and many people around Soba followed suit. 'Now, to dispel rumours that may be afloat. It is true that we have with us two emissaries from the Azure Angels.' The light of the flames revealed the leathery texture of the man's skin, beaten down by the elements.

Soba's heart soared, her chest filled with light. Topper Luxo had spoken truly. The Azure Angels were here. She glanced at the people sitting near her, the flickering firelight casting their faces in shadow. A wave of murmuring and whispers arose among them.

Gambit continued, 'I know that we have history with the

Azure Angels, but it is my hope that we might let bygones be bygones and listen to what they have to say. We have more in common than it might seem. I'll let them introduce themselves when they see fit, but please when you come across them, treat them like family.'

He nodded to the far end of the table, where a large tree trunk obscured Soba's view. She squinted, making out two people with large grey hoods shadowing their features. Could they be the terrorists?

Soba leapt to her feet, trying to push through the crowds to get a closer look at the hooded figures, but a group of Azure teenagers blocked her way as they cleaned the tables and took the empty plates. When she finally made it to the spot where she'd seen the two cloaked people, they were nowhere to be seen.

Soba cursed under her breath, scanning the area. It was impossible to see clearly in the flickering light of the flame torches. The mantras drilled into her from Inspector Academy ran through her mind.

Patience is a predator's primary tool.

Watch unseen, arrive unannounced.

She examined the nearest watchtower, a rickety structure built around two tall fir trees. No one was manning it at this hour. Unlike the watchtowers at the perimeter of the camp, this one was only operational in the daytime. These hapless rebels complained about shadowbirds and then went on to surveil their own people. Pathetic.

As the fools around her imbibed more Peri-wine than anyone with sense would, Soba disappeared into the shadows and began to climb the watchtower as carefully and silently as she could. The climb was nothing in comparison to what she was used to doing, but the control required to avoid crunching hidden branches or rustling leaves left her core on fire.

Casting her eye over the Dissidens, she located Gambit exchanging words with Lazlo and Linda, while the youths sat around a campfire regaling lurid stories. A flicker of movement at the edge of the clearing had Soba's heart beating double-time.

Two hooded figures were slipping away from the crowds, heading down the pathway that led back to the centre of the camp.

The Azure Angels.

It had to be them.

As quickly as she could without drawing attention, Soba climbed back down to the ground and made chase.

Leaving behind the warmth of the bonfire and raucous voices, she crept down the pathway, giving her eyes time to adjust to the darkness. With her oculary ability, this would've been so much easier, but as she tuned into the sounds of the forest, she found that a part of her enjoyed the challenge. The thrill.

Up ahead, she spied a single lit-up cabin. With large windows, an extensive treehouse terrace and gabled dormers it was much grander than the hut where Soba was staying. A spiral staircase wrapped around a large oak tree, leading up to the hut.

An orange glow bathed her face as she neared the cabin. Had the Azure Angels come this way or had someone forgotten to turn off the lights before going to the party? Soft footsteps creaked on the wooden slats above her. With no other leads, she had little choice but to investigate.

One foot on the stairs, then another, then another, until she reached the mid-level terrace and an ornate wooden door. The cold glass of the door pane pressed against her cheek as she peered inside. Cosy armchairs, a smouldering fire, a thick woollen rug on the floor. Perhaps she was wrong and they hadn't come this way.

Her heart raced as a shadow moved at the far end of the room – a figure in a grey hood.

She rested her hand against the door handle, contemplating her next move. Then the cool metal of a blade pressed against her throat.

CHAPTER 21
TRAITOR

SOBA

A wave of silky black hair tickled Soba's face and the scent of sandalwood and smoke filled her nostrils.

'Who are you?' the stranger whispered in Soba's ear.

'M-Millie,' she croaked, concentrating on keeping her breaths steady and her neck intact.

'What're you sneaking around for? Did Gambit send you?'

Slowly, Soba tried to manoeuvre her arm into her coat pocket to retrieve her knife. A sharp pain flared in her ribs as the stranger jabbed her with her elbow.

'Don't try anything,' the stranger said, a light accent curling her words. 'Now tell me, why are you here?'

Soba wracked her mind for an explanation. Without a doubt this woman was one of the Azure Angels. Her fierce demeanour was completely at odds with every other member of the Dissidens Soba had met so far. But while she wanted to ingratiate herself with them, she also wanted to keep her head on her shoulders. 'Lazlo ... took something from me. Something I need. What are you doing?'

The woman pressed up tighter against her, blade steady. 'We're trying to find out if Gambit can be trusted.'

So, this was Gambit's cabin. The camp leader hadn't exactly spared any expense constructing this wooden monstrosity. 'And ... can he?'

Heavy footsteps resounded from inside the cabin. A man in a grey hood came into view.

The woman spun Soba around to face her, keeping the blade flush to her neck.

Heart-shaped lips, large opal eyes, tawny skin.

'How do I know you aren't one of his lackeys?' the woman asked, baring her teeth.

Finally, Soba placed the accent, she must be from the archipelago of Arq-Tao. That made sense. The Inspectors had always suspected that the Azure Angels' strongest base was located in Arq-Tao.

Soba raised her hands, slowly placing her fingers between her exposed throat and the blade. The light from the cabin shone across her face. 'Relax, do I look like one of Gambit's inner circle to you? There's a serious melanin deficiency in these parts.'

Her aggressor's lips curled down, and a glimpse of mirth flashed in her eyes.

The man exited the cabin and began conversing with the woman in a rhythmic language that sounded like Tagal. After the conversation got heated, he spun around, his hood falling to his shoulders to reveal heart-shaped lips and the same opal eyes as the woman. Could they be siblings?

'Who the ock are you?' he spat, not a trace of a Taoan accent in his words. If anything, he spoke with a Densolid Azure lilt.

'I am Millie Kuti. I arrived here yesterday after fleeing my performance troupe in Sumavig, I—'

The man cut her off with a dismissive wave. 'I don't give a weld-wolf's balls-sack who you are or where you're from. All I care about is that you stay quiet about what you saw tonight.'

Soba's heart raced as she reached into her coat, taking comfort from the cold metal of her small knife.

The Taoan woman adopted a fighting stance, oozing power and violence from every pore. If Soba had met her in any other circumstance, she would've sworn the woman was an undercover Obsidian.

Soba snatched her hand out of her coat and placed her hands together in prayer position. 'Look, there's something I need from Gambit's cabin. I don't want him knowing that I've been here, either. He'd kick me out and I've only just arrived. I'll keep quiet if you do the same.'

The Taoan woman's face hardened. 'Prove it. Go in and get what you're here for.'

With the weight of the terrorists' gaze on her back, Soba entered the cabin, going straight for the room at the back where the man had been. A small smile curled up her lips. It was overflowing with coats, small weapons and other objects.

This night was going better than she'd planned. Even though she'd nearly had her throat slit, she was pretty sure she'd just introduced herself to the emissaries of the Azure Angels. Now, she had to get them to trust her. She cast her eye over the weapons and at the last minute took a small bronze dagger.

As she walked out, she displayed the dagger in her palm, offering it up for the siblings to inspect.

'And what do you need something like that for?' the man sneered.

Soba rolled back her shoulders. 'I only arrived yesterday, I'd be a fool to believe this place was all love and harmony without proof. Until I know I'm safe, I need to be able to defend myself. It's never wise to relax in this pale man's land.'

Shadows flickered on the woman's face, her posture relaxing slightly. 'I almost didn't catch you,' she said, 'you crept up so stealthily, like a jaguar in the night,'

Soba shrugged. 'I'm a performer, I've learned to be soft on my feet.'

'I'm Blink,' the man said, voice flecked with ice. 'And I hope we don't cross paths again, for your benefit.'

'Tala,' the woman offered curtly. 'And don't forget, we're watching you, jaguar. If you say a single word to Gambit about this, you'll regret it.'

The days spent in the forest blended together, blurring into a monotonous chain of mundane activity and banal conversation. Another day spent chopping wood. Another evening of tasteless food. Another empty night of restless sleep.

Soba moved through the camp intentionally, aware that there was always at least one set of eyes on her. Studying her.

Lazlo's observers were easy to track. Though the forest was their home, they moved with distinctive patterns that Soba had come to recognise. One watcher favoured their left leg. Another had a continuous cough, which they tried to muffle as best they could but not well enough. Still, it was the other set of eyes that piqued her interest.

An observer who moved through the forest almost imperceptibly, blending their breaths to the sound of the forest. Timing their steps with hers. There was no doubt in Soba's mind that this person was Tala.

If Soba was a jaguar, then Tala was a leopard.

Since their first dramatic meeting, Soba had crossed paths with the Azure Angels several times. Tala often sat across from her for lunch or breakfast, her features harsh and unsmiling, and Blink had volunteered for wood-chopping duties alongside Soba. Even though she yearned to strike up contact and try to form a relationship, her gut told her to wait.

Blink and Tala weren't like the rest of the people here. Compliments and light conversation about the weather wouldn't cut it with them. They were wild cats. And the only way to gain the trust of a wild cat was to wait for it to come to you. So, though the days of relative inactivity stretched out before her, Soba knew she had to be patient.

The flames of the bonfire twirled and swayed in front of her as she stuck out her legs, warming her boots. Perched on a log, she gazed at the hypnotic dance of the fire. Without the distractions of the city, the demons of her past had grown louder.

In her normal life, the noise of Densolid drowned them out, while the constant stream of tasks and missions kept the demons silent and small by driving her to be better.

Faster.

More.

Out here in the forest, with time and space to think, the roots of memories long buried were stirring; pushing out small, fermented shoots that smelled sickly-sweet, like overripe pomegranates.

A flicker in the corner of her vision drew Soba's attention away from the flames.

'Another day in paradise, am I right?' Tala said, taking a seat at her side.

The leopard had arrived.

Ignoring the twinge of excitement in her chest, Soba schooled her face into a docile smile. 'I'm enjoying the time away from the city. The hustle and bustle of a performer's life is incessant. It's nice to be able to breathe. To relax.'

'Oh, yeah?' Tala said sarcastically. 'Because I think you're bored. I think you're as frustrated by these people as I am. You see how ineffective their movement is, don't you?'

Perceptive as well as stealthy.

'I understand why you might think that,' Soba said, 'but you don't know me.'

Tala kicked out her legs, sparks flying near her boots. 'I know more about you than you think.'

Soba raised an eyebrow, this woman was presumptuous. 'We've barely exchanged more than a few words, and most of them were with your knife at my throat.'

Laughter burst from Tala's mouth, a joyous staccato sound. The light of the fire highlighted subtle navy tones in Tala's dark hair as she looked at Soba from under thick lashes, opal eyes glinting with mischief. 'I know you like to start the day with a run. That you push yourself in every physical activity, almost as if exhaustion could drown out your thoughts. I know that in spite of your sweet smiles and nods, you feel lonely here. You feel lost. Because something inside you tells you that you're destined for more. And as much as you try to hide it, you're arrogant. Every time you catch me watching you, your lips crease into a smug grin. I know there's more to you than meets the eye.'

Tala's observations disturbed her, tugging at something deep in her core, but she couldn't let it show on her face. 'You've been watching me?'

A figure stepped in front of the fire, blocking the warmth and the light. 'Gambit's ready for us, come on,' Blink said.

Tala nimbly rose to her feet.

Staring daggers at Soba, Blink spoke. 'If Gambit breathes a single word about the other night, we'll know it was you. And you'll be sorry.'

Soba raised her hands, then made a gesture of locking her lips. 'You can trust me.'

'We'll see,' Blink responded before pivoting on his feet and storming off into the darkness.

Tala followed close behind him, but Soba didn't miss the furtive glance back her way before she disappeared into the forest. Silent on her feet, like a leopard.

Soba was going to kill someone.

The sharp edge of the axe swung down, piercing its target with a loud thwack. The frisson of satisfaction was short-lived. Soba lifted the axe high in the air, enjoying the burn in her biceps.

It had been fourteen days since she'd arrived on the outskirts of the Asabrek forest, a full half-cycle. Fourteen days since the first injection of Azuserum had chemically burnt her

Obsidian eyes into submission. Fourteen days since she'd felt the call of the soundwaves.

Since she'd seen Elias.

The axe swung sharply down, making a satisfying crunch as it sliced through a ropey branch. Sweat beaded on Soba's forehead, the salty warmth almost instantly cooling in the chill of the air. She'd been at this for hours.

Reaching down and pulling the blade free, she widened her stance, preparing to swing again.

'Just as I thought.' Blink appeared from the brush behind her, forcing her to pause mid-swing.

Soba had the core strength and stamina to chop wood all day and night, but Millie Kuti, the runaway performer, did not. While performers engaged in elaborate physical stunts, it wouldn't come close to the challenges Soba's body had endured.

Embodying the frailty of Millie, she collapsed to the ground, panting. The smell of wet earth made it easy to feign sickness. Blink looked down at her, still smiling.

Good, he feels superior. That meant he hadn't detected the danger behind her fake Azure eyes.

Blink knelt and whispered in her ear, 'I don't buy the meek-little-Millie act.'

'What do you mean? You surprised me, that's all,' she said, smiling shyly.

'Drop it,' Blink said. 'We've been watching you, we know who you really are.'

In the space between one heartbeat and the next, Soba allowed panic to spread through her limbs, then the moment was over. If he truly knew what she was, he would not be smiling.

'And who is that?' she asked.

'You're strong and you're smart. I don't know why you pretend to be so weak and sweet in front of the Dissidens. You're more than that.' He reached out a hand to help her up. 'Tala said you almost always catch her watching you. You're observant and stealthy, like a jaguar. You have your own head, too. I can tell you're not convinced by all this living-together malarkey.'

Soba cocked her head. 'But if you don't believe in the Dissidens' way, then what are you here for?'

Blinks brow furrowed. 'There's one group that's suffered more than the rest. For Azures to live free, we need upheaval. Total revolt. What Gambit's doing here is measured, controlled. Works for him but not for us.'

He's confiding in you. The plan is working.

Soba mulled over her words. This part was crucial. She was well on her way to winning both Blink and Tala's trust, but she couldn't push it. If she asked too many questions she could break the spell.

'Why are you telling me this?' she asked, injecting feigned naïvety into her words.

'Because you kept your word. Now, humour me, why are you acting like you're someone you're not?'

The rope-like trees seemed to tangle and grow thicker around them.

'You know how it is, Blink,' she said, staring him straight in the eye. 'I am Azure. Too many here consider us the weakest of the pack, even though they pretend we're equals.'

Blink nodded, eyes alight.

She continued. 'I am also Octengion. I have not missed the way our pale brothers and sisters look at my skin. My body.

Even rebels have prejudices, and these Albiners are no different from the rest. They resent me for what I represent, a country that has thrived under the Empire in the face of their failed ambitions. Their lack of progress.'

Blink appraised her, expression hard. He still didn't believe her, not completely. 'Come on. You look exhausted. Let me help you carry this wood back to camp.'

Soba nodded, then collected the chopped wood so they could start the hike back to the central encampment.

They walked in silence for half an hour or so, pushing through trees until they reached a clearing. From here, it was less than ten minutes to camp. Blink stopped, taking a moment to rest. Soba wasn't tired, but she pretended she also wanted to rest.

He handed her a piece of bread, a knife, and some nut-butter from his packsack. 'I'm sorry I was so hard on you,' he said. 'I'm pretty deep in something and I've got to have my wits about me. Can't afford to trust the wrong people.'

Poor, naïve fool.

'It'sh m'okay,' Soba said through a mouthful of bread and nut-butter.

Blink's eyes widened.

In a moment of madness, she opened her sticky mouth and stuck out her tongue. Blink's face contorted and he burst into hysterical laughter. After a good few minutes of shared giggles, they regained control.

'Ahh, Millie, you're something else. I understand why Tala talks about you so much.' Blink wiped tears from his eyes.

'Tala talks about me? What does she say?' Soba asked. A strange glow filled her chest.

Blink tapped his nose. 'She'll kill me if I tell you. Anyway, was nice chatting. We won't be here much longer, I'm afraid. Can't afford to waste more time.'

Soba wanted to ask him where he was going next, but she restrained herself. She didn't want to scare him off, not when she was finally forging an emotional connection.

She had much less time than she'd thought to get the terrorists to trust her fully. Yet try as she might, she could only think of one way to do so.

It was unfortunate that it involved further sullying her tarred, rotten heart.

CHAPTER 22
PETITION

SOBA

'Do you want a top up?' Soba asked, proffering a bottle of berry-infused Peri-wine to Tala.

'Millie!' Tala laughed coyly. 'Go on, then.'

Soba filled Tala's cup to the brim, catching the scent of sandalwood as she leant forward. Warmth curled inside her lower belly. She put it down to the homemade Peri-wine.

'So,' Tala said, lying back on the picnic blanket and looking up at the stars. They shone brightly through the canopy of trees, decorating the branches like fireflies. 'Are you going to tell me why you invited me out here for a night-time picnic?'

Readying herself for sin, Soba licked her bottom lip. It drove Elias crazy every time she did that. 'Blink told me you'd be leaving soon. I wanted to spend some time with you before you go.'

'Alone?' Tala raised her eyebrows. There was nothing harsh

about her features in the moonlight. With her smooth skin and glowing eyes, she resembled a living sculpture.

Soba's silence made Tala laugh out loud, butterflies of joy escaping her lips. Soba liked the way her mouth fluttered open and closed. It was cute. Almost adorable.

Never look back, only forwards.

Not that she was feeling drawn to the past, or even to the future. Today she'd simply existed in the present. Inviting Tala for an evening picnic was an efficient way to glean more information from her without Blink overhearing.

Or was it something more?

No, of course not. She was in love with Elias. There was no room in her heart for anything else.

Tala sighed. 'It's not a secret. You know I've been watching you. And I like what I see. Now ... what do *you* like?'

Frowning, Soba thought through her response. Coming on too keen would draw suspicion. Millie's persona was principally timid, reserved. She couldn't break character. On the other hand, she wanted Tala to trust her, and the best way to engender trust was intimacy. She didn't feel comfortable betraying Elias, but he'd understand. The same way she understood he had to maintain appearances with his high-society courtesans.

'I ... I've never been with a woman before,' Soba said, coupling truthful words with direct eye contact. Surprisingly, it was easy to infuse her voice with desire. Easier than it should've been.

'But you've been with a man?' Tala pressed.

'Only one,' Soba replied.

'Was it serious?'

'It is ... *was* ... intense ... complicated,' Soba stuttered.

'Tell me more.' Tala took a large gulp of Peri-wine. 'Who was the lucky guy?'

'Well, he was older ... and higher status than me. My mentor, actually.' Soba cast her eyes to the glowing crescent of the moon, its light burned through the thick canopy of pungent eucalyptus and pinecones. The moon's face howled down at her.

An expression of pain. Or a warning?

'Oh, wow. Who would've thought? Millie the career-whore!'

'We were in love,' Soba said, unable to keep the irritation out of her voice.

'Calm down, I was joking, Mils. I'm sure you were. And I'm sure it wasn't your fault at all. Sounds like he's a bit of a creep. How old were you?'

'No, no. It's not like that. I mean, I was fifteen, he was twenty-one. His family had high hopes for an arranged marriage. Some kind of alliance or something. But he loved me,' Soba said, losing track of where truth bled into falsehood. She shouldn't have drunk this much Peri-wine, it was impeding her judgement. She'd have to watch her words.

Tala frowned. 'Must've been some high up Azure then to have had an arranged marriage. Was he Az-Sec?'

Realising her mistake, Soba tried to backtrack. 'No, just part of a successful performance troupe. Marrying to bring two outfits together.'

'Oh, yeah, which ones? Blink might know them. He spent his younger years growing up in Densolid, you know. Poor dragonbee. Wouldn't you have hated growing up in this wasteland?'

Soba hadn't known that... Interesting. That must have been why he'd met with Daezen Trovit. Perhaps Daezen was in the city right now, plotting the terrorist attempt. Now *that* intel would buy her favour with the directorate, with Elias.

'Why did you come here if you hate it so?' Soba asked.

'Well, if it was up to me, we would've stayed in Arq-Tao, but Blink has other ideas. Big ones. And what kind of sister would I be if I didn't help?' Tala sat up, the soft Peri-wine aura fading from her face. 'Wait a minute. The wine's going to my head. Did you say your ex approached you when you were a child? That's ... that's... That's wrong, Millie. If you were fifteen, then he was taking advantage of you. Temples burn. Especially if his family has wealth. You know that it's not normal for an adult to show interest in a child, right? It sounds like he was grooming you. Did he ever pressure you for sex?'

Anger, denial, rejection. Soba choked on the emotions accumulating in her throat, sweeping through her body in flashes of sticky discomfort.

Memories of Elias came forth unbidden. He'd encouraged her to share her body, explaining that there was natural attraction between them, a law that could not be broken. The images shot through her mind, leaving a trail of doubt in their wake. But Millie couldn't share any of these details. Millie could not confide in Tala because Millie was a demure Azure woman, and anyway, these things hadn't happened to Millie – they'd happened to Soba.

She swallowed, ignoring the lump in her throat to focus on the mission. Later, there'd be time to think about what Tala had said. 'Maybe you're right,' she said. 'I don't want to talk about it.'

'Oh, temples burn. Millie, I'm so sorry. I should not have intruded so. We've only just met and I... I'm sorry, it must be the wine. I ... I'm not normally so... Well, I was going to say pushy, but that's a lie. I'm not one to hide my opinions. Or my feelings.'

Tala moved closer to Soba as she spoke. A curtain of dark silky hair flopped forwards, inches from Soba's face. Her eyes locked on Tala's full, parted lips, her heart racing.

Tala caught her staring and leaned closer. 'I don't want you to do anything you're not comfortable with. I like you, but I won't push it if you don't feel the same. Relationships are about mutual consent, equality, not dominance. I want you to choose. I want you to listen to the way you feel.' Tala's light Taoan accent curved her words until they turned into smoke, clouding Soba's vision.

Clouding her mind.

She had to press the advantage, but this didn't feel like a mission anymore.

It felt...

It felt...

Blinking slowly, Soba moved towards her, drawn like a moth to a flame, stomach burning with complex and conflicting desires. A coil of warmth curled tightly in her lower stomach. They were so close they were sharing air. Even without her access to her oculary, the sound of Tala's breaths was music to her ears. Twisting through the space between them.

A forbidden dance.

A dangerous choice.

What should she do?

Tala's words wrapped around her mind, glowing in her chest.

'I want you to listen to the way you feel.'

The music reached a crescendo. Soba's stomach flipped as she leaned forward and pressed her mouth to Tala's.

The taste of amber roses. The silken feel of Tala's lips. Her mouth opened, moving deeper, enveloping her body in a golden warmth that almost made her forget why she was here. What she had to do.

She pulled back, lips alight with flames.

Soba told herself she was just playing her part, just doing her job – whatever it took to get the intelligence and keep her cover. Then, she lifted a hand and stroked Tala's velvet cheek, fingers tingling at the touch. Her stomach tightened. Blood thumped in her ears.

'Are you okay with this, Millie? Tell me to stop if you're not.' Tala breathed against her mouth. 'I mean it, we can finish off the drinks and head back. I don't want you to do anything you don't want to.'

'I want it,' Soba replied, and somewhere deep inside, in a place she'd promised herself she'd never look, her words rang with deadly truth.

A lie that wasn't a lie.

Tala placed her hands gently on Soba's back and pulled her on top of her. They kissed, softly at first; an ember catching the wind, burning higher and higher. Before she knew what she was doing, Soba's hands tangled in the silky blackness of Tala's hair. Their bodies curled against one another, desperately, hungrily. She was falling. Falling inside herself.

Falling into a land where wrong and right didn't exist.

A world where sensation was the law, and the only thing she needed was the feel of Tala's hands on her body.

Pushing thoughts of Elias out of her mind, Soba inhaled, taking in Tala's scent and embracing the soft warmth of their intertwined bodies. They stayed like that for what felt like an hour, or maybe it had only been a minute.

Soba's head was unscrewed, unfocused. An effect of the wine, or something else? She jerked away, rolling off Tala and positioning herself at her side.

Tala went to stroke Soba's hair, pausing when her hand was inches from her braids.

'May I?' she asked.

Soba didn't reply. She didn't know how to. How could she articulate the gratitude, the confusion, the empowerment of having her feelings and desires placed at the very centre of this interaction?

Taking her silence as a no, Tala withdrew her hand. 'We can stop here, you know. I meant what I said. I don't want to pressure you into anything.'

Soba flinched. 'I want to help.'

Tala laughed, a trill that made Soba's heart sing. 'Help? With what? My libido?'

'No,' Soba said, not having to feign embarrassment. 'I mean with your mission. I want to help you and Blink. I want to make a difference.'

Tala sat up straight. Her face suddenly became sharp, angular lines hardening.

'Have I offended you?' Soba asked.

'No,' Tala said. 'It's not that... You just reminded me of more serious matters. For a second there I'd forgotten all about the blinding mission. It was just me and you.'

'I'm sorry,' Soba said, and she meant it.

'No, don't apologise. I'm thinking.'

'Okay.' Soba waited as Tala stared off into the distance.

'I will talk to Blink about this. I have an idea of how you could help. And I know that he, like me, will be honoured to count on your support with this.' Tala sighed. 'I can't give away much, but our plan aims to right a great wrong. To empower Azures like you and me and give us a chance to fight for our rights. We can't do it alone.'

A perfect fifth.

Shaking free of the moment of madness, Soba regained her focus. Like Tala, she had an important mission – one that couldn't be forgotten.

'Anything I can do to help,' she said, giving Tala a sweet Millie-type smile.

'I'll let you know, Mils. Anyway, we should get back. Blink will be wondering where I am. The last thing I want is him walking in on us like this. I wouldn't hear the back of it for several cycles,' Tala said, getting to her feet and returning the food and wine to her packsack.

Soba rose to help her.

They shared a brief kiss before starting the hike back to the Dissidens' encampment. The rebel and the Inspector were holding hands.

Azure and Obsidian.

Water-wielder and sound-bender.

Tala's small, soft fingers interlaced with Soba's strong grip, and as they navigated their way through brambles and over uneven tree roots, they never once let go.

Soba ran through the forest at full pelt. Branches smacked into her, and brambles scraped at her face. She didn't care. She needed the release. She needed to sweat.

The evening spent with Tala had left her spinning. Emotions gurgled in her gut.

As much as she hated to admit it, she'd enjoyed their kiss. She'd revelled in every touch and caress. But she wasn't attracted to women, was she? And it wasn't like Tala was an average Obsidian woman. She was an Azure. A rebel.

Most importantly, she wasn't Elias.

The sun had almost set, the forest's inhabitants awakening with the promise of dusk. Soba's skin crawled as the crippling cold deepened. Even the rustling of the leaves around her sounded flat. Off.

She was supposed to be concentrating on the mission, not losing her mind over it.

Her heart rate increased, blood pounding at her temples.

The mission.

Soba had completely forgotten the promise she'd made to Tala this morning. She and Blink were planning on making a petition to the Dissidens' camp leader, to Gambit and his inner circle. It was the siblings' final chance to win over support for their plot – whatever it was.

Soba still hadn't had any luck gleaning further information from the pair, though she was well on her way to winning their trust. In fact, there was a very real chance that Blink would reveal all the details to Gambit at this meeting; all she had to do was accompany them and listen.

They'd said the meeting was scheduled for sundown.

Artium be merciful.

The darkening sky was just about visible through a dense canopy of pines and fir trees.

She was late.

Ignoring the fatigue in her legs, Soba pushed off the ground and sprinted back towards the Dissidens' encampment.

Once she reached the clearing outside the town hall, she

charged through the double doors, interrupting Blink mid-speech.

The orange rays of the setting sun poured into the cavernous space through large arched windows. Blink and Tala stood alone at the far end of the room looking up at the raised platform where Gambit sat upon an embellished wooden chair.

Linda sat on his right, and Lazlo, the sallow-faced Sepia she'd met the first day, sat on his left.

'Welcome, Millie,' Gambit beamed. 'I hope you're here to convince our Taoan friends to stay?'

Soba rushed to stand next to Blink. A wave of Tala's amber perfume engulfed her, and she struggled to stay focused. Everyone was staring at her. Blink's eyes narrowed in suspicion while Tala smiled encouragingly, triggering a traitorous burst of warmth in Soba's chest.

'I stand with Blink and Tala. Their hearts are true. I trust them,' Soba said, careful not to overdo it. She didn't want to accidentally convince Gambit to help.

Blink's face relaxed, and he continued his pitch.

He spoke of injustices, of the resistance, of the Azure Angels and their belief in him and his people. The resistance was losing men, losing them fast. Soba held back a smile as Blink talked of an unknown weapon that allowed Inspectors to infiltrate their ranks.

The irony.

To her annoyance, he didn't outline any specifics about the plan. All he said was he'd been trusted to come to Albin, create his own crew and stage a mission that would change the tide of the rebellion.

Soba needed more than that. She needed details. So, she risked pressing the matter. 'Perhaps Gambit would feel more assured if you explained the mission in more detail.' If she could find out everything she needed now, there would be no need to stay with the Taoans. She could leave her fraught feelings for Tala far behind.

'I cannot do that, Millie. The details are irrelevant.' Blink brushed her off, turning back to the Dissidens' leader. 'Wouldn't you like the whole of Albin to have a chance at living the way you do here, Gambit? Don't you want to change the world?' He spoke faster, almost tripping over his words.

'Ah,' Gambit said. 'Changing the world...' He flexed his lined hands. 'I see a lot of myself in you, Blink. I really do. In some ways, I envy you. I miss that spark. That hope. The certainty that I, and I alone, will be able to make a difference. In the end, it all comes down to faith. To trust. To belief.'

Blink flinched. 'You're saying you don't trust us? Well then, trust your own. Millie, tell him!'

Soba stepped forward, meeting Gambit's eye. The Sepia was hiding something, of that she was sure. A secret smile danced behind his solemn eyes.

'Blink and Tala are trustworthy people. I would stake my life on it,' she said, hoping she hadn't gone too far.

Blink smiled at her. Good, the fool believed her act.

Gambit cleared his throat. 'Your actions will fall on deaf ears, and you will be caught. I cannot risk putting this community in danger.' The Sepia leader gestured towards Lazlo and Linda, then to Soba. 'I could not risk them. My people. No, I cannot help you.'

Blink erupted. 'Well, what do Linda and Lazlo think about this? What do the rest of the Dissidens say? You can't just sit up there on your mock throne and make judgement on something that affects everyone.'

Lazlo's face was unreadable, but Linda's green eyes swam with regret. She would be the problem here. She was all bleeding heart, and Soba could tell she saw merit in Blink's words.

Tala cleared her throat. 'Gambit, we mean no offence.'

'No offence taken, dear. I admire the lad's passion. Look at us,' Gambit continued, 'you're young, I'm old. We can't expect to share the same perspective on everything.'

'I don't see how age comes into this,' Blink said, gritting his teeth.

'Permit me an observation?' Gambit asked.

Blink took a surly step back.

Ever the antagonist.

'When you're young, life is more intense, more black-and-white. Emotions have sharp, serrated edges. Relationships, friendships ... why, they dominate your life. You think they're your people and always will be. You love fiercely. Hurt crashes down on you like a tidal wave on a shallow pool. But as you get older, the blade dulls. The pool deepens. Love becomes less urgent, more patient. People enter and leave your life like water through a mill. The wheel begins to turn faster, until suddenly you blink, and you don't know how you arrived where you are. You find you can longer shake the earth with a look. But you've carved out a plot of land and you're learning how to tend it. I realise that you will not yet understand what I'm telling you. But one day you will. Take my word for it, your fury will fade. And then you'll understand why I am refusing your petition.'

Soba's hair stood on end, her heart racing. Wasn't she as much of a fool as Blink? Thinking herself superior, thinking she could change things? She'd let her obsession with her career, with Elias, rule her heart. Sticky heat poured down her neck. She didn't know how she'd got here.

It was a zero-sum game. There would always be Azures like Blink. There would always be people like her own dead mother, unhappy with their lot and drawn to self-destruction. Drawn to the forbidden.

Tala's bright features twisted Soba's insides. She hated this feeling. It made her no better than her mother. An Inspector was not supposed to feel such things for a lighter colour, let alone an Azure terrorist.

Soba closed her eyes, taking strength from the darkness. She wasn't going to let the Sepia's words get under her skin.

'Fine,' Blink said. 'Linda, Lazlo ... *Gambit*.' He said the Sepia's name as if it pained him. 'Thank you for your time. My sister and I will not trespass on your hospitality much longer.'

He turned on his heel and exited the cabin. Soba and Tala followed close behind.

'So?' Tala asked, walking at double-time to keep up with Blink's angry strides. 'What's the plan?'

'Same as it always was,' Blink declared. 'Change the ocking world. Millie, you with us?'

Soba willed her eyes to glisten the way Blink's always did when he spoke about rebellion. 'I'm with you. I want the chance to make a difference. Even if Gambit won't back us, I'm in.'

Blink's eyes creased.

'I told you we could trust her,' Tala said, 'Millie's one of the good ones.'

Soba was acutely aware of the irony. Tiny mites crawled through her veins.

'Good. Get your stuff ready and get some sleep. We leave at dawn,' Blink stated.

'Where are we going?' Soba asked.

He turned to her, his cerulean eyes alight with purpose. 'We're going back to Densolid to meet with my crew. These idiots weren't my only bet. I've got someone way better in mind and unlike Gambit, I know they can be convinced.'

Sparks of excitement ran through Soba's veins at the thought of spending more time with Tala.

No, that wasn't it at all. It couldn't be. She loved Elias. They were in love.

Tala had no idea what she was talking about when she'd accused Elias of taking advantage of her. If anything, it was the other way around. Soba relied on him. He took care of her.

The tingling in her fingers was anticipation. She was nearing the end of the mission. She would receive great accolade from her superiors for exposing the plot.

Yes, that was it. It had nothing to do with Tala.

Nothing.

Soba neared the edge of the forest. Scanning each tree, she searched her surroundings for signs of the shadowbird. Not for the first time, she damned the Azuserum running through her veins, wishing she could access her oculary sight and sound out the area.

A flap of wings from the branches overhead. The dark beady eyes of a shadowbird stared down at her.

A perfect fifth.

The bird fluttered down from the branch, landing on her outstretched arm, staring straight into her eyes, unmoving. The bird's beak twitched and emitted a strangled response. 'Speak your message, Inspector Nite.'

Soba scrunched up her face. These birds set her on edge. But they were a necessary evil. She couldn't risk carrying her Inspector-issue Tile in case it was discovered. The birds were her only form of communication.

'I located the Azure Angels, a pair of siblings known as the Panaligans. They were refused aid from the Dissidens' leader. They're heading back to Densolid at dawn to attempt an attack of some sort. I do not yet know what the plan is, but they have powerful contacts in the city. I have won their confidence and will soon be on my way back to Densolid, masquerading as one of their crew. I will report in when I can.' She rushed through the details, keeping one eye on the forest around her.

The bird gave an uncanny nod, then took off into the air. It flew high, past the forest ceiling, swooping toward Densolid.

Something rustled behind her, setting her hairs on end. She tightened her fists, spinning to face the unknown threat. If someone had overheard her, the entire plan would be over. She couldn't let all this work go to waste.

A wiry man pushed through the brush, coming into the clearing where Soba stood. Squinting in the fading light of the dusk, she made out the man's features.

'Gambit?' she said in confusion, looking up to see the Sepia camp leader stood before her. Her bottom lip trembled.

He'd caught her.

Had he seen her talking to the bird? Did he know who she was? She was so close to exposing the entire terrorist plot. She couldn't let Gambit ruin things for her now.

But, she couldn't get away with murdering the camp leader, could she?

Yes, she could.

She would do whatever was necessary. And a part of her, a hazy poisonous part of her, wanted to cut down this man. His speech had unnerved her, and she couldn't afford to doubt. It was time to silence his meddling mouth once and for all.

Gambit gave a low chuckle. 'I suppose this is the moment when I tell you angrily to watch where you're going. Though it's hardly necessary. I know where you're going. And why.'

She stepped back, legs tensing, heart rattling against her ribcage.

'Then, I got to thinking,' he continued. 'Millie, have you ever wondered why the Empire needs Inspectors?'

What had he just said?

No. It couldn't be. It didn't make sense.

Even as her mind rejected the idea, her mouth opened and spoke the answer to the Inspector's code-phrase, the phrase only to be used when undercover agents needed to make themselves known to one another.

'To create peace and harmony. To arrive unannounced and leave unseen,' she said, intonation flat.

She inhaled, desperate to feel the acoustic waves, desperate to cool the white-hot panic.

Gambit was an Inspector's informant. Soba almost laughed at the thought of how Blink would react if he knew. Then, she realised. Gambit could not be entirely trustworthy, or Elias would never have needed her to come here. He would've trusted Gambit for information.

But he didn't. So, neither could she.

Slowly, almost imperceptibly, she readied herself to grab the knife. It pained her to be in this position. Stuck without her power, left with only her combat skills to fight this Sepia filth.

Gambit's eyes flashed amber and the ground underneath them trembled slightly.

'Forgive me, *Millie*... Yes, I know that's not your name.' His mouth twitched. 'I'm not supposed to make contact. But, you see, I'm worried. I need to ensure that you report to your superiors that the truce remains intact. I did not offer support, and I will never engage in activity that threatens the security of Albin, as per the truce agreement. In exchange, your forces will stay away from my people.'

Soba scanned his face for a lie, a twitch of deception, a tightened muscle. Gambit was not happy with his lot, that was clear. But he wasn't lying.

'Of course, Gambit. Now, I must go,' Soba said quickly, still ready to pounce at a moment's notice.

Gambit nodded tersely. 'As you wish,' he said, then looked back up at her, eyes pleading. 'Make sure you stop them, Inspector. I do not want to see my people drawn into battle. I've lost enough, already.'

'Of course. We've got this under control,' Soba said. She didn't buy his act. He wasn't doing this for his people. He was doing this to save himself.

Pathetic. Blink and Tala might be terrorists, but they had more backbone than this excuse for a leader.

Gambit's smile didn't reach his eyes. They were pools of swirling mud that held an undefinable hint of an uneasy feeling.

By the time she returned to her lodgings, she'd finally interpreted Gambit's emotion. His eyes had been full of darkness, swimming with untapped rage and frustration. She'd seen the very same look on Elias's face, countless times.

Needing to clear her head, she changed into loose-fitting clothes and began to do sit-ups, then lunges, then one-armed press-ups. Once she'd completed the entire routine, she dripped with sweat, her core on fire. The desired outcome had been achieved.

She was too tired to think.

No longer haunted by Gambit's strangeness, nor her phantom feelings for Tala, she collapsed into the uncomfortable, hard wooden bed, and fell into darkness; the only place she felt at home.

CHAPTER 23
DEBT

DAEZEN

Daezen dropped into a crouch, rolling left to narrowly avoid a blow to the head. Pushing himself to his feet, he blocked a second attack aimed at his stomach. The side of his arm burned from the impact.

Wincing, he pivoted, pushing his whole body behind a punch aimed at Topper Luxo's smirking face. The assassin dodged him with ease, catching Daezen's shoulders and taking advantage of the forward momentum. With barely any effort, Topper threw him unceremoniously to the ground. The wind rushed out of him, and within seconds, Topper was on him. Daezen was trapped.

'I yield,' he panted, struggling to catch his breath.

Topper grinned, relinquishing him and rising gracefully to his feet. His breath was steady, his face relaxed. Nobody would've guessed that he'd been sparring with Daezen for the past few hours.

They were at one of Topper's boltholes in a large hall full of weights, weapons, gym equipment and even a climbing wall. It'd been nearly a half-cycle since their meeting at Tavern Blue, and this was where Daezen came every morning to prepare for the mission.

His new Duty.

He no longer travelled to the San-centre, relieved from his honour-bound Duty for the Empire by a sick note Topper had forged on his behalf.

Daezen scrambled to his feet, eyes fixing on the more extravagant pieces of Topper's collection. An engraved curved blade, gold-plated throwing stars, a heavy-edged longsword, a scythe. Vintage, low-tech weapons filled the entire wall.

Noticeably, there was not a single Tile-tech weapon. Decades ago, the Octengions innovated oculary-based software prohibiting Azures and Veridians from accessing the full capabilities of any Tile device, especially weapons. Even Sepias were limited to weapons that caused minimal damage. In the absence of high-tech weaponry, Topper and his colleagues had scoured The Pipes for antique weapons and ancient designs.

Taking in the wall of steel and sharpened wood, it wasn't hard to see why Topper was constantly looking for new jobs. He might be paid handsomely for the dirty work he performed, but the tokens disappeared almost as fast as he earned them. The equipment in this room must have cost at least a million tokens, and it wasn't even half of Topper's stash.

A flask of water came hurtling towards Daezen. Only his finely attuned oculary sense saved him from a blow to the head. Raising his hand, he commanded the water to slow. For a second, it hovered several inches from his head, then he let it drop, catching it in his uninjured hand.

'Shame you can't fight as well as you water-wield, brother,' Topper said.

Something about the comment stuck in Daezen's mind. 'What makes the Obsidians and Sepias so much better than us, Tops?' he asked.

'Cos they can melt our ears, launch boulders at us and fry us with their tech, Daeze,' Topper replied, irritated by the direction the conversation was taking.

'Exactly.' Daezen smiled bitterly. 'It's not because they're better fighters than us, or because they're smarter than us. It's the way they use their oculary powers.'

Nights spent poring over the mechanics of breaking into the Empire Hall had left Daezen with a pretty good idea of how they could get inside. But the part that still haunted him was how to handle the Inspectors once they were in. If only there was some way of blocking the Inspectors' access to their oculary power, then they'd almost be on an even footing. No Obsidian power meant no way of charging their laser guns or sonar strikes.

If he could think of a way to do it, the plan might not be so impossible at all.

'Something on your mind, mut?'

'What makes you say that?' Daezen took a sip of water, then threw the flask back to Topper.

The assassin raised his coloured eyebrows as he caught the flask. 'I've been training you for over a half-cycle now, covering your rations so you can stop being a sewer rat and start being a rebel. But today your technique was nearly as bad as the first day you stepped into my training hall.' Topper chucked the flask into the air and caught it again. 'That enough of a reason for you?'

Daezen clenched his jaw. He wasn't any good at fighting.

Topper had been uncharacteristically kind with the insinuation that Daezen's technique had worsened. That in itself implied he'd made some progress, which he hadn't.

Irritation prickled his neck, fuelling a tension headache at the base of his skull. 'I don't know if I can do this, mut. I can't work out how to get us into the Empire Hall, let alone get us out. What's Blink going to say if he gets back and I don't have a plan ready?'

'Oowee, the Ice King thaws. Never thought I'd get that level of emotion from you, mut.'

Daezen stilled, pondering his next move. 'I want to settle my debt with the Health Centre. I need those tokens, now.'

Topper cocked his head but remained silent.

Daezen's lip curled upwards into a snarl. 'Are you going back on your word?'

'And what if I said I was? What are you going to do about it, huh? If I add enough interest, I've already covered off one diamond with the sick note and your rations. Forgery doesn't come cheap, brother.'

Closing his eyes, Daezen counted to ten, willing his blood to cool. By the ice, he couldn't make Topper do anything, the only leverage he had over him was the location of his training hall, and it wasn't like he was going to out Topper to the Inspectors and claim the reward. He needed Topper. Without him, Blink might swindle him completely.

'Try stopping this with your oculary.' Topper went to a corner of the room and withdrew a large sack, tossing it through the air as if it weighed nothing at all.

Daezen stepped back, dodging the bag as it landed heavily at his feet.

Topper laughed, 'You see, you're still spry.'

Unbelievably, the sack was filled to the brim with tokens.

'That should untwist your panties, Daezey-boy.'

Daezen buried his hands in the sack, feeling the cool plastic of each one, squeezing to ensure they were real. 'And they're untraceable?'

'Don't be silly, mut. All tokens are traceable. A merchant owes me a favour. He's actually the guy who owns this place, would you believe? Anyway, if anyone looks into it, they'll see you sold some family heirlooms for this haul.'

That was all he needed to hear. Daezen tightened the drawstring on the sack and heaved it over his shoulder, heading for the door.

He'd meant what he said. Every day that he failed to come up with a foolproof plan set his hairs on end. His patience with himself was wearing thin, and without any solid progress for his family, so was his belief in the mission.

'Where you going? We ain't done yet.'

'I'm done. For today, at least.'

'All right, all right, I'll see you tomorrow, though?'

Daezen nodded absent-mindedly. Then he left the training hall, bracing himself for the cold air of dusk.

The smell of fresh pie greeted Daezen when he opened the door to his apartment, warming his already bright mood.

Before coming home, he'd stopped by Densolid Major to visit the Health Centre. To settle the family debt. Once the transaction was complete, he'd left the domed sterile building, the sack of tokens almost as light as the weight that usually pressed upon his chest. Even if he couldn't get Blink into the

Gala, he'd succeeded in one thing. The Trovit family was free from a life of regular payments to the people who'd let Pa die.

One step closer to freedom.

He may be nothing but a pawn on this chatrang board, but he was one square closer to his opponent's side.

One square closer to transformation.

Kain was hunched over the stovetop, plating up food.

'What's up with you, snotnose?' Daezen quipped.

'Is that your way of saying "Thanks, brother"?' Kain retorted, placing three plates of food on the small wooden dinner table.

'No, it's my way of saying, "What's up with you, snotnose?"' Daezen pulled out a rickety chair and took a seat. 'What's this then?'

'Fish pie and tayters. Rosa had some leftover pastry from her cousin's bakery, and I caught the fish farmers on their way back to Widgerwood. It's their unsold stock.'

'Nice one, mut.' Daezen rubbed his hands together, relishing the warm glow of momentary triumph. Then he noticed the third plate of food. 'Where's Ma?'

Kain shrugged, sitting down and cutting his pie in half. Steam rose from the gooey insides.

'I'll go get her,' Daezen got up and stepped out of the kitchenette and into the living space. He did a quick scan: old red facsleath sofa, stained imitation-Parsian rug with a couple of new burn marks. No sign of Ma.

'Must be in her room,' Daezen mumbled, approaching the door of the master bedroom. 'Ma,' he shouted, waiting thirty seconds before banging several times.

Not now, Ma, he thought. *Not now.*

He'd spent the day getting the shit kicked out of him by

Topper, and now, after settling the debt, his spirits had finally lifted. The last thing he needed was another reason to be angry again.

Another reason to hate his broken life and broken home.

Tension built in the front of his head. Still no response. That explained Kain's terrible mood, at least. The sour taste of chemical regret surfaced at the back of his throat. His mother was using, again.

'I'm coming in, make sure you're decent,' he called as he opened the door.

A heady synthetic smell oozed through the doorway. Cathy Trovit was sprawled on the unmade double bed, a plume of white smoke floating above her. In one hand, she cradled a large glass pipe, in the other, a photo of Pa.

A lace nightdress, dirtied with ash and yellow stains, hung from her skeletal shoulders. Her lingerie reached her upper thigh, leaving her birdlike legs exposed. Her chest was sunken, collar bones jutting out. Daezen's lip quivered but he held in the pain.

After Flint's death, Cathy had smoked away her sorrows with opine. Aside from short-lived periods of recovery, this was the mother Daezen had grown used to. But no stretch of time would make it easy to see her like this.

Two glazed eyes slowly focused on him.

Daezen grasped her thin wrists and pulled her to her feet. Paper-like skin brushed against his calloused hands. When she stumbled, he let his gaze turn inward, calling up the water from the half-full glass on her bedside table. The particles rushed toward him, then splashed onto Cathy's face.

A bit of tough love never hurt anyone.

Cathy blinked. 'Flint? Is that you?'

Daezen's jaw tightened. 'No, Ma. It's Daezen. Your son. Now, come on, Kain's cooked dinner.'

'Kain? He'll go far, you know, Flint.'

Go far? Anger clenched like a fist in his chest. Daezen was the one holding their family together. His mind, and his alone, was responsible for their survival. Kain might've cooked dinner, but he did little else to help their case. He wasn't the one who'd settled the debt.

He wasn't the one who was fighting to change everything.

'It's Daezen, Ma. Pa's dead and you know it.'

He hated that word. Dead. It was so final. So absent of hope.

Cathy's head rolled from side to side as Daezen led her out of her room and into the kitchenette.

'I can't sit there. That's your father's chair,' Cathy exclaimed, shaking her head violently at the place Kain had set for her.

'Well, we can move it,' Daezen replied, holding her up with one arm. 'Can't we, Kain?'

Kain didn't respond, he just carried on eating his pie like an insolent little twack.

Daezen's head throbbed. 'Kain?'

'I can't deal with her tonight. Tomorrow, the day after, the day after that, yeah. But not tonight.'

Daezen waited for Kain to come to his senses and apologise. He didn't. Something haunted his brother's narrow face. Something dark. What on Shariza did the little snotnose have to worry about? He wasn't the one gambling everything for a way out of this cursed life.

'Fine!' Daezen led his mother back to the living space and onto the sofa. 'You're going to eat here tonight, Ma. That okay? I got a few things to talk about with Kain.'

Fetching the plate of food and a set of cutlery, he placed a pillow on her lap so she didn't have to rest the dish on her bare legs.

'My Kain cooked this? Oh, he'll go far, you know,' she wheezed.

'Yes, Ma. Now, eat up.'

He stormed back to the kitchenette. 'Well?' he said, keeping his voice low.

'Well, what?'

'What was that all about? Treating Ma like that?'

Kain dropped his cutlery onto the table, letting his head fall into his hands. 'Daeze, you've been working such long shifts recently. There's no one around to help. I come home from academy, a gazillion tasks to do, final exams to prep for, and she's there. Like always. Sucking on that ocking pipe. I always handle it. I *will* always handle it. Just. Not. Today.'

Daezen sat back and began to eat, mulling over his little brother's words. He hadn't realised Ma's situation was getting to Kain so much. Ever since he'd met Jantsia, he'd seemed his usual jolly self. What had changed?

'Mmm. It's good,' Daezen said, mouth full.

'Mmm-hmm,' Kain grunted.

When they finished, Daezen placed his elbows on the table, appraising Kain. Taking note of his hunched shoulders and overt scowl. 'So, time to tell me what's up.'

Kain clenched his fists. 'Nothing.'

'Then why do you look like someone smacked you in the face?'

'Ocking Jantsia,' Kain grumbled.

'Jantsia smacked you in the face?'

'No.' A reluctant laugh tumbled from Kain's lips. 'She's

avoiding me. She has been ever since that night at Prenderghasts. I wanted to talk things out, you know. It was her first time trying psychs and she said some brutal things. But I know what it's like, sometimes the drink goes to your head.'

Daezen rolled his neck, easing the tension that clenched in his chest at the thought of Jantsia. There was more to her than met the eye. If only he could see what it was, then he could stop thinking about her for good. It wasn't natural to think this much about his brother's best friend. 'Well, have you apologised?'

Kain's bright eyes met his. 'Me? What do I need to apologise for? She should be the one apologising.'

Daezen leaned back, patience hanging by a thread. All this drama because of one stupid drunken night. Kain needed to grow up. If he was ever going to stand a chance with Jantsia Brittle, he needed to buck up his ideas. 'Mut, at Prenderghasts you let Flossie manhandle you like there was no tomorrow. You have to have caught on to how jealous that made Jantsia?'

'I doubt it.' Kain hung his head. 'She was having too much fun with those Laminosian losers. Anyway, when I tried to talk to her, she told me to leave her alone. To give her space.'

'And you listened?' Daezen ruffled Kain's hair, irritation calming into brotherly affection. In this, at least, he knew how to help, though for some reason, he didn't want to. He shook his head, remembering where he was. Who he was. 'How naïve you are, little brother,' he continued, 'what I wouldn't give to be as blissfully ignorant. Want me to take the Savin Seductress off your hands? Keep you pure for the princess?'

Kain pushed him away. 'Oh, shut your piehole!' His expression darkened, shoulders rounding.

'She won't wait around for you forever, you know,' Daezen said softly.

Kain's head jerked up. 'What do you mean?'

'You know what I mean. Now, if I were you I'd—' The smell of burning reached his nostrils. 'Can you smell smoke?'

Kain's eyes widened in terror. 'Yep.'

They rushed out of the kitchen.

Cathy lay limp on the sofa, the untouched plate of food spilt down her legs, staining the ragged carpet. The glass pipe had fallen from her hand and smashed on the floor. Embers scattered across the far side of the sofa. Smoke rose from the small patches where they'd set alight.

Kain went straight for their mother, hauling her up and dragging her to her room. Daezen forced his breaths to calm, shifting into the unseeing. Through the door to the kitchen, he zeroed in on the glasses of water on the table. Located the central groupings. Called the particles towards him. Eyes straining from the effort, he twisted the peripherals into a bubble, then let the water fall onto the sofa, putting out the little fires.

He gritted his teeth. Transporting water from a distance like that took it out of him. Too many instructions to remember. Too many variables.

Later on, he sat in his room, moving wooden pieces across his chatrang set, playing against himself, as he did every night. Every move had a real-life comparison. His opponents' wall of defenders represented the Inspectors, his Knights were the rebels. By the time he finally completed the game, checkmating the darker set of players with a Fishing Pole trap, his eyelids grew heavy. He lay back on his bed, a spring poking into his side, and watched shadows dance on the damp, stained ceiling.

While he wasn't any closer to a feasible plan to get Blink and his rebel friends into the Gala, it had been a good day.

With a yawn, he unfolded his Tile, searching for the document that confirmed his triumph. He located the file, a smile creeping onto his lips as he reread the words.

DEBT PAID IN FULL.

Then he squinted, noticing something strange in the small print.

Patient admitted by Benyamin Brittle, suspected case of poisoning. Standard procedures failed to yield improvement in vital signs. Sent home with medication and instructions for palliative care.

His heart leapt into his throat.

That wasn't right. It couldn't be. Ma had told them that Flint had contracted the wasting sickness. Daezen had seen it with his own eyes. He'd watched on as the man who'd taught him right from wrong became little more than a bag of bones; barely recognisable. Then one day, he died. And on that same day Ma disappeared into a haze of opine smoke.

The day Daezen had left the academy without graduating to get an entry-level Duty. To try and keep their family afloat, abandoning all his dreams and desires for them.

He read and reread the small print.

It had all been a lie.

His father, Beny, perhaps even Ma. They'd all lied to his ocking face.

Daezen threw the Tile to the floor, knuckles whitening as he clenched his fists.

Should he tell Kain? Should he share the burden of this life-shattering information?

He didn't know what to do. The walls of his boxroom drew closer. Thoughts scattered into chaos.

A rush of blood to the head as he leapt from bed and stormed into his mother's bedroom without knocking.

Dull unfocused eyes shifted in his direction.

His heart iced over. 'I paid the debt today, Ma.'

Ma blinked slowly, lips quivering as she pulled the bed covers tighter over her.

He walked closer to the bed, leaning down to whisper in her ear. 'I saw Pa's files.'

Cathy let out a small groan, trying to cover her face with a grubby pillow.

Daezen pulled it from her, features breaking into a snarl. 'When were you going to tell me, huh? You knew, didn't you? Didn't think I deserved to know why I had to throw my life away? Didn't cross your ocking drug-addled mind?'

'Please,' Cathy croaked. 'I'm sorry. I ... I ... I promised... I...' She reached out a trembling hand.

Bone-white, skeletal, yellow broken nails.

Daezen jerked back, heart exploding in his chest. He made himself sick. What kind of son was he to speak to his mother in that way? Who did he think he was?

He ground his teeth together. He needed to get out. He needed to see the open sky, smell the merchants' smoky bonfires on the street. The world was closing in on him and he didn't know what was real anymore.

He didn't know anything.

Without looking back at Ma, he rushed out to the hall, drew his facsfur coat tight around him, and headed out into the frozen night.

CHAPTER 24
LIES

JANTSIA

'Right, Level Tens, we're entering the final stretch. Only fourteen days remain before exams are upon us.' Educator Leanne placed her hands on her hips, her expression serious. 'This is the chance to really go the extra mile and set yourself up for the best possible starter Duty.'

Before her sham awakening, these words would've taken root in Jantsia's mind. She would've been overcome with pure dread as she tried to figure out how she could pass her Oculary Practice, spiralling into doubts over what the future held for someone like her.

But now?

Now she couldn't care less.

While the other students wrung their hands, shoulders tight and faces pale with nerves, Jantsia stretched out her arms, propping her elbows lazily on the desk. One of the perks of sitting alone at the back of the class was that she had plenty of space: physically and mentally.

By the time exams rolled around, she'd be travelling down the Empire to the beaches of Laminos with her parents and Luz. And while the idea of never seeing Kain again tugged at her heart, the chance for a true, fresh start shone brightly at her centre.

The evening after those horrid Az-sec soldiers marched Educator Vortil out of class, Baba had returned. As angry as she'd been with him for abandoning her and her mother, his return had lightened a weight on her chest.

Later that night, she scrolled through her Tile, trying to find out more about the Varzesh Clause and why merely talking about it had got Vortil into so much trouble. She chewed on her lip, frustrated at the lack of any reference of Varzesh. It was too much of a coincidence. Maman had been talking about it, Vortil was imprisoned for merely mentioning it. And now, not a single file on Varzesh on the entire network? Something was amiss. She just hadn't worked out what.

A knock came at her bedroom door.

'Am I disturbing you?' her baba asked, coming into the room.

Jantsia's cheeks warmed as she closed down the search page. 'No, not at all. Good to see you back.' It was about time she stopped searching for the night. Although she'd taken great care to use one of the untraceable applications that Kain had shown her a while back; she didn't want to risk raising a digital alert at the Inspectors' Cyber Centre. 'I was worried about you. We both were. Where on Shariza did you go?'

Her father's lips tightened, posture stiff. 'I'm sorry for

making you worried,' he said. 'I needed some time to think. Your mother's plan was ... difficult to come to terms with.'

'Why?' she asked, genuinely curious to hear his response. She would've thought he'd be as happy as any of them to get out of Densolid and start afresh. To live together as a real family without having to pretend.

'You know that my family has lived as indentured servants of the Rostamani Riviera Elites for decades, don't you?'

Her nose scrunched up. What did that have to do with any of this? 'Sure.'

'Well, it won't be easy for me to go back to that family. I know your mother's come to an agreement with them, but no matter what they say, I'll always be a slave in their eyes. Here at least I have my performance troupe. Here I have a degree of status. Of power.'

Jantsia's chest tightened. She hadn't thought about that. Hadn't considered how much it would cost her baba to return to a place he'd only visited as a slave. 'And what do you think now?'

He sighed. 'I've realised it's the only viable option. We can't get any more of your medicine while we're here and we've already drawn enough unwanted attention from the Densolid Inspectorate. There's no other choice, we have to go.'

She could see how much this decision had cost him from the twitch of his lips and his white-knuckled fists. But in spite of his obvious discomfort, her shoulders relaxed. Relieved to know that they all agreed on their next steps. One family united, no matter what.

She let out a breath. 'Thank you.'

He opened his mouth as if he were about to say something, then changed his mind. With a smile that didn't quite reach his eyes, he started again. 'Your mother told me she gave you meditation exercises to help with strong emotions until we find a permanent solution for the medicine. I can help you with that. I've had my fair share of difficulties in the past.'

He must be talking about his time living with the Rostamani Rivieras.

It can't have been easy to serve a Great Elite family, to see his parents' lives consumed by the whims and fancies of stuck-up Obsidians. Jantsia swallowed back emotion. Now wasn't the time to feel guilty for her part in this. They had to think of the future, not the past.

A fresh start.

'I'm fine,' she said. 'I've got enough pills to last me till we get to Laminos. Maman says she knows people there who'll be able to help.'

His eyes hardened. 'No, Jantsia, this is important. You should ration the pills as much as you can, and if the doc is right, meditation could dull the severity of the conflict of your blood...' He shook his head. 'We can't rely on anyone else. We have to work with what we've got.'

Since then, Baba had helped her run through breathing exercises and visualisation techniques to calm her heart rate. At first, all she'd succeeded in doing was crashing back to the horrible blood sickness-fuelled hallucination. The hall of mirrors, where she confronted thousands of versions of herself shouting and pleading for release. But with time, she'd got the hang of it.

It had helped that Kain had kept his distance like she'd asked. The last thing she needed was an emotionally-charged confrontation. Although, from the progress she'd made with the exercises, it was possible she'd be able to handle it.

Educator Leanne's voice broke through the memories. 'Jantsia, how're you getting on today? Any progress?'

Jantsia smiled serenely. 'No, but it's okay.'

Leanne raised a bright pink eyebrow. 'What's been going on with you this past half-cycle? If I didn't know you better, I'd say you'd completely stopped trying. With an awakening as powerful as yours, I can't quite comprehend why.'

She shrugged. 'I guess I just don't feel the need.'

It had taken time to come to terms with her loss of power. But with her medicine supplies running short, she couldn't risk experimenting further. From what she'd gathered, any activation of the ocularies in her blood worsened her disease, necessitating higher doses of medicine than she could afford to take. The supply was limited. At least until they located another source of medicine, she had to be careful.

Stay invisible. Stay alive.

Educator Leanne lowered her voice. 'Does this have something to do with whatever happened between you and Kain?'

Jantsia's stomach flipped, cheeks heating. 'Why would you think that?'

'It doesn't take an oculary scientist to see that you went from being attached at the hip to barely looking at one another overnight.'

Jantsia pursed her lips. 'No offence, Educator. But I don't think that's any of your business.'

Her teacher laughed. 'Humour me, Jantsia. This new, relaxed attitude of yours may actually come in handy. I always had an inkling that you were pushing too hard in this class. I've seen your grades for other subjects. You're an overachiever. But oculary skill is not something that can be forced. It is as much art as it is craft. Why don't you give the filtration task a go, just for me?'

Jantsia's admiration for the Educator warred against her better judgment. Even though she no longer needed to prepare for exams, she didn't like disappointing Leanne.

'Okay,' Jantsia said, 'I'll give it a go.'

It wasn't like anything was going to happen. Peace emanated from her core, and she'd taken a double dose of the new medicine that morning. There was no harm in putting on a show for her favourite Educator.

Jantsia turned her attention to the bowl of dirty water on her table, struck by how the light reflected off the surface of the muddy liquid. Even in this form, water was a beautiful thing to behold. It flowed to fill whatever container it was kept in; formless and shapeless in the way it occupied space. What must it feel like to be so malleable? So adaptable? To be water?

A vivid image rose to the fore of her mind. The dark-lipped woman with seafoam hair, her lithe body dissolving into a bubbling stream. In water form, she trickled past the confinements of the mirror cage.

Jantsia's vision slipped, perspective flipping on its head. The greasy feeling of being covered in dirt prickled across her body. She broke into a sweat. This was horrible. This was disgusting. She had to get the dirt off her. She had to—

The muddied water of the bowl swirled into a vortex, forming a bubble above her head. Grit separated from water, falling onto the desk in uneven clumps. The bubble popped. Purified water gushed back into the bowl, crystal clear and transparent.

A sharp pain cut through Jantsia's temples.

Oh, my eyes, what have I done?

'You see,' Leanne said with a bright smile. 'I knew you could do it.'

Jantsia got to her feet, nausea curdling her stomach. 'I need to go. I'm not feeling well.'

As she rushed to the door, she momentarily locked eyes with Kain. He'd stopped what he was doing to watch her. Big blue eyes glistening with concern. Oh, how she wanted to embrace him, to apologise. To tell him she hadn't meant anything she'd said. But she couldn't risk getting into it right now. She had to get home and take more pills. It had been arrogant not to bring her supply to the academy. She'd grown far too confident in her newfound meditative glory.

Luckily, Oculary Practice was the last class of the day, so she didn't need to worry about explaining her absence to any of the Educators. One of the reasons she kept coming to the academy despite her family's plans to leave, was for fear of raising suspicion among the academy staff. It only took one report to Az-sec and she'd be wading through trouble yet again. She'd seen how quickly Vortil had been disposed of. No one knew what had happened or where he'd gone. It was like a dirty secret that everyone had silently agreed to never speak of.

Though her temples pounded like drums, and her stomach churned, she made it home without losing consciousness. As soon as she swallowed down another two pills, her breaths slowed, headache dissipating. After running through her meditation exercises twice, the web of pain at her crown disappeared entirely.

She ran her finger over the blister pack of pills. Only twelve remained. That'd be enough, just about.

A buzzing sound vibrated from the corner of her bedroom. She ignored it, continuing to mentally plan her schedule of medicine going forward. If she could reduce the dose to a single pill a day then she'd be fine. That should be manageable, as long as—

A sharp claw pierced through the bedcovers, puncturing the sole of her foot.

'My eyes,' she exclaimed. 'What do you think you're playing at, Luz?'

The firecat swished his tail, communicating indifference to her rage, then he padded to the top of the bed, her buzzing Tile in his mouth.

'You want me to look at this?' She sighed. 'All right, all right. We all know who's boss around here.'

> **Kaino**
> Brown got you down mut?

Her breaths quickened, heart rate rattling. Before her mind could catch up with her fingers, she tapped out a message.

> **Jantsy**
> Same old cack, ice-eyed twack.

She clicked send. No going back now.

> **Kaino**
> What happened to you in OP? I was worried :/.

So, he still cared about her? Her chest tightened. She didn't know how to respond. It was unlikely she'd have another oculary explosion after taking a double dose of pills, but still. Was talking to him worth the risk?

> **Kaino**
> There's something I want to tell you. Can I see you? Think you can get to mine tonight?

Jantsia wanted to see Kain more than ever. While the past half-cycle had been peaceful and uneventful, it had also been lonely. Heat crept up her neck. This could be a chance to make things up with him before she left. To spend their last days together. Meeting him would doubtlessly trigger a series of intense emotions, emotions she wasn't sure she was ready for. But then again, she'd just taken the pills.

Surely she could handle it.

Jantsy
I'll be there.

She logged off the messenger app, heart racing. Luz sprawled on his back, his little belly distended from gobbling down his dinner in such a short space of time. If things got tense with Kain, she'd need comfort. She'd need a friend. Maybe a dose of frozen Densolid weather would finally calm Luz's zoomies a little.

'Ready, Luz? We're going on an adventure.'

Winter was coming. Thankful for the furry ball of warmth hiding inside her jacket, Jantsia shivered as she waited for Kain. Sleet landed on her nose, her bare hands, and on Luz's head.

'Get down,' she said, pushing him back into the shelter of her facsfur layers. Firecats were all but extinct, she didn't want to start a riot in Azure Minor, or worse – tempt opportunistic thieves to attempt a catnapping.

Two icy hands clamped down over her eyes. She drew in a sharp breath, readying herself to scream.

Could it be the Inspectors? Maybe they'd lied to her mother, and they still had her under surveillance.

'Brown got you down, mut?'

Jantsia's fear simmered into irritation. She pushed Kain's hands away. A million and one retorts melted on her tongue as she took in his wide smile. He really *was* happy to see her. With a rush of appreciation, she pulled him into a tight hug.

'Yeooooooiaw!'

'Oh, my eyes, Luz. I'm sorry. Are you okay?' Jantsia squealed, stepping back from Kain. She'd completely forgotten Luz was there; she'd almost crushed him with the force of her embrace.

Kain raised an eyebrow but didn't comment on her feline companion.

'Come on, it's freezing out here,' he said, beckoning her to follow him to the apartment. As the rusty front door creaked on its hinges, Jantsia realised that Kain had never invited her to his home, instead often asking to meet her at the door or at Mrs Naz's Teahouse. Though she couldn't fathom why, it'd become one of those unspoken parts of their friendship.

She wouldn't ask, he wouldn't tell.

Once they were safely inside, Kain brewed a pot of chai and set out a dish of nut-cream for Luz.

'So, boss. Can we talk?'

Her stomach churned. 'About what?'

'About what happened at Prenderghasts.'

Daezen's face flashed to the front of her mind. The tingling on her cheek as he'd placed a strand of hair behind her ear. Her breaths quickened. She hadn't let herself think about that until now. Locked it away in a secret space. Heat crept up her neck.

It was nothing.

Not yet ready to answer the questions burning behind

Kain's eyes, Jantsia scanned the apartment, taking in the claustrophobic air of the square space, the peeling paint, the tattered burnt-out sofa. Kain hadn't invited her over before because he'd been ashamed. Shame wedged itself into her throat like dry bread. All this time, she'd been so obsessed with her own secrets that she barely spared a thought for how Kain must feel.

'Is your mother in?' she asked.

Kain pulled out two mugs, then grated some ginger into the simmering pot.

'Opine,' he said curtly.

Darkness seeped into her chest. 'Oh, Kain. I'm so sorry.'

'Don't be. It's nothing I haven't seen before.'

When they'd first got close, Kain had confided in her about his mother's addiction. Since Flint Trovit had died, Cathy had gone through cycles of recovery and relapse. In the brief periods of recovery, Jantsia, too, had shared Kain's tentative hope. And she'd been there to cushion the subsequent crushing disappointments as the grieving woman returned to the pipe.

Kain had confided so much in her. And yet, here she was, keeping secrets. More shame bubbled inside her, rising and sticking to her tongue like opine vapour.

Kain filled the mugs with chai and brought them to the table.

She took a sip of the milky, spiced drink, trying not to let the awkwardness of the silence get to her.

'Is Daezen around?' she asked, hoping he'd say no. That man got under her skin, twisting her thoughts and feelings until she wasn't sure which was up or down. She needed a clear mind for this. She needed to remain calm.

Peaceful.

'Nope,' Kain said.

Her stomach dropped. 'On the late shifts, then?'

'No idea. I think there's a lot of things he's not telling me at the moment.'

She bristled, heart clenching. Worry and fear dripped down her neck like icy rain. 'What do you mean?'

Kain sighed. 'I don't think he's going to his Duty anymore.'

'What? Have your rations been halved?'

'No, nothing like that. Just, the food he gets is different. More expensive than the standard ration-issue food.'

'He's probably found himself a rich, performer girlfriend or something,' Jantsia said, surprised at how uncomfortable it felt to say those words.

'I guess,' Kain said, examining his hands as if they held the answers. 'I'm worried, Jantsy. About him, about Ma. I think ... I think he might be into some bad stuff.'

Regret tangled her tongue. 'I'm so sorry, Kain. We should've spoken sooner. I can't believe I made things worse for you. You have so much on and I ... I ... I was so cruel to you.' Tears welled at the corner of her eyes. She wiped them away with her sleeve.

Kain was her best friend. He told her everything. Could she take a chance on him?

Stay invisible, stay alive.

She took a deep breath. She had to keep her emotions under control, but that didn't mean she could live with herself if she disappeared on Kain without a word. 'I'm leaving, Kain. The day before exams, I'm gone.'

'Leaving the academy?'

'No,' she said. 'Leaving Densolid, this will be my last lunar cycle in the city. My patron is relocating and obviously, Baba and I will go with her.'

He flinched as if he'd been shot with a laser gun, hunching

over and taking a step back. Then he looked directly into her eyes, an ocean on fire. 'Well, boss. I'm not going to let that happen.'

Jantsia's heart pounded against her ribcage, breaths coming quicker.

Kain took hold of her shaking hands. 'We're going to work this out. We'll find a way for you to stay.'

'That's the thing,' she said, pressure building in the front of her head. 'I don't want to stay. And before I go, it would mean a lot to me if we could put everything aside and be friends again.' A tear rolled down her cheek. 'I could really do with a friend.'

He fixed his jaw. 'But I don't want you to leave. And I don't want to act like that night didn't happen. I want to be more than your friend.'

More than a friend?

Sparks of anticipation flew up her body, exploding in her toes and dancing across her fingertips. She had never believed that Kain might like her in this way. Especially since he'd been spending his days surrounded by tall, blonde beauties like Flossie.

Could this be real?

'If you can't stay in Densolid,' he continued, 'then I'll go with you. Even if we have to run away and live like ice bears in the forest. I've thought about what you said, and you were right. I get why you got so angry. I didn't notice you. Not properly.' He gripped her hands tightly. 'But I see you now. I really see you. And I want you. I *choose* you.'

His words saturated the air, intoxicating her mind and making her giddy. Daezen had been right all along. He'd told her to be patient with Kain and she hadn't listened. But the plan was in motion now. She had to leave. Had to follow her family to Laminos.

Didn't she?

Kain scanned her face, searching for a reaction. Then he placed a hand on the back of her head and gently nudged her towards him.

'Will you come with me, boss? We could leave this mess behind. Just me and you. Us against the world.'

Their faces were so close now, the heat of his breath warmed her lips.

Slowly, so, so slowly, as if any sudden movement might break the spell, he inched closer. Closer. Closer. A skip of her heart. A frisson of heat in her lower stomach. She was falling. Falling into him.

Their lips touched. Softness enveloped her mouth, spreading sensation through her like molten lava that lit her up from the inside. A pale light bathed her face in gold, bleeding through closed eyelids. She grabbed his waist, holding him tight as if he might disappear. He wrapped his arms around her, squeezing her gently as if he felt her doubt and wanted to comfort her. His hair was soft and silky between her fingers, his body warm and supple. He pressed against her until all she knew was him.

His softness.

His scent.

He wanted her.

He'd chosen her.

The front door swung open and Daezen stumbled into the room. Jantsia drew back instinctively, her heart a melting pot of fear and confusion. Daezen inspected them, his face a mask of neutrality.

A traitorous twist of desire wormed through her at the sight of his piercing eyes and square jaw.

Daezen cocked his head, not a glint of warmth in his gaze. 'Well, well, well, the Princess Brittle has finally decided to grace our humble abode with her presence.' His eyes fell on Luz who was curled up on their faded facsleath sofa. 'And she's brought her royal firecat. I guess extinction isn't a problem for people like you and your pa. That Obsidian gets you anything you want, doesn't she?'

Ice-cold shame flooded her body, freezing over the warm glow that had ignited her only moments ago.

Kain cleared his throat. 'Daeze, didn't think you'd be back so early.' He turned to Jantsia, taking her hand and squeezing it tight. 'Come on, let's go to my room.'

Daezen's mouth curled into a cruel line; his voice was deceptively soft. 'I don't think so. If you're going to stay in my house, you'll answer a few questions first.'

Kain dropped Jantsia's hand, squaring up to his brother. 'Back off.'

Unease saturated the air, unleashing a waterfall of doubts and fears in Jantsia's mind. Daezen had always been cool and standoffish in a certain way, but never cruel.

'She and her father are hiding things from us, Kain. Beny knows things about Pa's death and never told us. Probably because they don't think we're good enough.'

Kain gaped, looking at Jantsia with wide eyes.

Jantsia stuttered, 'I have no idea what you're talking about, I—'

Daezen cut in, 'I don't believe you. I've seen how easily you lie. I can see past your act. And frankly, I don't want you messing with my brother. Not until you come clean.'

'Don't talk to her like that. Don't—' Kain started.

'I can fight my own battles,' Jantsia bit back. 'Daezen, you're not making sense.'

'Well, tell me what makes sense, then,' Daezen replied. 'For once in your life, say something real. Something that isn't a lie.'

And the worst thing was, he was right. Jantsia was lying to Kain, just not in the way Daezen seemed to think.

Guilt slithered through her guts. What had she been doing kissing Kain like that? Letting him confess his feelings when all along she was a fraud. He wouldn't have those feelings about her if he knew the truth. He didn't see the real her. He saw only what he wanted to.

The girl he cared for didn't exist.

The real Jantsia was a dual-oc, a liar, an aberration.

The real Jantsia wouldn't be easy to love.

Dark ice cut through her temples, conjuring a black mist that sailed before her eyes. Deep inside her, something snapped, throwing her back to the endless hall of mirrors where a cacophony of voices deafened her. At the far end of the hall, a fist crashed against a mirror, cracking it in two.

The Trovit apartment went dark. Even the grey sun that had shone weakly through the window disappeared. Suffocating blackness enveloped them.

'Jantsy, what the—'

Bright light pounded her head. Oh, for Fladden's sake, not again. She had to get out of here. She couldn't have an episode now. She needed to get home. She *needed* to be safe. Completely at odds with how to proceed, she did the only thing she could think of.

She ran.

After taking a second to call Luz to her, she blindly pushed past Daezen, fumbling to get her coat on and exit the apartment.

Light rushed back into the air. The throbbing coldness dimmed. The arctic wind roared.

Jantsia dashed down the road, wincing as she heard someone call her name. Cursing under her breath, she turned a corner.

One of the Trovit boys was following her. She just wasn't sure which one.

CHAPTER 25
PIPES

JANTSIA

She ran until the stitch in her side became unbearable. Until her breaths burned her lungs. Then she slid into a tight alleyway, planning to run through meditation exercises in an attempt to calm her boiling blood.

White hair stuck out of Luz's giant ears, bristling in the cold. Two large golden eyes held her in their gaze, cooling the blaze in her head and slowing her heartbeat. Allowing her the mental space to run through what had just happened.

Kain had kissed her.

He wanted to be with her.

He'd offered to run away with her.

Then Daezen had come in and ruined it all by reminding her of the poisonous secret eating through her blood and accusing her and Baba of... What exactly did Daezen think had happened? This was all so unexpected, she didn't know how to process it. Could Baba really be hiding things about

Flint's death? And if he had, what did that mean for her and Kain?

A cool voice in her head cracked a whip. *Kain doesn't want to be you, he wants to be with the idea of you. Even if Daezen was wrong, and Baba had nothing to do with Flint's death, once he finds out the truth, he'll run in the other direction.*

'Jantsia! Jantsia!' Kain sprinted down the street, not noticing her hiding place.

Luz mewled softly in her ear.

Her heart knew what it wanted.

Us against the world.

'Kain, I'm over here,' Jantsia called, stepping out of the alleyway to wave.

He paused, shaking as a gust of glacial wind blew a dust of frosting down the slushy road. The moment he spotted her, he sprinted towards her and scooped her up in his arms.

Flutterbies swarmed in her stomach as he spun on his feet, swinging her round and round. Just as she was about to complain about getting dizzy, he released her. Without the tight hold of his arms and the warmth of his body, she felt cold. Feet planted firmly on the ground, she pressed against him, her head resting on his chest so she could hear the rapid drum of his heartbeat.

This wonderful boy had chosen her.

He shivered violently and she drew back, realising that he wasn't even wearing a coat.

'Where's your coat?' she exclaimed.

He shrugged, teeth chattering together. A giant grin was plastered across his face, and the way he was looking at her made her brain foggy. She felt herself going red.

'Jantsy,' Kain said, savouring her name as if he could taste it.

'You didn't have to leave. Ignore Daezen, he's ocking paranoid about everything. He'll be okay. Look, I meant what I said. Whatever happens, I want to be with you.' He grasped her hands tightly, still shaking from the cold.

'It's not that simple,' she said, pulling away from him. 'You should go back. You'll get sick out here without a coat. I need some time to think about all this.'

Kain gripped her by the shoulders, Luz crawled out of his hiding place in her coat and leapt to the floor. 'I don't care about the cold,' he said, trembling fingers tucking a curl behind her ear. 'I don't care about Daezen's paranoia.' He cupped her face in his freezing hands, forcing her to look him straight in the eyes so she could see that he meant every word he said. 'And I don't care if it's complicated,' he breathed against her lips.

A wildfire burned her from within. Heating her breaths, her cheeks, her chest, her stomach.

Before Jantsia had time to process his words, his mouth was on hers. And it was nothing like the first time. Gone was the caution, the reluctant fear that pushing too hard might break the spell. This was a kiss of desperation. Of hunger. His arms clamped around her waist, pulling her tightly against him with a strength she couldn't defy, even if she wanted to. Her hands tangled in his mess of hair as he pressed into her, devouring her as if she were the last drop of water in the desert. The scent of elderflower and sage filled her nostrils, her heart raced, and a throbbing pleasure built in her lower stomach.

Then she felt him shaking, and remembered how cold he must be. 'I want it, too. I want to be with you. I think I've wanted it for a long time.' Tentatively, she traced a finger down his jawline. It felt strange to touch him like this. Like she was dreaming, and at any moment she might wake up. 'You're freezing, Kain, you should get back home. I should, too. We can talk more tomorrow at the academy. I ... I ... need to ask Baba some things.'

Kain's brow creased. 'You really think Daezen was on to something?'

'I don't know, but I plan on finding out. You and Daezen deserve to know.'

It took a little more nudging to convince Kain to leave. A few times he pretended to go only to sneak back and cover her neck in kisses. And although she pretended to be annoyed, she enjoyed every single one of his fake goodbyes. After telling him for the tenth time that she didn't need him to walk her to the pod-stop and that she'd be fine getting home, he finally left. But not before giving her a particularly salacious look that had biting her lip and looking away in embarrassment.

As soon as he'd gone, guilt slithered through her like an oily snake. Was she really going to abandon her parents to run away with Kain? How was she expected to choose between him and her family?

She watched as Luz sniffed every inch of the alleyway, following him as he went around the bend. Her parents had always made the choices. They'd always made the decisions. It was time for her to choose her own path. And to do that, she had to find some way of becoming independent.

Past the darkness of the lane hung a dark navy canopy. Dim, brass light glowed through coloured vials. In her mad rush to escape, she'd ended up running straight into The Pipes. She crept closer to the market stalls. People said that anything could be found here. Illicit medicine included. Perhaps, there was something in that. Perhaps, this place was her way out.

Without access to her medicine, any escape with Kain

would be short-lived. But was this yet another thing she could take into her own hands? Could she find her own solution to the blood sickness without having to rely on others?

'Luz, come here.' The firecat shook the light dusting of snow from his fur and jumped back up to bury himself in her coat. 'Stay down,' she whispered as they entered the black-market maze.

Luz buried himself deeper, nose pointing upwards so he could appreciate the full range of strange smells and odours. Fried fish, purple smoke, resin-heavy clothes. A veritable olfactory buffet.

The stalls brimmed with merchandise, bizarre contraptions overspilling into the small pathway that ran through the centre of the market. Customers bartered, merchants sang and the smell of roasting nuts filled the air.

Every tiny square of her vision was filled with detail. A large hourglass of bright green liquid and golden bubbles. Labels that read 'Instant Lust' and 'Oculary Boost' – even a dark, viscous liquid called 'The Widow's Revenge'. One merchant sold blueprints for torture weapons, a balaclava over his head, eyes masked by highly illegal darkened lenses that hid his oculary denomination.

Jantsia paused, running her fingers over a turquoise hand mirror. Veins of copper wire glowed beneath its surface. Clasping her fingers around the warm brass handle, she felt a strong desire to check her appearance, and lifted it up to her face.

'I wouldn't do that if I were you, little blue.'

A wide-faced Veridian woman grinned down at her. Dirty yellow hair streaked with silver and pulled into a long braid, fell across a brown facsleath tunic with vein-like copper wires embedded in the fabric, just like the hand mirror.

'Oh hello,' she said, 'I wonder if you could help. I'm looking for something ... illegal.'

The merchant's eyes sparkled. 'Well, you've come to the right place. What can I do you for? Poison? Coloured contacts? Ask, my dear, and Morgan will provide.'

Jantsia hadn't met many Veridians before, the segregation law meant that Azures rarely came into contact with their green-eyed counterparts. She'd heard the rumours, though. Masters of produce, apothecaries of the earth. It was said that talented root-renders could create anything from plant extracts, even the stuff of her wildest dreams.

'How about a cure for the blood sickness?' she asked, throwing caution to the wind.

The merchant Morgan wheezed, laughter laced with opine vapour. 'Very funny, pickle. I only make what my clients want. And I've never had anyone ask for such a thing before. All the dual-oc critters are long gone before they're old enough to pay the price I charge.'

Jantsia mulled over the woman's words, placing the hand mirror back on the stall. She hadn't exactly said no... Maybe if she got on the woman's good side, she'd open up a bit more.

Jantsia gestured at the copper-veined contraptions. 'What are these things?'

The woman smiled, a shark's grin full of teeth the same colour as her hair. 'Something new I've been working on, little blue. You've heard of Tile-tech, yeah? Well, this is Root-tech.'

Jantsia frowned. 'Root-tech? You mean like, some kind of Veridian-powered tech?'

Tile-tech had been engineered by Obsidians for Obsidians.

The restricted access given to Sepias, Veridians and Azures meant that most of the time they could only use the simplest of features. Most likely that was why Jantsia hadn't had any luck searching for the Varzesh Clause on her Tile.

If this woman really had created a version of Tiles keyed to Veridians, well that would be a miracle in itself. A partial cure for the oppression and power inequality between Obsidians and the other oculary orders.

The woman raised her bushy eyebrows. 'Well, ain't you a smart one, pickle.'

Wonder washed through her, a thousand questions on the tip of her tongue. Then she noticed the merchant's face crease in confusion as she ran her thick tongue over chapped lips. Now she really did look like a shank-shark.

Jantsia's heart fell into her stomach as she followed the woman's eyeline. Luz crept between the stacks of potions and instruments, sniffing everything enthusiastically.

'Luz, get back here, right now,' she said through gritted teeth.

On hearing his name, the cat chirped. No longer watching where he stepped, he proceeded to place a fluffy white paw right on top of the turquoise mirror.

The mirror lit up, sending bolts of golden energy into the sky. Luz leaped high in the air, floating with his hairs on end, feline eyes as bright as two miniature suns. The Veridian merchant shouted down the brass pipe at her stand, her voice deep and dark like a death knell.

'Firecat in section fourteen, Morgan calls forty per cent finder's fee!'

The woman launched herself at Jantsia, her great bulk knocking down the stall between them. Glass jars and vials crashed to the ground, creating a tarry puddle of bubbling violet that seemed to eat through the stone floor.

Jantsia didn't have time to move. She didn't even have time to think before the massive woman knocked her to the ground.

Her breaths quickened as she struggled to inhale. The giant woman was crushing her airways.

Inhale.

Luz yowled.

Exhale.

The woman smelled like facsleath and fish.

Inhale.

'Oh, my ocking eyes,' she whimpered, as Morgan withdrew a copper-veined knife and placed it at Jantsia's neck. It was cold and sharp.

It was death.

Her exposed throat flickered.

She couldn't let them take Luz.

He was the only creature that never judged her. That was always by her side.

She couldn't lose him.

But she was powerless.

'Call your beast off and you'll leave with your life,' Morgan wheezed, her spittle decorating Jantsia's face. She craned her neck slightly, careful not to touch the blade and saw that Luz was no longer floating in the sky. He was falling. Claws unsheathed and outstretched. It looked like he was aiming for—

'ARGHHHHHH. THE MONSTER'S GOT ME!' Morgan cried out in pain as Luz fastened onto her neck.

Newfound strength poured through Jantsia's limbs as she rolled Morgan off her. Luz dashed forward, nudging Jantsia urgently. Steeling herself, she clambered to her feet, making a platform with her hands so the cat could jump up and burrow back inside her coat.

Unfortunately, the scuffle had not gone unnoticed. Morgan's message had blasted down the interconnected brass pipes that gave the market its name. From every direction crowds of people rushed to see what had occurred. The sharp and lustful look in a few of the merchants' eyes was not one of innocent curiosity.

'Give us the beast, girl. Give us that firecat,'

She stiffened, holding Luz tight against her. 'No,' she cried. 'You can't have him.'

Her vision wobbled, a faint trace of the hall of mirrors superimposing on the scene in front of her.

'I'm here,' called the dark marble version of Jantsia from behind her mirror. 'Let me out.'

She doubled over. Nausea flaring.

The Obsidian version of her stepped through the mirror. 'Use me,' she said. 'Show them what happens when they disrespect us.'

The sounds around her burst to life with terrifying clarity.

'An Obsidian dares to walk through our market,' called the merchant in the balaclava. 'Let's show this black-hearted kid why The Pipes are an Obsidan-free zone.'

What was he talking about? She wasn't Obsidian. Her eyes were blue.

A knife flew through the air, inches from her head.

The dark Jantsia's black lips pulled back to reveal spiked teeth. 'Make them pay.'

Jantsia dug in her heels, letting her rage rise up to the fore. *'Leave us alone.'* Her voice crackled with power.

Many of the aggressors dropped their makeshift weapons,

faces growing vacant as they turned on their feet and shuffled away.

They're getting away.
They should suffer.

Power sizzled in the air, and Jantsia found herself wanting to give into the voice. To harness whatever was happening to her and knock these people to the ground.

To make their ears bleed.

Sharp teeth clipped her collarbone.

It was Luz.

Taking one last glance at the chaos around her, she rushed down the clearest route. The people around her seemed so confused that they barely noticed her.

Once she was far enough away to be safe. She slowed her pace, ducking into a side-street. Her breaths came heavily, scalp coated in sweat. Raising trembling hands, she wiped her brow and pulled her wild hair into a ponytail.

The turquoise hand mirror from Morgan's stall lay on the ground, a large jagged crack running through its centre. She glimpsed her reflection and flinched. In place of the dull blue eyes, were two burning coals.

The eyes of an Obsidian.

Her heart leapt into her throat.

Then she was plunged into darkness as a sack was thrust over her head, her arms were yanked behind her back, and the cold metal of handcuffs clasped around her wrists.

CHAPTER 26
TRUTH

JANTSIA

Her captor shoved her through the market, taking twists and turns until she had no idea where she was. She tried to shout. To fight back. But her headache returned with a vengeance. Breaths coming hard and fast against the rough canvas of the sack. Luz howled, scratching at the sack from the outside and trying to free her.

'Keep your monster under control or I'll shove him in a sack, too,' spoke a gruff voice.

'Luz, it's okay. Stay calm,' Jantsia stuttered, head pounding so hard she tripped and stumbled.

They came to a stop. A strong smell of incense reached her nose.

The man pushed her to the floor, and by the sound of his footsteps she could tell he was walking away.

Was he an Inspector? Had they been watching her and seen her eyes change colour? The metal of the handcuffs dug into her wrists as she struggled, trying to shake the sack off her head. Spikes of pain stabbed through her temples. She couldn't think straight. Couldn't rationalise anything that was happening. Inspectors had been known to raid The Pipes but never alone.

Luz's rough tongue licked her hand, easing her breaths.

There was nothing he could do but provide comfort. No one could save her now. And if she really had been taken by Inspectors, she was as good as dead.

More footsteps.

This time it sounded like several people were approaching.

'I heard the commotion down the way and went to investigate, sir. You were right, the Inspectors do have people on the ground. Though I have to say I didn't expect them to send a girl.'

'That's all right, Mungo. Good work. You can leave us now.'

Jantsia stiffened at the sound of the second man's voice. Had her headache distorted her mind? There was no way it could be who she thought it was.

No ocking way.

The sack was pulled from her head. Curling smoke from burning incense danced in front of her eyes. She was inside a fortune-teller's tent lit up with candles.

Looking down at her, a troubled expression creasing his face, was her father.

'Baba,' she sobbed, relief and confusion tying her stomach in knots. 'What's going on?'

He bent down, taking stock of her black eyes and removing the handcuffs from her wrists. He pressed his lips together. 'Have you got any of your pills on you?'

She nodded weakly.

'Take them.'

She withdrew the pack from her coat and popped two pills in her mouth. What an A-rate twack she'd been to not have thought of doing this earlier. With all the commotion at the market, and the confrontation with Daezen, she'd been too distracted to think straight.

Less than a minute passed before she started to feel more like herself. More like one version of herself, at least. Even if the hall of mirrors was nothing but a hallucination. It was a powerful one. A hallucination that influenced reality.

'Good, your eyes are back to normal. The pills are working. You should be more careful, Jansty jaan. We can't afford to let the blood sickness take hold like that.' Benyamin helped her to her feet. 'You shouldn't be here.'

She clenched her fists together so hard her nails dug into her skin. 'Neither should you. What in Fladden's name is going on here? Who was that guy? And why did he call you sir?' Adrenaline ebbed away from her body, leaving her tired and weak. 'And why did he cuff me and put an ocking sack over my head,' she spat, taking a step closer to her father until they were almost nose to nose.

He settled his hands on her shoulders. 'I'm sorry that happened to you, love. Mungo was only doing what I asked him to, keeping the area under surveillance and looking out for Obsidians. It was just bad luck that he was doing his rounds when you ... did whatever it was that you did.'

'I had no choice,' she said through gritted teeth. 'They were trying to take Luz from me. I needed to make them stop and then...' She trailed off. And then what? She'd activated the

Obsidian power coursing through her blood? She'd let the blood sickness run rampant through her mind?

'Take a deep breath, Jantsia. Remember the meditation exercises.'

She snorted. 'Meditation exercises? I'm not the one lounging around a secret hideout in The Pipes and shoving sacks over people's heads.' She caught sight of two shadows at the entrance of the tent. 'Are those guards?'

His expression turned steely. 'I can't just run away to Laminos like the past seventeen years never happened. I refuse to turn my back on my beliefs.'

Her bottom lip quivered, legs trembling. 'So, everything you said to me and Maman was a lie? You were never going to come with us?'

The hypocrisy of her statement didn't escape her. Hadn't she just been planning her own getaway with Kain?

'No, it wasn't a lie. Not really. Wherever you two go, I'll follow. But there's something I have to do first.' He paced back and forth. 'Have you ever heard of the Varzesh Clause?'

Her heartbeat quickened. Of all things she'd expected him to say, that wasn't one of them.

'Sort of,' she said. 'I don't know much about it. Only that it's dangerous to talk about, and that if it's activated it could trigger a change in the Empire's hierarchy.'

The candles flickered, illuminating the lines around Benyamin's eyes. 'And do you know how to put it into action?'

'Sort of,' she repeated, fists tightening. This was all far too strange. This was unbelievable. What did her father know about Varzesh and how did it relate to whatever he was doing here?

Benyamin continued, 'A call for Varzesh has to be issued by

a descendent of one of the Great Elite families. If done correctly, it will set in motion a series of trials that will determine a new set of Great Elite families. I wanted your mother to call for Varzesh at the Gala. To make a statement in front of the world. To show the people of the Empire that not all Obsidians side with the establishment. She refused. So ... I'm taking things into my own hands.'

Jantsia frowned, her neck slick with sweat.

His eyes glinted with a fervour she'd never seen in her father before, transforming him from an Azure servant into someone to be feared. The man looming over her wasn't her baba. This man looked more than capable of doing terrible things.

Terrible things, like lying about Flint Trovit's death?

He rolled back his shoulders. 'If all goes well at the Gala, we'll still travel to Laminos, but I will have secured a permanent source for your medicine, and the balance of power will start to shift away from the Obsidians. Azures will have a chance to fight back. To be free.' His eyes went distant, as if looking far beyond the striped canopy of the tent into another world. 'Your mother had the same dream long ago, but the responsibility of keeping you safe has twisted her mind. She can't see beyond the welfare of our family. She can't see that the only way to really keep you safe is by changing the world.'

Jantsia took a step back, almost tripping over Luz. What her father was talking about was treason. He was talking about rebelling against the ruling class. About organising some crackpot operation that would somehow lead to full-blown revolution. She had no idea what he was planning to do, and she didn't want to know. The only thing clear in her mind was that whatever it was, it would endanger them all.

The Obsidians were too powerful to take on. And if he upset

the status quo, perhaps the Rostamani Rivieras would renege on their deal to shelter their family.

She glanced at the opening in the tent. 'I take it I'm free to go?'

He paused for a moment too long.

She took another step back, nearing the exit.

Benyamin's hands twitched, prompting Luz to hiss and bare his fangs. 'Jantsia, please. Think of the Trovits, I know you're fond of Kain. Do you really think they deserve to live the way they do? In a constant struggle to make ends meet?'

She paused, remembering the state of Kain's apartment. His pained expression as he spoke of his mother's addiction. Her heart clenched as she remembered everything he had said. The way he'd kissed her. The way he'd offered to leave everything behind for her.

Her stomach churned. She couldn't let him abandon his family. Not without knowing they'd be okay. It didn't matter what he said. His family meant the world to him.

One more step and she'd be out of the tent, back in the bustle of the market. Free to think this through properly and evaluate her choices.

Benyamin stilled, never once taking his eyes off her.

Jantsia took a deep breath. 'What you're planning, it would help Kain and Daezen? It would help Cathy?'

He nodded, his lips pressed tightly together.

Luz rubbed against her legs, pawing at the floor. Kain and Daezen weren't the only ones who needed help. What she wouldn't give to be free. Free from secrets.

Free from hiding.

Free from the threat of the blood sickness that darkened every thought.

The time to hide and stay invisible was over. She'd never be safe, not in this Empire. And people like her deserved a chance. Her life was only getting started, she wasn't going to let anyone take away her choices anymore.

'Tell me,' she said. 'Tell me everything.'

CHAPTER 27
BROTHERS

DAEZEN

Daezen shifted a piece forward on the chatrang board. An idea brewed in his mind. A way of disabling the Inspectors' oculary.

When the power had gone out, just before Jantsia fled, Kain hot on her heels, Daezen had struggled to find the fuse box, fumbling in the dark. The moment he'd turned it back on, the light had burned through his eyes, making it almost impossible to see for a few seconds.

If he could blind the Inspectors, they'd be powerless.

But how?

Kain stormed through the door, breaking Daezen's focus. He was shaking, fingers practically blue.

Daezen turned up the heating and rushed over to brush the frost off his brother's hair and back. 'What on Shariza were you thinking, rushing out there like that? And why the ock didn't you take your coat?'

Kain glowered at him. 'If you cared so much you could've brought me one.'

'I had no idea where you went, you idiot. The lights went all weird and by the time I worked out how to restart the fuse box you were gone. I had a little look down the street and back but I didn't see you anywhere.' The truth was that Daezen hadn't looked that hard. Shame at the way he'd spoken to Jantsia had been eating him up inside.

He stood by his assessment. Jantsia and her father were hiding things, but he could've had a bit more tact. Since he'd paid off the Health Centre debt and discovered that Pa had been poisoned, he hadn't been able to sleep properly. He spent his days getting the shit kicked out of him by Topper or puzzling over the impossible goal of breaking into the Gala. And his nights were haunted by the mystery of what had happened to Pa. He was worn thin. Bone tired. But that wasn't an excuse for the way he'd acted.

'Jantsia isn't some criminal mastermind. She's just a seventeen-year-old girl – so why on Shariza did you go at her like that? Are you jealous or something?' Kain clicked his knuckles menacingly. 'Why are you so set on ruining the only good thing in my life?'

It unnerved Daezen to see his brother act like this. Especially when he was right. Daezen had spoken out of turn. And in some place, underneath the exhaustion, jealousy niggled at his soul. The moment he'd walked in to see Jantsia and Kain's faces pressed together, it had cut through his weary heart, though he hadn't stopped to consider why.

'Kain, be quiet. I'll explain everything. Just take a breath,' Daezen said in a low voice.

Their mother's bedroom door creaked open.

Daezen braced himself for the brutal combination of pain and shame that always rushed through him when he saw his mother under the influence. But it wasn't the opine-zombie version of his mother that greeted him.

Freshly showered, a grey towel wrapped around her head, Cathy Trovit stepped out of her bedroom, a clean but faded T-shirt and thermal tracksuit pulled over her birdlike frame. The clothes hung off her, revealing how much weight she'd lost in these past cycles.

Wrinkled and pinched as it was, her face brightened. She narrowed her shrewd ocean-blue eyes, which darted from Daezen to Kain then back again.

'Far be it from me to cast judgement on anyone,' she said, papery cheeks turning pink. 'But as I still seem to be your mother, in spite of all my failures, I have to ask...' She puffed up her chest as much as she could, her lips pinched, and her ocean gaze froze over. 'Am I witnessing my sons fight over a girl?'

Daezen's eyes widened in shock. From the corner of his vision, he saw Kain's head hanging like a deflated balloon between his shoulders.

'Ma, it's not—' Daezen began. But even as the words were leaving his lips he tasted the mistake.

'Do not insult my intelligence by saying "it's not what it looks like" please, Daezen. I thought I raised you better. I'm an addict – not a simpleton. I know I owe you answers.'

Daezen flinched. 'What?'

'I remember what you said to me the other night. About the debt. Now, take a seat, I've got a story to tell you both.'

Three knocks at the front door. Daezen's heart raced.

'Well, don't stand around like a pair of melting snowmen,' Cathy said. 'Answer the door, one of you.'

Snow tumbled from the sky, and the blue light of the lampposts illuminated Benyamin Brittle's silhouette, a navy hood shadowing his features.

'May we come in?'

'Er... Hi,' Jantsia said, stepping out from behind Benyamin.

Daezen stepped aside, ignoring the light tingle in his temples at the sight of Jantsia's reticent smile.

Benyamin scanned the apartment, lips tightening as he eyed the burnt-out sofa.

'Please,' Daezen said with a sneer. 'Take a seat. Our humble abode may not be what you're used to, but I promise you won't contract any diseases here. There's not a *poison* in sight.'

Kain's neck turned red.

'Daezen,' Ma admonished, 'that's no way to talk to a guest.' She smiled. 'Beny, it's so good to see you again.'

'It's good to see you, too, Cathy. Did you get my message?'

'I did as a matter of fact. I've been preparing for this moment for a few days.'

Why was Ma talking with Beny like that? Full of warmth. After what he'd done. Let down Flint, his father, her husband? Daezen paced the edge of the room, watching Beny with suspicion as he took a seat next to Ma.

'Daezen,' Jantsia warned, 'don't let your pride get in the way of this. It's too important.' She stuck out her chin and rolled her shoulders back. She looked imperious. She looked ... *powerful*.

Questions pricked behind Kain's wide eyes.

Benyamin cleared his throat. 'Cathy, if I may?'

Ma nodded, lips tightening.

Beny continued, 'I need to tell you some things about Flint

that you're going to find upsetting. But I want you to know, my only intention has ever been to honour him. He requested that I keep this information from you, and I'm sure he asked Cathy to do the same.'

'What's going on?' Kain asked.

Jantsia took Kain's hand and whispered something in his ear. Nausea seeped into Daezen's blood, making him feel unsteady on his feet. Not wanting to sit, he leant against the damp-stained wall, trying to focus his eyes on Beny.

Beny continued, 'We were out playing water-darts when Flint began to experience symptoms. Naturally, I rushed him to the Health Centre right away. It was only once the healers gave their diagnosis that I realised he'd been poisoned.' Benyamin wrapped an arm around Cathy's shoulders as she started to sob.

'At the time, I thought he'd stopped with all that rebel nonsense,' Cathy said, shoulders shaking. 'He'd told me that you'd both left it all behind you.'

'Left what behind?' Kain asked, his question directed at Ma, but his eyes firmly on Jantsia.

Numbness overtook Daezen. He should've been the one to ask that question. To interrogate Benyamin for every last detail. But he couldn't find the words.

'Flint and I headed up a rebel group known as the Azure Warriors. We specialised in intercepting Obsidian shipments as they crossed over the border from Parsia to Albin and distributing them among the people who needed them most.'

Daezen found his voice, mind whirring as he processed Beny's words. 'What kind of shipments?'

'Mainly food and clothing,' Beny said. 'Up here in Densolid, many Azures and Veridians go hungry and cold in the winter.

Entry-level Duty rations don't cover the high price of Parsian imports.'

He didn't need to explain this to Daezen, who had firsthand knowledge of the struggle that families like his went through just to keep themselves fed and clothed.

'But one day,' Beny continued, 'we happened upon a store of weapons by accident. They were locked for Obsidian use only, of course. But Flint had the idea of getting in contact with other rebel splinter cells to see if one of them had the knowledge to unlock the weapons for Azures. It turned out there was a real market for the weapons among rebels across the Empire, especially the Azure Angels. They wanted to stockpile them so that they were prepared for the day someone succeeded in unlocking Obsidian tech. For the day they could mount an armed revolt.'

Kain's mouth dropped open. Daezen didn't blame him. It was hard to reconcile the memories of their father with who Benyamin was describing. Flint Trovit had been a soft-spoken and gentle man. Daezen remembered how he'd encouraged him and Kain, soothed their fears as they'd learned to ride a hoverbike. The way his eyes creased when Kain said something outrageous, lips trembling to hold in the laughter while Ma berated him.

All that time, he'd been running an underground weapons network, helping Azure, Veridian and Sepia rebels prepare for war.

'So why did you stop?' Kain asked.

'Because I bleeding well told them to!' Cathy said, wiping the tears from her eyes. 'They were in over their heads. I told them that if they kept this up, they'd end up putting you both in danger. It was only a matter of time before the Inspectors worked out who was behind the robberies.'

'Yes, that,' Beny said, a faint smiling creeping onto his stern face, 'and the fact that Zuleikha was getting suspicious. I couldn't risk putting Jantsia in jeopardy by incurring her wrath.'

Jantsia snorted.

Daezen's rage spiked. 'You find something funny about this?'

She crossed her arms. 'Of course not. I only found this out today. And I'm the one who convinced him to come here, so watch your mouth.'

'It's true,' Benyamin said. 'Jantsia knew nothing of this. Anyway, I later discovered that though we'd both agreed to retire from the business, Flint had continued running missions. He'd expanded the operation. By my count, he must've armed more than half of the rebel groups in the Empire, from Arq-Tao all the way down to Octengion. And along the way ... he recruited someone he shouldn't have. An Inspector infiltrated the operation. And once they knew the locations of the other rebel sects, they poisoned Flint.'

'Why didn't you tell us?' Daezen blurted out. 'We deserved to know the truth. He was part of our family.'

Beny raised an eyebrow. 'So, you're of the opinion that one's family should always know what their loved ones are involved in?'

Daezen stiffened. Beny couldn't possibly know about the Gala mission, could he?

'We know what you're up to,' Jantsia said. 'So you can get off your high hoverbike and get down to telling *your loved ones* the truth.'

'What's she talking about, Daeze?' Kain asked, his face creasing with confusion.

Daezen gaped. That little Brittle bitch. How dare she talk to him like that. How dare she force him into this situation. Beneath the waves of anger, a small glimmer of respect burst to life. She'd played her pieces well, this girl.

There was definitely more to her than met the eye.

'That's enough, Jantsia,' Beny said, his pained expression making him look older. Much older. 'People have many reasons for keeping secrets. Protecting those they love being the highest of those reasons. Flint didn't want any of you to be at risk. And knowing what he was doing would've put us all in danger. He kept this from you to keep you safe.'

Despair drowned the flames of Daezen's rage. They'd backed him into a corner where the only way out was the truth. 'Blink's back in town,' he said coolly. 'He's on a mission for the Azure Angels, and me and Topper have agreed to help. Everything's already in motion, and I've got us a good deal. If we pull this off, we'll never have to worry about tokens again.'

'You look just like him when you talk like that,' Cathy said between sobs. 'Just like Flint.'

Kain's eyes blazed with defiance. 'I want in.'

'But Kain—' Jantsia said.

Kain cut her off. 'I'm not rotting at the academy or some shitty Duty while you go out there and fight for Azures. I want to make a difference. Nothing you can say will stop me.'

Jantsia's shoulders sank, her powerful stance bleeding away until she seemed to shrink in stature.

'I'm not here to try and stop you,' Beny said, standing up and making his way to Jantsia's side. 'Blink came to me when he first arrived in town. He'd been given my name by his commander. At first, I refused. I had my own plans in motion and didn't want to risk involving people I didn't know. But once I learned you were involved ... I had a change of heart. I'm here to help, we both are.'

Daezen watched Beny take Jantsia's hand, a heavy ache growing in his chest, as he wondered if, in another world where Pa had lived, he'd be standing at his side, just like that.

'Daezen,' Jantsia asked softly, 'have you found a way to sneak into the Gala yet?'

'Yes,' he said. 'There's a weakness at the top of the forcefield. We're going to skydive onto the terrace. I just need to find someone stupid enough to fly us up there. I was actually thinking of your pa's friend, Glent, the barman.'

Beny cocked his head. 'You know what, that might just work.'

'And how will you handle the security once you're in?' Jantsia asked.

Daezen looked down at the chatrang board. 'Well, I've got you to thank for that part, actually... Beny, do you know where I could find a light flare? Not a standard one, a powerful one. A flare with enough force to blind a hall of Inspectors?'

Beny shot him a wicked smile. 'I can definitely help with that. That's smart, Daezen. I'd never thought of flipping the oculary advantage on its head. We may not be able to use their weapons, but the oculary lock affects them, too. Without their power, they'd have to rely on steel and fist.'

Jantsia chewed on her lip. 'It's a good plan, for sure. A great plan. But won't there be guards watching the entrance to the hall from the terrace?'

'He could use the light flare trick, right?' Kain piped up.

Beny shook his head. 'I'll only be able to get one light flare with that level of power. And if you use it too soon, you risk alerting the rest of the Inspectors before you can locate the targets. That's still the plan, isn't it? Take high-profile Obsidian hostages?'

Shame burned Daezen's cheeks. 'Yeah, that's the plan. And I don't know what to do about the Inspectors guarding the terrace,' he admitted, 'we might just have to risk taking them down with force.'

A spark of rebellion smouldered in Jantsia's eyes. 'And what if there was somebody already inside that could cause a distraction?'

CHAPTER 28
CREW

DAEZEN

The players stacked neatly on the board.

Knights, pawns, bishops.

Exactly where Daezen wanted them.

The rook inched forwards, leath boots blazing with rubies, and tapped his iron-tipped nails on the service door at the back of Prenderghasts.

Heartbeat even.

The door swung open. Faux-flame lamps lit up the narrow metallic hallway.

Hands steady.

Inside a plush office, Blink, Tala, and a woman with cool brown skin and long braids were sitting at a round table. The newcomer seemed scared, demure. Where did he know her from?

Breaths soft.

On this board, everyone was a player.

But for which side?

'Hey, muts, long time no drink or whatever,' Topper announced. 'As I live and kill, Blinky my old boy. When Daeze said you were back I thought he was playing me for a greener.' He locked eyes with the woman at Tala's side. 'Didn't think I'd see you again, you tease.'

Tala's mask of stone cracked. She leant over, furiously whispering something into the woman's ear. The woman responded in a voice too low to distinguish.

Ice flecked Blink's laugh. 'Thanks for coming, Topper... And Kain? I hadn't expected you, but it's great to have you here.' He shot Daezen a bemused look before steadying his expression. 'I'd like to introduce you all to Tala, my sister, and the newest member of our crew, Millie. Although it seems some of you already know her. We picked her up at the rebel camp. She was the only one brave enough to volunteer for the mission.'

Suddenly, Daezen remembered how he knew the woman. She'd approached them in Tavern Blue when he'd first met with Topper to bring him in on the mission. A worm of doubt wriggled through his stomach. This woman didn't fit into his plans. Nor did coincidences. Chance was a cruel master, more likely to take the coat off your back than bestow good fortune.

'Well, gents, ladies. I'm all ears. And eyes.' Topper said, pointing at the two bright red rubies sewn into his irises.

Blink picked up the large jug of Fireglug that sat in the centre of the table and poured the newcomers a drink. Daezen curled his lip as the assassin took a large mouthful of the lava-like concoction, and Kain followed suit.

Nice to see his brother and friend going back on their agreement to stay sober within the first minute of smelling a drink.

Blink proffered a glass to Daezen. 'A little something to whet your tongue before I get on with the serious stuff?'

He shook his head, even if Topper and Kain chose to drink themselves silly, he wanted a clear mind for this. It was too important. This was the moment he presented his plan to the group. The moment he showed them what he was capable of.

Blink shrugged, taking the glass for himself and glugging it down, shaking his hands out and trilling his lips. 'Here we go. So, most of you already know this, but our mission is to kidnap a series of high-value hostages from the Inspectors' Gala. I was hoping we'd have a bigger crew, so I had a pretty long list of targets, but seeing as there are only five of us, I've narrowed it down to the two most valuable marks.'

Tala spread her Tile on the table and brought up three photos before exchanging a loaded glance with Millie. It almost looked like she was apologising with her eyes. They were close, very close. His breaths remained even. Not a trace of jealousy passed through his heart. Tala was beautiful, but at some point he'd stopped thinking about her and started thinking of someone else...

He hardened his neutral expression, stiffening every facial muscle that might give away his emotional state. Matters of the heart had no place in this room.

Blink swiped through the images, enlarging the photo of a bald man with dark brown skin and large glasses. 'Meet Dr Alhaadi Popoola, Octengion's leading ocular scientist. We've had tip-offs that he was involved in the last chain of rebel arrests, and that his research into ocular enhancers and blockers is the most advanced in all of Shariza.'

He swiped again, zeroing in on the image of a young man with golden-brown skin and spiky pink hair. 'And this is Zentich

Quispe, an oculary hacking genius. He was arrested at the age of eleven for recoding his Tile into a miniature laser gun, but the Laminosian Inspectors soon found a better use for him. They say he's capable of hacking anything and has little loyalty to anyone. That's why they keep him under lock and key.' Blink spoke faster, tripping over his words in excitement. 'Can you imagine what we'll be able to demand from the Council of Great Elites in exchange for returning them? More rights for Azures, less restrictions. Who knows, maybe we can convince one of them to help us unlock Tile-tech weapons for Azure usage, and then ... and then...'

'Rebellion,' Kain said softly.

Like Daezen, he must be wondering how many of the weapons his father had distributed around the Empire were still under rebel control. The Inspectors couldn't have found them all. His eyes grew wet as he thought about the significance of this mission. If they could somehow convince one of the two hostages to help, they could complete Pa's dream. They could unlock Tile-tech weaponry and build an Azure Army. They could fight for a free world.

Topper pouted. 'Doesn't sound too bad to me, but I have a question.'

'Ask away, Tops, but be brief. Daezen still has to present his plan.'

Nerves shot through him like electricity. Everything relied on his plan going smoothly. But how much should he reveal with Millie in the room?

Topper pointed a sharpened nail across the table, straight towards Millie. 'Why the ock is this chick here? Last time I saw her, she was in Tavern Blue, drooling over yours truly. Doesn't that seem like a bit of a coincidence to you?'

Finally, someone other than Daezen saw reason. Beny had been right to doubt Blink's judgment. He was hot-headed and stubborn. Great qualities for a soldier, but not for a leader.

Tala's thin lips curved downwards. 'Your friends have excellent manners, Blink.'

Topper clicked his tongue. 'Maybe, I'd be a bit more polite, sweet cheeks, if I wasn't putting my pert ass on the line so you and Blinky boy can make your way up the greasy rebel pole.'

'It's fine.' Millie placed her hand on Tala's shoulder. 'He's right, he should know who he's working with.' She turned to the group. 'My name is Millie Kuti, I joined the Dissidens rebel group after leaving my performance troupe in Sumavig. While on my way to the Asabreks, I stopped off in Densolid, and drank far too much Fireglug to drown out the nerves. I apologise for my behaviour, Topper. I was very scared about going against the Empire. In my inebriation, I hung onto you for protection. If you doubt my words, Blink and Tala can vouch for me, as can the Dissidens' camp leader. Because in spite of the shelter and safety the Dissidens provided, I've decided to risk my *own* pert ass for the cause.'

The tension broke, and they shared a brief moment of laughter.

'All right, Daezey,' Blink said. 'It's your time to shine. Let's hear the plan.'

Daezen rolled out his neck, deciding at the last minute to withhold vital parts of the plan from the group. Not everyone needed to know everything. 'All right, this is what I've got so far. There are four key challenges. First, we have to get inside. The Gala will be held at the Empire Hall in Densolid Major. It's surrounded by a forcefield with only one checkpoint in and out.' He opened a new page on Tala's Tile and made a quick sketch of the building. 'At first, it looked hopeless, but thanks to our friendly neighbourhood assassin, I've learnt about a weakness in the forcefield structure. It won't be easy, but if we enter right through the weak point, we can access the Imperial terrace.

'The next problem is getting from the terrace into the building. Inspectors will likely be guarding the door. One of our contacts on the inside is going to cause a distraction, but then it'll be up to us – and by us, I mean Topper – to disable the guards on the inside before they can sound the alarm.'

Topper rapped his nails on the table. 'How many will there be?'

'It's hard to tell, but based on the intel Blink shared they won't be able to spare more than two.'

'It's doable. Blink, Tala – can I count on you to back me up?' Topper asked.

'Of course, mut,' Blink said.

'All right,' Daezen continued, 'so we've made it in, disabled the guards, then we need to locate the targets. Once we've found them, we'll set off an uber-powered light flare, blinding everyone who isn't expecting it – and causing chaos among the guests. Then we'll have two minutes to take down the targets, use the commotion to rush out the front door and remote call our hoverbikes to escape. I've practised it myself. For two minutes exactly, none of the bastards will have access to their oculary powers, that means no laser guns and no sonar attacks. And that, ladies and gentleman, is how we infiltrate the most exclusive gathering of Inspectors in the whole of Shariza.'

Blink clapped slowly, catching Daezen's eye. 'Never doubted you, mut. I knew you could do it.'

Kain patted him on the back. 'We can do this.'

Tala pursed her lips, staring into the distance as if

visualising it all happening in front of her. 'Okay,' she said, 'I think we could pull this off. I can help Topper disable the guards. Mils, will you help? We might need back up.'

Millie remained silent, her lips twitching slightly.

'Millie?' Tala repeated.

She shook her head as if waking from a trance. 'Yes, of course. I'll back you up.' She turned towards Daezen. 'Who is the inside man? Are they Obsidian?'

Daezen shook his head. 'I can't divulge that. Their condition of participation was secrecy. But I promise you, they can be trusted. They will not fail us.'

Millie narrowed her eyes. 'And how exactly will we break through the forcefield? You said you found a weakness, can you share that with us?'

'No,' he replied, suspicion crawling up the back of his neck. Betrayal was a disease that plagued mankind. A disease that killed his pa. He wasn't going to take any more risks than he had to with this. 'Trust that if I withhold information, it is for the good of the mission, nothing more.'

'Fair enough,' Blink said, eyes glinting in the lowlight. 'Well, that's enough for tonight, friends. Tops, shall we meet at yours tomorrow to begin preparations.'

Topper smiled like the firecat that got the cream. 'I look forward to it.'

CHAPTER 29
TRAINING

SOBA

It was nearly noon, and inside Topper Luxo's training hall, the air thickened with perspiration.

The crew had been sparring for several hours, and Soba's patience danced on a knife edge. Her muscles twitched to let loose and throw herself into the fight. But she couldn't. She ground her teeth together, every inch of her focus zeroed in on holding back. On restraining Inspector Soba Nite. Millie Kuti had no combat experience, and Soba had to act accordingly.

She'd been paired with Daezen, neither of them had been trusted with a weapon, and it was probably for the best. After hearing his master plan to disrupt the Inspectors' Gala, Soba's fingers itched to carve him a new mouth. It was brilliant, and she hated him for it. Part of her even feared him...

If she hadn't been there to run interference, the mission would probably have been a success. Though, irritatingly, he hadn't expanded on every detail. She could arrest them all now and bring the whole mission to an end, but that would mean leaving too many loose ends.

It would mean leaving Tala...

All this time, she'd thought the resistance a helpless bunch of lighter colours, too stupid to know which end of a sword to stick someone with. But this small group of Azures were posing a real threat.

Luckily, though, Soba *was* there. And she would report every detail to Elias at the next opportune moment. Regardless, too much of the Inspector's advantage relied on chance. The chance Soba would set up surveillance on the Trovits. The chance she would form a connection with Tala.

Luck was a lazy man's word.

Soba didn't want to deal in chance. She wanted certainty.

When Soba had arrived that morning, Blink and Tala led her straight to Topper Luxo's home, a location the Inspectors had relentlessly searched for and yet never found. The large sandstone mansion boasted decorative turquoise tiles and engraved pillars. Not exactly an underground fort, such as Jenna Rutkitz had suggested in their last debrief. Topper had been hiding in plain sight this whole time.

The property wasn't registered in his name, of course. The Inspectors had thought it belonged to an Azure family of merchants who only took up residence in the summer.

Of course, upon entering the high-roofed training hall, it became clear that this property no longer belonged to the merchants, if it ever had. The inner wall was lined with contraband. Low-tech steel weapons, wooden staffs, curved blades. Soba couldn't take her eyes off them. The points she'd receive for confiscating a haul this large would easily take her to the next level of seniority. When you paired that with the arrest of Topper, the foiling of the rebel's plans, and the intelligence ... well, she was easily looking at a promotion to Senior Inspector, if not more.

This operation would do wonders for Elias's career. Director Greta Vox might finally name him as her shadow, and in a few solar loops, he'd ascend the ranks to become the most powerful Inspector in Albin.

'Keep going!' Topper shouted.

Daezen scowled at the assassin, sweat dripping from his brow. He was struggling to keep pace with Soba, even though she'd significantly dialled down her speed and the strength of her impacts.

Elsewhere in the hall, Kain was holding his own against Topper, face reddening as he dodged the assassin's punches.

'Come on, Daeze. If things get icy in there we're going to be fighting and running for our lives. We can't afford to have a weak link. Keep going,' Topper called, keeping track of Daezen's sluggish moves while he sparred.

Topper danced around Kain, a true master of the fight. Soba would've liked to spar against him. To have had a real challenge. But that wasn't possible, not without breaking her cover.

Topper's admirable skill aside, the younger Trovit's potential surprised her. As far as she knew, Kain had no formal training, but his instincts were good, and he was light on his feet. If he'd been born Obsidian, Soba would've considered taking him under her wing.

Daezen's fist shot towards her. The movement was sloppy. She waited until he was close to making impact, then sidestepped the blow, tripping over her feet for effect.

'For Fladden's sake,' Daezen exclaimed, putting his hands on his knees and breathing heavily. 'I thought I'd got you that time. You sure you haven't done this before?'

Soba smiled demurely. 'It must be all the performance training. Of course, I have never fought like this before.'

Tala and Blink were sparring on the other side of the training hall, the clashing of swords echoed around them. The siblings panted, heads dipping, but the rhythm of the fight stayed on beat. They jabbed and blocked with their itak-blades as if their lives depended on it. Rays of sunlight shone through the large arched windows, reflecting off the weapons.

Daezen stood up straight, eyes narrowed.

He didn't believe her. Not entirely. *She'd have to change that.*

With renewed vigour, Daezen rained blow after blow down upon her. She slipped out of his reach yet again. On his final desperate attempt, he threw his body behind the strike, leaving his left side completely open to attack. She didn't press the advantage. Instead, bracing herself for impact, she slowed her dodge and stumbled.

Daezen's clenched fist connected with her cheek, making a sick crunching noise.

It hurt. But not much.

Soba cried out in mock-pain and let her body crumple to the floor.

An itak-blade crashed to the ground, and footsteps echoed across the hall. Tala rushed to her side, bending to stroke her face.

'You faked it,' Daezen snarled. 'You let me hit you. You could've dodged it easily. I've seen your speed.'

Soba rubbed the side of her face, trying her best to ignore

Tala's smoky scent. The softness of her touch. Her simmering opal eyes.

Tala scowled at Daezen. 'We're supposed to be training. Not trying to mutilate each other.'

Topper walked towards them, hands up in a gesture of peace. 'It's okay, team. This is good. It's good for Millie to get used to the pain, and for Daezen to understand what it feels like when a blow strikes true. Millie's a tough'un, she'll be all right, won't you Mils?' Topper said, eyeing her and Daezen with caution.

'I'm okay,' Soba said, letting her voice quaver.

'She faked it. I'm telling you, she did.' Daezen glowered.

Soba looked up at him, schooling her features into a sweet smile, then gripping Tala's hand. 'I was tired, Daezen. I tripped. You won, fair as snow,' she said.

'I don't believe you,' he retorted.

Tala sprung to her feet and strode towards Daezen. 'Why, you little sand-licker! You get off on hitting women, do you?'

Kain stormed in front of Tala. 'Don't you dare talk to my brother like that.'

'Enough,' Blink called. He stepped between Tala and the Trovits. 'Enough,' he quietly repeated. 'Look, I know you and Tops don't know Millie, and I know the stakes are high. I see why you'd be worried, but Tala vouches for her. That's enough for me and it should be for you, too.'

Daezen sneered. 'Yeah, it would be. If I thought she was thinking with her head instead of her—'

'STOP!' Topper boomed, 'Tala, go with Millie to the bathroom, second door on the left. I've got a healing kit under the sink. You can clean her up and put salve on her face. Stop a bruise forming.'

Tala nodded, helping Soba to her feet.

They walked through a tiled hall to a spacious bathroom with high ceilings. Mosaics lined the walls, depicting imagery of feminine Azures kneeling under a stormy sky. In place of hair, each had a mane of water tumbling down their naked body.

Soba sat on the turquoise lid of the toilet, letting Tala search the cupboard under the sink for Topper's healing kit. She didn't like being alone with Tala. Even staying in adjacent rooms at the dingy hotel they lodged in made her feel uncomfortable.

Tala approached her, a cloth and salve in her hand. As she reached over to apply the lotion to Soba's cheek, her silky black hair flopped in front of Soba's face.

She shut her eyes. Attempting to conjure up images of Elias to avoid thinking about Tala's lips.

But it was too late.

All thoughts of Elias shifted, his beautiful face appearing sinister, juxtaposing harshly with memories of Tala in the forest.

'Did he ever pressure you for sex?'

The cold metal of his rings digging into her sides.

'You know that it's not normal for an adult to show interest in a child, right?'

Frankly, Soba, you look disgusting.

'Relationships are about equality, not dominance. I want you to choose. I want you to listen to the way you feel.'

You know the deal. You keep your end of the bargain, and I'll keep mine.

'Are you okay, Millie? I'm not hurting you, am I?'

Soba opened her eyes. Tala's smooth skin creased in concern.

'No. It's fine. You're not hurting me.'

A lie.

Tala's presence hurt Soba to the very core, making her doubt everything she held true. Her devotion to Elias. Her low opinion of Azures. The dirty nature of cross-oculary fraternisation.

No, Soba would not make the same mistakes as her adulterous mother. She and Tala were an impossibility. A crime. Soba was just getting caught up in the moment. Nothing more.

Never look back.

'Okay,' Tala said. 'I think we're done here.'

Her eyes locked with Soba's.

Soba shut her eyes tight.

But all Tala did was kiss her lightly on her injured cheek.

The place where she'd kissed Soba burned, as if her lips had imprinted onto her skin.

'Shall we get back?' Tala asked sweetly. 'We can't leave the boys alone for too long or they'll come up with another crazy plan.'

Soba nodded, getting to her feet.

They walked back to the training hall where Daezen crouched over a pool of water on the floor, while the others stood over him.

'All cleaned up. What's next? Should we practise the jump?' Soba announced as they entered.

The men flinched.

They were up to something.

Topper was the first to recover, adept at artifice as well as battle.

'Let's call it for today.' He grinned, revealing his spiked canines. 'We can come back fresh tomorrow and pull this shitshow together.'

Tala gathered up their stuff and readied to go, but

something about the shifty look in Daezen's eyes gave Soba pause. As they exited the training hall, she kept Daezen in laser focus as he and Kain turned in the other direction, leaving their hoverbike parked up outside the mansion.

Her heart raced. If there was something going on that she didn't know about, it could put her whole mission in jeopardy. She couldn't knowingly give Elias incomplete information. She had to do everything in her power to keep the whole operation firmly under control.

Hating every inch of herself, Soba wrapped her arms around Tala from behind, peppering small kisses up her velvet neck. 'There's something I have to do before tonight,' she murmured, before lightly nipping the soft part of Tala's ear.

She felt the Azure's knees shake and buckle against her legs.

Tala rolled her hips, pressing herself against Soba. Desire stirred in her lower stomach. She didn't want to do this.

She wanted to do this.

She didn't want to do this.

Tala spun around, arching an eyebrow. 'What are you waiting around for? Hurry up and do whatever you need to do. I'm going to have a word with the receptionist and see if they can turn up the heat in your room.' She licked her lips. 'That's where I'm going to be waiting. For you.'

Soba's heart skipped a beat, mind conjuring up an alluring image of Tala curled up in her bed. Soft curves, golden skin, tight muscles, satin hair.

Her heart beat erratically. Then she rushed in the other direction, in pursuit of Daezen and Kain.

It wasn't dark yet, so she couldn't risk pursuing them on the street. The uncomfortable flush and undesirable feelings for Tala faded as she turned her mind to the problem. Her dark brown skin stood out among the pink-and-white sickly faces of the Albiners, if she followed them on the ground they'd spot her easily.

So, she did what she did best. She climbed into the sky where she tiptoed across rooftops, skipped between the shadows of sulphurous chimneys and crouched behind choking generators.

It wasn't easy to follow from this distance, but Soba didn't like easy tasks.

Sinking into the rhythm of her breath, matching the drip-drop sound of the rain against the tin roof, she tracked them all the way to The Pipes.

Kain's bright blond head bobbed in the crowd. Artium be merciful, she didn't want to hurt him. He was just a boy. In honesty, she wanted to grip him by the shoulders and shake him. He was throwing his life away with this mission. He was making a mistake. He deserved more.

Soba slid down a drainpipe, ignoring the friction burn on her bare hands, then circled the market, reaching the rusty ladder at the back of the Red Ruins.

Sixty rungs later, she was atop the building.

A perfect fifth.

From this height, she tracked the duo all the way to a striped tent with uniformed guards at its entrance.

She leapt from the building, cushioning her fall against a large navy canopy. *Now that was pain.* Daezen's pathetic little slap was nothing in comparison.

Soba rushed through the market, elbowing bumbling merchants and shoppers out of the way. But as she approached the tent, she slowed.

Feline steps.

Silent breath.

The striped tent held secrets.

Focusing on the empty space where her oculary should be, Soba zoned in on the voices coming from inside the tent. If only she could use her echolocation skill, she'd know exactly who was inside and what they were doing.

She bit her bottom lip. Spots of glacial rain spattered her forehead. When it rained, all the filthy, foetid smells of this place floated up to make themselves known.

She couldn't waste any more time.

Elias was waiting for her.

And so was Tala.

On the approach to the Inspectors skyrise, Soba made her way to a back entrance, eyes cast firmly to the ground to avoid anyone spotting their pale colour.

She keyed the code into the door's internal Tile, then placed her fingerprints against it.

The Tile blinked, capturing her image. The door slid open.

Soba hurried through the corridor, senses on high alert. She didn't get far before a pair of strong hands gripped her shoulders and dragged her into a room. The door slammed, lock clicking into place.

She wasn't scared, she'd known him by his scent alone. Velvety spice and harsh citrus cologne. Elias had come to meet her.

'So?' he drawled. 'Have you missed me?'

Elias's sultry lips creased into a confident smile, telling her he already knew the answer to his question. She'd missed him the way an addict misses a high. Like poison heading straight to the heart, Soba couldn't forget him.

But why?

'Of course,' she breathed. 'Shall I debrief, Chief Inspector Vox?'

'You shall.'

She faltered. Tala crept into her mind, stroking her face, laying herself bare.

Could she really betray her?

Elias tapped his foot.

Ignoring a sickly sense that she was making a terrible mistake, she spoke. 'I successfully infiltrated the Dissidens' encampment and met the Azure Angels, two Taoan terrorists. The Dissidens refused to give aid and the truce was upheld. The Taoans returned to the city and met with the Trovits – and Topper Luxo.'

'Interesting. The traitor's children follow in their father's footsteps. Continue.'

Her blood crawled with tiny mites. Her voice caught in her throat. To reveal this to Elias would be to draw a line in the sand. A line that would forever separate her from Tala.

She clamped her lips together.

'For Artium's sake!' Elias exclaimed. 'Do we really have to do it this way? You always did like to play hard to get.' He stepped closer, towering over her. '*Speak.*'

Soba's lips fell apart and words tumbled from her mouth. 'They plan to kidnap Dr Popoola and Zentich Quispe on the night of the Gala. Their plan is surprisingly impressive.' In a monotone, she continued, telling him the full details of the plan. Then she halted, unsure why she'd given in. Had she chosen to tell him all of that, or had he made her do it?

Elias grinned. 'Very interesting. This will do wonders for the Inspectorate's reputation. Though, I have to say, I was surprised to hear you're still undercover. The mission was to locate the terrorists and ensure they didn't receive aid.' He spread his long-fingered, ringed hands wide. 'You've achieved both of these goals. So why not arrest them and be done with it?'

Soba coughed. Conflicting emotions rattled together, constricting her throat.

Arrest them? Arrest Kain? Arrest Tala? Would she even be capable of—

Stay calm, said the strong, indomitable voice inside her, the voice that kept her alive. *He's testing you. Explain your rationale.*

'Thank you for your kind words, Chief Inspector Vox,' she replied, falling back on formality to escape the discomfort. 'Though I fear that I have not yet gleaned enough intelligence on their operation to say the mission is complete.'

'How so?' His voice trickled like dark honey, eating away at her defences. Leaving her raw. How could he dismantle her entire being in just two words?

'Daezen Trovit has a man on the inside and refuses to reveal who they are. We could arrest him and force him to tell us, but I fear it would give the traitor time to flee. Considering the fact that this person obviously has access to our inner circle, we must discover who they are and capture them. The security risk of them escaping is too high. Until I know what they're doing, I ask permission to continue with the operation.'

'Very interesting. I will allow you to continue the mission. Perhaps we'll even let them play it out to the end. Yes ... why not have them think they've won? They'll share boundless intelligence in their elated stupidity. And finally, when they're in the belly of the beast – we'll cut their fun short. We could make quite the spectacle of it.'

Soba's heartbeats quickened at the thought of Tala's face when she realised her betrayal.

'Inspectors will attend the Gala from all over the Empire, Soba. I thought we might use the night to finally announce our relationship.'

His voice was thick and sweet with a bitter aftertaste. Soba could feel each syllable unravelling her insides. He wanted to go public with their relationship. He wanted her at his side, both in private and in front of the world. It was all she could do to stop herself dropping to her knees.

His eyes swirled with thick night. She wanted to touch his golden wavy hair, feel his broad shoulders, and hear *that voice*.

'Don't touch me,' he said. 'Not when you look like that. I won't have a wet whelp in my bed.'

The harsh words hit her like bricks. Crushing the hope, the desire, the need that, only seconds ago, had burned bright in her chest.

Elias surveyed her. 'It looks like, after all that time spent with the vermin, their weakness is rubbing off on you. You're losing your edge, Soba. We'll have to restart those hunt challenges again when your mission is over.' His mouth twisted cruelly as he handed her a folded golden Tile. 'Take this, you'll need to inform me at every stage of the mission. I can't risk causing a scandal at the Gala.'

'Yes, Chief Inspector. I'll be going, now.'

Her head spun. She had to get out of here. She had to come to terms with what she'd just done. She'd practically signed Tala's death warrant to cement her place as Elias's partner. She had to warn her.

'*Not. So. Fast.*'

Each word gripped her heart like a vice, the melody behind them making it impossible for her to move an inch. A hint of anger infused Elias's voice. She'd forgotten that he always liked to tell her when she could leave. She'd disrespected him.

'Just because I don't want you to touch me, that doesn't mean I don't want to see you. After all, I've missed seeing your lovely legs. I want to see them. I want to see them *now.*' His eyes shone with a malicious kind of lust. 'Now, turn around, and *take off your clothes.*'

The force of the command took hold and she immediately acquiesced. A ringing sickness pounded in her head. Thoughts of Tala flashed through her mind, followed by her concern, her words. *Did he ever pressure you for sex? That's wrong, Millie. Did he ever pressure you for sex?*

She closed her eyes and counted to ten. Goosebumps rose on her naked flesh. She shivered.

'Such a filthy little Inspector, aren't you?' His words were whispered on her neck, his body pressing against hers from behind.

Her voice quavered. 'Yes, Elias.'

So he didn't mind touching her after all.

Readying herself for what would inevitably come next, Soba banished thoughts of Tala's amber scent, ignoring the void her absence left in her chest.

Instead, she forced herself to think of how grateful she was for all Elias had done for her. How much of an honour it was for him to connect with her in this way. How honoured she would be to be named as his partner. After all, she'd been a helpless child, on the brink of death. She'd trusted Elias for nearly a decade while Tala had been her life for less than a full lunar cycle.

And now look where she was, an Albin Inspector entrusted with a high-level mission, a spy, Elias's protegee. He didn't care about her family's disgrace. He didn't care that she didn't have unscarred, soft and pale skin like his courtesans. She was his fantasy. She was his desire.

She ... was *his*.

CHAPTER 30
WATER

DAEZEN

Incense filled Daezen's nostrils as he entered the tent with Kain. Jantsia and Beny lounged on satin cushions next to a low table with three glasses of water at its centre. The air was thick with candlelight and vapour, casting Jantsia's face into shadow and reflecting off her eyes. Something was changing. A difference to her demeanour that he couldn't place.

Jantsia caught him looking and gave him a strange smile that filled him with the overwhelming urge to move closer to her. To examine the depths behind her strangely fierce eyes. Then Kain pushed past him, smiling dumbly as he rushed towards her, lifting her up and embracing her in a tight hug.

That secret smile hadn't been for Daezen, it had been for Kain. Heaviness took over his limbs as he knelt down next to Beny.

Beny cleared his throat, causing Jantsia to pull away from Kain and resume her place. He couldn't see properly in the flickering light, but Daezen bet her cheeks were turning pink, highlighting the freckles on her nose.

'How did it go today?' Beny asked.

'It was amazing, sir,' Kain said, shifting awkwardly on the satin cushions that lined the Parsian rug beneath them.

Their first group-training session had destroyed Daezen. And it didn't help that Kain was taking to combat so easily. He should've felt proud to see his little brother dodge Topper's attacks, but instead he'd felt useless, insignificant.

Topper had been training him for nearly a full half-cycle and he could still barely fight, whereas Kain had jumped in and taken to it like a fish to a stream.

'You got my message?' Daezen asked Beny, keen to steer their conversation away from combat training.

'I did. The plan is solid. I'm sure we can make it work.'

Daezen puffed out his chest. 'Good, let me know if you need any more information.'

'There is one thing,' Jantsia said, gripping Kain's hand in hers. 'I was wondering if there might be a way you could go unnoticed, just for a short while.'

'What do you mean?' Daezen asked, trying not to stare at the place where Kain's hand touched hers.

She chewed on her bottom lip. 'Well, the other day in The Pipes, I came across a vendor of coloured contact lenses. I know they don't last long, and they'll go for a high price, but isn't it safer if your crew wear them? The mission relies on speed, anyway, and this way, we might be able to avoid some confrontation, at least.'

Admiration filled his core and it took all his willpower not to let it reach his face. It was obvious that Jantsia and Kain had escalated their relationship. Beny may not have noticed, but that hadn't been the hug of a friend. Their hands hung softly together under the table. Daezen had to ignore his emotions or risk ruining the most important relationship in his life.

'It's a good idea,' he said. 'I'll get Tops on supply duty.'

Kain nudged Jantsia playfully with his elbow. 'Oh, I think I have an idea, too,' he chirped. 'If we have the lenses, maybe we can skip the whole skydive part and disguise ourselves as workers, go in through the front door?'

Jantsia's eyes widened in an expression of incredulity. Daezen caught her eye and raised an eyebrow. She giggled, expanding the bubbles of light in his chest.

'What?' Kain demanded, face screwed up in frustration. 'All right, how about this. We could get performer passes and go in with Mr Brittle!'

'I'm sorry, Kain,' Beny said, 'that won't be possible. Everyone on my crew has been subject to strict background checks. They don't let Azures into the building without heavy surveillance beforehand.'

Kain's face fell, shoulders hunching over.

'It was a good idea,' Jantsia said to him under her breath.

Beny frowned, perhaps starting to notice the new dynamic between his daughter and Kain. 'Right, shall we get down to business?'

The brothers leaned forward, eyes laser-focused on Beny. A tingling sensation rushed down Daezen's body like rainwater. Being the brains of the operation wasn't enough. Words would only get him so far. And if Daezen couldn't fight with his fists, he'd have to learn how to do it with his eyes.

Benyamin explained that during his time serving the Rostamani Riviera Elites, he'd picked up valuable information about how Obsidians connect with their power. While most Albiners preferred to create strict formulas for oculary use, the most powerful families in Parsia, Octengion and Laminos had found ways to unlock new depths to their power.

Benyamin believed the information was purposely restricted, with lighter-colour academy curriculums severely curtailed to ensure this ability didn't reach those with eyes of the wrong colour. He even went so far as to suggest the information had been held back from many Obsidians in Albin, to punish the Albiners and prevent them from pursuing their previously failed imperial ambitions.

If what Beny said was true, it would change everything. Currently, there was no way to control water without latching on to the central grouping, holding the peripherals in check, and relaying clear commands down the connectors. So many variables. So much effort.

But if that part could be circumnavigated by Beny's method? Well, almost anything would be possible.

'Speeding up turns water to steam, to vapour. And slowing down transforms it into ice. I wish I could tell you how to do this, but it's more of a feeling than a sequence of commands,' Beny said. 'You have to feel the water. Be the water.'

Daezen stared at the glass of water, the light of the candle flames dancing on its surface.

Be the water.

He squinted, shifting into the state of unseeing and tracking the trajectory of the particles.

Be the water.

Daezen worried he might be going insane. The more he stared at the glass of water, trying to *be* it, the more ridiculous he felt.

Kain harrumphed. 'I don't get it. I'm so good in OP class, why can't I do it?'

'You'll get there in the end,' Jantsia said.

'I know it's hard,' Beny said, 'but it's also the simplest thing in the world. A child could do it.'

Daezen gritted his teeth. 'You're not helping.'

'You have to try to forget everything you know. Think of something you don't understand, but feel to be true in the depths of your soul. Something that communicates before it is understood, like poetry.'

Daezen scoffed. He didn't give a rat's arse about poetry.

Something you don't understand, but feel to be true in the depths of your soul.

He rested his eyes on Jantsia. Her small body seemed to contain a multitude of layers, of personalities. He didn't understand her, but she made him feel something deep inside. It intoxicated him to see her morph into someone who demanded respect and wouldn't back down.

He zoned in on the periphery particles, tracking their movements, imagining how they must feel. Jantsia's defiant face burned into his mind.

There was something odd about her.

Something intriguing.

Something he couldn't make sense of but knew to be true.

Something that communicated before it was understood.

A nauseating flip overtook his sight. He was no longer inside his body, he *was* the fast-moving particles, tracking up and down the surface of the water in the glass. Taking in what he saw, he gauged the disconcerting sight of himself, brow furrowed, eyes glowing bright turquoise. Then, he made an effort to slow.

The coldness spread rapidly. He felt it in his fingertips, his eyes, his soul. The feeling overwhelmed him.

Somewhere he became aware of a sound. What was it? It was familiar. Yes, he knew it. It was…

Ocking avalanches.

With a curse, he was thrown from the glass. His sight was limited to the field of vision of his own two eyes. Slowly turning his head, he saw Kain waving his hands.

Beny ran his fingers over the soft layer of ice that coated the glass on the table. 'Well done, that's excellent for your first try.'

Kain tapped Daezen's shoulder. 'What's the secret? Come on, share!'

'There's no secret, mut. It's like Beny said. You have to be the water.'

'Well done, Daezen,' Jantsia said.

'Thanks,' he replied, 'and let me know if you want help working out your part of the mission. I don't want you to be in any more danger than necessary.'

'I'll be okay,' she said, 'Kain, don't be upset. I can't do it, either.'

Kain turned away, his expression darkening.

Daezen didn't have time to entertain some petty rivalry. He had to do everything within his power to master the skill in time for their mission. Time was running out. And he wasn't going into an event filled with Inspectors from all around the Empire without a secret move up his sleeve. Without a solid defence.

A fantasy of walking through a crowd of Inspectors, twirling daggers of ice, came to his mind. He'd make it a reality.

He would, or he'd die trying.

CHAPTER 31
PROMISE

JANTSIA

The moon winked, nearly full in the smoky sky as the end of the lunar cycle approached.

The Gala was tomorrow.

Tomorrow, everything would change.

'You ready, boss?' Kain asked, helping her onto the dark hoverbike.

She pulled her facsfur coat tighter around her, wrapping her arms around Kain's waist and resting her head on his back. 'As long as you promise you got Daezen's permission to borrow the bike this time.'

He peered over his shoulder and flashed her a mischievous grin. 'Unseeing eyes, unhurt heart, right?'

Jantsia shivered, and it had nothing to do with the cold. 'Right,' she said.

The engine roared to life as they rose through the glacial air until they were high above ramshackle streets. She tightened her grip on Kain and let the bittersweet feeling of their closeness wash over her.

Wind buffeted her face as they soared over the city. The sight of the tin roofs and twisting, coloured paths tugged at her chest as they crossed into the wealthier Azure suburbs. Blue lanterns lit up the navy-tiled streets, but from this height, they looked like cerulean stars embedded in the ground.

Though she'd spent much of her life hating this city, the idea of never seeing it again brought tears to her eyes. No matter how alone she'd felt in this place. No matter the darkness that tinged her memories of growing up ... this place was the only home she'd ever known.

Kain lowered the hoverbike, reaching a sandstone mansion with a mosaic-tiled roof situated at the top of a hill. He landed on a large balcony, from which the whole of Azure Minor was visible. They dismounted.

'What is this place?' Jantsia asked, wanting to ease the heavy silence that hung between them.

'One of Topper's hideouts – and before you ask, he said I could bring you here.'

She raised an eyebrow. 'You know I don't really care about that stuff, don't you?'

'Don't say that!' he protested, 'You're my sweet little rule-stickler, and you always will be.' He wrapped an arm around her shoulder, pulling her closer. 'You see those canopies there?'

She squinted. 'I think so.'

'Well, just above it, those pointy, tower things, that's the Red Ruins.'

'Pointy, tower things? You mean minarets?'

He grinned then planted a soft kiss on her forehead. 'You see,' he said, 'you love telling me off.'

'You love it, too,'

His eyes brightened. 'Well, it was there, on the Red Ruins next to one of the *minarets* when I first thought I'd lost you.'

Her chest tightened, breath catching in her throat. Emotions swirled beneath the surface, but she couldn't afford to let them rise up and take her over. 'Yeah, and whose fault was that?' she quipped, breaking the tension.

'I was such an idiot,' he said, shaking his head. A strand of white-blond hair fell across his eyes.

She leant in, heart racing as she brushed his hair out of his eyes. 'But you're my idiot. My loveable idiot.'

The words were out of her mouth before she really thought them through. Oh, Fladden be merciful. He knew how she meant it, right? It wasn't like she'd said she loved him. She'd just said 'loveable'.

His eyes widened, face paling. 'I want to tell you something,' he said, expression uncharacteristically guarded. 'It's about the running-away thing.'

Her stomach dropped. 'It's okay, Kain. I know. I can't ask you to abandon your family. And the truth is, I don't think I can do something like this to Baba...'

His lip quivered. 'We'll find a way. Once we get settled with the rebels, I'll find a way to come to you. Or maybe you and Beny can run away from that horrible Obsidian witch and come and join us.'

She swallowed past the lump in her throat. 'Maybe.'

'I don't want to be apart, but I'm starting to realise how hard all this has been on Daeze. I can't abandon him.' He looked up, electric-blue eyes piercing straight through her. 'I'll find you. But just in case something happens, I want to get everything out in the air. I don't want to leave anything unsaid.'

'Nothing is going to happen to us, Kain.'

'I know, but I never told you how much I appreciate everything you've done for me. When Pa died, I thought I'd never know happiness again. And then you appeared with your bright red face and those lovely little freckles on your nose, singing that stupid song.' He laughed, tears in his eyes. 'He's the boy that never smiles,' he sang off-key, bringing tears to the corner of Jantsia's eyes. 'I thought you were too good for me, you know,' he continued, 'for a long time, I was just waiting for you to realise that you could do better. Find a friend with more connections, more influence.'

'Don't say that, Kain. You've done far more for me than I ever did for you. Before my awakening, I felt so alone.'

'But you've awoken now, and you are a beautiful Azure woman.' He grasped her hands and stuttered. 'Jantsia, I think I love you.'

Her stomach flipped. Breaths coming fast and shallow. 'Kain, I—'

'You don't need to say anything, I know. I know everything,'

His lips gently met hers, slowly opening her mouth, lighting her up from the inside. If only she could lose herself in this moment. If only she didn't feel so awkward, aware of everything.

She pulled back. This was wrong. She was a liar and a terrible person for leading Kain on like this. Her secret burned at the back of her throat, choking her.

'What's wrong?' he asked.

Tears rolled down her cheeks. 'I ... I never thought you'd like me this way. I mean ... look at me, I'm not like everyone else. I'm not like Flossie and Pixa.'

He traced the line under her chin, leaving a tingling warmth that travelled down her neck and took root in her chest. 'You don't need to be. You're perfect just the way you are.'

'I wish we could leave. Run away now, just you and me, but...'

'The mission is too important,' Kain said with a sad smile.

She blinked tears from her eyes. 'It's bigger than us.'

His fingers interlaced with hers. 'Hard to believe anything could be more important than this.'

A maelstrom of emotions warred within her. The hall of mirrors encroached on her awareness. She took a deep breath, pushing the hallucination far away. 'I wish we had more time.'

He smiled kindly, wiping the tears from her cheeks. 'Don't speak like that, we'll have more time.'

Jantsia rose to the tips of her toes and pecked him on the lips, making a silent promise to herself. If they survived the mission and somehow found their way back to one another, she would tell him the truth.

Not now.

She couldn't ruin this moment and didn't want to risk upsetting him with everything else on his mind.

He'll understand, she said to herself. *But for now, it's better to keep it to myself.*

Unseeing eyes, unhurt heart.

Time was running out.

A flame of uncertainty flickered in Jantsia's mind, threatening to set all the paper lies she told herself on fire and burn them to a crisp.

Luz purred on her lap as she lounged on the cream armchair

in her hallway, her messenger app flashing on her Tile. Should she message Kain? Tell him she'd changed her mind and wanted to run away with him? As she scrolled down her contacts, she found herself accidentally clicking on Daezen's name instead of Kain's. Her cheeks flushed, remembering the strange twinge of desire she'd felt as he'd interrupted her and Kain's kiss. The jitters in her stomach when she'd learned of Daezen's brilliant plan to infiltrate the Gala. She didn't know where these feelings were coming from, but it couldn't be more than respect.

She admired his strength of character. His resilience. That was all.

She closed down the messaging app with clammy fingers.

Kain loved her. But running away wasn't the solution. It would only cause more hurt. She couldn't take Kain away from his mother, from his brother. And even though her parents had written the book on silver lies, she didn't want to be like them.

If she was going to take things further with Kain, it had to be from a place of truth. A place of honesty.

Paper lies weren't the foundations of a strong and meaningful relationship. Besides, without a confirmed supply of medicine, she'd be cutting her own lifespan short. She'd be turning her back on everything her father had shared.

On the opportunity to change the world.

For the first time in hundreds of solar loops, there was a chance to rebalance power within the Empire, improve the lives of thousands of families living from hand to mouth like the Trovits. Was she really so selfish that she'd prioritise her own desires over that?

An idea sparked in her mind, one that set her pulse racing so fast the world around her swayed. She withdrew the blister pack of pills from her pocket.

There was only one left.

Her vision swam as full-length windows transformed into reflective surfaces. Cream carpet morphed into a sticky grey substance. Her gorge rose. She was back in the hall of mirrors.

The mirrors shuffled and shifted, flowing and rippling like a tidal wave until a single pane of glass stood before her.

Her pulse slowed.

Hands steady.

There was nothing to fear from this place.

She knew it like the back of her hand. *The inside of her mind.* Just like she knew every version of her that whispered from behind each mirror. They couldn't hurt her.

They were part of her.

She was one of them.

Obsidian eyes glinted with triumph from inside the mirror cage. *'One pill is all you need.'* Dark-marble hands placed arrogantly on full hips. Legs wrapped in dark leath. *'Let me out. Use me.'*

Jantsia gazed at the woman. So similar to her, yet so different. Eyes burning like hot coals, hands reaching out with long nails painted the colour of midnight. A cruelly twisted mouth. A woman who knew what she wanted.

And Jantsia knew what she wanted.

She extended her hand towards the glass, heart skipping as her arm passed straight through as if the mirror's surface were made of water. Cold crept up her arm, travelling into her bloodstream and numbing each and every part of her. Chilling her to the bone.

When she opened her eyes, she didn't have to check them. From the rigid quality of her vision and the sound of her breaths in the air, she knew they were black. Finger hovering over the

Tile, Jantsia let her power ooze into its smooth surface. The display blinked twice before switching to dark mode.

The Tile had recognised her as Obsidian.

Then she opened the search bar and typed two words.

Varzesh Clause.

Later that day, Jantsia found herself with another conundrum: deciding on the correct outfit for the Gala. For one thing, it had to be blue. Colour-themed dressing was standard practice for elite events to ensure the easy distinction between workers and guests. In theory, she was attending as Zuleikha's assistant, so she had to dress the part.

Luckily, though she'd never worn them, expensive blue dresses filled her wardrobe, all of them gifts from her mother.

Up until recently, Jantsia would've refused to wear anything Maman had bought her, but something had changed. It ate her up inside that the moment they'd finally bonded was now drenched with hers and baba's lies.

Soiled with guilt.

What would Maman say if she knew about the plan?

But hopefully she never would. If everything went smoothly, Maman would never know of her and Baba's deceit. At least not until much later.

After hours of indecision, she decided upon a silk turquoise halter dress with delicate beading and transparent lace. When she spun in front of the mirror, she glittered, like light reflecting off the surface of a frozen lake. Maman had suggested it, telling her that it had been ordered from a Shizari tailor, an old man who still made clothes using the old Parsian techniques.

Jantsia twirled. 'What do you think, Luz?'

Luz chirruped and made to jump on her shoulder, but she raised a hand. She wouldn't issue a command – no living thing deserved to be treated like that – but she would make a request.

'Please, Luz. Not tonight. I can't have your fur all over this dress.'

Luz's wide golden eyes stared up at her in the betrayal and he scurried off to hide under the bed. He probably sensed her nerves and perceived the change darkening the air. The uncertainty of their future pulsed beneath them.

Jantsia's reflection was wholly different from the night she'd gone out with Flossie and Pixa. Her hair hung naturally; curls spruced up by a few sprays of her mother's essence of suavizant. Instead of plucking her brows and lightening her face tone, she'd accentuated it.

Golden face-shine shimmered on her cheekbones and black powder thickened her eyebrows.

'Everything packed? We're leaving in an hour. Don't forget anything,' her mother called.

Jantsia scanned her room. It was bare. Most of her belongings were already packed up and placed into the back of the pod. Whatever happened. Whatever she decided. This would be the last time she saw her room. The last evening she'd ever spend in Densolid.

She knelt down, careful not to tear the delicate hem of the dress.

Luz's ears flattened, tail close to the floor.

'We've got to go, Luz. I've set up a cat zone in the back of the pod. You'll be safe there. And I'll be back in no time for our next adventure.'

CHAPTER 32
GALA

JANTSIA

The Empire Hall was a beacon of light.

Inside the giant glass atrium, float-lights filled the air, bobbing up and down and gently cycling through colours. The stage was large and domineering, marked by two glass pillars, engraved with the symbol of Obsidian eyes.

Jantsia and Zuleikha watched the party unfold from the safety of a high-up box, metres above the melee of Obsidian high society. Their side of the atrium was filled with boxes and cubes, small floating rooms, decked out with chaise longues and plush armchairs. They served as seating areas for the audience and provided a perfect view of the stage.

Jantsia peered down at the stage with clenched fists. Metal eyes blinked down at them from the ceilings, red lights blinking at their centre. Cameras that would livestream the event to every Obsidian household in the Empire.

Below the stage, a dark-marbled floor heaved with the

Obsidian glitterati of Albin. They wore enormous fascinators, gold-enamelled dresses, and brightly coloured suits. The extroverted style of the VIPs contrasted almost comically with the sombre Inspectors who prowled the floor in formal uniforms, medals and epaulets marking which country they served. The aristocrats laughed and snaked their way around the central area, delicately nibbling on canapés and elegantly sipping tall glasses of smokewine and goldfizz.

What would her mother say if she knew about the plan? Jantsia's breaths quickened. If she didn't relax, Maman would realise something was up.

Zuleikha turned to Jantsia. 'Now, a quick warning, Beny had no choice about the outfits – *Elias chose them.*'

The scent of lavender perfume spread across the balcony, swirling inside Jantsia's stomach.

Twelve scantily clad Azures marched on to the stage, assembling in triangle formation. Among them, she spotted her baba. Pale, muscled bodies tumbled across the stage. Water droplets floated in the air, transforming into the shapes of dragonbees and flutterbies, reflecting rainbow patterns onto the black marble floor.

'I told you he was good,' Maman whispered, a small smile relaxing her usually pinched lips.

Jantsia's heart raced as several performers cartwheeled off to the wings, her father among them.

This was the moment.

The remaining performers conjured bubbles into the air, taking turns to move into the spotlight and perform their signature moves.

Jantsia chewed on her bottom lip, ruining her lipshade. 'Maman, did you say where the bathroom was?'

Not shifting her gaze from the stage, her mother replied, 'Hold on a bit longer, the finale sequence really is something to behold.'

Guilt wedged in Jantsia's throat. 'I can't wait. I'm desperate.'

Her mother waved a hand dismissively, lips tightening into a thin line. 'Well, hurry up, then, it's on the floor below, down the hall. But be quick. The performance will be over soon and I'll be escorted to the stage. I don't want to leave you here by yourself. It's crawling with Inspectors.'

Jantsia nodded weakly. Her back itched from the detail in the bodice and her shoes pinched her feet.

As she ducked out of the door, panic swirled in her stomach. If Daezen's plan had any chance of working out, she and Beny had to distract the Inspectors standing guard at the door to the Imperial terrace. If they didn't succeed in this, the team would get inside only to be confronted by a squad of heavily armed Inspectors.

Clunk. Clunk. Clunk.

Her stupid painful shoes announced her presence to everyone who cared to look. Trying to focus on the map of the Empire Hall she'd spent hours memorising, she repeated the steps to herself.

Up two floors. Down the hall. Through the double doors where there will likely be security. Baba will meet me there.

By the time she reached the double doors, she already knew what awaited her. Two voices echoed inside the room.

'But, Jenna, I don't understand what's so special about the Octengion Inspectorate's research facility, oculary science was born in Albin, after all; lest those savages forget.'

'Oh, get with the times, Babitut. The only reason we're so far behind is because of the Vox family's pride.'

Dread fell on Jantsia's chest like a ton of bricks. Where was her father?

Strong hands grasped her shoulders, spiking panic through her core.

She spun around.

'It's okay, Jantsy jaan. It's me.'

Relief washed through her at the sight of Beny. He'd changed out of the skimpy performance outfit and into his navy servant's suit.

He shot her a pained smile that didn't reach his eyes. 'You ready?'

She nodded, attempting to maintain a semblance of confidence, while her traitorous heart beat like a drum in her ears. 'Just another show, right? Another pretence. I've got this.'

He squeezed her hand. 'We've got this.'

With a final nod, they burst through the double doors.

Two Inspectors stood guard by the door to the terrace. A male Inspector with ruddy cheeks and a female Inspector with long red hair. The man met her gaze, lips curling down. 'What are you doing here? This room is off-limits to servants.'

She ignored him, letting her face screw up with rage. 'You see?' she shouted at her father. 'I told you this was the wrong room. Our Master Musika will kill us for this!'

Beny curled up his fists, face going red with feigned anger. 'What do you mean, you stupid girl? I told you we should go down another floor. None of this would even be happening if you'd remembered to pack her pre-performance supplies.'

The red-haired Inspector narrowed her eyes, paying full attention to their show.

Jantsia gritted her teeth and placed two hands on Beny's

chest, shoving him backwards. 'I'm still in training, Baba. You're the one who's supposed to be checking all my work!'

'Need some help over there, Babitut?' called the female Inspector with long red hair, her hand resting on the laser gun in her holster.

The ruddy-faced Inspector shook his hand. 'Stand down, they're only Azure servants having a squabble. I can handle it.'

The woman resumed her guard position, losing interest in the spectacle.

Sweat beaded on Jantsia's forehead. It wasn't working. They needed to distract all of the Inspectors to give the crew the best chance at breaking in. She locked eyes with her father and gave him a curt nod.

'Handle it?' Jantsia screamed, turning to Inspector Babitut. 'Handle it? So you're going to tell the Chief Inspector that the Gala performance was ruined because my stupid father forgot to bring our Master Musika her purified water and voice-cleansing tablets?'

'Don't you dare talk to an Inspector that way, insolent child,' Baba shouted, opening his palm wide before slapping Jantsia hard.

Her face stung from the blow. Adrenaline coursed through her, she took two steps back and collapsed at Inspector Babitut's feet.

'Get off me, whelp,' he said.

She rose to her feet and ran at Beny, pushing him so hard that he crashed into the long table in the middle of the room. It was covered in drinks and canapés for guests on their way to the terrace. Broken glass and mushed up food littered the floor.

'Oh, it sure looks like you have it handled,' the red-haired Inspector said, storming towards them. 'Help me clean this up,

Azures. You too, Babitut. The chief won't be pleased if someone important walks in and sees this chaos.' She shook her head, scowling at Jantsia. 'If you weren't the servants of that Rostamani Riviera bitch, I'd have your ears bleeding by now.'

Jantsia glanced at the door to the terrace. It was completely unguarded.

Her stomach writhed with nausea. Where were Daezen and his crew? This was their chance. If they didn't make it here soon, then everything they'd planned would be for nothing.

CHAPTER 33
SKYDIVE

DAEZEN

The deafening rush of the air and the biting swirl of icy wind dominated his senses. Daezen closed his eyes, ignoring the itch of the black-coloured lenses, and concentrated on visualising the plan. No time to be nervous, nor think of all the things that could go wrong. He patted his jacket, checking the light flare was safe inside.

That small square would be the key to their success.

'This is as low as I can drop her,' Glent shouted, his thick Sumavig accent making the words all blend together, or perhaps that was the jittering noise of the old pod engine.

An ex-pod pilot turned criminal, Topper had met Glent on one of his first jobs and said he owed the man his life. Since Beny had also vouched for the man, Daezen had been happy to involve Glent in the first stage of the mission. Breaking into the Empire Hall.

Blink pulled his goggles over his eyes, checking his watch.

'Okay, we're running slightly behind schedule. But now that Obsidian idiot has finished his smokestick and gone back inside, the coast is clear. Get ready everyone, we'll be jumping in five.'

The rusty door of the antique pod flapped on its hinges.

Daezen's stomach flipped as the vehicle dropped several feet then teetered left.

He caught Kain's eye, expecting to see his own fear reflected back at him, but all he saw was steely determination. At his side, Tala and Millie finished checking their packs and joined the rest of the team at the jump point.

Dressed in black leath jumpsuits, with black jump-packs and tinted goggles, they looked more like a team of Inspectors than a group of teenage rebel upstarts. Daezen allowed a small smile to creep onto his face. It had been smart of Jantsia to think of the lenses, hopefully it would help them avoid needless confrontation.

Topper slapped Glent on the back and whispered something in his ear.

'You'd better, young'un, or the Inspectors won't be the only ones on your tail,' Glent growled back.

'Ha-ha, Glent, I would rather stab myself seven times in each eyeball than double-cross a messed-up ocker like you,' Topper shouted. 'Let's go.'

Blink held up his hand, fingers splayed.

Daezen's grip tightened on the pack, grinding his teeth together and forcing himself to focus. No time to change the plan. No time to do more preparation. No time for anything. He couldn't let the poisonous doubts infect his mind. Not now.

Four.

He linked arms with Kain on his right and Blink on his left, squeezing Kain's arm twice.

Three.

They might splat on the roof of the terrace.

Two.

If he hadn't calculated the drop right, they'd be fried by the forcefield.

One.

A pull. A yank. A hastily whispered prayer lost to the wind.

And he was falling.

No, he was flying.

For a second, all his worries became insignificant, the details of the plan seemingly inconsequential. An overwhelming urge to let go of Kain's arm, to spin and look at the stars screamed in his mind.

Arms linked in formation, the team of five spun through the air. His stomach dropped, hands flailed in the wind, euphoria brightening his bones, burning through his flesh and tearing up his insides.

But they were getting closer. Closer. Closer.

They passed the shimmering edge of the forcefield. A flare of heat washed over his skin making it itch, but not causing any lasting damage. His heart soared, they'd made it through.

The ground rushed up to meet them.

He yanked down on the string from his pack, and a small black parachute exploded into the air. The others followed suit, never breaking formation.

He pulled his knees tight into his chest, bracing for impact.

The white stone of the terrace smacked into his knees. He rolled, rolled, rolled. Absorbing the impact, like they'd practised.

A quick scan around the roof. Millie was already on her feet, feline in her movements while Tala helped Blink stand. Kain was on his knees, a giant grin taking up most of his face. Daezen winced as he stood, a sharp spearing pain burned at his kneecap, but he couldn't worry about it now.

The first stage of the plan was completed. Now he had to hope Beny and Jantsia had distracted the Inspectors inside, or they'd be shot down with laser guns the moment they entered the building.

He hobbled into position behind one of the pillars, gesturing to the others to follow suit. Topper clinked two short swords together and bared his teeth, moving to the front of the formation, stance wide and low.

Daezen's heartbeat was in his temples. In his throat. In his guts. His eyes flicked to the door.

Topper crept forward, waving his hand to indicate they follow. Hands on their weapons, the team lined up behind him, before storming through the door.

CHAPTER 34
BETRAYAL

SOBA

As they crashed through the door, Soba took stock of the scene before her.

Inspector Babitut stood between Jantsia and Benyamin Brittle, who were screaming at one another. A scowl contoured Inspector Rutkitz's face as she cleaned broken glass from the floor.

Not wasting any time, Topper shot two throwing stars in the direction of the Inspectors. Inspector Rutkitz sidestepped, narrowly dodging one of them, but the other steely weapon hit Inspector Babitut square in the chest. He fell to his knees, hands shaking as he reached for his laser gun. Benyamin Brittle spun in the air landing a roundhouse kick to Babitut's head before he could charge his weapon.

Soba's heart raced.

Jantsia and Benyamin Brittle were working with the rebels.

She struggled to maintain her cool composure, as

adrenaline pumped through her body, mind moving at a hundred miles per hour.

Bright pink spots speckling her cheeks, and opal eyes obscured by the illicit black contact lenses, Tala raced towards Inspector Rutkitz, itak-blade held high. Seeing her like this pulled on strings buried deep in Soba's heart. If only this weren't all pretend. If only this game wasn't destined to a gory, bloody end.

Luckily Soba had let the Azuserum fade from her system before the mission, making excuses to avoid Tala's notice. Otherwise, she would've feared taking on the rebels at this moment. Though she knew her oculary gave her an unbeatable advantage, she still didn't want to hurt Tala. Neither her body nor her heart. And yet, she would do more than hurt her.

By following through with Elias's plan, she wouldn't just be breaking Tala's heart, she'd be signing her death warrant. Could she do that?

Would she really be capable of watching Tala die?

A cramp spasmed in her chest as Tala called to her. 'Back me up, Mils!'

Soba didn't respond, instead she fell inwards, twisting the soundwaves in the air until they formed a sonar charge.

Time slowed as Tala dived at Inspector Rutkitz, blade angled for a killing blow.

Soba let the sonar strike fly.

Tala's body slumped and hit the ground, blade clattering to the floor. Soba spun, shooting off another enormous wave of sound that knocked Topper, Blink, Kain and Daezen to their knees. Blood dripped from their eyes as they screamed.

Inspector Rutkitz's chest heaved up and down as she charged her laser gun, pointing it at Benyamin Brittle's chest.

She cast Soba a disdainful glance, fear glinting in her dark eyes. 'That was a bit too close for comfort, Bloodbat. What's going on? Why are Obsidians attacking us?'

'They're Azures, Jenna. They're wearing coloured contacts. They'll disintegrate soon enough.'

Before the rebels could regain consciousness, Soba and Inspector Rutkitz bound the rebels' hands and relieved them of their weapons.

'That one's got a light flare in his jacket,' Soba said, pointing at Daezen.

Rutkitz nodded, retrieving the flare. 'Is Babitut all right?'

Soba checked for the junior Inspector's pulse. 'Out cold.'

'Is this one a threat?' Rutkitz jabbed her laser gun in Jantsia Brittle's direction. The Azure girl rocked back and forth, hands clasped around her knees, her turquoise dress ripped at the edges.

'No,' Soba said, not certain this was true, but not wanting more blood on her hands.

'Good,' Rutkitz replied before smacking Benyamin Brittle over the head with the end of her laser gun and knocking him to the ground.

Jantsia let out a pained cry, tears flowing from her red eyes.

'Well, that was unnecessary,' Soba said. 'Come on, round them up, Elias is waiting for us in the VIP room.'

Tala was the first to stir. Without realising, Soba must've gone easier on her, pulling back on the strength of the sonar strike at the last minute.

She took it all in. Soba's glowing coals for eyes. Her own bound hands.

A dark and heavy mist descended upon Soba as she met Tala's gaze. Burning anger seared through the opal windows to her soul. That hateful gaze smothered her, it drowned her. Soba's breaths tripped over one another, unable to keep pace with her lungs.

'I'm not who you think I am,' Soba said quietly.

'No ocking shit,' Tala shot back. 'You're one of them, aren't you?'

'My name is Inspector Soba Nite,'

'How did you fake it? How could you do this?' Tala screamed, baring her teeth. 'You're a lying demon whore!'

'Shut up, Azure,' Rutkitz spat, kicking Tala in the side.

A spike of nausea had Soba retching. Her throat burned with phantom acid and twinges of sharp pain twisted between her ribs.

She fought the urge to apologise. To reach for Tala and caress her bloodied cheek. Instead, she knelt at her side, heart splintering into fragments of black ice as she bound her legs. 'Tala, I can explain—'

Tala's eyes shot open. 'Get away from me!' she shrieked. 'Don't look at me! Kill me if you must but spare me the sight of those evil eyes.'

'Tala, please. I ... I—'

Tala roared, straining at her bindings, then easing off. She raised her chin and laughed bitterly. 'If I survive this, the next time we meet, *Inspector Soba Nite*, it will be with my blade at your throat.' She spat out blood, fixing Soba in her sights. Eyes dull and empty. The wings of her soul had burned to ashes, and it was all Soba's fault. 'I will bathe in your blood you black-eyed demon!'

She would not let tears fall from her traitorous eyes. 'Tala, if you calm down, I won't have to hurt you.'

'Hurt me?' Tala cackled. 'Now imagine such a thing. Well,

I'm sorry to disappoint you, Inspector Soba Nite, but I'm not going to go easy.'

A heavy weight settled on Soba's chest, pouring liquid lead into her blood. With a twist of her fingers, she spun a screech-note out of the air and shot it towards Tala. Towards her own broken soul.

Tala writhed in agony as blood dripped from her ears, her nose, her eyes.

Tala's pain was her pain.

Tala's blood was her blood.

Soon enough, she stopped struggling and lay limp on the ground.

Soba checked her pulse. Faint but still there.

Is any of this real?

She went through the motions like a robot, unfeeling and dead inside as she unfolded her Tile to call Elias.

'It's done,' she said, careful not to let any emotion into her words. As long as she didn't look at Tala's limp body on the floor, at her bleeding head, then she was fine. This was fine. 'We're bringing them in. The Brittles were working with the rebels.'

Elias's soft voice echoed through the Tile. 'Good work. I have to say I'm glad to know we don't have an Obsidian traitor on our hands. *Be swift.*'

Ignoring the shadow monster swallowing her soul, Soba and Rutkitz roused the Azures, tying them together and directing them towards the door. Without letting her gaze stay on Tala for too long, she hauled her body over her shoulder.

'What have you done, Millie?' Blink croaked as he was ushered past her.

Kain's eyes bled red, his face contorted in agony.

'How could you?' His gaze shot to Jantsia Brittle, who swayed unsteadily on her feet.

Rutkitz heaved Benyamin Brittle over her shoulder with a groan. 'Let's go.'

Only Daezen didn't react, remaining preternaturally still from the moment he awoke. Blood streamed from his nostrils, but his expression was a mask of stone.

Never mind him, Soba thought. *There's nothing he can do now.*

She'd done it. She'd earned Elias's approval and successfully caught two traitors with access to the Albin Obsidian inner circle.

So why did she feel like she'd carved out her own heart?

CHAPTER 35
VORTEX

DAEZEN

Panic punched Daezen in the gut.

Millie Kuti – or whatever her real name was – had delivered them to the VIP box, where a smarmy-looking, golden-haired Inspector loomed over them, smiling like a weld-wolf at the butcher's. Behind him, surrounded by guards, were none other than Dr Popoola and Zentich Quispe.

A set up.

An ambush.

'Very good work, Inspector Nite,' the smarmy Inspector said in a dark voice infused with malice. 'Very, very good work.'

Fiddling with the lapels of his bright white suit, Dr Popoola whispered something to Zentich, before raising his voice. 'Chief Inspector Vox, you've proved your point. May Mr Quispe and I leave? You can be sure we will share this with our superiors. The Laminos and Octengion Inspectorates are in your debt.'

'Not quite yet, Dr Popoola. I have some very specific

requests of yourself and Mr Quispe.' The Chief Inspector said, raising a hand.

The guards tightened the circle around Zentich Quispe and Dr Popoola.

Zentich's eyes darted back and forth, assessing Daezen and his crew with interest. *'Está bien,'* he said. 'I would like to know more about these people. I will hear your request, Elias. All I ask is for a few minutes with that one.' He pointed in Topper's direction. 'He is *the* Topper Luxo, no?'

Topper grinned, revealing bloody gums. 'The one and only.'

Elias turned around and began conversing with Zentich in a low voice.

Daezen gritted his teeth, assessing the severity of the situation. They were lined up on their knees, every single one of his crew bound and bloodied. Locked in a large room encased in crystal with only one way out. The door was guarded by the red-haired Inspector and Millie, the traitor.

They had no weapons and no escape plan. Beyond the crystal walls, the party continued in full swing. Obsidian guests fawned over one another, with their ridiculous, expensive outfits and overpriced drinks, completely unaware of what was occurring above them.

Blink spat blood, yelling curses at the Inspectors, while Topper remained uncharacteristically quiet, feline eyes darting around the room. Like Daezen, he was probably trying to work out a way to escape. Tala's head hung low, her eyes haunted as if someone had sucked her soul from her body. On his left, Kain was as white as snow, mouth agape as he stared in Jantsia's direction.

Jantsia.

In spite of everything, she looked beautiful. Thick curls piled high atop her head, her lovely halter-neck turquoise dress emphasising her wide shoulders and accentuating her angular collarbones and pale golden skin.

Slowly, she raised her head. 'Baba,' she croaked, 'we need to—'

'Not now, Jantsia,' Beny whispered. Other than Topper, he was the only one who'd kept his cool, but he wasn't fooling Daezen.

Things were most definitely not under control.

A commotion came from behind the door and Zuleikha Riviera Rostamani swept in past the Inspectors in a swish of purple silk.

'Elias,' she said, 'would you kindly tell me what is going on? What are you doing with my servants? I've been looking everywhere for them. I can't be expected to perform without my supplies.' She paused, locking eyes with Dr Popoola. 'Alhaadi,' she said, 'what are you doing here?'

'Ah, Zuleikha,' Elias drawled. 'How kind of you to join us. Inspector Soba Nite has been on a very important mission. One that concerns your servants. Not only has she tested the latest invention given to us by Dr Popoola, but she has also managed to foil a terrorist plot.' Elias turned to Millie – no, *Inspector Soba Nite*. 'Would you enlighten our prestigious guest, Inspector?'

Millie, or Soba, or whoever the ock she was, smiled tightly, Obsidian eyes opaque and unreadable. *Unforgiving black eyes ringed with white.* He'd been a fool to think contact lenses could have that effect. She withdrew a vial of bright blue serum from her jacket, holding it high for everyone to see.

Zuleikha gasped, a strange expression flickered on her face.

Soba spoke mechanically, eyes focused on some distant point of the room. 'This is Azuserum. I was the first Albin

Inspector to try it. It allowed me to masquerade as an Azure, changing my eye colour and even bestowing upon me minimal water-wielding oculary control. I passed retina scans and infiltrated a terrorist group, uncovering a plot to kidnap the Empire's most valued scientists. I regret to inform you that your servants were collaborating with these rebels.'

'No,' Kain breathed.

Blood pounded in Daezen's temples, panic warring against reason. He had to think of a way out. Think of the plan.

But how could he think straight when he'd led Jantsia and his own brother to their deaths?

Of all the plans he'd put into place, Millie being an Inspector hadn't been one of them. He cursed his short-sightedness. His arrogance. The chatrang board in his mind upended, knocking all his players to the floor.

Zuleikha's eyes widened, her lips pressed together in a thin line. 'There must be some mistake.'

Beny raised his chin, unwavering. 'It's true, Master Musika, I am what he says. But Jantsia had nothing to do with any of this. Let her go.' Despite the circumstances, his voice was steady, the only indication of his nerves was a slight tick in his jaw. Daezen would be like him. He would not cave. He would not panic.

He would get them out of here.

As if hit head-on by a sonar bullet, Zuleikha's spine went concave. Though she recovered quickly, Daezen didn't miss her panicked glance in Jantsia's direction.

'So be it,' Zuleikha said, a queen of ice. 'You can take my manservant, but give me the girl.'

Elias grinned, eyes gleaming with violent intent. 'I don't think so. My Inspector insists that the girl was part of the plan, and I'm inclined to agree.' He walked over to Soba and gripped her by the waist. 'Hasn't my Soba done such wonderful work? All in honour of keeping the Empire safe.' He turned to Daezen and his crew. 'I think this deserves a round of applause. *Applaud Inspector Soba Nite, now.*'

His words hung in the air, impossible to ignore or deny.

Daezen's hands moved back and forth, slamming against each other robotically. He hadn't wanted to do that, had he?

'Millie, what are you doing?' Kain pleaded. 'Stop this. Stop this, now. You know us.'

Millie Kuti might know them, but Millie Kuti didn't exist. Daezen could see it now. Inspector Soba Nite cared little for him or his brother. Her dark gaze sent abject fear tingling down his spine, as unforgiving as the arctic wind.

Zuleikha's musical tone filled the room without needing to raise her voice. 'I do not appreciate the theatrics, Elias. If you do not give me back the girl, I will be forced to find Director Greta Vox and demand your dismissal.' There was something strangely familiar about her. The way she spoke, her wide-set eyes, they reminded him of—

Elias smirked. 'Go ahead, she's aware of this plan. I've kept her abreast of every detail. In fact, I believe she would like to bring you in for questioning. Shall we fetch her, she's only round the corner?' He indicated the balcony next to them where a hardened woman with a scar on her face surveyed the crowd.

The light dimmed, clotting the air and transporting Daezen into a nightmare-scape. The Inspectors knew every detail of their plan. He was trapped in a room full of Obsidians, and with no clear way out.

They were going to die.

The moment despair crossed Daezen's face, Elias gave a guttural laugh.

A cool, calm voice echoed in his head.

Don't freeze up, now. You may not have prepared for this exact scenario, but your mind and your oculary will help you escape. Stay calm.

He closed his eyes, bringing the mental image of the chatrang board back into focus, carefully returning the pieces to their squares, playing out moves and judging their current situation.

They were trapped, but it wasn't a checkmate.

There was still one move, a play, that the Inspector didn't know about.

I have to be the water.

He caught Beny's eye.

'Now!' Daezen shouted. Falling into second sight, he focused on his bindings, willing the moisture within them to cool and freeze. Ice burned through those around his feet and hands, with a howl, he tore himself free.

Beny broke free a second after Daezen, and with a jerk of his hands, he called all the liquid in the room towards him. Pools of spilt drinks formed a hovering bubble and the air grew dry. The bubble stretched into streams of liquid that swirled around them, encompassing the crew with a vortex.

'Don't let them get away,' Elias boomed.

Weakened sonar attacks grazed Daezen's skin, fractured by the wall of water that encompassed them. Daezen took advantage of chaos to free the rest of his crew from their bindings. Topper grinned, eyes alight with a fervour Daezen didn't understand. Then he reached down to his boot and withdrew a sharp knife.

'Let's get out of here, team,' Blink shouted. 'Can you hold the vortex while we dash to the door?'

'I could do with a little help,' Beny said in a strained voice.

The vortex roared around them.

Daezen nodded, refusing to let fear rise into his thoughts, letting his gaze fall inwards. The twirling vortex expanded in front of his eyes, becoming a stream of interlocking particles, wrapped in a swirl of blue light. A tendril of power extended from Beny's chest. And somehow, Daezen knew that this was his oculary signature. The energy came from his soul.

Reaching out to trace a finger through the blue light, he felt Beny's fearlessness, his resolve, his love for his daughter.

Beny hadn't commanded the water to move this way.

He was the water.

Now, Daezen had to do the same.

Sinking further inside himself, his perspective flipped, and he threw his oculary power into the particle rush. He spun round and round and round, fuelling the vortex. Being the water.

From this new viewpoint, Daezen saw the Inspectors readying their sonar shields and charging their laser guns, but Zuleikha hung back, eyes wild as she searched the room for something – or someone. Dr Popoola cowered in the corner while Zentich placed his hands on the crystal glass wall where ice was spreading like a web.

Benyamin's energy tore parts of Daezen away, freezing the wall and moulding a spray of liquid into daggers of ice. They sliced through the air and crashed down at the Inspectors' feet. Elias spat blood onto the floor, then took a step back, indicating his minions do the same.

One of the Inspectors didn't heed Elias's command and took another step closer to the vortex. A ball of ice slammed into his head, knocking him to the ground. Cracks appeared on the glass walls. It was working. They were going to smash their way out of here.

'I can't keep this up much longer, Zuli. I'm going to need your help,' Benyamin called over the rush of the water.

As he spun and spun, Daezen caught sight of Kain slipping through the wall of water.

'The scientist and the hacker are here!' Kain cried. 'We have to get them, or this will all have been for nothing. He made a mad dash towards Dr Popoola and Zentich while Daezen and Beny shifted the vortex so he could get past.

At the last minute, Elias turned his attention away from the vortex and towards Kain. The glass wall splintered further, cracks deepening.

'No!' Daezen howled, dropping to his knees as large beads of blood leaked from his eyes. He crashed back into his body, becoming aware of a dull ache that throbbed behind his eyes. The vortex halted, so he pushed himself back into the water, leaving his body once more. But his strength was waning.

The Inspector had Kain in his filthy hands. Nausea overtook him.

'Beny ... I'm losing it,' he said through gritted teeth.

His body sucked him back in for the final time, slamming his vision back into two bleeding human eyes.

'Run!' Beny shouted.

The vortex crashed to the ground at the same time as the glass walls of the box shattered into pieces.

CHAPTER 36
LIGHT

JANTSIA

Ear-splitting screams sliced through Jantsia's already shattered heart as the whole Empire Hall erupted into chaos.

Her mother grabbed her and started dragging her towards the door. 'Come on,' Zuleikha said, 'let's get out of here while they're distracted.'

Tala and Blink were already sprinting to the edge of the box, getting ready to jump, while Topper bared his teeth, jabbing his knife at one Inspector while kicking out at another. Beny wasn't far behind, shooting daggers of ice through the air at Elias, trying to give Kain a chance to escape. Daezen froze the boots of their aggressors, stopping them from advancing. Golden light filled Jantsia's chest, driving her onwards. Even as blood streamed from Daezen's nose like a red waterfall, he wasn't giving up.

And neither could she.

'Stop this nonsense, if you want the boy to live,' Elias drawled, one hand tight around Kain's neck while the other flicked a small blade across his fingers. 'You are all going to pay for causing such a scene.'

Jantsia's eyes settled on Elias. The man who'd invaded her home. The man who'd humiliated her mother, condemned her father, and put her friends in danger. He held Kain tightly, the way you would a lover, but there was nothing loving about his tight-knuckled grip and sadistic smile.

Show him who you are.

'Release him, demon,' Daezen howled.

All across the hall, guests made for the exit while Inspectors gathered together, approaching the shattered box with glowing black eyes.

Jantsia's breath caught in her throat. Her mother intensified her grip. 'Jantsia we must leave, now.'

But Kain's life hung in the balance.

Her heart hardened, rage slithering like a serpent, coiling up as it prepared to strike.

The sounds of laser guns charging. The air rippled with sonar waves.

Jantsia's gorge rose.

She broke out in sweats.

She couldn't let this happen.

And she had the power to stop it.

To stop it all.

'Don't you dare!' Jantsia shouted, breaking free of her mother's grip to join the fight.

Cold black eyes focused on her.

Topper withdrew another knife from his boot and shot it forward with brutal accuracy. The revolving weapon caught the light, spinning towards Elias. The Inspector stepped to the side, narrowly avoiding the steely flight of the weapon, and bringing his own blade flush to Kain's throat.

Time slowed, wrapping around Jantsia like a vice. Voices echoed at the edge of her awareness. From behind the mirrors, a thousand versions of her called out in unison.

Set us free.

Déjanos libres.

Āzādemun kon.

Set us free.

Jantsia's stomach cramped, dark stars dancing across her vision.

'If the boy dies, you're next, you tarry filth. I'll make it long and slow.'

'You can break out of this, Kain. Fight it!'

'Elias, you told me you had it all under control!'

'Jantsia, we must run.'

She could stop this.

She could stop it all.

Her consciousness fell inwards, and the chaotic scene before her faded away, shifting to a familiar hall of endless mirrors. The floor cushioned her descent, wrapping her in a shiny shroud that warmed her from the inside. At the far end of the never-ending hall, a single mirror glowed as brightly as the sun.

Even if letting her power free was going to kill her.

Even if this place was nothing but a hallucination borne of the rapidly advancing blood sickness.

Even if this was the end.

She wouldn't let Kain die.

She wouldn't let any of them die.

Jantsia broke into a sprint, buoyed along by the bouncy

surface at her feet, and flew down the hallway. She passed the Obsidian Jantsia, the Azure Jantsia, thousands of versions of herself wearing an array of Laminosian, Parsian and Albin clothing.

But they weren't really different versions of her, were they?

Each and every girl trapped inside the mirror *was* her.

The real Jantsia couldn't be encapsulated by any single one of them.

The real Jantsia was anything but ordinary. And it was time to accept that. Because ordinary wouldn't save her family and friends.

Ordinary wouldn't change the world.

She continued chasing the light, head pounding as she neared it.

The glowing mirror shone so brightly it seared an image into the back of her eyes.

'I set you free,' she screamed, blindly reaching forwards, letting the glass of the mirror dissolve in her hands. 'I set us all free.'

All along the endless hall, mirrors cracked, smashed, exploded.

At her very core, a thousand voices merged into one.

She'd spent so many years protecting herself, protecting her secret, protecting a lie. And without realising, she'd cut parts of herself away, little by little, trying to shape herself into someone else. Someone the world wanted her to be. The parts she didn't want to be there flashed through her mind; the parts that brought her shame.

No more.

She raised her voice over the chaos, knowing that the others would hear her, even here, trapped inside her mind. More mirrors cracked, bleeding light into the ever-growing ball of power in her chest. 'My name is Jantsia Riviera Rostamani Brittle and by order of the Great Elites, I call on you to stand down.'

Her body rippled with power. Her eyes burned in their sockets.

This was it.

She snapped back to the Gala, back to her body. The fighting had stopped. All eyes fell upon her.

Her limbs vibrated.

The blood sickness was taking hold.

She'd run out of time.

A crushing pressure built in the front of her head.

She took a deep breath, filling her lungs for what might be the last time. 'I call upon the Great Elites to activate the Varzesh Clause. I call upon the Council to confirm the validity of my request. I am Jantsia, daughter of Zuleikha Riviera Rostamani, former heir to the Rostamani and Riviera Great Elites of Parsia and Laminos. I will bleed so others can live.'

The earth shook as if the very foundations of the city had heard her request.

Voices and images faded further into the background until the knife pressed against Kain's neck was the only thing that existed. The sharp edge of the blade slipped nearer to Kain's exposed throat.

A white-hot thread of light sliced through Jantsia's mind as the final parts of her broke free of their mirror cages, joining the ball of light at her centre. The air around her burst into life. Particles swarmed her vision, consuming every single space. Her consciousness split into a million different fragments surging through the hall. Every fibre of her being lit up like a flare.

Shattering, heating, exploding, destroying, unmaking, exposing.

A silver sun was summoned from the sky, breaking through the night to envelop the entire Empire Hall, covering the approaching Inspectors and the remaining panicking guests in fiery light.

The knife clattered to the floor.

Jantsia's heart rattled in her chest, straining under the weight of her body. Her blood.

Through the dizzying spin of particles, she saw Kain's chest rise and fall.

Another surge of power coursed through her body.

The crystal walls cracked, splintering all the way down. Screams filled the air as the domed ceiling of the atrium exploded into a shower of glass, and a horde of shadowbirds dived into the hall, raining down on the guests in a nightmare of talons and flapping wings. Somewhere far in the distance, she thought she could hear Luz yowling.

The creatures of Shariza had heard her call.

For the Varzesh Clause was not simply one enshrined in law, it was a protective measure written in blood. In the spirit of the forefathers, of Shariza Farzhad, of Fladden Scope, of Artium Jansen. The cores of power situated across the Empire would always recognise the call for Varzesh.

Another wave of power erupted inside her, launching her high into the air. Silver light streamed from her eyes as she took flight, pouring all her anger, her rage, her frustration out through the particles around her.

Power burned up inside her. If this was the end, it was going to be a spectacular one. Let these Obsidians see what should really scare them about dual-ocs. What should really scare them about the blood sickness. It had given her the power to do this.

She swirled higher. In the periphery of her vision, Daezen ducked and pulled Kain from Elias's grip. She pushed more energy into the network of veins in the ground and the force-field around the hall blinked and disappeared. She caught Daezen staring up at her as if she were an angel, silver light reflecting back at her from his eyes. But Jantsia only had eyes for one face. A beautiful, pale, delicate face. A crestfallen face, wracked with betrayal and hurt. Hurt so razor-sharp it cut with jagged edges. The face of her best friend.

Her light faltered. Her stomach cramped. And she spiralled down and down. Nothing could stop her. Not even the earth.

She hoped she'd done enough.

She hoped she'd freed her friends.

And with all her heart, she hoped that Kain would find it in his heart to forgive her.

But as she fell back to the ground, not even the solidity of the floor could save her. She'd pushed things too far.

And she didn't have any way of halting the blood sickness now.

She was done for.

A supernova consumed every part of her, every mirror, every self and immersed her in a cold, empty darkness.

CHAPTER 37
VARZESH

SOBA

Light burned through Soba's core, shedding her skin and transporting her to another time. Another life.

The silver supernova had smashed her crystal belief system, pounding the shattered pieces of everything she thought she knew into a palmful of sand. She reached out to touch the line of dark light that shed, layer after layer, from her being. A rush of emotions, emotions not her own, crashed through her soul. Power-hungry lust. An unshakeable sense of superiority. An insatiable hunger for violence.

Elias's persuasive, oculary energy dripped from every inch of Soba's body. Like sickly honey washed away with water, heavy tendrils of his power were stripped from her heart. From her mind. Oculary power that was not her own was blasted from the fibre of her being. Oculary power that belonged to Elias.

The truth choked her.

She'd been drowning in a pool of Elias's persuasion power for so long she'd never even noticed it shackling her mind. He'd used his oculary speciality to keep her in line, to make her think he was someone she could love, to make her subjugate herself to him. Persuasion power wasn't supposed to last long, but something inside her, inside Inspector Soba Nite, had wanted to believe his lies. She'd *wanted* to love him.

She'd wanted him to wash away her secrets.

But secrets were open wounds. The longer they were left to fester, the more likely they'd become infected. Until one day, untreated for so long, the scabs rotted. The damage untreatable without cutting away chunks of flesh to stop the infection spreading.

She remembered.

She remembered the parts of herself she'd cut away.

She remembered what it meant to be Lola.

The dead roots of her past sprung to life.

Her Obsidian mother had fallen in love with a Sepia man, a man who wasn't her father. To flee the rage of the Sàlàkọ́ Great Elites, they'd moved far out to the desert to live in peace. Then her mother had given birth to a dual-oc baby. A baby Lola had thought would die before adolescence.

But that wasn't true, was it?

Jantsia was a dual-oc and she was alive.

That meant her dual-oc sister, Tiwa, who was taken and killed by the Inspectors, could have lived.

Blood pulsed in Soba's ears, and her stomach writhed and twisted as if filled with maggots.

She blinked past the searing light burning into her eyelids to take stock of her surroundings. Inspectors and guests lay strewn across the room, some of them were wounded, all of them blinking rapidly, trying to restore their sight. Shattered glass boxes coated the marble floor of the hall. Amongst it all, she spied Tala, every inch of her body emanating fiery hatred. A mess of emotions wound up so tightly within Soba that she felt she might break apart entirely.

'The forcefield's down,' Daezen shouted, 'Topper, call the hoverbikes.'

In a heap of rubble and shattered glass, Zuleikha held Jantsia to her chest. 'Beny, go with the rebels, I'll look after Jantsia.'

Inspector Soba Nite owed nothing to Zuleikha. Nothing to the girl. Her only allegiance was to Elias.

But she wasn't Inspector Soba Nite.

Perhaps she never had been.

It's time to look back.

Time to answer the call.

Soba issued a silent anguished cry, drowning in the depths of everything she'd lost as a result of this baseless lie. The lie that Jantsia Rostamani Riviera Brittle disproved simply by existing.

At the edge of her awareness, three riderless hoverbikes descended through the gaping hole in the atrium. Blink and Tala leapt onto a bike and zoomed off into the distance. Topper, Daezen and Kain mounted the second hoverbike, following close behind them. Sonar strikes clapped in the air and laser guns shot in their direction, but it was too late. They were gone.

Kohl dripped from Zuleikha's wild eyes, mixing with face-shine and tears. Her previously coiffed wavy hair was plastered to her scalp. 'Beny,' she howled, 'save yourself, I can't protect you both.'

Zentich Quispe approached Beny, wobbly on his feet, and

whispered something into his ear. Beny's face steeled as he mounted the final bike, helping Zentich up behind him. 'I'll find you,' he said, before taking off into the air and disappearing through the shattered dome of the hall and into the night sky.

Rage spun a protective barrier around her heart, as Soba raised her voice. 'As the former heir of the Sàlàkọ́ Great Elites of Octengion I recognise the call from the Rostamani Rivieras and request safe passage to inform the Imperial council. I will bleed so others can live.'

A crack opened up in the marble floor of the Empire Hall, swallowing up many of the guests and Inspectors that hadn't already fled to safety.

Zuleikha shared a look with Soba, zeroing in on the white rings of her eyes – recognising the truth in her words. 'I recognise you, *Lola Sàlàkọ́*. Varzesh has been called,' she said.

Exhaustion clouded her vision and she dropped to her knees. No longer Soba Nite, but Lola Sàlàkọ́ once more. An eerie silence descended upon the ruins of the Empire Hall, as the screams dissolved into broken whimpers and murmurs. The shadowbirds amassed around Zuleikha, forming a protective circle.

It was done.

The call for Varzesh would spread, reaching to the ends of the Empire.

Lola took a deep breath, her first real breath in years. Then a cold, dark voice cut through the peace.

'The rebels might've escaped, but I still have you in my grasp. You stupid insolent bitch. I would've made you my bride. I would've made you my queen.'

Lola jerked her head up to see Elias advancing on her.

His knees shook and by the way he was blinking his eyes, he still couldn't see properly.

'Enough,' boomed Director Greta Vox, hobbling through the wreckage. 'You will hold fire, nephew. The Varzesh Clause has been called and these women are protected by law. They must participate in the trials, or we will all perish.' She cast an irritated look at the flock of shadowbirds, unmoving and unblinking.

Elias pointed a blade at Zuleikha. 'What about her? She's fair game, isn't she?'

'I will serve as my daughter's mentor,' Zuleikha said hurriedly, holding Jantsia's limp body close to her. 'So keep your paws off me.'

Director Greta squinted, trying to see past the light seared into her mind to survey the wreckage, an abyss had opened up in the centre of the Empire Hall and the remainder of the floor was covered in broken glass and blood. Survivors clung to one another, extravagant dresses ripped into pieces and faces smeared red.

'What a mess,' Director Greta said. 'Elias, you'll be on clean-up for this one. Now, as much as it pains me, it is my duty to the Empire to see the contestants are kept safe. We must begin preparation for the Trials.'

Lola laughed at the absurdity of it all, and the sight of Elias's horrified, bleeding face only made her laugh harder.

Her skin pulsed and vibrated in the biting cold of the night air.

Inspector Soba Nite had died tonight, and with her death Lola Sàlàkọ́ was free.

EPILOGUE

The mirrors were melting.

Broken shards of melting glass pooled at Jantsia's feet, forming a puddle of liquid silver that spread across the vast emptiness, until the place where the hall of mirrors had once been was filled by an expansive silver sea.

Somehow, she didn't sink. She didn't drown.

She walked.

Each step triggered ripples across the silver sea, emitting melancholic notes and harmonic chords. An overwhelming sense of peace emanated from her core.

She wondered if this strange world of water was the afterlife. Lilting music cast light on the soft waves. If this was death, she would accept it. She only wished she could know if her friends and family were safe. If she'd done enough to help them...

A strange, rough sensation in the crook of her elbow. It almost felt like Luz was licking her but that couldn't be real, could it?

Then the silver sea faded away, taking the sense of peace and tranquillity with it.

∽

Light bled through the heavy curtains, and a purring ball of fluff warmed Jantsia's side. She blinked her eyes open, surprised to see Maman hunched on an armchair at her bedside, snoring softly.

Something was off.

The divots of the mattress weren't the same as in her bed, and the placement of the room was unfamiliar.

Luz chirruped and licked her face, his golden eyes gleaming. For a second, she lost herself in his gaze, assaulted by a deep sense of understanding. Not thoughts or language exactly, but something deeper. Memories hurtled back, slamming into her mind.

'Maman,' she whispered.

Her mother didn't stir.

'Maman,' Jantsia said again, louder this time.

'I'm awake,' Zuleikha replied, only opening one eye.

Fear filled her mind. 'Where's Baba? And Kain? And Daezen? Are they okay? Where are we?'

Luz yowled, echoing how Jantsia felt inside.

'That's a lot of questions, love,' her mother said. 'Baba, the Trovit boys and their friends all escaped safely. We're in Albin City under the protection of Director Vox.'

Jantsia's skin grew clammy. 'What? Why would she want to protect us?'

Maman massaged her temples. 'Your call for Varzesh was recognised by the power core of Densolid. Everything has changed now. The Varzesh Clause is in play. Once the Council has met to set terms, the Trials will begin. And you will be one of the participants.'

The Trials.

Something was wrong with her vision, everything looked ... brighter, more vibrant. The added detail and heightened colours made it difficult to interpret what she saw. 'That thing that happened in the Empire Hall... Why am I still alive? What about the blood sickness?' Jantsia's voice faltered.

'I don't think you were ever sick, Jantsia. I think we were lied to,' Maman said, a quiver in her voice the only indication of her exhaustion.

The words sank into Jantsia's skin. 'Lied to? My eyes aren't blue, are they?'

Maman's hand stretched out to grasp her shoulder. 'No, *miha.*'

'What colour are they? Are they black? Am I Obsidian?'

'No, *miha.*' This time she could hear the crack in her mother's voice.

'Well, surely I'm not Sepia... Or Veridian... My eyes aren't brown or green, are they?'

Her mother cleared her throat again. 'No.' A bloodied tear rolled down her cheek, red mixing with black. 'Ask me the question, Jantsia.'

Jantsia bit her bottom lip, running a hand through Luz's fur.

'What colour are my eyes?' She paused, letting the question float in the air. Then she asked what she really wanted to know. 'What am I?'

ACKNOWLEDGMENTS

I always thought of writing as a solitary activity, but the process of writing and publishing *The Girl with the Fierce Eyes* has taught me that the opposite is true. Without the support and influence of my parents, this book would never have been possible. I owe my love of reading and poetry to my dad who read me Greek myths and classics (with his own safe-for-kids edits) from a young age, and who gave me a book of T.S. Eliot's poetry when he saw me start to struggle through adolescence. To my mum, who has always been there to advise, listen, and support me through my bouts of madness, and who is one of the kindest and most compassionate people I have ever met. And, of course, my brother, whose unwavering confidence in my abilities and incredible pep talks made all the difference when I felt like giving up. To my husband, who not only supported me financially and emotionally through many writing freakouts, but who also thought up the incredible tagline 'Your eyes decide your destiny'; thank you for being there with me on this journey and believing in my story when I couldn't.

I am blessed with an extensive, vibrant, characterful family. Maman, whose strength and resilience inspires me every day. Baba, whose love of life and joyful laughter live on in me and all the people who knew him. To Grandad and Cath, I'm immensely pleased that I made you both proud by writing this. To Nanny, a fierce force of nature and probably the person whose reading taste is most similar to mine, thank you for being an inspiration to women everywhere. To my aunties and uncles; Mehdi, Emma, James, Joe, Amy, Mitra, Marmar, Kate, Alan, Ben, thank you for being there for me from my precocious beginning to my highly strung present self. And, of course, to my pack of cousins, of which I still claim the right to be the chieftain, Izzy, Sam, Katrina, Jamie, Gabriella, Rhys, Sonny, Buddy, Willow, Sadie and Sam.

Alas, I'm one of those incredibly lucky people who has as much of a found family as a blood-related family. Lulu, Rachel, Alexandra, Hannah, Caro, Sharoll, Leo, Alex, Sammy, the Annas, thank you for sticking with me through thick and thin. To Pav and Clinto, new friends that have been wholeheartedly behind me in this wild publishing ride. To my new family, Norelkis, Felipe, Luis, Dani, Maria-José, Vero, Ale, Gabriela, Sara, Edicson, and the indomitable Carmen, you have welcomed me in as if I were one of your own.

And finally, to my community of writers, publishing professionals, and, of course, the many teachers who've inspired me throughout my education. Laura, thank you for seeing the potential in my work and choosing me to be a part of Team Laura. Demi, Gabi and Kat, for being the first readers of this story and for helping me to grow as a baby writer. And to Bonnie, Aje, Charlotte and the whole One More Chapter team for taking a chance on me and transforming my first-ever manuscript into the beautiful book that it has become. And most of all, thank you to the Shooters and Rollasons for inviting me into their family writing club. Without the weekend Zooms and the one-hundred-plus warmups, this story would have remained forever in my head and never reached the page.

There are so many more people, places and institutions that

have inspired this story – too many to name. My school family, my Bolivian family, my Venezuelan family, my Iranian family, my Gloucester family, my Welsh family, my writing family.

Family is everything to me, and much like writing (and life) it can be messy, complicated, and doesn't always look the way you think it's supposed to. But there's nothing I would change about my many families and communities.

Thank you all for your part in making this dream a reality.

The author and One More Chapter would like to thank everyone who contributed to the publication of this story...

Analytics
James Brackin
Abigail Fryer

Audio
Fionnuala Barrett
Ciara Briggs

Contracts
Laura Amos
Laura Evans

Design
Lucy Bennett
Fiona Greenway
Liane Payne
Dean Russell

Digital Sales
Laura Daley
Lydia Grainge
Hannah Lismore

eCommerce
Laura Carpenter
Madeline ODonovan
Charlotte Stevens
Christina Storey
Jo Surman
Rachel Ward

Editorial
Kara Daniel
Charlotte Ledger
Ajebowale Roberts
Jennie Rothwell
Sofia Salazar Studer
Caroline Scott-Bowden
Emily Thomas
Helen Williams

Harper360
Jennifer Dee
Emily Gerbner
Ariana Juarez
Jean Marie Kelly
emma sullivan
Sophia Wilhelm

International Sales
Peter Borcsok
Ruth Burrow
Colleen Simpson
Ben Wright

Inventory
Sarah Callaghan
Kirsty Norman

Marketing & Publicity
Chloe Cummings
Grace Edwards

Operations
Melissa Okusanya
Hannah Stamp

Production
Denis Manson
Simon Moore
Francesca Tuzzeo

Rights
Helena Font Brillas
Ashton Mucha
Zoe Shine
Aisling Smyth
Lucy Vanderbilt

Trade Marketing
Ben Hurd
Eleanor Slater

The HarperCollins Distribution Team

The HarperCollins Finance & Royalties Team

The HarperCollins Legal Team

The HarperCollins Technology Team

UK Sales
Isabel Coburn
Jay Cochrane
Sabina Lewis
Holly Martin
Harriet Williams
Leah Woods

And every other essential link in the chain from delivery drivers to booksellers to librarians and beyond!

ONE MORE CHAPTER

One More Chapter is an award-winning global division of HarperCollins.

Subscribe to our newsletter to get our latest eBook deals and stay up to date with all our new releases!

signup.harpercollins.co.uk/
join/signup-omc

Meet the team at
www.onemorechapter.com

Follow us!

 @OneMoreChapter_
 @onemorechapterhc
 @onemorechapterhc
 @onemorechapterhc

Do you write unputdownable fiction? We love to hear from new voices. Find out how to submit your novel at
www.onemorechapter.com/submissions